COACH FROM
WARSAW

A Novel

Irene Magers

Shady Tree Press
New York, New York

Published by SHADY TREE PRESS
136 East 64th Street, 7th Floor
New York, NY 10065
U.S.A.
www.shadytreepress.com

PUBLISHER'S NOTE
A first edition of this book was originally published with
the title, *Ticket to Berlin*. A work of fiction, all names, characters,
incidents stem from the author's imagination, except where
historical figures or locales enter into the story.

ISBN: 978-0-9841211-5-1 *(Hard cover)*
ISBN: 978-0-9841211-1-3 *(Paperback)*

OTHER BOOKS BY IRENE MAGERS
Night Crossing to Athens
Last Train From Berlin
Down And Out in Manhattan

Cover design by Sonja Lohmeyer and Dennis Kreibich
Interior Layout & Design by Scribe Freelance Book Design Company

Published in the United States of America

COACH FROM
WARSAW

First Book in a Trilogy

*For my parents who gave me the tools
and for Julian who gave me the time*

Chapter 01

Dorrit was crouched by the side of the bed. Her hands—a child's hands typically refusing to be still—were kneading a corner of the bedclothes, her lips twitching in prayers over the man who lay prostrate on the cot in the sleeping alcove next to a small living room two floors above a greengrocer.

"Please God," she murmured, her voice tight with fear. "Don't let Papa die. Please..."

Somewhere in the dark apartment a clock chimed the hour of eight, the jingle followed by others pealing the hour, for whatever the flat lacked in fine appointments it housed a number of rare timepieces. The cheerful bell-like concert sounded incongruous on this terrible night. The girl shivered, her teeth made clattering noises in her mouth. She clamped her lips shut, which made praying difficult. Maybe it didn't matter. God was probably tired of listening; it might behoove her to concentrate on Dr. Kozlowski. In Dorrit's present state of mind, the two were one and the same.

"Please hurry!" she now begged the doctor, letting God off the hook.

Outside, a storm raged. Sleet scraped against the slanted roof where a skylight rattled on its rusty hinges with each blast of the icy wind. Dorrit was about to get up and stuff a towel around the edges to stop the noise, when her heart lurched in panic as her father struggled for air a moment before another violent spasm consumed his chest. She remained by the bed, too frightened to move.

"Papa!" she cried after his seizure passed. "Papa!"

He didn't answer.

Using her sleeve, she dabbed at the beads of moisture on his furrowed brow. His feverish eyes were closed, his thin lips quivered, and his gray-streaked beard shuddered with his labored breathing.

"Papa?" she tried again, whispering. He didn't respond.

Alarmed by his silence, exacerbated by the shadowy corners in the apartment, Dorrit reached toward the oil lamp on the bedside table, turning its knob for more light. Warming her fingertips against the flame, she stroked her father's flushed face and ran her hand over his balding pate to rouse him. If only he'd open his eyes she wouldn't be quite so afraid. Of course, he had suffered these disabling spells before and survived, she told herself over and over again. Winters were hard on Herman Zache's lungs, this winter of 1895 more so than others. January had dumped three feet of snow across Poland and now February brought ice storms. Dorrit didn't know which was worse but realized the weather was the reason the doctor was late. The streets of Bialystok were choked in arctic ice, slowing traffic with what some said was a glacier forming underfoot. Pedestrians—wrapped to their cheekbones in woolens—purchased footing on slippery sidewalks at great expense to knees and elbows.

Resting her head on the edge of the horsehair mattress, dank with sickness, Dorrit again implored Dr. Kozlowski to hurry, her patience evaporating as the minutes ticked by; it was difficult to be understanding of bad road conditions when her father was so ill.

Herman Zache was a physician as well but didn't practice. His daughter didn't know why because he never talked about it. Once, when she asked him, he became melancholy, drawing his lips into a tight line indicating some deep-rooted sorrow. As she couldn't bear to see him unhappy, she never again pried, which was also why she hadn't asked for clarification the time she came across some papers and discovered he'd shortened their last name from Tzacheroff to Zache. Moreover, one document stated that she was born in Saint Petersburg, a city he never mentioned, not even in passing. She wondered about the discrepancies, but assumed there was a perfectly good explanation.

A loud rap on the front door tore Dorrit from her musings.

The doctor!

She let go of the corner of the bed cover she'd wadded into a clammy ball and struggled to her feet, brushing lint from her blue plaid frock; her legs were stiff, her knees numb from the hard floor.

"The doctor is here, Papa," she announced with overwhelming relief. Their downstairs neighbor, Frau Weiss, was obviously as good as her word when she promised to send her husband out in the storm to summon help. As Dorrit now ran toward the door, wrapping a knitted shawl around her slim shoulders, she decided to show her appreciation by giving Frau Weiss the begonia from the windowsill in the kitchen. Despite the weak winter light, two pink blooms were about to unfurl. Surely, a flowering plant ought to please the landlady.

Dorrit threw back the latch and flung open the door to the hall.

"Good evening," Dr. Kozlowski wheezed, short of breath from his climb up the stairs. He stepped into the small foyer, ice particles dripping from his beard, awakening a musty tobacco redolence on his lapels. He reached out to pat Dorrit's head. She shrank back, not because his gloves carried the rank smell of wet leather, but because of habit. People invariably tried to stoke her hair, something she minded only because it made her father uncomfortable. He became particularly upset if anyone commented on her appearance. Once, when a neighbor in Minsk suggested it was odd that a father and daughter didn't resemble each other in the least, Herman Zache became visibly agitated. The next day he made plans to move.

"Good evening." Dorrit curtsied and closed the door against the draft from the stairwell before taking the doctor's coat and hat, items she hung on a hook behind the door. Dr. Kozlowski kept his scarf around his neck against the chill in the flat.

"So, what seems to be the trouble?" he said, bending down to retrieve the black bag he'd deposited on the floor. He had been here once before, about a month ago.

"Papa has trouble breathing." The words tumbled out with the impatience of the girl's youth. "He's running a fever. He's coughing. He can't speak. Do you have the medicine? The syrup? It helped him the last time." Without waiting for an answer, she turned and dashed into the living room to a clock perched on a shelf that also held books. Standing on tipped toes, she opened the front of the ancient timepiece and reached into the pendulum well, losing the grip on her shawl in the process. She removed her hand from the clock and was holding two crumpled bills. "I hope this is enough for the medicine and your visit," she said, handing the money to Dr. Kozlowski before retrieving her wrap from the floor.

"It'll do." The doctor tucked the bills into his waistcoat pocket and produced a bottle of dark liquid from his black bag. "Use it sparingly," he cautioned.

"Oh, I will. One tablespoon every hour as needed." Dorrit repeated the instructions from his previous visit to prove she remembered. Clutching the precious medicine to her chest she also remembered her manners. "Thank you," she said, frowning with gratitude.

A frown clouded Dr. Kozlowski's face as well. He was dismayed that a child of twelve should fret so. He had four children of his own and among them had never seen such anxiety. Not even last summer when his youngest fell from a tree and the others ran to fetch him at his clinic, reporting that their brother's arm hung at an odd angle.

"Your father has suffered bouts of congestion before," he now said, compelled to calm the girl's fear. "All things considered, he's a sturdy individual. Worrying yourself sick serves no purpose." His eyes swept over Dorrit's thick red curls so shiny they glimmered like fire in the dim lamplight. "Besides," he reached out and patted her cheek before she could step away and avoid him, "if you persist on frowning, you'll get ugly lines between your eyes." *Unusually fetching,* he was thinking; *a color peculiar to the Romanovs.* Out loud he said, "Tell me, child, who did you inherit those vivid green eyes from? Your mother?"

Dorrit raised her thin shoulders and let them fall, indicating she didn't know. Her mother had been dead for years. She had no memories of her and no photographs, something she'd never admit to a virtual stranger. In the same manner that Herman Zache refused to explain why he had quit the medical profession, he never mentioned his wife. This left Dorrit free to tinker and fabricate, something she didn't mind. Making up an imaginary person was exciting and she nurtured the idea that her mother had been as beautiful as an empress and as kind as God.

Dabbing at the melting ice crystals in his beard, Dr. Kozlowski crossed the floor of the sparsely furnished living room and looked askance at the girl running ahead of him. Although she was much too thin, she was remarkably pretty. The man in the sleeping alcove was quite the opposite.

As the doctor bent over the bed, Dorrit prayed her father hadn't overheard the comments about her eyes. It was precisely that sort of talk that upset him and, sick or not, might prod him into another move.

She didn't want to move again and certainly not in the dead of winter. They had a wonderful apartment; a living room plus an extra chamber next to the kitchen that her father insisted she use for her very own, declaring he preferred to sleep in the alcove near his books. She was happy with the arrangement; this was the first time she'd had a room all to herself and she would hate to leave it. Moreover, this building was close to both the synagogue and the university. Her father could walk to *shul* on Saturdays as well as to the medical college where he substituted for professors on sabbatical.

While Dr. Kozlowski fumbled with his pince-nez and prepared to examine the patient, Dorrit fell to her knees on the other side of the bed. She groped under the blanket for her father's hand. "The doctor is here, Papa," she whispered.

"You'll be fine now. And look!" She plucked at his sleeve. "Here's your medicine." She held out the dark amber bottle so that he might see it.

Dr. Kozlowski positioned his stethoscope on Herman Zache's chest. As he listened, his grave mien didn't escape Dorrit. She bit her lips. *Please God*, she prayed silently, *please make Papa well*. Despite her misery, she remembered to pray in German. Her father would like that. Although he had taught her a smattering of several languages, he favored German. She suspected that he was hoping to live in Berlin some day. He often spoke of its great university, and the many moves he'd embarked upon all had one thing in common: they invariably pointed west.

Chapter 02

"*Whoa!*" *Johann pulled* rein so sharply his stallion flared its nostrils, whinnied and stumbled backwards, its hind legs digging into the soggy forest floor, its front hooves boxing the air.

The sudden groan of splintering wood had shattered the rainy silence, alerting horse and rider to danger a split second before a massive tree trunk toppled to the ground in front of them, bringing down lesser growth in its crushing plunge. Roots tore from the wet soil and, flailing in the unaccustomed environment, spit sod and last summer's rotting leaves in all directions.

Clamping his thighs into the sides of the rearing animal, Johann dared the beast to unseat him. It didn't. It wheeled in a tight circle, tossing its black mane, before yielding to a will stronger than its fear. The minute all four hooves found solid footing, Johann eased up on the reins.

"That's a good fellow," he said, reaching down to pat the horse's shiny neck before brushing at the splashes of mud on his suede jacket, which only managed to spread it around. Cursing under his breath, he turned up his collar for what little comfort it afforded against the steady rain plastering his dark brown hair to his head and seeping down his back. His square jaw clenched, his gray eyes glinted with irritation. Why hadn't he grabbed a hat before going out in this sour weather? Johann von Renz was never at the mercy of the elements; this was a first, a very unpleasant anomaly and decidedly uncomfortable. Mentally flogging himself for stupidity, he guided his horse around the fallen corpse of the ancient oak.

Some days it didn't pay to get out of bed.

Actually, the morning had started out well enough. Things only began to fall apart when his mother succumbed to hysteria because his father didn't return from his ride as expected. By midday, having worked herself into a blind frenzy, Annedora von Renz ordered every ambulatory servant out in the rain to search for the baron and, in a burst of democratic impartiality, dispatched her son as well.

Caught up in the charged atmosphere that ensued whenever the baroness raised her voice to the employees, Johann had rushed from the house without dressing properly. But at least he'd had the presence of mind to bring a pistol. Fingering the cold metal securely tucked into his belt, all the while listening for the menacing snorts of wild boar known to roam these woods, he urged his horse on. If only the rain would let up. April showers? *Hah!* This was a deluge of prophetic proportions. The entire county lay under water obscuring fields, meadows, and roads. And why in heaven's name had his father gone out alone in this weather?

Actually, Johann knew the answer to that. Their land manager along with a number of grooms had fallen victim to a fever sweeping the countryside, giving new meaning to biblical plagues and leaving Baron von Renz with no escort. After days of being housebound, he suddenly refused to truckle to inclement conditions, brushed aside all caution, and rode out at the crack of dawn to inspect the damage to his lands.

Shivering involuntarily, Johann huddled his broad shoulders inside his jacket, the gloomy weather underscoring his mood. He felt a strange premonition of doom. But why? He was twenty-one years old, healthy, strong, sole heir to a noble title and a large parcel of Prussia which had supported his family in splendor for generations. Particularly since the Battle of Leipzig, where his great-great grandfather, an illustrious *Generalfeldmarschall,* had served Emperor Frederick Wilhelm III with such distinction that it cost him his life, but added a princely number of wheat-growing acres to his estate.

Emerging from the woods, ducking under branches drooping with new foliage hanging wet, limp, and dispirited, Johann came to a road that originated in Warsaw and meandered lazily through Bernau—the village of his birth—before straightening on its last leg toward Berlin some twenty-five kilometers directly west. His brow crimped, he glanced at the flooded ruts in the old road; there were no tracks, no clues to follow. However, since others involved in the search had probably gravitated toward the Black Wolf on the green in Bernau to swap stories and inquire about the whereabouts of the baron in total comfort, Johann decided on the opposite course. He turned his horse east toward Ladeburg and a tavern where he, too, could get in out of the rain. Days of monsoons had postponed planting throughout the region, causing boredom to reach epidemic proportions, a bonanza for establishments serving spirits. Karl-Heinz Konauer, friend since the cradle, was no doubt addressing his malaise at the Ladeburg Inn, but Johann figured he could be persuaded to relinquish a warm chair for a wet saddle and join the search. Eager for company, he forced his horse into a fast lope, no small feat on the muddied road.

Chapter 03

Minutes later he rode up to the inn. A lackey, draped in oilcloth, stepped out from under a roof overhang where he'd taken shelter. He touched his grimy cap respectfully, for although this rider was soaked to the skin like any other mortal in this ungodly weather, his garb was of a finer quality and his saddle was studded with silver.

"Want your horse stabled?" The old man gummed the words behind a grizzled beard and took the reins.

"No." Johann swung down from the saddle. "I'm only staying a minute."

"I shan't bother the blacksmith then."

"On the contrary. I suspect my friend is inside. He'll need his horse."

The lackey knew the inn's regular customers and it didn't require any guesswork to identify the friend of this well-heeled individual. "I'll fetch Herr Konauer's horse," he said, securing Johann's black brute to a post, before sloshing across the courtyard to the stables.

Johann took the steps to the tavern in one easy leap and, hand poised on the doorknob, shook himself like a shaggy dog before going inside, where he spotted Karl-Heinz at a corner table with a svelte gypsy girl on his lap. The golden hoops in her ears glinted as she threw her head back in a guttural roar at something he was whispering.

Raking long, slender fingers through his wet hair, Johann strolled across the uneven plank floor, nodding to the proprietor behind the bar counter and to several idle farm workers sitting astride three-legged stools near the source of their newfound contentment. The smoky heat in the place felt good. Johann figured his clothes would dry quickly in this warm environment.

Karl-Heinz looked up the minute his friend's shadow fell across the table, put his wine goblet down, and discharged the wench with a slap on her ample posterior. As she slipped away, she gave the tall, lean, and exceptionally handsome newcomer a sultry look. It was rare to see a clean-shaven man among the inn's clientele.

Johann sat down, reached for Karl-Heinz's glass, and sampled the wine.

"Hey, get your own!" the latter protested, motioning toward the bar for service. "How about some food?" Sniffing appreciatively, Karl-Heinz eyed the huge stone fireplace near the kitchen, where half a pig was rotating on a spit. A large, bubbling kettle hung over the hearth at the other end of the room, and the entire place smelled of burnt pork rind and cellar cabbage boiling in sugar and vinegar. Rubbing his hands together, Karl-Heinz licked his lips. He was coping with the wet weather the way he knew best: eating, drinking, and keeping company with females his family wouldn't approve of.

"I don't have time." Johann wiped his mouth on the back of his hand and pushed the wine goblet back across the table. "I'm looking for my father. Have you seen him?"

"Sure, but not here. He and my father were wading knee-deep in mud earlier, lamenting the loss of their fields."

"Where were they?"

"Where?" Karl-Heinz pursed his lips and studied the low-hanging beams overhead. "At the old crossroad . . . I think. Yes, near the Kaiser's game preserve."

A serving girl approached with a pitcher of hot, spiced wine. Karl-Heinz checked it for floating flies before she poured. "Want any?" she asked, turning to Johann.

He shook his head and, as she walked away, he again pressed Karl-Heinz. "About what time was that?"

Karl-Heinz worked up a fine resonant belch. "Huh? What did you say?"

"When did you see them?"

"Earlier. Around nine . . . I think. Maybe it was ten o'clock? Or thereabouts." Blowing across the top of the glass to cool it, Karl-Heinz sipped gingerly. "Your father seemed impatient to be off."

"Where was he going?"

"Search me."

Swallowing his impatience, Johann persevered. Karl-Heinz could be a trial when bingeing and he was no sage, but he had something else going for him. He was loyal to the bone. "Did you at least see which direction he took?" Johann asked one last time. "East? West?"

"Didn't notice. And I haven't seen him since because I've been right here. Had a game of cards earlier with that Polish fellow. What's his name? That new manager over at Hotzendorf's place?" Johann shrugged; he didn't keep track of the local work force. "I took five marks off him." Karl-Heinz patted his breast pocket. "Money I was about to spend on that morsel over there." He nodded toward the gypsy girl at the bar and looked disgruntled. "With this interruption I will have to woo her all over again."

"Sorry," Johann murmured.

"You didn't actually expect to find your father here? Did you?"

"No."

Karl-Heinz leaned back in his seat, hooked his thumbs into his belt, and looked around a room in dire need of some human kindness. "I didn't think so. This place is strictly for the likes of you and me. So, what's the matter? Is the baron missing?"

"Not officially. But he's been out too long in this weather. My mother is worried and has sent everyone but the dogs out to look for him. I just spent an hour combing his favorite haunts in the woods. Damned near got killed doing it."

"I can tell." Karl-Heinz perused his friend's appearance; hatless and soaked, there was mud on his clothes. "You look like the devil. Got thrown? Huh?"

"No." Johann decided not to elaborate on his close call with a ton of timber. It was more expedient to rouse Karl-Heinz to the search, and if he wasn't quite sober, so be it; the rain would work like a slap in the face. "Look," he said, "I need your help. If my father is stranded with a lame horse, which I'm beginning to think is quite likely; two good Samaritans are better than one. How about it?"

"Uh, well, yes, I suppose I could come along." Karl-Heinz's stomach was growling so vigorously it interfered with a prompt response. He threw a regretful glance toward the sizzling meat and the wench now busying herself at the bar, dallying with another customer. It was with precious little enthusiasm that he finally got to his feet and reached for his coat hanging over an empty chair. "All right, I guess we might as well be off." He dropped some money on the table and followed his friend outside to where the lackey was tending two horses.

When Karl-Heinz saw his gelding, saddled and ready, he griped at Johann, "You sure took a lot for granted."

Chapter 04

The two riders were soon plodding across fields stripped of topsoil, Karl-Heinz carrying on *ad infinitum* about the prospects of a poor harvest come August. Johann shrugged. Farming was a tiresome occupation, one he was glad to leave to others. Physical science intrigued him and were it not for his parents, who made no demands on their son except that he present himself at the dinner table regularly, he'd be attending the university in Berlin.

The search had used up a perfectly good hour when Karl-Heinz, who had the liveliest respect for his own welfare, concluded he was near death from starvation. He halted his horse at the crest of a hill near the Konauer spread, second in size only to the von Renz property. Low plumes of wet clouds drifted across a meadow—now a fine lake—where some stalwart trees stood up to their armpits in water. Beyond, obscured by the mist, the gorged and swollen river dragged its contraband of rich topsoil to the sea. There was no pleasant twittering of returning songbirds; they were obviously extending their southern hiatus until the weather improved in these parts.

"You know what?" Studying the dismal view, Karl-Heinz tried to extricate himself from this wild goose chase. "The baron has enough sense to get in out of the rain. He's probably taking shelter in my father's library. Feet to the fire and a good bottle of port between them, I'll wager they've lost track of time and simply forgot to send word."

"You could be right." Against his better judgment, Johann let his horse nibble on last summer's leftovers, slimy tufts of yellow grass poking through the mud.

"Of course I'm right!" Karl-Heinz snorted, removed his wide-brimmed hat and, tousling his matted blond hair with unnecessary roughness, beat the hat against his knees to shake off some water. "For all we know, they're as sodden as the soil. No one's at home to keep them sober. Mother went to Oranienburg this morning." Karl-Heinz made a fist and reshaped the top of his hat before replacing it on his head.

"Oranienburg? Why?"

"Cousin Hilda is failing."

"Hildegard Gersdorf?" Johann knew the frail, widowed Konauer relative and was not surprised to hear of her decline.

"Yes. Gerlinde sent word last night. She was frantic."

"I can imagine," Johann agreed, bored. Hildegard Gersdorf's daughter, a nervous thin girl of bland appearance, was easily frightened. He knew her to be seventeen but she could pass for twelve. "What's the complaint this time?" he asked without the slightest interest in the ailing woman or her plain daughter.

"That nasty fever making the rounds has all but done her in."

"She's dying?" Johann straightened in the saddle, his indifference vanishing.

"I'm afraid so. Mother is leading the death knell, which leaves no one at home to keep my father out of trouble. Given the bad influence of yours, one can expect the worst. Want to ride over to my place? If he's there, it will save you some trouble."

Johann shook his head.

"All right, suit yourself." Home and hearth lay a short distance away; the road was easily accessible from here and Karl-Heinz's stomach insisted he take it. He shifted in the saddle and held his chin at a stubborn pitch, figuring he'd given more than enough of his time in the name of friendship. "This is where we part ways."

"You break my heart," Johann grinned, flashing a row of glamorous white teeth. He fished a handkerchief from an inside pocket and wiped at the rain seeping under his collar. "I'll continue the search a while longer. I want to check along the river."

"Are you daft? You'll sink into the swamp and into oblivion in less than a minute. You and your horse. And that, my friend, would be a shameful waste of an expensive animal." Karl-Heinz eyed Johann's mount with a touch of envy, every black ounce of it thoroughbred.

"I'll loop around to the left," Johann said, frowning at his friend's priorities. "Close enough to home so someone will hear me holler if I begin to sink."

"Why go at all?"

"I'm curious to see if the beach has survived the high water. My father pays a fortune to have sand hauled in. I'm sure he'd appreciate a report. He might even be there himself. He takes great pride in maintaining white dunes a hundred kilometers from the Baltic."

"Eccentricity runs in your family," Karl-Heinz sniped under his breath, forgetting the many summers he'd spent swimming and lounging on the river beach. But hunger made him testy. He clucked to his horse and, fighting gravity, turned right, negotiating a slippery downhill path. "I still say he's at my place."

"If so, send him home. Pronto!"

"Count on it." Without turning, Karl-Heinz raised a fist, thumb pointing up.

Chapter 05

Baron Edmund Bernhard von Renz was not at the Konauers'. Johann found him some twenty minutes later, lying face down on a grassy knoll near the river, a magnificent roan stallion sprawled nearby, thrashing and foaming at the mouth in pain. One glance told Johann there was no hope for the animal and quickly taking the pistol from his belt, he aimed and pulled the trigger, putting the animal out of its misery before jumping to the ground, tethering his horse to a dwarfed spruce. Kneeling, he now carefully turned his father over.

The breath caught in his throat at the sight of an ugly abdominal gash, a laceration that along with a subsequent loss of blood had rendered the baron unconscious. But he was alive. Johann glanced around for whatever vile beast had ambushed horse and rider and might still be lying in wait. Reaching for his pistol for the second time in as many minutes, his eyes flicked over the immediate area, site of a furious struggle, evidenced by the trampled patches of muddied grass. Spotting a trail of blood, he saw the boar, its sharp tusks jutting menacingly from underneath the shrubs where it had crawled with his father's hunting knife still plunged into its gray-mottled belly swarming with bloated ticks eager to abandon their dead host.

Putting the gun away, Johann turned his attention back on his father, speaking to him, trying to rally him; alas, to no avail. He dug into his pockets, found a clean handkerchief and pressed it against the wound. The white linen absorbed the blood like a sponge. Leaving it in place, Johann ripped off his suede jacket, turning it inside out to expose the dry lining before placing it under his father's head. Shivering and pelted by rain, he tore pieces of material from his shirt and stemmed the flow of blood as best he could with a makeshift bandage. The elder von

Renz moaned and opened his eyes. The minute he recognized his son, a shadow of a smile passed over his sallow face.

"What happened?" Johann asked in a raw voice, posing the question only to test his father's faculties, because it was obvious that he had been thrown and gored.

The reply came in a rasping whisper. "A . . . a boar . . . mad as anything . . . came out of nowhere. Hamlet spooked. I think he broke a leg. Maybe two . . . He's in agony. Put him down."

"I already have." How typical of his father to concern himself with the stallion before anything else, Johann thought and again eyed the hefty boar lying belly-up in the bushes. He hoped to God it wasn't rabid. "Does it hurt when you breathe?" he asked, trying to dispel a mounting alarm. In the past couple of weeks there had been several reports of hydrophobic animals in these parts.

"Terribly . . ."

Johann realized his father had broken some ribs and couldn't ride, even if he could get him up on his horse. A stretcher was needed. He was a big man. It would require several people to carry him back to the house. "I have to go for help," he now told him. "I won't be long. Try not to move while I'm gone."

"Don't worry. I won't budge." Baron von Renz grasped his son's warm hands and held on tightly for a moment as if attempting to draw strength from them.

Johann smiled reassuringly even as his silvery-gray eyes dulled and the muscles in his jaw tightened with the seriousness of the situation. He swung up on his horse and with no concern for his own safety, galloped off, taking dangerous shortcuts across slippery fields and driving a priceless stallion into death-defying jumps over high hedges and rain-swollen ditches.

It was an hour before the baron was brought home. A doctor had been summoned and stood ready to examine the patient the minute he was placed in his bed.

Much later when the doctor left, he was grim-faced. Word quickly spread and villagers began assembling outside the tall iron gates marking the entrance to the barony, an enormous red brick residence covered in places by ivy and climbing roses. A beautiful fountain stood in the center of the courtyard, trickling water into a reflecting pool where schools of goldfish swam in lazy circles under the lily pads.

Johann and his mother spent the night, keeping their vigil by the bedside. Eventually Johann dozed off. He was awakened before dawn by Annedora's heart-wrenching sobs.

His father was dead.

It was barely a month after the baron's funeral, when Annedora von Renz took to her bed, a victim of the fever still cutting a merciless swath through the countryside, a virulence that left the strong weak and the weak dead.

The baroness did not recover and was soon laid to rest next to her husband under the ancestral tombstones in a secluded corner of the cemetery behind the Bernau Parish Church.

Chapter 06

"Where the devil were you?" Karl-Heinz barged into Johann's library, unannounced, and in such a state of anger that he neglected to notice the large chunks of dirt flaking off his boots, leaving brown spots in the pastel Aubusson. His rudeness this morning in July included slamming the door behind him with a thud, sending the papers on Johann's desk flying. "Where were you last night?"

"Last night? Where was I supposed to be?" Johann looked up, spreading his fingers over his paperwork to keep it in place against Karl-Heinz's temper. Narrowing his eyes, he glared at his friend, not at all happy with his visit. He had to wade through his father's investment portfolio before the solicitors arrived from Berlin; due at noon, they took pride in being punctual and so would probably be early. Attorneys and accountants were doing their damnedest to assure he had no peace and now it seemed that Karl-Heinz was joining the conspiracy. Admittedly, Johann had neglected their friendship during the past months when, along with mourning his parents, he had to get a grip on his new responsibilities. Everything on the estate needed his attention and every employee expected him to have quick answers when, in fact, he hadn't the foggiest idea what made the place run, nor did he care; something he wasn't about to acknowledge, of course. The family residence in Berlin needed his attention as well. But for now he simply sent bank drafts in the hope that the caretakers—a husband and wife team by the last name of Schmidt—would be motivated to keep the roof tight and the basement dry. They lived on the premises, and he trusted they enjoyed that comfort enough to want to maintain it.

"Last night . . ." Karl-Heinz persisted, his voice rising, "you, of all people, were conspicuously absent!"

"Absent from what?" Johann still looked puzzled.

"From *what?*" Karl-Heinz rolled his eyes, wondering if Johann had been simple-minded all these years without anybody catching on. Leaning across the desk, he planted his palms on a pile of documents while his angry blue eyes bore into a person he'd known since creation. "The Konauers throw an elaborate soiree to proclaim the end of my bachelor days, and guess who doesn't bother to show up?"

"Wait! Wait a minute!" Johann's dark eyebrows snapped together; Karl-Heinz finally had his undivided attention. "Did I just hear correctly? You're getting married?"

"That's right." Karl-Heinz began to rummage through the sea of papers on Johann's desk, invading private territory bold as you please. It's got to be here somewhere, he thought, all the while wondering how a person so meticulous about his own appearance that shaving was a daily obsession could tolerate such a mess. "Ah-hah!" he shouted triumphantly a moment later, having found what he was looking for. "Here it is! Unopened!" He held up a gold-edged envelope.

Johann snatched it from his hand and tore roughly at the wax seal, his eyes skimming the contents written in Ursula Konauer's neat hand. He swore under his breath. To have ignored this was unforgivable. He would have to apologize to Karl-Heinz's mother forthwith. "I am terribly sorry," he said, looking contrite. "As you know, I've been distracted lately. If it'll make amends, I'll sack Rolf for failing to bring this particular invitation to my attention."

"Nah, keep the old boy on. Senile or not, butlers are hard to come by." Some of Karl-Heinz's petulance had left him the minute he spotted the unopened letter and realized that negligence, not intent, accounted for any insult.

"So tell me, who are you marrying?" Johann wondered how an experienced rogue like Karl-Heinz had been fool enough to get himself trapped; a pregnant bride was obviously the explanation for this sudden engagement.

"Gerlinde."

"Who?" Stealing a sideways glance at the porcelain clock on the black marble mantelpiece, Johann saw that precious time was passing.

"Gerlinde Gersdorf."

Johann still looked confused.

"Come on!" Karl-Heinz scowled; it was unlike Johann to be so thickheaded. "You know Gerlinde. Remember Hildegard? She died in April. Gerlinde is her daughter."

"Oh, yes, of course." Johann was connecting the dots.

"There ought to be a prize for such swift comprehension," Karl-Heinz groused under his breath.

"But wait . . . ah, wait a second!" Johann cleared his throat and cherished the hope that he had misunderstood. "Are you telling me that you're marrying *that* Gerlinde? Gerlinde Gersdorf from Oranienburg?"

"None other."

"Why?"

Annoyed with his friend's reaction, Karl-Heinz was furthermore irritated that he had to explain himself. "I'll tell you why," he began slowly as if addressing an underachiever. "Hildegard in her dying breath made my mother promise we'd look after Gerlinde. You know, make sure she didn't fall into the clutches of some ne'er-do-well looking to improve his prospects. And how, I ask you, how better to foil a greedy suitor than have Gerlinde marry me?"

Johann could think of a dozen but said nothing. Instead, he got up from his desk to stand by the bay windows facing acres of sloping green lawns. He pushed at the satin drapery, pretending something outside had caught his interest while his mind slowly absorbed what he'd just heard. Try as he might, he couldn't recall Karl-Heinz even liking the girl. Marrying her was preposterous. She was so pathetic, so colorless; small . . . bone thin, the proverbial runt; the one that's drowned at birth. A doorknob had more personality. "You consented to this marriage?" he finally said, turning around.

"Consented?" Karl-Heinz brushed at the knees of his tan jodhpurs and fell into a chair. "My friend, you are looking at a happy man."

Johann didn't believe that for a minute, but kept his peace as he rounded the massive oak desk and walked over to one of the bookcases in the library, where he opened a false front revealing a liquor cabinet. "Well, then I suppose felicitations are in order," he said. "It's uncivilized to drink before noon, but I think we can make an exception in this case. What'll it be?" Silently, he acknowledged that he needed a drink to help this disaster sink in. He was quite familiar with his friend's taste in women and had Gerlinde been a boy she couldn't have been further from the mark.

"I'll take some brandy. A splash of that rare Napoleon you're hoarding." Karl-Heinz shrugged out of his riding jacket, threw it on the sofa, loosened his collar, and prepared to enjoy himself. "And for once try not to be miserly with it."

Johann poured liberal amounts into two crystal snifters, handing one to Karl-Heinz. "To your bride," he said and sat down on the corner of his desk. "And to your happiness!" The first did not impact the latter, but he lifted his glass and tried to be cheerful. "When's the wedding?"

"Early September. In Oranienburg. You'll get the details in a letter." Karl-Heinz propped his dirty boots up on a pristine white damask ottoman and leaned back in his chair. "So I suggest you open your mail once in a while." He accepted the slim cheroot Johann offered him.

As Johann struck a match and held it out, he eyed his friend for signs of a twisted arm. There were none. If Karl-Heinz was being railroaded, he sure didn't show it.

Chapter 07

Small of physique but having compensated for any lack in stature by amassing an enormous fortune, Viktor Gersdorf had spent his youth and most of his middle years in South Africa, too preoccupied with investing in gold mines to be practical in the ways of the flesh. Marriage never occurred to him until he suffered an illness that brought dreams of immortality into the harsh morning light. He retired to Germany and acquired a house so large it cried out for a mistress. A trusted friend introduced him to Hildegard Kollmer, a mature woman of such cardinal virtues that she'd been overlooked by less discriminating gentlemen.

Settled into domestic bliss, Viktor Gersdorf, sadly, did not have years in which to enjoy it. He lived just long enough to see his child born. However, his daughter would not lack for attention. His two maiden sisters arrived for his funeral, carrying large suitcases; woe be it for them to turn their backs on a bereaved sister-in-law in her hour of need. And so, the three women set about to raise the fatherless infant; a responsibility they took to heart and carried out admirably, drawing on their combined inexperience.

Gerlinde was fourteen when *Tante* Angelika died. *Tante* Amelia passed away two years later, and this past April when Gerlinde's mother followed the aunts into the grave, she was so inconsolable that she agreed without deliberation when Ursula and Karl Konauer suggested that she marry their son. She was not the slightest bit fond of Karl-Heinz, but was even less fond at the thought of living alone.

The marriage took place on a brisk September day bursting with the first rich colors of the approaching autumn. Standing next to her robust groom in an ornate four-centuries-old church, the diminutive ashen-faced bride was completely overshadowed by the splendor of her surroundings and would have faded into the background altogether, if not for the twenty meters of sequined ruffles in her wedding gown that screamed for attention.

Following the ceremony, at the evening gala in the Gersdorf's large sensibly decorated home, Johann claimed the perfunctory dance reserved for the best man, drawing Gerlinde into the salon where musicians were playing slow waltzes in respect for the bride's recent loss.

"I hope you'll like living in Bernau," he remarked when it became clear that Gerlinde wasn't going to inaugurate the light conversation the dance required. In fact, she demonstrated a rare gift for silence; a trait he grudgingly admired; chatty women did not appeal to him. "I suppose it'll be quite a change for you. Our sleepy little village can hardly compare with the metropolis of Oranienburg."

Gerlinde stiffened, unwilling to admit that she knew little about her birthplace because she'd never been allowed to venture about except to attend church with her mother and her aunts. Teachers had come to the house to instruct her in reading, writing, needlepoint, and whatever dance steps were required of a girl of good breeding.

"I expect Bernau will suit me," she said, lowering her eyes lacking in both sparkle and wit. Moments later when Karl and Ursula Konauer brushed by, and Gerlinde heard her father-in-law humming the music, she wished she were dancing with him. Or, better still, ensconced in a corner of the salon with Ursula. Older people tended not to unnerve her. "Ursula will be a wonderful companion," she added in the next instant.

Johann raised his eyebrows. *Ursula?* This girl had married Karl-Heinz, not his mother. But he said nothing. It was none of his business if she preferred an old woman to a young husband. Inwardly he chuckled. Karl-Heinz had his work cut out for him. No wonder he was honeymooning in Sicily where no one from these parts would bear witness to her maidenly protests.

"Once we return from Taormina, I hope you'll be our first guest," Gerlinde said softly, her voice quivering as if she'd read Johann's mind about the wedding bower.

"Nothing would please me more."

"Then I shall expect you to come regularly and without ceremony," she added and lifted her pale blue eyes. Emboldened by what she took to be sincerity in his expression, she stretched her lips into the semblance of a smile. "It'll be ever so nice to have family nearby."

"Family?" Johann said, surprised. He didn't realize Gerlinde had any. Why else had the Konauers made the supreme sacrifice of tying this pitiful creature to

Karl-Heinz? They didn't need her dowry and could have pawned her off on a more suitable soul without breaking any deathbed promises.

"Oh, forgive me." Gerlinde blushed a deep crimson clear to the roots of her beige hair. "I'm being presumptuous, of course. But . . . uh, Ursula told me that you and Karl-Heinz are like brothers. And I . . . I just . . ." The rush of blood to her face accompanied by a sudden roar in her ears interfered with her ability to continue.

Amused with her discomfort, Johann's face broke into a grin. "By all means, consider me brother Johann," he quipped. "It sounds a bit pious though. I'm afraid I'm not blessed with any corroborating qualities."

A nervous giggle, like a polite hiccup, escaped Gerlinde's throat. Intuition told her that he spoke the truth. Johann von Renz was no member of the clergy and seemed proud of it. She lowered her head while her embarrassment subsided.

Before the dance ended and although it was awkward to lead a girl around on the floor when she was determined to study her shoes, Johann found he was warming toward this nondescript person drowning in shyness and ruffled silk. Her flaming cheeks pulled at a man's heartstrings, if not his passion. He finally conceded that Karl-Heinz, the quintessential scoundrel, might possibly get a rise out of such a timid creature.

Chapter 08

Traveling back to Bernau the following day, nursing a world-class hangover, it occurred to Johann that in the span of one short summer he'd been stripped of all companionships that mattered. His parents were in their graves and although Karl-Heinz was still his neighbor, he suspected their friendship would never be the same again. Karl-Heinz was now a married man. His priorities and obligations would change. He might even be a father before a year passed. Johann arrived home uncharacteristically depressed, which he attributed to his lingering headache.

Frau Erdmann, cook and housekeeper on the von Renz estate, had prepared a sumptuous meal for his homecoming. But although he had eaten little since breakfast, Johann had no appetite and stabbed abstractedly at his plate, soon pushing it away. The large dining room felt oppressive. The tapestries on the walls seemed to close in on him. The double doors stood open to the terrace where a cool September breeze flapped the curtains, giving proof of circulation; still, he experienced a crushing lack of air. He finally rose as if he'd broken bread with the devil, and pushed his chair back with such force the tapers in the silver candelabrums flickered, spilling splotches of hot paraffin on the table's rosewood surface.

Frau Erdmann whisked her rotund bulk through the swinging doors from the pantry with uncanny grace and, using the blunt edge of a knife, began to scrape at the wax before applying lemon polish; her synchronized grunts reminding the maids—whose dewy eyes were following the handsome baron—of their immediate duties.

Grimacing at the strong smell of lemon oil, Johann left the dining room, crossed the hall in a few long strides and settled down in the library with the evening papers. However, his bleak mood, as acute as it was bizarre, stayed with him. He couldn't concentrate and eventually threw the papers aside, now glancing aimlessly around. This room had been his father's domain but since his mother had been partial to pastels, the sofas and chairs were upholstered in white damask, strewn with plump pink pillows. The draperies framing the bay windows were the color of sea mist, the identical shade of the leaf pattern in the border of the rose Aubusson on the floor. Only the mahogany-paneled walls and bookcases filled with leather-bound editions ensured that, despite Annedora's best efforts, the room was respectably masculine.

Loosening his tie and toying absently with the gold chain on his waistcoat watch, Johann felt at odds with his world, a trespasser in a familiar milieu. His headache had dulled; nonetheless, he experienced an unremitting sense of restlessness. He couldn't read and he couldn't get comfortable. Unbuttoning his vest he balanced himself on the edge of the chair and reached behind him for a superfluous pillow, tossing it on the floor. Leaning back he pushed his legs out in front of him, crossed them at the ankles and finally confronted the baffling mood that had dogged him all day and could no longer be ascribed to a hangover.

Galling as the idea was, he realized that in some inexorable way he was utterly bored. As he puzzled with this revelation, repeatedly opening his pocket watch and clicking it shut, he came up with no answer that satisfied him. Only one thing was certain. Life on the estate presented little challenge. The dormant season was about to quiet the landscape, and Klausen—the new manager he'd hired when the former man failed to regain his health—had proven himself capable of running things. The workers respected him; one stern word, and the laziest among them were galvanized into activity. The spring floods, the funerals, the change of command had been unsettling for all, but normalcy had returned and everyone had again fallen into an established routine that Johann didn't fit into. Of course, he had long realized that with regard to agronomics he was not cast from the same mold as his ancestors. When all was said and done he could expect to maintain the status quo and grow old, knowing he had held the estate together for his heirs with embarrassingly little effort.

Heirs? He glanced around the room where family portraits were prominently displayed, reminding him of his duty. Whereas he'd never before wished for any siblings, he suddenly did; a brother would ease the pressure to produce heirs. Shrugging wearily, he supposed that marriage was inevitable although he had yet to meet a female sufficiently fascinating not to irritate him any sooner than absolutely necessary. Even the ones who were good sports and enjoyed a roll between the sheets quickly lost their allure.

That said, he got up, stretched and sauntered over to the fireplace. He took a cheroot from a gold case on the mantelpiece, lit it and leaned a shoulder against the black marble. Studying the rows of books along the walls, he recalled the time when he'd outgrown his various tutors and had fully expected to attend Humboldt University. However, every time he broached the subject, his mother had looked stricken with the thought of losing him to Berlin. Apparently, his father didn't like the idea any better because he always found one reason or another to postpone any decision about advanced studies.

Clamping the cheroot between his teeth, Johann bent down, lifted a log from the brass bin and tossed it into the fire. A shower of sparks rose in a frenzied dance as the flames retreated under the heavy bulk before regrouping to lick the new morsel. Wiping wood chips from his hands, Johann walked back to his chair, sat down and continued mulling over his circumstances. He had no family to consult. No living relatives to set up roadblocks. Any determination about his future was now entirely his own.

He made a snap decision. At first light tomorrow he would move to Berlin, enroll at the university, and if he were older than other newcomers to the hallowed Humboldt halls, so be it. He'd take competency exams and catch up with his peers. Johann Maximilian von Renz was not the least bit vain except in matters of intellect. There he considered himself above the fray.

Chapter 09

Berlin, five years later . . .

"*Gott im Himmel*, I believe the temperature is dropping." Rubbing her hands together, Frau Schmidt walked briskly into the library and over to the red velvet drapery, pushing it aside in order to squint at the thermometer attached to the outside of the window; it confirmed what her middle-aged bones were telling her. "Only November, but I dare say a fur-lined coat will be necessary for anyone venturing out tonight." Smoothing her white, starched apron, she patted the tight curls of a new permanent wave and continued peering out toward the dark street, searching for the elegant carriages that normally drove along Lindenstrasse. There was no traffic this evening; something she pointed out to her employer before turning away from the windows to stoke the fire and rearrange the pillows in the supple red leather sofa and chairs. That done, she pinched some wilted blooms on the chrysanthemum plant on the coffee table and attended to other housekeeping details that might justify her presence.

From his place at his desk, Johann made an unintelligible sound. Frau Schmidt regularly busied herself within his earshot to inform or opine, and during the handful of years he'd now lived in Grunewald—a fashionable residential section west of the general hub of Berlin—he had perfected a deaf ear to the noise of traffic as well as to that generated by his housekeeper's vocal chords. Still, despite these irritations, he'd never once regretted that decisive September day in 1895 when he arrived unannounced, giving the resident caretakers pause; a substantial raise helped them recover. Schmidt starched his collars, acquired new black butler attire and a smart livery uniform with top hat for when he drove the coach. Frau Schmidt hired additional maids and delighted in lording it over her brood of inferiors, occasionally forgetting her own station when she waltzed into the sanctuary of the baron's library without a summons, such as tonight.

"Might you have plans for this evening, *mein* Herr?" she finally asked when her circuitous comments about the weather failed to elicit a response and nothing else in the room required her attention.

"No."

"You won't be needing my husband then?"

"That's right."

Frau Schmidt hurried from the room, tugging at her apron, glad that her husband was not needed to drive the baron on this bitter night.

Johann went back to his reading as relieved as the meddlesome housekeeper to be spending a rare evening at home. The "season" was in full swing with the usual abundance of soirees and balls. He glanced across the desk at a pile of letters, put his book down, and reached for an envelope Schmidt had placed on a separate tray, indicating its importance. Turning it over, he recognized the seal of Kaiser Wilhelm. Since moving to Berlin and because of his family's peerage, Johann was regularly invited to receptions at the Imperial Palace on Unter den Linden. Putting the gilt-edged note aside for the moment, he flicked through the less important invitations, deciding he would send his regrets to most of them. He had long since become bored dancing attendance to debutantes whose zealous mothers—determined to have marriageable daughters off their hands—were prone to sycophant behavior. The fact that he was twenty-seven years old and still a bachelor chafed the *grand dames* of Berlin.

Silently praising Schmidt's attempt to make order from the chaos on the desk, Johann picked up another envelope, which, like the invitation from the palace, lay apart from the clutter. Recognizing the cramped handwriting he immediately knew it was from Gerlinde and, since his reading about infectious tropical diseases was now interrupted anyway, he might as well attend to it now.

He opened the letter. After reminding him that he was again expected for Christmas, she devoted two pages to her son's latest mischief. Johann leaned back in his chair as he read, a smile tugging at the corners of his mouth. He was immensely fond of the lad, his godchild, a charming boy with straw-colored hair and sturdy legs. Born a year to the day of Gerlinde's and Karl-Heinz's marriage, Hans' birth had brought great joy to the Konauer household, although his entrance into the world almost became Gerlinde's exit. She'd hovered between life and death for months, her son turning four before she reclaimed her premarital state of delicate frailty.

With the passing of time, Johann had come to love the unassuming Gerlinde. Small of body, she owned an uncommonly large heart, one that embraced all of God's creatures with democratic zeal. Johann, who would have liked nothing more than to have talked Karl-Heinz out of the marriage, now occasionally found himself envying his friend such a philanthropic wife.

Chapter 10

Dorrit walked across the floors in the apartment for one final check to make certain nothing was forgotten. She felt a touch of sadness at leaving. She and her father had lived in Warsaw for five wonderful years, the longest they had remained in any one place since abruptly moving from Bialystok in the spring of 1895; a move Dorrit suspected had something to do with Dr. Kozlowski who had treated her father's recurring lung infection during the winter. Come spring, and despite Herman Zache's restored health, the doctor nonetheless continued to stop by. Dorrit thought he was being awfully nice because he never charged a fee for those visits. Her father, on the other hand, wondered about a hidden motive and grew increasingly leery; his suspicions bearing fruit the day Dr. Kozlowski brought along his sixteen-year-old son. The boy had a terrible complexion, stared rudely at Dorrit, and asked personal questions not warranted on a first visit. Knowing how much her father hated any kind of probing into their private affairs, she was not surprised when he very politely cut the *tête-à-tête* short.

When a matchmaker came calling the next day, Herman Zache was no longer polite. Trying to eavesdrop on an exchange she was not allowed to participate in, Dorrit stood behind the closed door to her room, her ear pressed against it.

"Ivar Kozlowski is prepared to marry your daughter in three years when she comes of age," she heard the *shadchen* explain.

Dorrit's heart dropped. She strained to listen to her father's response, but he was speaking too rapidly; still, she garnered enough from his harsh tone to realize that he would have none of it. Relieved, she sank against the door and heard the woman warn that he might never receive a better offer.

"You ought to be grateful that a family of property is willing to accept a bride without a dowry," she admonished him, at which point Herman Zache's pride came into play and he all but tossed the woman out the door.

The minute the *shadchen* was gone Dorrit tore from her room.

"Papa! I'm so glad you didn't consent!" she cried and threw her arms around him.

He held her tight, stroked her hair, and allowed himself a small smile of satisfaction with his decision. "Then I was right to assume that you don't care for the young man?"

Dorrit nodded, burying her face in his chest. "Even without the spots on his face, I could never marry him," she said, heatedly. "Besides, it would mean leaving you. Something I could never do!"Herman Zache's smile vanished, replaced by a dark cloud spreading across his face. He let go of his daughter and turned away, but not quickly enough for her to miss seeing it. She attempted to forestall any further eroding of his mood with a cheerful suggestion. "I'll make some tea," she said. "With biscuits and marmalade."

Indeed, the visit from the matchmaker had taken its toll on Dr. Zache. Before going to sleep that night, Dorrit heard him pace the apartment. The next morning he severed his professional ties in Bialystok. "It has become necessary to move," he stated simply and without elaborating.

Dorrit was not surprised. This sort of thing had happened before. Without demur, she packed her things and helped her father box his clocks and his books. He squared his bill with Frau Weiss, gave her the two extra months on the lease, but no forwarding address.

Chapter 11

Heading west, Dr. Zache found a part time teaching post at Warsaw University. The following year it became full time, and three years later he took over as head of the department of medical history when the present man died of advanced age and the professor next in line succumbed to a liver complaint. It was a meteoric rise that Herman Zache had never dreamed possible.

Warsaw suited him, proof being that although the winters were as severe as in Bialystok, he was ill less often. Once when Dorrit commented on this wonderful new development, he revealed that the distance he had finally put between himself and Mother Russia was the reason for his improved vigor. However, when she asked him to be more specific, he immediately fell silent and disappeared behind that wretched expression she recognized but didn't understand. And now they were leaving Warsaw as well. She should have known it wouldn't last. Still, this move was different from all the rest. There was no sense of urgency. Her father wasn't fleeing. He had carefully planned this change over several months.

Opening and closing the drawers of a tall bureau in the living room, Dorrit confirmed that they were empty. The bureau belonged to the landlord, who had come over this morning to determine that none of his furniture had suffered damage beyond normal wear and tear. Handing Herr Kmetz the keys to the apartment, Dorrit walked over to the windows and glanced down toward the street below. Her father was standing on the curb with the suitcases. He had gone ahead to hail a public coach, so far without success. He looked up and saw her. She waved, indicating she'd be right down.

"I'm afraid coaches are scarce this morning," she mumbled, buttoning her coat.

"Yes, it's a shame about the rail strike." Herr Kmetz knitted his brows and looked sufficiently concerned. However, a moment later he was smiling at the seventeen-year-old girl pivoting gracefully for one last look around the living room. Her green cloak was plain, but one scarcely noticed its lack of style when the morning light filtering through the windows put such an unusual glow in her auburn hair and a lovely pink tinge on her smooth cheeks. She was exquisite. The landlord wished himself twenty years younger and, mesmerized, followed her as she turned her back on the apartment and walked into the hall and down the stairs. Closing the door behind him, Herr Kmetz was tempted to apologize for the modest flat that she and her father had rented from him.

"The rail strike is a real nuisance," he commented again as they reached the ground floor where he held open the door to the street. "Nonetheless, I trust you and the professor will have a good trip." He extended his hand. "Best of luck in Berlin."

"Thank you." Dorrit turned dazzling green eyes on Herr Kmetz, said good-bye, pulled her hood securely over her head and stepped from the doorway. Hurrying across the sidewalk to the curb, she linked arms with her father still anxiously eying the street for a public conveyance to the depot. They had tickets on the noon coach to Poznan. From there, it was only a day's journey to Wielkopolski and the German border.

Dorrit glanced up at the sky. Clouds were blowing in from the west, dulling the sunlight and further chilling the air. Except for the constant worry about her father's weak lungs, she was excited about the trip. Unfortunately, trains sat idle across Poland and if the job action spread into Germany, they'd be obliged to ride a horse-drawn rig the entire way.

"I hope the coaches aren't too drafty," she said, huddling close to her father to keep warm.

"Whatever the mode of transportation, my dear, December is not a good month for traveling." Herman Zache patted her hand. "But if I'm to assume my new position first thing in January, we have no choice. Pray there are no delays along the way."

Herman Zache had campaigned hard and long for his post at Humbolt University; a crusade that included sending copies of books he'd co-authored while in Warsaw, never profited from, but which had apparently tipped the scales in his favor. Dorrit was not surprised at his resolve to move, or at his defiance of the season. Of course, some might question his sanity. He was giving up a tenured and distinguished position in Warsaw for a part-time opportunity in Berlin, a step down on the professional ladder. Still, it was a dream come true for him.

Chapter 12

After picking up broken branches and other debris that the wind had scattered across the property during the night, Schmidt swept the sidewalk and harnessed the baron's city coach with horses from the public stables across the street in Grunewald Park, a forest which ran the length of Lindenstrasse and lent the neighborhood its name. The morning was unpleasantly cold. Schmidt put hot bricks under the floorboards and otherwise made sure that the coach was ready to depart for Bernau on schedule; hopefully before the storm broke loose. The clouds were thick as thieves and as menacing. Why anyone would want to set out for the country with a blinding blizzard just waiting to test one's holiday spirit was beyond him. But it was not his place to counsel Herr Baron. As it turned out, the storm held off just long enough for Schmidt to deliver his employer in Bernau and complete the roundtrip before it unleashed its fury at nightfall, leaving drifts of snow across Germany.

Come morning the sky was making no frivolous promises. But it was the day before Christmas; Johann was expected at the Konauers' and was not about to beg off because of inclement weather. The light coach he kept in Bernau was for summer driving and would have a difficult time on the snow-packed roads. Rather than chance getting stuck, he simply decided to ride. He instructed Rolf to pack his clothes and other particulars in saddlebags, and shortly after breakfast headed for the stables.

Otto removed his cap respectfully the minute his employer walked into the compound. When he realized the baron wanted Asmodeus saddled, a stallion not known for caution, he volunteered to ride along.

"Supposing he was to step on an ice patch and come up lame," he said, bending down to pick up a net of hay. "You'd be out there alone in this crotchety weather where a body could freeze and not be found till spring." Otto hung the feedbag over a stall where a horse was making loud noises, signaling hunger. "I best tag along."

"Thanks, but no, Otto." Johann smiled at the old loyal groom. "You stay here. I'll just take an extra horse to carry my gear."

Muttering under his breath about some folk's lack of regard for ornery weather, Otto knew better than to press his point with the baron. Instead, he yelled at a groom to saddle Asmodeus, while he went to the stalls to personally choose the spare. The conditions this morning required a slow, sure-footed animal.

Minutes later, putting a booted foot into the stirrup, Johann swung up in the saddle and with the extra horse in tow, rode off, wryly noting the latter had legs like an elephant. What on earth had possessed Otto to trouble a poor plow horse on a day like this?

Prudently deferring from snow-covered shortcuts, Johann stayed on the barony's private lane lined on each side by poplars brandishing their naked limbs like tongues lashing at the leaden sky. Once out on the main village road, he bore left and straight into a nor'easter. It was a grueling trek before he finally caught sight of the Konauers' approach—similar to his—marked by rows of trees that offered guidance but no protection against the needles of ice stabbing at his face. A layer of snow covered his hat and coat like goose down but offered no warmth. He dug in the spurs. The stallion responded and set a good example, but it required repeated black threats and violent tugs on the reins to convince the lagging beast of burden that it was in its best interests to keep up.

At long last the Konauer residence came into view at the end of the lane, looming like a huge apparition, gray and blurred by the hostile elements. It was noon, but the weather did a good job of simulating dusk. Entering the courtyard, squinting through frozen eyelids, Johann caught sight of lights burning in all the windows.

Instantly the surrealistic scene took on a wonderful aura.

Chapter 13

The horses were taken to the stables and Johann was ushered into the great hall, where a roaring fire was burning in the large stone hearth.

"Welcome, Herr Baron!" The butler relieved the guest of his heavy outer clothing and travel bags, stiff and crystallized with ice. "I trust the trip was not too punishing."

Flexing his fingers in front of the fire, Johann grimaced at the frozen articles the butler was passing to a valet. "I've been out in worse, Gunther," he sufficed and pushed a hand through his matted hair.

Accepting a folded towel from the man, Johann ran it across his wet shirt collar before brushing the remaining ice particles from his well-fitting black riding breeches. He rearranged his neck cloth, rolled up his sleeves and unbuttoned his suede vest, completely unaware of the devastating effect his masculine primping had on two maids watching from across the foyer.

Hearing voices in the hall, Karl-Heinz thundered down the stairs. The two friends embraced enthusiastically.

"You continue to thrive. Even in winter," Johann laughed and slapped Karl-Heinz none too gently on the back, noting his complexion was as ruddy as when he'd last seen him at the end of the summer.

"It's the good, clean country air," Karl-Heinz said, landing a couple of reciprocal blows. "I've said it before. You're wasting away in the city. You ought to come back to the land." Karl-Heinz had felt swindled since the day—five years ago—when he returned from his honeymoon and discovered Johann's defection to Berlin. From that time on he never missed an opportunity to protest. Now, true to form, he again aired his grievances as he led the way to the library where another roaring fire chased the last chill from Johann's bones. Pushing a couple of winged armchairs close to the fireplace, Karl-Heinz plunked himself down ahead of his guest. "Lillian has returned from Switzerland," he announced, stretching his feet toward the flames. "She's back in Berlin. She and my aunt and uncle will be joining us for the holidays. They'll be here by evening."

"How nice." Johann sat down, only now remembering that Karl-Heinz's cousin had been away at a finishing school in Zurich.

"How nice?" Karl-Heinz echoed. "That's all you can say? Lillian's a peach. You could do a lot worse."

"I suppose," Johann dawdled, eying a bowl of nuts on the coffee table. No longer cold, he realized he was hungry. "Do you have a nutcracker?"

"Huh?"

"A nutcracker?"

"Oh, yes." Karl-Heinz got up and walked over to the Louis Quatorze desk in the corner of the wood-paneled room with intricately carved cornices and moldings. "Catch!" He threw what looked like a pair of silver pliers at Johann. "Now, as I was saying..."

"I know what you were saying." Johann cracked a plump hazelnut and popped it into his mouth, discarding the shell fragments into an ashtray. "You want me to seduce Lillian."

"No! That's not what I was saying." Karl-Heinz frowned; after all, Lillian was family and should be treated with the appropriate respect. "I merely meant to suggest that you ought to look her over. Being that she's just finished all that schooling, you two educated types might get along like peas and carrots."

"Actually, I was tempted years ago when she was a tomboy."

"Pervert!" Karl-Heinz snorted.

Johann grinned. "At least she was spunky back then. Remember the summer she arrived for a visit just as we were stretching rabbit entrails across your courtyard?"

"We?" Karl-Heinz reached for the bowl Johann was balancing on his knees, grabbed a fistful of walnuts and proceeded to crack them with his bare hands. "As I recall, you were the weird one measuring the stinking mess." He separated out the nutmeats and tossed the shells into the fire.

"Who was doing what is not the point. Lillian didn't throw a fit or faint. It impressed me."

"So now you're telling me you like women with strong stomachs?"

"Not necessarily. I simply prefer more than a pretty face. The last time I saw Lillian she'd become decorative without any *esprit de corps*. Believe me, Berlin has plenty of pretty ornaments. Bright and shiny on the outside but tap them and all you get is a hollow echo. Forgive me for being so blunt."

"Never!" Karl-Heinz promised. Chewing vigorously, he sucked his teeth, reached for more nuts and wondered if he ought to be insulted on Lillian's behalf. "So remain a bachelor," he shrugged. "Let that be your punishment. I still say Lillian could be your ticket to happiness. She likes Bernau. We could be one big happy family out here."

"Do you really believe a nonpareil city girl like Lillian would be content living in the country? Prefer it over Berlin?"

"Unless she'd prefer a broken neck."

Johann laughed. "Don't trouble yourself. Besides, Berlin, *not* Bernau, is in my blood. And you're on my back. Let's drop the subject of my heart."

"Only while I tell you some great news."

"I'm listening . . ." Johann put the bowl on the table and brushed shell remnants from his lap.

Slouching in his chair, savoring the moment, Karl-Heinz looked enormously pleased with himself. "Gerlinde is expecting," he said. "The baby is due in June."

"What?" Straightening, Johann stared at his friend. "You can't be serious. *That's* your good news? If I remember correctly, having Hans nearly killed her."

"That was ages ago. Dr. Speckmaier claims she's stronger now. He says women have an easier delivery the second time around."

Johann raised his eyes to the ceiling as if begging God's forgiveness on behalf of this mortal blunderer sitting next to him. "You know better than that," he said soberly, "even if Dr. Speckmaier doesn't. Gerlinde is no stronger today than she was four years ago. Another baby might . . ."

"All right! All right!" Karl-Heinz held up his hands to silence him; he had expected a pat on the back, not a lecture. "What do you want me to do? Gerlinde has had her heart set on another child for a long time. It's all she ever talks about. She goes all mushy whenever she sees someone else's baby. She'd like to have a baker's dozen!" In an attempt to further exonerate himself, he added, "There's no one around here more excited about this than the little mother herself."

"I don't doubt that," Johann said. "And of course it's too late for second thoughts. Just promise me one thing."

"Sure. What?"

"Bring her to Berlin when her time draws near. Admit her to Wirchow."

"A hospital? Why? She's not sick. She's just having a baby."

"Yes, but for whatever it's worth, I'll be on hand. I start my residency there first thing in the New Year." Even as he was saying this, Johann feared that some higher power would have to intervene on behalf of one of God's most deserving creatures.

"Residency? They're sure cranking out doctors fast nowadays," Karl-Heinz observed, glad to change the subject.

"Not really. I've been doubling up on lab work. It has allowed me to move along at a quicker pace."

"What happened to your internship?"

"Over and done with. By special imprimatur at Charite."

Karl-Heinz whistled, impressed.

Chapter 14

Hans darted into the library, jumped up on Johann's lap, and immediately engaged him in a guessing game about his Christmas present. Tousling Hans' blond hair affectionately, Johann managed a fair amount of evasiveness, keeping the boy in happy suspense.

When Gerlinde followed moments later, Johann rose to greet her but was almost knocked off his feet as she stepped through the door and his eyes fell across her bird-like form. Her pregnancy didn't show yet except in her face, which was like a death mask, cheekbones protruding unnaturally, her blue eyes sunken into deep purple circles. Her pale hair was pulled into a severe bun, which didn't improve the picture. As he walked toward her, his arms outstretched, he managed not to communicate his shock.

"Johann! How wonderful to see you!" she cried. "I am sorry I wasn't on hand when you arrived. Ursula insists I take a nap before lunch. Most of the time I just lie in bed, watching the clock. Today I actually slept." Gerlinde tilted up her small, plain face. "How were the roads? You must have had quite a time getting here. I'm so glad you made it."

"Nothing could keep me from spending Christmas with my favorite girl," Johann grinned, kissing her and keeping her cold hands in his, surreptitiously checking her pulse. "Moreover, I've just heard some exciting news," he said with genuine cheer because her pulse seemed normal.

"You mean about the baby?"

"Yes. Congratulations!"

"Thank you. We're all so happy about it. But I'm afraid it has turned the house upside down. Karl and Ursula tiptoe around as if a loud noise will knock me over."

Just then, Ursula and Karl joined the group in the library; Ursula bubbling with excuses as to their tardiness.

"I had to finish arranging bedrooms for everyone tonight," she explained after welcoming Johann warmly. "I couldn't relax till the job was done. But now, come along. Let's have lunch." She took his arm and led the way across the hall to the dining room. "You must be starved," she said before also commenting on the roads. "I hope they'll be plowed by tonight. I'm worried about everyone getting here safely."

The midday meal was an unequaled feast. The cook had formerly been in the Kaiser's employ; something Ursula never tired of reminding one and all and, of course, no one was sufficiently tactless to question why he no longer held the royal post. Today, however, his delicately seasoned pheasant in a rich butter and wine sauce did not sit well with everyone. As the meal concluded and the group prepared to leave the table for the solarium where coffee and dessert would be served, Gerlinde rushed from the room, white as a sheet, hands clapped over her mouth. Ursula, quick on her feet for a woman of fifty-five, gave chase. She knew where chamber pots were hidden from view and where the poor girl could discreetly retch.

With the abrupt departure of his mother and grandmother, Hans followed the men into the solarium, crawled up on Johann's lap, and was soon revealing his plan to raid the kitchen to supplement the bread he'd stuffed into his pockets during lunch.

"I'm gonna steal some raisins and bacon," he was saying. "Then I'm gonna mush everything together into balls and hang them in the pine tree outside the living room window. You know, the one that's as tall as the house." Hans raised his hands above his head for emphasis. "It's got birds living in it. Lots of them. You wanna come watch them eat?"

"Sure." Johann smiled, not surprised at the youngster's concern for the sparrows that wintered in Bernau. Hans was softhearted like Gerlinde and had been known to beg that a window be opened to free a fly beating its wings against the glass.

"You, too, *Opa*?" Hans looked toward his grandfather bent over a humidor, sniffing the tobacco appreciatively while making a selection.

"Absolutely. I wouldn't want to miss it." Karl Konauer nodded, chose a cigar and once it was lit, told Johann how Hans had come upon a dead bird in the courtyard and, convinced it had perished from hunger, became determined to feed its surviving relatives.

"Nanny Kruse thinks the bread and stuff will only attract ru . . . ah, ro . . ."
Hans stalled. "What do you call them, Uncle Johann?"

"Rodents."

"Yeah! Rodents and rats." Hans suddenly ran off, sliding like a skater across
the hall and down toward the kitchen.

"Thievery will require a bit more stealth!" Johann laughed and held out his
cup for a refill when a maid came around with the coffeepot.

"What do you say we go exercise some horses?" Karl-Heinz put his cup down,
stood up and stretched. He walked over to look past the pots of red geraniums
hanging by the mullioned windows, where they bloomed in spite of the season.
"The weather looks pretty good."

"It does?" Johann raised an eyebrow. "You obviously haven't been outside
today." But that said, he finished his coffee and got up. He was game. Besides, Karl
Konauer's cigar was now making the air in the solarium unpleasant.

Chapter 15

"*Ladeburg?*" *Karl-Heinz* asked once they were saddled.

Johann studied the sky. "As good a destination as any, I guess. As long as the weather holds."

Karl-Heinz glared at the gray clouds pressing down on the landscape, daring them to spoil his plans. "It won't snow again for hours," he said stoutly.

"I wouldn't bet on it."

"I would!" Karl-Heinz happily placed wagers on the most trivial. "Snow by four o'clock and I'll pick up the tab. No snow, you pay."

"Fair enough."

Once out on the main road the horses set a steady pace, their snorts sending puffs of white mist billowing into the wintry air; otherwise, neither animal gave proof of exertion in the bone-jarring cold.

"Has the old place changed?" Johann asked after a while of riding along in silence, the air too sharp for conversation.

"No. Same crumbling decor. Same brew. Same greasy food."

"And the women?"

Karl-Heinz shrugged. "They come and go like the seasons. I suppose it's the gypsy blood in their veins."

"Any particular one these days?"

Karl-Heinz turned in the saddle. "What do you take me for?" he said, sharply. "Gerlinde is knocking herself out, bringing heirs into the world, and you're accusing me of forgetting my marriage vows." He rolled up his collar and looked as though he'd been vilely insulted.

"You're a good man," Johann chuckled; not at all sure his friend was being forthright.

There was no lackey at the inn to take charge of the horses. The holiest night of the year was fast approaching, business had tapered off, and to stand about in the cold would only generate frostbite, no tips. The riders took their mounts to the blacksmith across the way. He remained open, counting on trade from the public coaches that stopped here on their regular runs between Warsaw and Berlin.

Once the horses were sheltered, the two friends crossed the yard and climbed the steps to the inn, making use of the sturdy doorposts to knock ice and snow from their boots before entering.

It was hot as August inside. The stone fireplaces at each end of the taproom were hissing with fat dripping from slabs of meat hung above the flames. A skinny kitchen boy ran back and forth, cranking the spits to ensure an even roasting. He licked his lips. He'd get plenty to eat tonight because, except for the help, the place was nearly empty. From behind the bar counter, the minute he spotted paying customers, the proprietor motioned a serving girl to look alert.

The newcomers made their way to a place by a window, peeled off their gloves, removed their heavy coats and hats, and hung them over a couple of chairs before sitting down opposite each other. Karl-Heinz swept some dead flies off the wobbly table, broke off a chunk of wax from the candle burning on a tin plate, and tossed it across to Johann.

"Right the deck." He pointed to the corner on Johann's side where a leg didn't quite make contact with the worn floor planks.

"This tavern is unchangingly charming," Johann said and bent down to stuff the paraffin under the leg. Testing the table's stability, he wiped his hands on his vest before unbuttoning it against the heat in the room.

"Huh? What did you say?" Karl-Heinz's attention was honed on the girl approaching their table.

"I said the general state of disrepair is strangely appealing. The past century remains alive and well in this place. I hope the inn keeper never decides to modernize."

"Don't worry. The rafters will collapse from wood worm and other natural causes before it occurs to anyone to renovate." Karl-Heinz eyed the girl setting down two mugs. "What have you got in there?" He pointed to the pitcher resting on her generous hip.

"Mulled wine. House specialty."

"Is it good and hot?' She nodded and Karl-Heinz signaled that she go ahead and pour. "We'll both have some," he said before Johann could decide to order a more genteel drink.

She filled the two mugs, her heavy black mane obscuring half her face as she leaned over. "Want something to eat?" she asked, gathering her hair and twisting it into a rope that immediately came undone the minute she let go. When both men shook their heads, her warm eyes settled on Johann. She put the pitcher down on the table and reached unabashed for his hand, turning it palm up. "Maybe you want your fortune told?" she purred in a husky voice and appeared to be concentrating on his long slender fingers. "You don't work the land," she said, before tracing her thumb over the lines in his hand.

"That's right," he admitted with a grin.

"Hmm, your lifeline is not very long . . ." her face clouded an instant before brightening. "But I see a beautiful woman in your future."

"Thank you!" It was Karl-Heinz who spoke up. He shooed her away. "My friend is committed to a life of celibacy. No women. Beautiful or otherwise. And none of your prognosticating today. Leave us the pitcher and be off."

She gave Johann a dewy smile before walking away. "Maybe you'll change your mind later?" she said to him. "I also read cards."

"Perhaps next time," he smiled.

Testing the temperature of the wine with a finger, Karl-Heinz lifted the mug to his lips. "*Prosit!*"

"*Prosit!*" Johann took a gulp of the spicy brew and glanced around the tavern where an old gypsy fiddler was playing his viola with the same enthusiasm he'd bestow on a full house, stomping his feet and walking among the mostly empty tables. When he strummed old familiar tunes, several patrons belted out the words at varying decibels and levels of musical achievement.

Emptying their glasses, the two friends poured another round. It was getting on toward four o'clock and growing dark outside. Daylight didn't linger in December. The fiddler was taking a rest, and the serving girl, having found the palm of another customer, was promising him the moon.

Johann cleared a circle on the misty window with the cuff of his sleeve. Peering out into the semi-darkness, he spotted some carriage lights. A coach was approaching along the road from the east. He figured it was a mail coach and was probably carrying passengers as well. With no end in sight to the spreading railroad dispute, travelers were hopping aboard any vehicle that moved.

"Seems that I've lost the bet," he said after confirming that no snow was blowing across the beams of the flickering carriage lights. "You win. The weather appears to be holding. What do you say we get going?"

52

"Soon as you pay up." Karl-Heinz sloshed the last of his wine around the mug to incorporate the spicy sediment before swigging it down and reaching for his coat.

Johann dropped a larger than normal amount on the table before walking up to the bar to stuff a folded bill into the fiddler's jar and one into the kitchen boy's apron. The lad beamed.

Chapter 16

The coach Johann had seen through the window had come to a stop in front of the inn. Setting the brakes securely, the driver spit a stream of tobacco juice into a snow bank, where it melted, forming a small, discolored crevasse. Jumping down with a thud, he opened the carriage door and spoke to those inside the compartment.

"This will be our last rest stop before Berlin," he announced, reaching under one of the seats and pulling out a mail sack, which he threw onto the landing where Johann and Karl-Heinz had stopped to button their coats.

"How long will we be here?" one of the passengers inquired; he spoke German with a Russian accent and experienced some difficulty climbing from the coach. No sooner did he have both feet on the ground, when he bent over, consumed by a terrible cough.

"An hour . . . give or take," the driver said, busying himself with his team of bays. "It'll be nice and warm inside. The place serves a hot brew. It'll soothe your chest."

Nodding, the traveler turned to help another passenger from the coach. They were the only two people onboard and as the latter stepped out, her feet missed the wheel ruts in the road and disappeared into the snow, which swallowed the hem of her coat as well. It was too late to save her shoes, but she quickly hitched up her skirts, took the older man's arm, and headed toward shelter.

Johann started down the steps ahead of Karl-Heinz, then stopped abruptly, his hand pausing on the last button of his coat as his gaze beheld the two travelers, one so exceptional he couldn't draw his eyes away. Everything about her held his attention. When the old man halted in mid step, succumbing to another coughing spell, Johann saw her brow crease in a worried frown that did not diminish the enchanting picture she presented.

"Papa," he heard her say as she let go of her hems to help secure the scarf around the lower portion of the man's face. "It's been a long day. There's really no reason for us to push on. Why don't we stay here tonight and continue on another coach tomorrow?" Her speech carried no noticeable accent; every nuance and intonation was unusually cultured for one so young. Intrigued, Johann remained rooted to the inn's warped, wooden steps. "Berlin can wait a day," she went on as she took the man's arm and continued walking. "You're not supposed to exhaust yourself." Glancing up to inspect the inn, she showed no sign of disappointment with its shabby exterior. Warm lights were burning in all the windows, she noted happily, and smoke was curling from two chimneys. "This looks like a comfortable place," she said, envisioning the cozy fires. "A far better place to spend the night than the drafty coach. We need only ask the driver to bring in our bags. And, oh, listen Papa! Do you hear the viola?"

The man made a comment that was lost behind the woolen folds covering his mouth and nose. His cloak and hat appeared travel worn. These people had come some distance, Johann surmised and continued to study them, particularly the girl. She was wearing a green coat of coarse cloth and common cut that for all its unflattering lines and best intentions did not conceal a lovely slender figure. As she walked toward shelter with her father, both carefully avoiding the snowdrifts—he with a downcast face and a clumsy limp—she moved with the natural grace of the aristocracy, although she carried none of the trimmings.

Mounting the steps, and the moment the girl raised her head to the light pouring from the windows, Johann saw her face clearly. It was a masterpiece of astounding perfection. Large, wide-set eyes, a straight nose, an elegant chin, and softly curved lips were balanced in a flawless translucent oval. Her harmony of features caused him a moment of lightheadedness. He cursed the proprietor's strong brew because women—let alone such a young one—had never before had such an effect on him.

When a sudden gust of wind swept off the roof, pushing back her hood and tossing her hair—the color of paprika—about her face, Johann heard Karl-Heinz on the step behind him whistle. His friend, a practiced roué, was not blind of course.

Hesitating to proceed, the girl looked squarely at the two individuals blocking the way, wondering if they were planning to move aside. Karl-Heinz, the consummate gentleman despite his many rough edges, retreated immediately, but Johann was slow to do so. The bright green of her extraordinary eyes and the charming sight of her windblown red hair caused him to forget manners fastidiously handed down over generations. He compensated with a broad smile.

"Forgive me," he said, finally stepping back and addressing both travelers. "I couldn't help overhearing your concerns about traveling to Berlin tonight."

"Oh?" The girl looked eagerly at the tall, dark-haired stranger; perhaps he could persuade her father to postpone the last leg of their journey; Herman Zache was a stubborn man and in a hurry. "Are the westbound roads bad?"

"They're practically impassable," Johann assured her. "My friend and I rode the main link only an hour ago. Not a stretch was cleared."

This news seemed to please her. "Did you hear that, Papa?" she said. "The coach could become stranded. Why take that chance? Let's stay here tonight. By morning the road will have been plowed."

"If our driver is willing to go on," the traveler rasped behind his scarf, "I see no reason why we should stay behind. It's only a couple of hours to Berlin."

"Yes, under normal circumstances," Johann pointed out. "But we had quite a storm last night and the blizzard conditions lasted right through the morning." As he spoke, he wondered why he was wasting time encouraging these people to remain in Ladeburg. For all the girl's allure, he couldn't stay at the inn with her. As it were, he and Karl-Heinz had quite a ride ahead of them and standing about inhaling this bitter cold was sure to invite a host of assorted ailments, something the traveler substantiated with another deep cough.

Once he was able to speak and as if he, too, worried about courting pneumonia, the man said from behind the wool across his face, "We'd better get inside." He pulled his daughter toward the door. "I guess we'll heed your warning and spend the night." Bidding Johann a cordial good-bye, he nodded to Karl-Heinz as he passed him on the landing.

A smile as radiant as a July morning broke out on the girl's face. "You've been very kind to trouble yourself," she said with the sweetest expression this side of heaven.

Johann's gaze followed her as she was ushered inside. Had she turned around, she would have seen sparks of silver flashing in his gray eyes. Unmindful of the frigid air, he took a deep breath to steady a strange pounding in his chest. He felt exhilarated. He felt as if he had just seen his future and it was a spectacular sight.

Chapter 17

It was after five o'clock before the riders returned home and found the Konauer household under siege by arriving relatives and friends, one and all bemoaning difficult journeys on snow-covered roads as if the discomfort suffered en route was equitable remuneration for the lavish hospitality they were about to enjoy. While Ursula and Karl were greeting guests in the front hall, Karl-Heinz and Johann made use of a back entrance, neither one eager to face the crowd until absolutely necessary. Climbing the servant stairs to their respective rooms, Karl-Heinz stopped by an arched portal that led to the guest wing. "See you downstairs at seven sharp," he said. "I fixed it so Lillian will be your dinner partner."

"I'll try to be charming," Johann said over his shoulder as he headed along the corridor to his room.

Sitting on the edge of the four-poster bed, he was pulling off his boots when a maid carrying pre-warmed towels knocked and asked if he wanted a bath run. Johann nodded and let her in. While she busied herself with the valves on the pipes feeding a freestanding tub behind a tapestry screen, he stepped into the adjoining dressing room to peel off his riding clothes. He emerged wrapped in a terry-cloth robe. The girl indicated his bath was ready and that he need only ring if he required more hot water. She pulled the drapes across the windows, took his coat and hat from the bed, hanging both into an armoire, before she curtsied and left.

Shedding the robe, Johann sank into the warm water; it relaxed his body but not his mind, which remained in turmoil, wondering about that girl at the Ladeburg Inn. He realized any interest in Lillian tonight would stand a better chance if only he could shake the vision of that beguiling face. *Who was she? Where was she from?* He knew she was going to Berlin but where in the city and for how long? *Dammit!* Why hadn't he asked for her name? He had wasted precious moments, talking about the weather, when he should have asked questions instead. Of course, personal overtures were not considered good form during short and incidental meetings between total strangers; still, he'd never been a stickler about protocol and should have managed an introduction.

Irritated with his neglect, Johann eventually stepped from the tub and reached for a towel, shivering for an instant before rubbing himself dry. Dressing quickly into the formal attire the evening required, he was running a comb through his hair with distracted detachment when a valet entered, carrying his black evening jacket neatly pressed.

"Good evening, Herr Baron," the man said, crossing the floor and hanging the jacket on a brass wall hook, after which he helped fasten Johann's neck cloth with a diamond pin before threading matching cufflinks through the shirtsleeves edged with the hint of a ruffle. The valet retrieved the jacket, helped Johann into it and stepped back to assess the final result, his trained eye telling him that the Baron von Renz employed the finest tailors in Berlin.

A tall grandfather's clock in the hall struck the hour of seven as Johann walked down the wide, carpeted stairs. Guests were already gathered in the drawing room, grouped into conversation clusters around a Christmas tree, heavy with ornaments and shimmering with tinsel. Johann remained standing in the open doorway for a moment, content to let his eyes roam the festive gathering before deciding which group to approach first. His eyes fell on the slim form of Gerlinde. He smiled inwardly. She was wearing an ostentatious cherry-red gown, totally out of character and deliberately worn, he suspected, to defy her weak constitution.

Hans, dressed in a blue velvet sailor's suit, was standing at her side, clutching her full skirts in awe at being the youngest among so many. His blond hair was slicked back with water, the track of the comb still visible. Several older children were hovering around the Christmas tree, touching the decorations within reach and pointing to the more delicate ones that weren't. Examining a tray of canapés a maid was passing around, Hans wrinkled his nose at the sharp smell of Camembert, smoked salmon, and dollops of caviar, all the while wondering why adults delighted in such revolting morsels. He looked away from the tray, spotted Johann in the doorway, and immediately barreled through the maze of colorful gowns and black tuxedos.

"The birds ate the stuff I put in the tree!" he said breathlessly, grabbing at the knife pleats in Johann's impeccable trouser legs. "There must have been a thousand." Hans' lower lip suddenly jutted out, remembering his disappointment that Uncle Johann hadn't been there. "You should have seen them."

"I'm sorry, Hans. I wish I had. It was dark by the time your father and I returned from our ride. How about tomorrow? I'll help you make the treats."

Hans cocked his head. "Promise?"

"I promise." Johann picked up the boy and gave him a flying tumble in the air. Hans squealed with delight and, forgetting his disappointment, ran off toward the older children eying the tree. He knew which foil baskets held chocolates, something they'd probably appreciate knowing.

Johann stepped into the drawing room and began mingling, involving himself in pleasant conversation as he worked his way around the room to where Lillian stood in a swirl of turquoise satin among a host of admirers.

Chapter 18

Considering the lateness of the hour when the festivities ground to a halt, Johann woke extremely early the next morning. Raising himself clumsily onto one elbow, he reached for his watch on the bedside table and groaned. *Seven-thirty?* It would be noon before anyone else stirred. Only servants and thieves were up and about at this hour on a holiday morning.

He tried to go back to sleep but couldn't and eventually threw off the covers, got out of bed and staggered over to the windows. He pulled on a drape cord. Instantly, the room was flooded in bright light, forcing him to clap a hand over his bloodshot eyes.

A moment later, carefully squinting, he again braved the glorious dawn. The heavy gray sky of yesterday was now a brilliant blue dome wherein the moon—a small wispy sphere—was fading in the glare of the rising sun tinting the landscape pink. Tall trees cast long amethyst shadows across the snowy scene, the sight beckoning Johann's recalcitrant soul. Making a rash decision, he found his riding clothes and made quick work of getting dressed. His boots had spent the night by the fire and were toasty warm. Grabbing his heavy coat, gloves and hat, he left the sleeping house.

The glistening snow squeaked under his feet as he crossed the courtyard with a briskness of purpose, the thought of his destination infusing him with energy. He took a deep breath of the morning air spiced with the pungent smell of burning wood, rising from the chimneys. The servants, bless them, did an excellent job keeping the fireplaces alive throughout the night. Johann strolled into the stables, surprising the lone groom on duty. His horse was saddled and he was shortly on the road to Ladeburg, formulating a plan as he went.

He assumed the dazzling redhead and her father were in the tavern having breakfast. Yesterday the man had been in a hurry to get to Berlin; they were obviously late for a family holiday and would want to catch the first coach this morning. Johann decided he would casually approach their table, inquire about the comfort of the inn, share a few words about the vastly improved travel conditions, and then introduce himself. Of course, if father and daughter were still in their rooms, something the inn-keeper could be trusted to divulge, Johann would make himself comfortable, order breakfast, wait until they appeared, and then commence with the introductions.

Digging in the spurs, he forced his horse into a trot. But although Asmodeus was fresh and eager, the animal was circumspect and balked where the ground was unsure, an instinctive and admirable prudence but one that grated miserably on the rider's impatient nature this morning.

Nearing the inn, Johann saw a mail coach pull away, the horses struggling to get traction in the snow. The driver laid the crop across their backs, they responded with appropriate alacrity and by the time they approached him, were going at a remarkable clip considering the slippery terrain. Before Johann was forced off the road and almost off his horse, when—startled by the flying coach— Asmodeus suddenly reared, he caught sight of the two passengers through the small carriage window.

Uttering a string of obscenities in tribute to his poor timing, he was sorely tempted to charge after the speeding conveyance. However, as quickly as that notion entered his head, he rejected it. He'd look like an idiot. Worse, he'd run the risk of being mistaken for a robber and shot.

Mail was more sacred than human life.

Chapter 19

Dorrit Zache ran down three flights of stairs as though her life depended on speed, which it didn't. She was sound of both body and mind. Her father, however, was not, and the noise of his labored breathing still roared in her ears as she reached the bottom steps, crossed the small vestibule, and flung open the door to the street. She dashed out onto the sidewalk in such a hurry that she forgot to close the door behind her, and was two blocks away before realizing her neglect. Fraulein Strutzenberger, the spinster who lived on the ground floor, would surely complain about lost heat, but Dorrit couldn't go back now. There was no time to waste. She would face the music later.

A newcomer to Berlin, Dorrit had not made the acquaintance of any of her neighbors except Fraulein Strutzenberger, who had taken an immediate dislike to the tenants from Warsaw, yet considered it her civic duty to be on speaking terms in order to confront them with any and all crimes and misdemeanors. Dorrit managed to avoid her as much as possible and took comfort in the fact that at least she was on good terms with the neighborhood grocer, Herr Ziegler, a kind man who never sold her inferior provisions and always inquired about her father. Best of all, he had a telephone he let his regular customers use.

Racing down the street, oblivious to the cold March wind, Dorrit's hair flew about her face like a firestorm, while her eyes were black and dilated with fear for her father. She burst into Herr Ziegler's small shop, her cheeks flushed from the mad dash, her lips white and pinched.

"Fraulein Zache?" The portly man behind the counter cluttered with candy jars and packaged edibles, looked surprised because this was her second time in the store today. His young and pretty customer was usually organized far beyond her years and always shopped with a carefully compiled list. "Did you forget something this morning?" he asked. "Perhaps the Ceylon tea the professor is so fond of?"

"No, Herr Ziegler. I need . . . that is to say, m . . . may I borrow your telephone?" Dorrit stammered, trying to catch her breath and quiet her heart. "My father is ill. He can't breathe. He's coughing. I have to call a doctor." She pushed the hair off her face and only now realized that she was wearing an old housedress and ugly slippers. In her rush she had forgotten to put on a coat. But if Herr Ziegler wondered at her neglect, he made no mention of it.

"Professor Zache has had coughing spells before," he said. "What makes you think he needs a doctor? Some lozenges might do the trick. Look," the grocer pointed to a bin under the counter, "I have some nice honey and licorice-flavored drops. If I remember correctly, they gave him some relief the last time."

Dorrit shook her head. "He needs something stronger today. Something only a doctor can dispense. He's worse this time. He needs real medicine."

"Surely he can't be that ill." Herr Ziegler arched his white, bushy eyebrows and looked over the wire rim of his spectacles. "I saw him yesterday. He looked quite fit when he passed my store on his way home from the university."

"I know, but he wasn't supposed to walk home yesterday. The weather was much too raw." Dorrit ran the back of her hand across her eyes, fighting tears of frustration that her father had decided to save money by walking rather than hailing a cab. "He got himself chilled to the bone. He didn't sleep well last night and now he's having trouble breathing. Please, may I use your telephone?"

"Of course." The grocer opened a flap in the countertop to let her pass through. "Now, take it easy." He patted her shoulder and pointed to the apparatus hanging on the wall next to a picture of Kaiser Wilhelm II that appeared to have been removed from a book and framed. "Go ahead. Help yourself."

"Thank you." Dorrit tore the receiver from the hook, praying for a quick connection. While waiting for the operator, she studied the Kaiser's blond hair, finely groomed mustache, and regal posture. He is a splendid looking emperor, she decided, awed with his exquisite persona and fancy regalia, which concealed the fact that he had a lame arm.

When Dorrit finally heard the nasal twang of the operator on the line, she blurted into the mouthpiece, "Please connect me to a doctor!"

"*Jawohl*," the voice responded in a bored monotone. "Who?"

"Who?"

"Yes, I need a name or a number."

"I don't have a name. Anyone will do. Please! Anyone!"

"I cannot connect you with . . . ah, *anyone*."

"Just a moment." Dorrit held her hand over the mouthpiece and looked toward the grocer scooping coffee beans into the grinder for a woman who'd come into the store. Sniffing the wonderful aroma, the woman indicated she wanted a full pound—ground twice—and just when Dorrit was in a terrible hurry. "The operator needs a name," she said over the noise of the grinder, even though she knew it was impolite to interrupt Herr Ziegler when was with a customer.

"Yes, of course. Don't you have one?" He looked over his shoulder at her and kept cranking the handle on the grinder.

"No."

"Well, then you'd better hang up and give me time to think." The grinder fell silent; Herr Ziegler weighed the coffee and sealed the bag.

Dorrit thanked the operator for her trouble and replaced the receiver.

The grocer put the coffee and the woman's other purchases into the net she held open. After he'd counted out her change and walked over to open the door for her, he turned and gave Dorrit his full attention.

"I gather it's Hannah's day off, or you wouldn't be in such a pickle?" he said.

"Yes. She doesn't work Wednesdays and Saturdays."

"Then the best thing to do is to run over to Wirchow."

"The hospital?"

"It's only a few blocks. It will be much quicker to fetch help rather than call and wait for a doctor to show up."

That made sense to Dorrit.

"Do you know where it is?"

"I . . . I think so." She sounded unsure.

Motioning her over to the storefront window, Herr Ziegler pointed through the glass. "Go along Niederlag. Make a right at the second intersection. Walk three blocks and you'll see the hospital on the south side of the street. You can't miss it. It's a huge red brick building."

"Yes, I remember seeing it once."

"Good. But don't go to the main entrance. Go to the emergency ward. It's clearly marked and there's always someone on duty. Explain your father's symptoms. If not a doctor, at least they'll send a nurse back to the apartment with you."

"Uh . . ." Suddenly embarrassed, Dorrit lowered her eyes.

"What? What is it?"

"Since it's such a big place, do they . . . do they charge an awful lot?"

"No more than a private practitioner. Probably less."

Relieved, Dorrit pulled open the door. A sudden blast of frigid air entered the store. "Thank you, Herr Ziegler."

"*Gott im Himmel!*" The grocer shivered and his gaze swept over Dorrit's inadequate housedress, which made her look awfully thin and vulnerable. He looked down at her bare feet in the worn slippers. "You've got to go home first and put on some warm clothing and some proper shoes."

"I don't have time," Dorrit said, anxious to be on her way. "I'm not cold."

"Well, at least take this." Herr Ziegler reached for a large woolen scarf some customer had left behind. It had hung prominently by the door for months but was so ugly that no one admitted to owning it.

Dorrit accepted the shawl, quickly wrapping it tightly around her head and shoulders. "Thank you. I'll return it later," she promised.

"Keep it. You'll be doing me a favor." Herr Ziegler looked around for something else she could have. "Hmm, let me see . . ." When he heard the door slam, he realized he was talking to himself.

Chapter 20

"Hey, *wake up!*" Dr. Eckart walked into the emergency ward where he found his colleague slumped over the desk at the reception station. He scanned the scheduling sheet and discovered that Johann had been on duty some eighteen hours. "For crying out loud!" Kurt Eckart poked his friend to rouse him. "Wake up and go home! You're doing overtime on your overtime."

Johann straightened in the chair and looked at Kurt with a glazed expression. He rotated his shoulders, checking for signs of life.

"Did you hear what I said?" Kurt jabbed him again.

"You told me to go home. You want my job?"

"No. I came down to see if you're hungry."

"Hungry...?"

"Forget it. In your condition you won't be good company. Go home. I'll cover for you till your replacement gets here."

"Thanks." Johann glanced around the empty room. During the night he had treated a gunshot wound and three drunks who'd gotten into a fight. One had fallen on his bottle and been impaled. Thankfully, the others had immediately set aside their dispute and brought him in before he bled to death. Early this morning there'd been several youngsters suffering fevers and highly strung parents. An elderly man with a sprained ankle had hobbled in alone, while a woman in false labor had arrived with a dozen relatives. But the cases had eventually tapered off. At the moment, the emergency room was empty, even of staff. The nurses had slipped down the hall for coffee; Johann seemed to remember one of them asking if he wanted some.

"Speaking of the devil, here he is." Kurt Eckart nodded toward another resident doctor coming down the hall. "Well, what do you know? It's Philip. He must have been evicted from the labs and ordered to report to ER for some real duty."

Johann, Kurt, and Philip had gone through medical school together and remained fast friends even though their interests were now taking different directions. While Johann preferred the emergency ward, Philip von Brandt favored laboratory work. He hailed from an aristocratic military family. His mother was a Hindenburg and his father, General Ludwig von Brandt, had attained great fame in the Franco-Prussian War of 1870. When Philip declined to follow his two older brothers in their distinguished military careers, he somehow landed in medical school where, repulsed by blood and gore, he soon gravitated toward research.

Kurt Eckart, on the other hand, came from a long line of physicians. His father was Chief of Surgery here at Wirchow and Kurt was being groomed to follow in his footsteps. However, he was given some flexibility last year when his sister married a physician more ambitious than he. Truth be known, Kurt's heart was not in medicine. Nonetheless, being a pragmatic man, he applied himself to the healing profession until such a time when he would come into his inheritance—old money on his mother's side—that would enable him to enter politics. To keep abreast, he regularly sat in the visitors' gallery at the Reichstag.

Struggling from the chair, Johann stretched, took off his white hospital coat, tossing it into the laundry bin before reaching for his overcoat in the metal locker behind the reception station.

"Where are the nurses?" Philip had walked in and was looking around, uncomfortable with the thought that he might be stuck here alone; it'd be just his luck to have a patient with a severed leg carried in.

"Relax," Johann said, reading his mind. "They'll be back. If not, hit the panic button and they'll be here in three seconds flat. Anyway, Kurt will keep you company."

"Wrong. I'm going to get something to eat." Kurt checked the enamel clock hanging on the wall behind the desk and prayed for fast service in the physician's lunchroom. He turned and headed up the hall before Philip could beg for mercy.

Johann bent over the roster taped to the reception station and signed out, handing the pen to Philip so he could sign in.

"Where did you say the nurses' call button is?" Philip ran his hands over the desk like a blind man.

"Right there." Johann pointed, stuffed his arms into the sleeves of his coat and with a wave over his shoulder walked through the swinging doors and out onto the sidewalk crowded with workers from local factories out and about during their lunch break. Fumbling in his pockets for his gloves, he bowed his head against the chilly March wind and hoped Schmidt had brought the coach around, something he generally did whenever Johann worked the graveyard shift.

He was rounding the corner and happily spotted his sleek black carriage, when someone brushed past him at bullet speed, knocking him off balance. Cursing under his breath, he turned to glare at the back of the rude fellow who hadn't stopped to utter a word of apology.

Huh? A girl? Barefooted in worn slippers, a hideous rag tied around her head and shoulders, she was obviously a street urchin. He saw her dash into the emergency ward but, judging from her speed and agility, didn't appear to be in need of medical attention. Johann shrugged. If she'd come to beg, she'd come to the right place. Philip was a generous chap.

Johann climbed into his comfortable coach and, dead tired, sank back against the soft leather upholstery and closed his eyes.

Schmidt pulled away from the curb.

Chapter 21

Minutes before the gold-tasseled red velvet curtains rose on the last opera of the season, Johann entered his private box with one of Berlin's well-bred beauties, the raven-haired Louisa von Tirpetz, on his arm. His loge had the enviable distinction of being adjacent to the royal parterre, regularly occupied by Germany's monarch and his empress; tonight proved to be no exception. Before the lights dimmed in preparation of the overture, Wilhelm and Augusta Victoria swept in followed by their glittering entourage.

An immediate rustling of satin gowns ensued on the floor below as everyone turned to watch the Kaiser and Kaiserin exchange greetings with the titled occupants in adjoining enclosures. Acknowledging the Baron von Renz with a cordial comment, Kaiser Wilhelm paid special attention to Fraulein von Tirpetz; her father, Admiral von Tirpetz, was his aide and personal confidant.

"My dear Louisa," using her Christian name, the Kaiser reached past the partition for her hand, "the hall is enhanced by your lovely presence this evening." He put her hand to his lips.

"Your Majesty. You are much too kind," Louisa protested demurely while executing a flawless curtsy and fluttering her fan to ensure that no one in the opera house missed the Kaiser's kiss, or her rose gown, a color that complimented her creamy skin and black hair. Both her mother's diamonds as well as her own were fastened around her throat and together fell like a sparkling waterfall to the very edge of her revealing décolleté.

During the main intermission, sipping champagne and strolling the grand mezzanine on the arm of her suave escort, Louisa continued to attract attention. Enjoying her popularity, she suspected one and all were trying to recall if she'd been seen with Johann frequently enough for them to assume that an announcement was imminent; she certainly did her best to give that impression. She clung possessively to his arm, dimpled prettily at his every word, and appeared as though there was a secret 'understanding' between them. She aspired to becoming the Baroness von Renz and had prepared herself for his declaration this past New Year's Eve during the Count and Countess von Beckstein's dazzling ball. However, much to her chagrin, the evening passed without a proposal.

In the weeks following, Louisa had given her disappointment some serious thought and realized that after returning from his Christmas holiday in Bernau, there had been something vaguely different about Johann. She couldn't put her finger on it, but he seemed distracted. During the Beckstein's New Year's Eve festivities, and considering the fact that he was her escort, he had danced with far too many other women. Furthermore, he'd gone to the smoking lounge to gamble shortly before midnight, leaving her to dance with a number of unattractive partners and watch the fireworks without him. But as if this snub wasn't bad enough, when the last dance was announced, Johann invited Lillian Schindel to the floor. During the waltz, which Louisa was obliged to suffer with Graf Zollern, she craned her neck to watch them. They appeared rather cozy, causing her to wonder if anything had passed between them in Bernau, where she knew they had spent at least two nights under the Konauers' roof. Of course, Louisa refused to believe that a silly goose like Lillian could hold Johann's interest for long. It was hard work keeping him charmed. Louisa had invested months in the endeavor and it never occurred to her that some anonymous girl had managed it in a matter of minutes and with no effort at all.

Indeed, three months had now passed since Johann's brief meeting with that nameless stranger on the steps of the Ladeburg Inn. Yet, her enchanting face and smile teased him to this day, a bedevilment that often interfered with a good night's sleep. There was no scarcity of beautiful women in Berlin, so it was nothing short of lunacy that he only wanted the one he couldn't find. The distinct possibility that she and her father had come to the city for a short stay and had long since left, did nothing to dampen his desire or ameliorate the strange bondage to a memory.

A practical man would have put the trifling encounter to rest long ago, Johann told himself time and again; yet, he had not been able to do so. Moreover, in January, he had gone so far as to send a private investigator to Ladeburg to interview the proprietor and have a look at the guest registry. Unfortunately, the ledger along with everything else about the inn was neglected, and the proprietor had not recorded a one-night stopover. He recalled the lovely Fraulein and her less than robust father, but as much as he was threatened, cajoled, and bribed, he could not remember any name; nor could he recall any pertinent information that might be traced.

Chapter 22

Karl-Heinz shifted restlessly in his seat as the carriage rattled through Schwanebeck on its way to Berlin. He glanced at the rapidly changing landscape where green fields were slowly giving way to clusters of plain houses sidling up to breweries and other buildings associated with the various industries thriving on the outskirts of any large city. With each passing minute, he prayed Gerlinde would experience a change of heart so he could order his driver to turn around.

"For heaven's sake!" he finally muttered, feeling increasingly trapped. "Why do you want to give birth in a cold, austere hospital among strangers rather than in the comfort of your own home?"

Gerlinde sighed and looked at her husband with a small, controlled smile. They had covered this ground many times, but since he enjoyed nothing better than bellyaching, she was not about to deny him some pleasure on a trip he was staunchly opposed to. "Johann is no stranger," she reminded him. "He has promised to be on hand."

"Yes, and isn't that just peachy? I suppose it doesn't bother you to have him see you . . . uh, well, you know . . ." Karl-Heinz was suddenly at a loss for words.

Pink spots crept into Gerlinde's cheeks; she was plenty bothered and inherently shy, but was far more afraid than modest. When Dr. Speckmeier told her that she was carrying twins, she realized she needed a medical miracle and hoped Wirchow could provide it. And if that meant Johann would see her in a state of total undress, so be it. She'd stand naked on a public street if it guaranteed bringing healthy babies into the world.

Karl-Heinz was still venting his spleen as the carriage skirted Wannsee Lake and entered the forested suburb of Grunewald, soon rumbling along Lindenstrasse. "I suppose you think it's strange that our Kaiserin gives birth at home?" he asked in a last ditch effort to make Gerlinde see reason. Having come this far, he was willing to spend a pleasant evening with Johann and then take Gerlinde back home tomorrow.

Studying a small imperfection in one of her lace gloves, Gerlinde mumbled something inaudible.

"Did you ever stop to wonder why the Kaiser's children are born at home?" Karl-Heinz pressed her.

She shook her head.

"Well, I'll tell you. It's proper. It's traditional. Hospitals are for the sick. God only knows what kind of diseases one might encounter there."

"With twins to consider, Johann says . . ."

Karl-Heinz rolled his eyes, stopping her in mid-sentence. "Sure! He says something and we all jump. Well, I say, not that anyone listens of course, but I say he has no business meddling in the private affairs of others. Living in Berlin has done strange things to him. City noises have rattled his brain and now he's on some absurd mission to upset the established order of things. What's good enough for the royal house is suddenly not good enough for the Konauers. On top of that, he's forcing me to abandon my lands during the growing season."

"You don't need to remain in Berlin."

"Oh? And how would it look if I didn't?"

"Anyone curious enough to wonder could be told that you have to stay with Hans."

"That would be insulting to my parents as well as to the employment of Fraulein Kruse."

"Yes, I suppose so," Gerlinde acquiesced softly. "But you don't need to stay in Berlin the entire time. My due date is not for another four weeks. You could travel back and forth."

"Are you suggesting," Karl-Heinz demanded hotly, "that I leave you alone in the house of a bachelor?"

"In my condition," Gerlinde giggled, "do you really believe anyone would talk? Besides, Lillian could come and stay with me."

"Lillian!" Karl-Heinz snorted. "That would only make matters worse. Johann escorts her around town occasionally. How would it look if they were suddenly cohabitating? City folk have an insatiable appetite for gossip. Lillian's reputation would be in shreds within an hour. Woe be it for us to blacken her fine family name. It's my mother's, too, don't forget."

Gerlinde smiled secretly. Ursula was not worried about gossip, except that generated by her son if he abandoned his pregnant wife for even a day.

Chapter 23

For *the past* half hour, Frau Schmidt and Nurse Gneist had kept their vigil by the front door of the massive gray marble villa on Lindenstrasse, Nurse Gneist anxiously eying the traffic, worried that the ride from Bernau might have started her patient's labor, in which case there'd be nothing for her to do except bring the mother-to-be to Wirchow, and then go back home and wallow in disappointment. Nurses vied for these plum private home assignments, and she was especially pleased to have landed one that might last for as long as a month. The accommodations were exceptionally grand, and with so many maids under foot no one would ask her to lift a domestic finger. Smoothing the pleats in her white uniform, she was adjusting her cap when she spotted a coach slowing down along the street. When she heard the rasping sound of brakes being set, she knew her patient had arrived.

"They're here!" she exclaimed, pushing Frau Schmidt aside as she now rushed down the steps; the housekeeper had been pleasant company during the wait but was no longer needed.

Shuffling along the flagstone walkway on sensible rubber-soled shoes, Nurse Gneist passed swiftly through the wrought iron gates and stopped at the curb, her arms folded across her ample chest as she watched Herr Konauer climb from the coach. She eyed him with a severe expression. Thirty years in the nursing profession, she'd seen many women die in childbirth and had developed a healthy dislike of men. To her credit, she'd managed never to marry one and now made short work of the required formalities with this male person, quickly edging him out of the way so she could assist Frau Konauer from the coach.

"There now . . . easy does it." Nurse Gneist used a kind tone as she helped her patient to the sidewalk dappled with splashes of a sudden, soft May rain. "I'm Nurse Gneist. Welcome to Berlin!"

Gerlinde smiled, and once her feet were securely planted and her awkward weight balanced, she offered her hand. "I'm so glad to be here."

"Well, I should say so. And now you just leave everything to me. Herr Doctor keeps long and unpredictable hours at Wirchow so I'll be available around the clock. But, dear me, let's not stand about on the wet sidewalk and chitchat. Into the house with you. We'll have a spot of tea. Then you must take a nap. I'll have to insist."

Gerlinde smiled at the domineering woman and wondered how Johann knew that this was precisely the kind of person she'd be most comfortable with. Nurse Gneist was an uncanny mixture of two maiden aunts she had once loved so dearly.

Walking up the path and climbing the wide marble steps to the front door, Gerlinde appreciated the scented air from a profusion of purple lilac growing along the side of the house and inhaled deeply. Paying no attention to fragrance or flora, Nurse Gneist was eying Frau Schmidt, wondering why that busybody was still standing there.

Unaware of the nurse's uncharitable thoughts, Frau Schmidt cheerfully offered her hand. "Welcome, Frau Konauer!" she said with a bright smile. "We've been eagerly awaiting your arrival."

Holding a palm over her heart, Gerlinde had to catch her breath before speaking. "I hope my husband and I won't be putting you out?"

"Not at all. We're delighted to have you," Frau Schmidt declared quite truthfully because this houseguest and her husband had been here before. This petite woman was easy to deal with and not the least bit demanding.

Brushing the housekeeper aside, Nurse Gneist led her patient into the rotunda-like hall where Schmidt took Frau Konauer's cloak before going out to the curb to help carry the valises.

"Don't forget, bring everything to the downstairs guest suite," Nurse Gneist called after him before smiling at her patient and saying, "We can't have you climbing stairs."

Eying the long curved staircase to the upper floors, Gerlinde was grateful for the nurse's wisdom.

Chapter 24

Gerlinde's water broke two weeks later just as she pushed herself away from the dinner table and stood up. Doubling over, she clutched her stomach and turned deathly pale as a puddle spread in a circle under her skirts.

"Dear God!" she moaned, mortification buckling her knees as she eyed the stain on the priceless blue Persian carpet. "Johann, I . . . I'm so sorry."

"Nonsense," he said and was at her side in a flash, his arms around her to prevent her from falling.

"Hey! What's going on?" Karl-Heinz roared when he saw Johann embracing his wife. Stymied in Berlin, he felt entitled to some excesses, had polished off an entire bottle of wine with dinner, and was now slow to grasp the situation. However, the minute he saw Johann lift Gerlinde clear off the floor, he rose to the occasion. "Unhand my wife!" he bellowed, following the duo into the hall where Johann placed Gerlinde in a chair before giving orders. Karl-Heinz collapsed on a bench next to her. Schmidt left the house to harness the coach, and Frau Schmidt went to summon Nurse Gneist. The commotion flushed several maids from their rooms on the third floor. Leaning over the banister, they witnessed the whirlwind of activity, glad that Frau Konauer's time had finally come. For the past week the poor thing had barely been able to walk.

After fetching her wrap from a hall closet, Johann bent down to speak to Gerlinde. "I'll be taking you to the hospital," he said and knowing that Karl-Heinz was in no condition to leave the house, told him to stay home for the time being. "It'll be hours before you have anything to celebrate. As soon as Schmidt has dropped us off, he'll come back and the coach will be at your disposal. I'll telephone you from Wirchow. Don't set out until you hear from me."

"All right." Karl-Heinz had no problem with that. He didn't like hospitals and was in no particular hurry to see the inside of one. This business of his wife giving birth in an institution for the sick had not been his idea.

Carrying Frau Konauer's valise, packed days ago, Nurse Gneist came running and took her patient under her wing with excessive kindness. But the look she directed toward the husband spelled useless man so clearly she might as well have shouted.

Gerlinde had been in labor a number of hours when Johann concluded that a caesarean section was her only hope. However, he had no seniority and came up against a stonewall when he tried to convince the attending physician to consider it. One baby was in the breech position, yet Dr. Ercklentz—a man with years of experience—insisted it could be turned, although its twin left no room for the maneuver.

Cursing a system where vintage doctors were allowed to play God, Johann ground his teeth and continued to monitor the patient. The babies' heartbeats were strong, but Gerlinde's was growing weaker, and as agonizing time passed, he realized she would have been no worse off in Bernau with Dr. Speckmaier. Why had he upset the Konauer household and brought her to Berlin?

Half an hour later, when her blood pressure began dropping the same time her heart began racing, Johann recognized the signs of acute distress and, regardless of Dr. Ercklentz's opinion, knew she could not deliver these babies. Every second was now critical and insofar as he had already reasoned with the senior man to no avail, he seized command of the situation. It was time to broker a miracle.

"Let's get the patient into an operating room!" he barked, motioning the attending nurse to send out the alert. "Now!"

"Pardon me?" Dr. Ercklentz's face appeared almost comical as his head popped up from between Gerlinde's thighs. With a wave of his hand, he indicated the nurse was to remain at her station. He got up from the stool and walked over to the sink to dab cold water on his face. "The patient is fully dilated," he said. "She is making good progress. In a few minutes I'll be able to use the forceps."

"I respectfully disagree," Johann bit off.

"Oh?" Dr. Ercklentz looked annoyed but kept his professional composure and, above all, remembered to keep his voice down so that the one being discussed wouldn't hear him. Women in the throes of giving birth might be blinded by pain, but in his experience they rarely suffered any hearing loss. "Her condition is much too fragile for a C-section," he said under his breath. "She might not come out of anesthesia. She's too weak."

"Which is precisely why she can't go on like this," Johann said between clenched teeth, and was about to remind the senior man that he had suggested a C-section hours ago before the patient weakened. But he held his tongue, figuring Dr. Ercklentz was only months away from retirement and did not want to rock the boat and test the hospital's long-established procedures. Or . . . ? It occurred to Johann that perhaps he had never performed a caesarean. Of course he couldn't hold that against him, for neither had he, but he had observed several. One as recently as last week and every step was fresh in his mind. He flexed his fingers. He could do it. He was almost sure of it.

When Gerlinde sank into unconsciousness, he became absolutely certain. Of course he'd have to force the issue and it would probably mean dismissal, which was fine by him as long as he was fired after the surgery. He kicked the locked wheels of the gurney free. Sensing movement, Gerlinde surfaced to a feeble plateau of awareness. Her small fingers worked themselves free from the tangled sheets and grasped at the metal rails on the bed. What was happening? Exhausted, her hollow eyes searched her surroundings.

Leaning over, Johann took her hand, squeezing it gently. "We'll have to operate," he whispered.

"N . . . no . . ." She rolled her head from side to side, clutching his hand with both of hers.

"It's the only way."

"I . . . I don't want ether."

Johann realized that she had overheard Dr. Ercklentz's remarks about not coming out of anesthesia.

"Darling, don't be afraid. You'll be fine. I'll see you through it." Johann sounded more certain of the outcome than he felt, but it was key to be confident. "You've done enough work. Now it's my turn."

A ghost of a smile parted Gerlinde's white lips before another violent contraction tore through her body.

Johann pushed the gurney forward.

Dr. Ercklentz was at the door, blocking the way. "May I remind you of your position?" he all but shouted. "As a resident physician, you have no authority to . . ."

"That's right," Johann cut him off. "I have no authority to stand by while a life is ebbing away. Three lives!"

Dr. Ercklentz blinked.

Johann tasted victory. "I will take full responsibility. This patient is a close friend of mine."

"Which might be clouding your judgment." Dr. Ercklentz bent over the patient, placing his stethoscope on her swollen belly. He was suddenly tired and unsure of his own diagnosis. Forceps were of little help in a situation such as this and the patient would probably die regardless. Here or on the operating table. What did it matter? Her bone structure, her small brittle body, was not made for childbearing. And twins? Well, that was just her bad luck. Twins doubled the chance for disaster even for a more robust woman. He straightened and looked squarely at Johann. "All right. Go ahead. Perform the surgery," he said, thinking that perhaps one of the babies might be saved, and glad to wash his hands of this patient.

Chapter 25

It was several weeks later when Gerlinde was discharged from Wirchow with two healthy baby girls.

On the heels of the Konauers' departure from Berlin, Johann removed himself as well to spend the summer on his estate in Bernau. When he'd initially been offered the residency at Wirchow, he'd made it clear that he would not be on duty during the months of July and August, something of a brass announcement, and one that had given the administration pause. Had they objected, he would simply have accepted a position at Charite or at another more "understanding" competitor. Although the practice of medicine occasionally humbled him, it never caused him to lose the arrogance of his breed.

A day in August, a day of torrential downpours, Karl-Heinz rode to the barony and strolled into Johann's library, trailing buckets of water and tossing his wet cloak and hat negligently to Rolf. The butler removed the dripping garments, carrying them well away from his own person as if they presented an offensive odor.

"Being the mother of three has gone to my wife's head," Karl-Heinz scoffed and unraveled several blueprints he pulled from the inside of his shirt, where they had survived the rain. "Not only does she think she's entitled to her own house, it has to rival the Palace of Potsdam!"

"And why not?"

"Yes, why not?" Karl-Heinz concurred with a sly grin. "Which is why I spent an appalling fortune on that thieving architect you recommended."

"There's none better in Berlin."

"There's no one richer now that I've paid him for these!" Karl-Heinz waved the blueprints accusingly at Johann.

"Does Gerlinde like the plans?"

"She loves them."

"Then your money was well spent."

"I'll withhold judgment until I see the finished product." Karl-Heinz had mellowed over the years, but displayed a stubborn streak now and again for old times' sake. Using a heavy inkwell and a crystal cheroot tray as weights, he spread out the blueprints on Johann's desk. "All right, take a look." Pointing to several highlighted areas, he went on to explain each in great detail. "Of course, the children's playroom will be on the ground floor. Not tucked away near the attic as it is in my parents' home. Which, come to think of it, is a real danger in case of fire."

"Something the architect pointed out?"

"Huh?"

"I thought so," Johann laughed. "By the way, have your parents reconciled themselves to separate households? Or haven't you told them yet?"

"Being that I'm no coward, of course I've told them." Karl-Heinz cleared his throat, rolled up the blueprints and slipped the rubber band around them. "Actually Gerlinde broke the news," he said with a lopsided grin. "They were distressed at first but felt better once they learned we were planning to build right down the hill from the old manse. If they miss the sound of squabbling children, all they have to do is open a window."

Chapter 26

Over the course of the summer Johann came to the conclusion that he wanted to specialize; few in his profession did, but he felt it was the way of the future. Delicate and risky surgery intrigued him, something that was confirmed with Gerlinde's caesarean, and since he wasn't relying on the practice of medicine for a living, he could afford to be selective.

He returned to Berlin in September and began visiting his alma mater to hone his skills on cadavers and to observe new techniques performed by such world famous physicians as Theodore Kocher and Hugo Knonecker. It was on one such occasion, while watching from the observation gallery, that he heard about a weekly seminar dealing with the history of radical surgery. He decided to attend and rearranged his Friday schedule in order to do so.

As the professor pottered into the lecture hall the following Friday afternoon, Johann craned his neck to see past the seats in front of him. There was something vaguely familiar about this individual and Johann could have sworn he had seen him before. However, any familiarity, real or imagined, became unimportant once the lecture began. The man was a well of knowledge, produced illustrations to prove his theories, and claimed that blood vessel surgery and reconnecting severed nerves would one day become routine. Feverishly taking notes, still vexed by the feeling that he knew the man, Johann finally decided he simply reminded him of other professors he'd known. After all, members of the university community shared certain similarities: beards in need of a trimming, small wire-rimmed glasses, and baggy attire. This pedagogue fit that mold with his trademark rumbled tweed coat, frayed bow tie, and trousers without pleats held up by leather suspenders.

Throughout the fall Johann attended each of Dr. Zache's seminars, frequently remaining behind to challenge the professor with provocative questions. It was during one such discussion in mid December that Dr. Zache offered Johann the loan of several books he had co-authored while at Warsaw University.

"These translations are rare," he cautioned as he handed them over. "The publisher ran only a limited print run in the German language. If lost, it will be difficult to replace them."

Fingering the volumes, Johann promised to return them by next week's seminar. "Unless you'd like them back sooner?"

"No. Next Friday will be fine. In fact," the professor chortled, "I'd be insulted if you were finished with them before that."

Chapter 27

A *cold, pea-soup* fog had hung over Berlin for days and on the afternoon when Johann brought the books back to the university, he found a group of his colleagues milling outside the lecture room, reading a note pinned to the door, explaining that Dr. Zache was ill and would not be available until after the Christmas recess. As his colleagues scattered, Johann lingered indecisively. He felt uneasy about keeping the publications over the long holiday period, but to deposit them here in the professor's cubicle by the door was even more troublesome. Of course, with the lecture canceled, he had time to spare before reporting to his nightshift at Wirchow and could use it to deliver the books directly to Dr. Zache's home.

An administrative secretary in an office down the hall provided Johann with the address, writing it down on a piece of paper. Thanking her, he put the slip in his coat pocket, tucked the books securely under his arm, and left the university compound, walking through the Humboldt Gates out onto Unter den Linden.

A stiff wind was dispersing the fog, turning it into blowing sleet that almost obliterated the beautiful gothic-columned State Opera at the corner of Opernplatz, discouraging both pedestrians and pigeons from dawdling. On the opposite side of the square, the Royal Library and National Archives buildings rose in architectural splendor, outdone only by the opera house.

Shivering, Johann turned up the collar on his coat and glanced up and down the wide boulevard where a sudden coating of ice had now slowed traffic to a crawl. Spotting his coach parked half a block away he hurried along the slippery sidewalk, dodging in between other hardy souls in various stages of skidding.

"I need to make a stop before you drop me at Wirchow," he said to Schmidt, fishing the slip of paper from his pocket and handing it over as he got into the coach.

"Very well." Schmidt studied the address, closed the door and climbed back up into the driver's box. He clucked to the horses, turned right at the next corner and continued east for a couple of blocks. Progressing along Niederlag Strasse, he shortly pulled into a narrow street, the coach wheels rumbling over the uneven cobblestones.

Johann glanced out the window, surprised to learn that Dr. Zache lived in this dismal community. But he supposed it went hand in hand with the neglected attire. Those devoted to academia wasted little time on luxuries and although the teaching profession was a highly respected one, it was not particularly lucrative for a non-tenured professor.

Checking the address, Schmidt halted the horses in front of a three-story brick structure so ordinary it defied description. As he jumped down and opened the carriage door, pulling out the steps in one fluid motion, he contrasted this building to other residences where he normally dropped off his employer. He hoped the baron's business here would be quick; dusk came abruptly in December and this was no place to linger after dark.

"I'll only be a minute," Johann said, stepping from the coach and crossing the sidewalk. Once inside the building, he stopped at the base of the stairs to determine which apartment Dr. Zache occupied. Leaning close, he studied the names on the mailboxes, the unlit hall making the small print hard to read. A door behind him squeaked. Without turning, Johann knew he was being spied upon.

"Who are you looking for?" a sharp voice demanded to know.

Johann spun around and caught a glimpse of a shock of gray hair before the door slammed shut, followed by the frantic rattling of keys as the tenant made herself secure.

"I am looking for Dr. Zache," he said, addressing the locked door. "Can you tell me which apartment he's in?"

"Top floor. Door on the left."

"Thank you." Johann started up the stairs.

"Make sure the front door is closed before you go up," the woman said from inside her apartment. "And it wouldn't hurt to remind the professor's daughter to do the same. That girl is constantly running in and out, wasting a lot of heat, and God knows what street rabble is invited in when the door is left open. This used to be a proper building."

Ignoring the woman's complaints, Johann made his way up the dimly lit stairwell against the unpleasant smell of fried liver, coupled with the noise of brawling children behind closed doors. Of course, if what he smelled was their supper, no wonder they were testy. A moment later, when he tripped over a bicycle some thoughtless yokel had left on the landing, Johann began to regret his decision to come here. By the time he reached the uppermost floor and rapped on the professor's door, he realized he should have sent Schmidt.

A chubby girl wearing a stained apron and blond braids wrapped around her head like a crown answered his knock.

"Fraulein Zache?" Johann believed her to be the irresponsible daughter the woman on the ground floor had complained about. "My name is Dr. von Renz. May I see your father for a moment?"

"I'm not . . . uh, I'm Hannah. I work for Dr. Zache."

"I see. Well, I have some books for him."

"You can give them to me." The girl held out a hand while guarding the door with the other. "I'll see that he gets them."

"I wish to deliver them personally." Although she was probably following instructions not to let in strangers, her suspicious manner irritated Johann and he was not about to requite her lack of trust by handing over the books. The silly wench might put them down in the kitchen and forget to inform her employer of their safe return. Perhaps it'd been a mistake to come here, but there was no reason to compound it with another.

"The professor is ill," she said. "Wait here. I'll see if he can have visitors."

Before she could shut the door on him, Johann put his hand out against the insult, but only managed to keep it ajar because Hannah had planted her foot solidly on the inside. But, having challenged him, she was unsure about what to do next. Only one thing was certain, she could not leave the door open. An intruder gussied up like a gentleman had robbed the family a floor below and hadn't been caught yet. As far as she knew, this might be the same individual.

"Hannah?" A voice called out from inside the apartment. "Is someone at the door?"

"Yes!" Johann spoke up. "I would like to see the professor. I . . ." His voice died in his throat because even in the dim light of the small foyer, he recognized her the minute she came into view. "Good God!" he sputtered.

Frowning at the expletive, she approached the door.

Silent and strangely numb, Johann stared at the image that had haunted him for an entire year and, of course, he now instantly realized why Dr. Zache had seemed familiar at that initial seminar back in September. He was none other than the weary traveler at the Ladeburg Inn, whose face had been obscured by a woolen scarf. Astonished with the luck of coming here today, Johann failed to conceal his delight as his eyes raked over the professor's daughter. She had grown, he noticed. She was taller and standing in this dingy hallway—lush copper curls cascading freely over her shoulders—her face radiated such glamour that her plain frock and dull surroundings appeared even more so in contrast.

"Are those my father's books?" she asked the tongue-tied caller, her eyes on the bundle under his arm.

"Yes." Johann absorbed the shock he'd sustained with a couple of shallow breaths, freeing his vocal cords. "I came to return them."

"Well, please come in," she said, more trusting than the maid. "I'm Dorrit." She extended her hand. "Dorrit Zache."

As Johann reached for her hand and introduced himself, he wondered if she recognized him. It appeared she didn't. There was not the slightest trace of recollection in her lovely green eyes.

"My father is ill," she explained, ushering the guest inside. "But not so ill that he won't be cheered by company. Are you a colleague?"

"Actually, I'm one of his students." Shifting the books from one hand to the other, Johann shed his coat and gave it to the maid. She hung it in the hall closet before disappearing into the kitchen. "I attend his Friday seminars. Your father was good enough to lend me these books last week. When his lecture was canceled today, I decided I'd better bring them by."

"That's very considerate," Dorrit said, leading the guest along a narrow corridor. "I hope it wasn't too far out of your way."

"No, not at all. I'm on duty at Wirchow tonight. So this was very convenient."

"You're a medical doctor?"

"Yes."

"My father was a physician before he turned to teaching."

"Yes, so I understand."

"He was a very skilled surgeon at one time," she added with pride. "Of course that was long ago when his health was good. His lungs are weak. It would have been a disaster to let him go out in today's weather. I insisted that he cancel his lecture."

"A wise precaution," Johann nodded, thinking it was nothing short of a miracle. For how else—and by what possible means—could he have discovered that Dr. Zache was the father of such an amazing offspring? With all due respect and looking at the professor in the best light, one would never in a million years guess that he'd sired such a perfect child.

Dorrit brought Johann into the living room, a small rectangular parlor with a lone window that looked out onto the tiled roof of the neighboring building where a sagging, rain-filled gutter defied gravity with the help of a few rusty and loose nails. Dressed in a warm robe, the professor was sitting in the sofa with a tartan blanket spread over his knees and a pillow behind his back. His wire-rimmed spectacles lay on a small table set with two cups and a teapot. An open newspaper, strewn across a wing chair, suggested that Dorrit had been reading aloud to him.

Despite its lack of fine decor, Johann decided the room was wonderful. Wall shelves buckled under the weight of countless books haphazardly stashed amid a collection of old clocks, cranky with age, for not a single one kept the correct time. Among the clutter, he spotted some framed photographs of a child in various stages of development, plus what appeared to be a recent portrait of father and daughter. There was no woman in any of the pictures. Evidence of Dorrit's mother was conspicuously missing.

Chapter 28

After a nightlong shift in the emergency ward where he had free reign with whatever creative procedure he chose for victims of grisly crimes or accidents, Johann returned home, knowing that unless infection set in he had probably saved a life or two. Following a nap and a change of clothes, he was ready to tackle the mail, the newspapers, and the breakfast tray Frau Schmidt brought into the library. Placing the food on the table near his chair, she put another log on the fire and opened the red velvet drapes. The tall windows on each side of the fireplace were patterned in small diamond-shaped glass panes offering daylight and a pleasant view through a row of birch trees, past a patch of manicured grass and beyond to the sidewalk where the wrought-iron fence was embraced by clinging wisteria vines. On the opposite side of the street, groves of elm and chestnut marked the perimeter of Grunewald Park. The trees were bare and dormant at this time of year, but were embroidered each spring in a variety of lush greens.

On Saturdays, in addition to the regular Berlin papers, Johann had the London Herald and a Paris weekly delivered; reading them helped him keep up his French and English. There was always much to wade through and it was generally a labor of fascination, but today his interest was lacking. Each time he came to the end of an article, he realized he hadn't the foggiest idea what he'd just read.

Irritated, he finally tossed the papers into a heap on the floor and got up. He felt restless and needed to move about. Of course, he didn't have to exercise his legs to determine that it was Dorrit Zache who interfered with his concentration. Underlying his lack of focus this morning was a prickly feeling that something had not gone well yesterday. For although she had greeted him warmly, a short while later she appeared eager to be rid of him. He had barely sat down and accepted a cup of tea when she began to glance at the various clocks in the room, indicating his speedy departure would be welcomed.

Why the sudden change in her attitude?

Perhaps he shouldn't have accepted the tea, which in truth he had only done to prolong the visit, in retrospect, probably a mistake. But even if he had wanted to leave immediately after handing over the books, how could he possibly have done so without insulting the professor? A born rodomont, the man had seemed delighted to see him, talking nonstop from the moment Johann arrived, stopping only to cough, not a sterling time for a physician to withdraw.

"Dorrit has had more education than most males her age," Dr. Zache began boasting almost immediately and looked over the rim of his cup to discern the impact his words were having on the guest. The minute he noted Johann's interest there was no stopping him. "I had little in the way of material goods to give her, so I made sure she was properly schooled and able to converse in several languages." The professor held out his cup for more tea, saying, "Display your proficiency with French, my dear."

"Papa! Really!" She shook her head as she poured and, neglecting to offer Johann a refill, set the pot down on the trivet with a thud.

"There's no need to get testy," Dr. Zache smiled good-naturedly and turned back to Johann. "I'm a staunch believer in the mastery of languages. Years before we arrived in Berlin, I made sure Dorrit's German was as polished as that of a born citizen." Looking sly, he added, "Surely my daughter is far too pretty to have any harsh accents on her tongue. Wouldn't you agree?"

Johann agreed.

Dorrit rolled her eyes at a rather large wall clock.

Pacing the floor in his library, it now occurred to Johann that perhaps Dr. Zache's bragging had made her uncomfortable and getting rid of the guest was the only way to stop the conversation, which also taxed the professor's lungs. He had wheezed and coughed a great deal; indeed, his daughter had every reason to worry. Her father was not a healthy man. Johann guessed pulmonary disease was slowly ravaging his lungs. There was no treatment except rest and warmth and she obviously made sure he got plenty of both, which was why she was watching the clock.

Arriving at that conclusion, Johann stopped pacing and sat down to finish his breakfast. The eggs were cold; he pushed them aside, halved a *semmel* roll and spread it liberally with butter and strawberry jam. After pouring some coffee from the silver carafe, he took a sip, leaned back in his chair, and made plans for Dorrit Zache.

He would enjoy nothing better than to take her to a nightclub, loosen her up with champagne and commence with his courtship, something he intended to make as short as possible. Initially the professor would probably have to be accommodated, if only because Dorrit might not accept an invitation that didn't include him, which ruled out Ciro's, but left other options open such as an evening at the opera followed by supper at the Adlon. The old elegant hotel on Pariser Platz had an exceptional dining room, a favorite with the after-the-concert crowd. Johann assumed that Dr. Zache was a music enthusiast. Intellectuals generally were.

He got up from his chair, walked over to his desk and scanned his calendar. He had signed up for an inordinate amount of night duty at Wirchow in order to have Christmas week off. Next Thursday was his first free evening, but it was also December the 23rd, the day he was traveling to Bernau.

Sitting down, tapping his fingers on the desk, Johann deliberated his dilemma, finally deciding that he would cancel Christmas with the Konauers, remain in Berlin and woo Fraulein Zache, commencing with an invitation for the opera and dinner. Rummaging through the drawers for something other than gold-initialed vellum stationery, which might strike the Spartan educator as garish, he found some simple parchment sheets and formulated an invitation for next Thursday.

He summoned Schmidt. "Deliver this to Professor Zache on Niederlag," he said, handing the envelope to the butler. "Be sure to return with a response."

"*Jawohl,* Herr Baron."

"Let's skip all formality around the professor and his daughter. I'd like them to be comfortable."

"Very well, Herr . . . *Herr Doctor?*"

"Fine."

As Schmidt left the library his eyes skimmed the back of the envelope, where his employer had simply scrawled:

Johann von Renz
77 Lindenstrasse
Grunewald

Well, it can't get any less formal than that, Schmidt mused and left to do the baron's bidding.

Feeling nothing but confident anticipation, Johann went back to his chair by the fire and picked up a newspaper from the pile on the floor.

Chapter 29

H*is good spirits* were short-lived. Schmidt returned within the hour, bearing disappointing news. Fraulein Zache had declined the invitation.

"Why?" Johann asked, surprised.

"She gave no reasons, *mein* Herr."

Johann dismissed the butler with the flick of his wrist. Once he was alone he got up, took an iron poker and used unnecessary roughness on the logs in the fireplace. Showers of sparks flew out onto the marble fireguard, coming dangerously close to singeing a rug. Had he dispatched a similar note to anyone else in Berlin it would have been accepted at once. People rearranged their calendars to accommodate him, a hand-delivered invitation was nothing less than a social triumph, and in the event Dorrit and the professor were committed to a previous engagement, why hadn't she just said so? A clarification left the door open, whereas a plain *no* made suggesting an alternative date damned awkward. Hands on hips, staring at the fire, it occurred to Johann that she might have another suitor, a thought that caused jealousy to seep into the deep dark recesses of his soul. Areas never before tapped rumbled to life with ugly feelings as he visualized her in the company of another male, one who couldn't possibly be worthy of such a treasure.

Scowling, he turned away from the fire and glanced absently out toward the street. After days of a dense fog, followed by yesterday's icy mess, the sky finally showed patches of blue. He ought to go riding—a reliable tension reliever—and the public stables in Grunewald Park offered surprisingly good stock. He had plenty of time once he finished the newspapers. He was free until tonight when he was escorting Louisa von Tirpitz to a richly attended but conversationally destitute soiree. He grimaced at the prospect of the evening ahead. Louisa was increasingly playing coy, which irritated him. Expecting to wring a declaration from him and believing it'd hasten his intent, she flirted mercilessly, teased him with provocative gowns, but immediately became a pillar of virtue the minute he tested the sincerity of her dalliance.

Idly massaging the tight muscles at the back of his neck, Johann acknowledged he was in need of some pleasant diversion. Happily, the gathering tonight would be sprinkled with a predictable number of women who were bored with their marriages or angry with their husbands. Among them, one could usually be counted on to risk scandal. The evening need not be a total loss. And tomorrow? Tomorrow he would make a new plan for Fraulein Zache. That decided, he settled down in his chair and resumed his reading.

Frau Schmidt came into the library to remove the tray.

Dorrit Zache arrived in front of the house.

Chapter 30

Standing on the sidewalk for endless moments, peering at the huge villa, she was convinced she had made a mistake. A physician, even the most gifted, didn't live in a house as grand as this. Digging into her coat pocket, she took out the envelope with the invitation, turned it over and checked the address again.

77 Lindenstasse...

This was it. The number corresponded to the one on the gate. There was no mistaking it, just like there was no mistaking the fact that she hadn't wanted to come, yet had gone to considerable trouble to get here, taking both a trolley and a bus and walking the last stretch.

Again she stared at the large villa. Surely no ordinary mortal dared pass uninvited through these elegant gates. She, the most ordinary of mortals, definitely had no stomach for it and couldn't for the life of her understand why her father had sent her. Why would a man who shunned all social interaction suddenly become unreasonable about an invitation?

"*Mein Gott!*" he exclaimed when he returned home from synagogue and saw the note from Dr. von Renz. "The opera? Dinner at the Adlon? That's a pretty pricey place." Remaining in the hall, examining the invitation with intense interest, he turned to Dorrit. "What did you tell the person who delivered this?"

"Nothing, Papa."

"Nothing?"

"Only that we couldn't accept."

"That's all you said?"

"Yes. I didn't think it was necessary to explain that you don't socialize. You've always told me not to go into details about . . . well, you know, about anything personal."

The professor raised his eyes devoutly toward heaven. Had God seen fit to punish an old sinner by dulling his daughter's mind? "Let's hope no harm's been done," he sighed, putting the letter on a shelf in the foyer while he hung up his coat.

"Harm?" Dorrit seized on the word, puzzled at her father's odd reaction. She had expected him to be relieved the way she had handled the matter. "What do you mean, harm?"

Deep in thought, Herman Zache didn't answer. "We've got to set things straight," he mumbled to himself and went into the living room where, instead of sitting down, he paced back and forth, his right hand balled into a fist pounding the palm of his left. He had always hoped to make a good match for Dorrit and had finally found an excellent candidate, only to have her rudely rebuff him.

"I've got it!" he said at last, stopped pacing and faced Dorrit. "Listen! You must go at once and see the good doctor. Heaven forbid he mistakes you for a social ignoramus and thinks even less of me for not teaching you better. This situation might be salvaged with a personal visit. You'll have to go and explain yourself. Apologize for your failure to consult with me before turning him down. Tell him you acted rashly. Without thinking. If he offers the invitation again, go ahead and accept it."

"Accept it? Is that wise, Papa? Suppose in the course of the evening he begins to pry into our private affairs?" Dorrit was remembering past occasions when nosy individuals had chased them out of town.

"We're in Germany now. Things are different here. We can talk freely. We're safe."

"Safe from what?"

The professor didn't answer. "Go wash your face and comb your hair," was all he said. "Pull it back neatly. You're a lady of good breeding. Wear your navy blue suit with some proper shoes."

"The new suit? Why?"

"Don't argue! Just do as I say!" Uncharacteristically, Herman Zache raised his voice to his daughter. "Now, hurry up!"

Dorrit had rarely seen him so emotionally engaged and saw no reason for all this fuss, but didn't argue; it would never do when he was agitated. He might work himself into a bronchial attack.

Once she had changed her clothes and polished her appearance to his satisfaction, Herman Zache thrust trolley fare into her hands, helped her into her warm coat, and all but shoved her out the door. "Take a westbound trolley," he instructed, giving her the envelope with the doctor's address. "Grunewald is west of town. Ask the conductor for directions. You'll probably have to transfer to a bus at some point."

Not until she was seated on the trolley, did Dorrit realize why her father had acted so bizarrely. His odd behavior was obviously due to the new medicine he had taken this morning. It was supposed to clear his chest but had muddled his mind instead. Now standing on the pristine sidewalk of Lindenstrasse, she sighed in desperation. To turn around and go home, telling her father that no one had answered the door was an attractive option. But could she fib convincingly?

Again her eyes fell on the elegant house of marble and stone rising majestically behind a row of white birch. A neat flagstone walk led from the gate to the front steps and a massive oak door hung with highly polished brass hardware. The tall windows on the ground floor seemed to be staring at her, blank and unblinking, warning her not to come any closer.

Her spine went soft, sagging under the weight of inadequacy. Weak-kneed and miserable, she reached out to the wrought-iron fence for support, her fingers grasping the cold metal and the gnarled vines clinging to it. She felt breathless similar to the way she'd felt in Warsaw once when she'd come within a hair of being run down by a speeding coach. Another pedestrian had pushed her to safety a split second before disaster. Once the danger had passed, she had leaned against a lamppost, trembling and feeling light-headed, precisely like now. Of course, that incident was a foolish comparison, she told herself, for in spite of her present anxiety; neither life nor limbs were in danger here.

Chapter 31

"Ahem . . ." *Schmidt cleared* his throat and walked into the library. "Herr Doctor?"

Frowning, Johann looked up from his reading. Was there to be no peace today? Was a conspiracy at work to test his patience?

"The young lady," Schmidt said, economizing on words, something the baron would appreciate, "the one I delivered a note to earlier is at the door."

"Pardon?" Johann pinched his lips together to keep his jaw from dropping.

"The young lady, the one . . ."

"I heard you."

"Very well, *mein* Herr. Shall I take her coat and show her in?"

"Yes."

Resisting the urge to rub his hands together, Johann put down the newspaper, got up and walked over to the fireplace. Dorrit Zache had come calling? How convenient. She might not be so troublesome after all. He braced one hand against the mantelpiece while the other engaged the iron poker. Stabbing at the logs, he kept his back turned on the French doors, pivoting around only when he heard Schmidt announce the visitor.

"Ah, Fraulein Zache?" Johann arched a dark eyebrow, but although he was able to control his voice to a smooth faultlessness, chaotic flecks of silver flashed in his gray eyes as they raked over her standing in the doorway. "What a pleasant surprise." This was as truthful a statement as any he'd ever made.

"Good afternoon," she said in a tight voice, staring at the opulence all around her, now immensely glad that her father had insisted on the blue suit. "Forgive me for intruding."

"You're not intruding." Johann approached her, wryly noting that she took a step backwards and looked over her shoulder for Schmidt, who had disappeared, good man that he was. "Come in. Sit down." Johann took her arm and ushered her to a chair opposite his near the fireplace. Although she dragged her feet, it was pleasant to escort someone not a head shorter than himself. Most women barely reached to his shoulder, but Fraulein Zache was taller than most.

As Dorrit lowered herself onto the edge of the seat, silently declaring she wouldn't be troubling him long, her eyes flitted over the library with its floor-to-ceiling glass-fronted bookcases. A table in a corner held an exquisite chess set, its game pieces crafted in pink alabaster and green jade. Indeed, everywhere she looked she saw objects of art that appeared to be priceless. Recognizing a painting by a new and emerging French Impressionist, she was also drawn to a life-sized portrait of a young girl in a rose garden, which hung above the fireplace. Dorrit could identify a number of artists, but didn't recognize that work and decided this was not the time to ask.

"To what do I owe this pleasure?" Johann settled into his chair and lifted his eyebrows into a questioning arch.

"I, that is to say, my father . . ." Dorrit hesitated, feeling far less comfortable in this warm library than on the windswept sidewalk outside, an antithesis she blamed on Dr. von Renz who was staring at her in an odd sort of way. Yesterday, he had appeared quite the gentleman; today, he seemed the wily sort her father had often warned her about.

"You were saying?" Johann prodded when she seemed reluctant to go on.

"I was about to explain that my father was not home earlier today when your note was delivered. He was quite upset to learn that I had declined your invitation without consulting him. I did so because he never ventures out at night. Especially in winter when he has to avoid large crowds. As you know, he cancelled his lecture yesterday because of illness. Likewise, he might be forced to cancel a social event at the last minute. Which would be a shame if you'd already bought opera tickets and made dinner reservations. Of course, there's also the issue of our religion. We don't observe Christmas. Your holiday begins next Thursday and, being Jewish, we wouldn't be able to celebrate in the same spirit with your other guests."

"Other guests?"

"I assumed . . ."

"You assumed too much, Fraulein Zache. I was inviting no one else. And, for the record, next Thursday is the twenty-third. Not yet Christmas." Johann was relieved that, apparently, there was no other suitor; his only competition was her religion, which he had no objection to. He attended church sporadically, mostly to hear the famous choir at the cathedral on Kurfurstendamm, something *she* couldn't possibly object to. "I have an idea," he said. "Suppose we skip the opera and the Adlon and have dinner here."

"In your home?" Dorrit was troubled with that kind of intimacy on such short acquaintance.

"Why not? It would minimize the professor's exposure and in the event he must cancel, only my staff will be inconvenienced." When Dorrit remained silent, wondering what her father would say about this new venue, Johann added, "If you'd like, I can ask my housekeeper to plan a kosher meal."

"Oh, you needn't trouble anyone on our account. We don't keep a kosher home. My father follows the laws of the Torah but not the dietary restrictions. If we are having meat for dinner and he suddenly needs hot milk to soother his chest, he drinks it."

Johann took that as an affirmative. "Then it's settled," he said. "Dinner next Thursday."

"Well, all right. Thank you." Dorrit placed her feet squarely on the floor and moved forward in her seat. Mission completed, she was eager to be off.

But instead of rising and escorting her to the door, her host stretched his legs out in front of him, crossing them at the ankles, indicating the visit had not yet been concluded. With the skill of a pantomimic, he signaled Schmidt hovering outside in the hall.

Chapter 32

Within minutes, Frau Schmidt brought plates of smoked salmon, cold cuts, and goose liver pate into the library. She was accompanied by a nearsighted maid who eyed Dorrit bluntly as she put a basket of sliced bread down on a small table in front of her. Without preamble, the butler poured wine and left a carafe of coffee in a warmer. Everything came about so quickly and so efficiently, everything except Dorrit's departure, for how could she insult the staff by leaving before sampling their efforts?

"*Guten appetit!*" Frau Schmidt was last to leave the room.

"Thank you," Dorrit croaked, silently questioning if she'd be able to choke down a single bite. It had been a long time since breakfast and she hadn't had lunch; still, she didn't have the slightest interest in the food.

"My housekeeper likes to see people eat." Johann grinned at the wide array of edibles, which included small decorative cakes. "Are you hungry?"

"Um . . . yes . . ." Dorrit nodded and, pretending interest, slipped her fork under some salmon, taking a large mouthful before realizing she should have cut it first; the fatty fish stuck like glue to the roof of her mouth. As she worked the logjam free, she didn't dare swallow for fear of choking, but chewing meant displaying big lumps in both cheeks. Of course, spitting it out was even more unattractive.

The room grew oppressively quiet, and she became convinced the entire household could hear her struggle. It never occurred to her that so much noise was involved with the simple task of eating. When the salmon finally slipped down, the ensuing gulp echoed off the walls loud as a cannon. She cleared her throat but only managed to wake a ticklish cough that shook her shoulders in an unladylike fashion.

Out of the corner of her eye, she saw Dr. von Renz smile. He's laughing at me, she thought, and her mouth went dry. In desperation she reached for the wine. It was velvety smooth and lubricated her throat nicely. She felt better and took another sip, for although her father had cautioned her about spirits, she didn't believe something the color of rubies could be harmful.

It became easier to eat. She enjoyed a piece of pumpernickel with pate and truffles without incident and could even glance at her host without embarrassing side effects. *Gott im Himmel*, for all his devilish arrogance, he cut a grand figure. Yesterday she determined that she'd never before come across a more handsome individual; today—even at home—he was well groomed and clean-shaven. His gray slacks were pressed and his shoes were shiny as a new coin. His shirt was crisp and spotless, and although he had rolled up the sleeves, wore no tie, and his dark hair looked a bit ruffled, he was positively elegant. Of course he was also old— thirty if he was a day; still, there could be no question about the fact that he was enormously attractive.

Vexed by her silence, Johann finally broke it with a pointed question. "Tell me about your family," he said, depositing his empty plate on the coffee table, but keeping his napkin across one knee so she wouldn't get the idea that the visit was over. Her springboard position on the chair had not escaped him.

"Family?" She looked up from her food as if she'd been ambushed. "I don't have any. Only my father."

"You must have had a mother at one time. I assume your father is a widower?"

"Yes. I was barely two when my mother died. I don't remember her, so I really can't tell you anything."

"Your father doesn't talk about her?"

Dorrit shook her head and took another sip of wine; it was amazing how much better it made her feel. "No, but he thinks about her a great deal. Sometimes I wish he wouldn't. It makes him terribly melancholy."

"How long has he been a widower?"

"Sixteen years."

"That's a long time to be in mourning. What did your mother die of?"

"Consumption. There was an epidemic in Saint Petersburg at the time."

"Russia? You're not Polish then?"

"No." Dorrit suddenly wondered if she ought to be telling him this and if perhaps the wine was making her careless. Then she remembered her father saying it was safe to talk freely now that they were in Germany. She forged ahead. "We lived in Warsaw for five years before moving to Berlin."

"But you were born in Saint Petersburg? I detected a Russian accent in your father's speech."

"Yes, he spent the first forty years of his life there. Immediately after my mother died we moved to Minsk, then to Kiev, Bialystok, and eventually to Warsaw. We lived in other places as well but didn't stay long enough for it to count. In fact, we moved so often, I think my father became confused."

"I can't visualize the professor being confused. His lectures are so focused."

"Maybe he just gets his personal facts mixed up. When we lived in Kiev, he'd tell people our birthplace was Minsk. When we moved to Bialystok, he'd say it was Kiev. And so on. He never once mentioned Saint Petersburg."

"Why not?"

"I don't know. And I've never pressed him. Any talk of Saint Petersburg upsets him. It was quite by chance that I discovered I was born there. I also discovered that he changed our name after we left."

"He changed your names?"

"Yes, our last name was Tzacheroff, which he shortened to Zache. I suppose he wanted a more German-sounding name. As long as I can remember he's always wanted to live in Berlin."

"Well, I can understand that." Johann smiled. "It's a great city. But why sweep Saint Petersburg under the rug?"

"I don't know. For the sake of satisfying my curiosity, I couldn't distress him with questions. I accepted early on that he didn't want to talk about the past. I suppose it was too painful for him because it included my mother. She was the light of his life. There's never been anyone else."

"Except you."

Dorrit smiled; the green of her eyes took on a lighter shade. "I'd like to think he's proud of me."

"That's a safe bet in view of his campaign yesterday."

Despite herself, Dorrit laughed. "He was rather pompous. You'll have to forgive him. Believe me, he normally doesn't run on like that. I don't know what set him off. But I can assure you that little of what he said was true."

"I believed him." Johann switched deftly into French, testing Dr. Zache's claim that she was fluent. "I believed every word."

"Then you are extremely gullible," she responded in French.

"Fraulein Zache, I'm afraid you've exposed a weakness."

"One of many, I'd guess." Instantly, she regretted her repartee.

Johann leaned over and refilled her empty wine glass.

Taking a carefully measured sip to hide her blunder, Dorrit wondered how she could have let such an impertinent comment slip. Bold as brass, she'd implied Dr. von Renz was a man of weaknesses, which was the same as suggesting he enjoyed gambling, foolishness with women, and drinking. Plus she'd called him gullible! The magnitude of her indiscretions rushed to her cheeks. The unfortunate thing about having red hair, she agonized silently, was the inclination to blush. But at least she'd been spared the freckles. While her color subsided, she reached for a *petit four*, a brandied sponge cake glazed in rich, dark chocolate. It was so mouth-watering that she couldn't resist taking another. While doing so, she glanced at Dr. von Renz. He looked congenial. Perhaps he wasn't offended? Moreover, he topped off her wine glass, something she didn't think an angry host would do.

"Fraulein Zache," he said, putting the decanter back on its silver coaster, "did you know that we've met before?"

"Of course. Yesterday."

"No. Before that."

Dorrit stared at him; she didn't meet very many people and couldn't imagine that she could have forgotten such an imposing individual.

"When? Where?"

"In Ladeburg."

"Where?" She looked puzzled.

"A small town some twenty-five kilometers east of Berlin. It was about a year ago. Last December. Your coach stopped at a village inn. I advised you and your father about the poor road conditions."

"Oh? Of course! Now I remember!" she said, surprised, her eyes glowing as though the memory was a pleasant one. "That's a strange coincidence. But what brought you to Ladeburg?" she asked in the next breath.

"I was just killing time, sampling the tavern's brew with a friend. I was born in nearby Bernau and still keep a home there. I always spend summers and the Christmas holidays in the country."

"What about this year?"

"This year I have other plans." In silent tribute to those plans, Johann raised his glass.

Figuring he expected her to do the same, Dorrit did so and quite spontaneously smiled over the rim of her glass.

Johann felt her smile like a pleasant punch.

Chapter 33

Arriving home from Wirchow at six o'clock Thursday evening, Johann took a quick tour of the downstairs glad to see that his instructions had been followed to the letter. Logs were burning in all the fireplaces, supplementing a temperamental coal burner in the basement and ensuring that the drawing room, in particular, was warm despite its size. Strolling through the room, he frowned at the fragile French antiques upholstered in striped pastels with tasseled cushions not made for comfort. While guests seemed not to mind, Johann was partial to the more intimate alcove reached through an archway at the far end of the room, where the chairs were firm and comfortable and where the glass veranda doors provided a splendid view of the terrace and the garden beyond. Of course at this hour on a winter evening there was nothing but darkness outside.

Peering into the shadowy garden, Johann realized it had started to snow. Opening the veranda doors, he went out to light the gas lamps in the corners of the terrace, creating a view and a visually pleasing ambiance. Brushing wet flakes from his shoulders, he stepped back inside to admire the scene. The softly falling snow looked sensational, glittering like confetti in the yellow circles of the gaslights. This was where he would entertain Dorrit and her father before dinner. Walking briskly back to the center hall, he closed the doors to the salon opposite the library; it was for dancing and large crowds and would only draw heat away from the rest of the house, compromising the professor's comfort. A quick glance into the dining room told Johann a festive table had been set.

Being in exceptionally good spirits, he broke his own rules and intervened between two maids arguing over where to hang the last of the Christmas ornaments on the evergreen standing at the base of the long curving staircase. The maids were not accustomed to attention from their employer and his affable mood caused their argument to lose steam; they ran, giggling, from the hall. The clock in the library chimed, reminding Johann that it was time to dispatch Schmidt to fetch his guests.

After Schmidt left, Johann went upstairs to change. Flicking through his dressing room closets, he selected a gray velvet dinner jacket and paired it with black gabardine slacks. He tied a maroon ascot into the open neck of his white silk shirt, fastened it with a plain gold pin, ran a comb through his dark hair, and the back of his hand over the lower part of his face. Satisfied he didn't need to shave, he went downstairs to the library to await his guests. Pouring himself a shot of smooth English bourbon, he sloshed it around in the heavy crystal goblet before tossing it down in one quick motion.

Chapter 34

Schmidt returned with his passengers, ushering them into the foyer, where a maid stood ready to take their coats.

"Good evening!" Johann emerged from the library and reached for Dr. Zache's hand. "I trust the trip was comfortable?"

"Thank you, yes," the professor replied, sniffing appreciatively as he surveyed the hall, giving the large crystal chandelier suspended from the domed ceiling a second look. Dorrit had not embellished; this home was even grander than she'd described. "It was good of you to send the coach. I dare say it would have been difficult to find public transportation this evening."

Laughing at the very idea, Johann turned his attention to Dorrit. A rush of pleasure swept over him. She was removing a small black beret from her auburn hair, tonight fastened into a neat chignon glistening with the moisture of melting snowflakes that caused wispy curls to work free, framing her exquisite face. The maid was taking her coat and underneath the coarse garment, she was wearing a cream-colored lace blouse and a green wool skirt. Although unsightly boots peeked out from beneath the hem of the long skirt, the ensemble was adequate for the occasion.

"It's a pleasure to see you again, Fraulein Zache," Johann said as he took her hand and put it to his lips.

Reciprocating with a similar comment, she smiled, flashing her pretty teeth.

Taking full advantage of her accommodating mood, a far cry from her reticent arrival last Saturday, Johann placed her hand on his arm and with the professor pulling up the rear, escorted his guests through the drawing room to the alcove. Schmidt appeared with aperitif wines, bowls of exotic nuts, and the promise that dinner would be served at precisely eight o'clock.

"Welcome!" Johann lifted his glass.

"Thank you. It's awfully nice to be here," Dr. Zache said and with a shrewd twinkle in his eyes added, "Merry Christmas!"

"*Shalom aleichem!*" Johann pronounced with flair.

Chuckling, both men concluded that the evening was off to an excellent start.

The paintings in the library had impressed Dorrit last week and, minutes ago, when she walked through the drawing room the pictures on the pale blue walls caught her attention as well. Having worn the soles from her shoes, roaming Berlin's museums during this past year, she was astonished that such treasures existed in a private home. While her father and their host were discussing things of a professional nature, she was blissfully content to study the artwork in the alcove. However, the minute there was a lull in the men's conversation, she turned to Dr. von Renz, asking if the painting on the wall behind her father's chair was by the Dutch artist, Jungkind.

"It is, indeed." Partial to the courtyard scene, Johann was surprised she identified it because it was unsigned and eluded many a trained eye. "It happens to be a favorite of mine," he said. "But lacking a signature, it's not particularly valuable. I've been told it's a proof. I suppose that's why it was relegated to this far corner of the house."

"It's wonderful," Dorrit said. "An early morning scene."

"Early morning?" Johann leaned forward and squinted at the painting.

"The weak yellows would indicate that," Dorrit qualified. "The sky is very light. Later in the day, the colors would be more vibrant and the shadows longer."

"Hmm, I believe you're right." Johann looked at the professor. "I see you made sure your daughter studied art as well as languages."

"Actually, much as I'd like to take the credit, Dorrit pursued that on her own."

"With a great deal of help from curators," she added.

"Would you like to see a Jungkind that *is* signed?" Johann asked.

"I'd love to!"

Johann got up. "Professor Zache, will you join us?"

"No, thanks. I'll stay put and keep the wine and nutmeats company. Paintings are not my forte. My ignorance would quickly become embarrassing."

As Dorrit toured the drawing room with her host, she studied a Renoir, a Signac, and a Cezanne, new artists coming into prominence and attracting collectors.

"This home and its contents belonged to my maternal grandparents," Johann told her as they crisscrossed the room. "But my parents are responsible for the Impressionists. The entire house was originally hung with ghastly flat and somber family portraits that looked as though they'd been painted posthumously. Every wall was like a grim reunion of the dead. The one hanging over the fireplace in the library was the only one that didn't offend the eye and so was never replaced."

Dorrit remembered that she'd been curious about it last Saturday. "It's a wonderful painting. Who is the artist?"

"Unfortunately, some poor soul who drank himself to death before he could make a name for himself. But he left some fine work behind. That particular one is of my mother as a child."

"What happened to the other family portraits? The somber ones?"

"All were banished to the basement."

"Oh dear, such rude treatment. The damp can't be good for them." Dorrit grinned. "Aren't you afraid of ghostly visits?"

"No. I can't help but think that my ancestors approve of the new arrangement. Surely bright and colorful landscapes are preferable to dour faces. Even their own."

"Have you added to the collection?"

Johann shook his head.

"Are you planning to?"

"No."

"Just as well, I suppose." Dorrit glanced around. "Where would you put them? There's no space left on the walls."

"Yes, if I were to collect anything, it'd have to be something small. Something that would fit in a drawer."

"Insects?" Dorrit cocked her head.

"God forbid! My housekeeper has an abhorrence of bugs. Dead or alive, none would be tolerated."

"How about stamps?"

"Stamps would be practical," Johann acknowledged, walking up to the signed Jungkind.

Chapter 35

Dorrit was examining the painting, when she suddenly felt a hand on her elbow. It was warm, yet made her shiver. Was Dr. von Renz signaling that they ought to move on?

She turned toward him and surprised herself by colliding with his shoulder. He didn't step back and kept his hand on her arm, his touch causing a strange warmth to rush through her. But as pleasant as that was, her inexperienced soul suspected that he was acting improperly. He was certainly standing much too close for any meaningful conversation.

A heady silence fell between them.

Bewildered, Dorrit looked up at him. One corner of his mouth was pulled into a half-smile. The breath caught in her throat and, try as she might, she couldn't draw her eyes away. His amused and speculative gaze held her strangely captive. She felt his hand slide up her arm and cup her chin. For a moment he seemed to be studying her face as if something about it pleased him. Suddenly he bent his head down.

A drum began pounding in Dorrit's ears. Heat was rising in her cheeks and, realizing that she was holding her breath—becoming dizzy from the effort—she stepped back in order to requisition some equilibrium. It would be the height of bad manners to sink to her knees from lack of air. As she backed away, she saw a shadow of disappointment cross Dr. von Renz's fine features. His jaunty half smile vanished. His hand let go of her and fell to his side. As she widened the distance between them with another step, she too felt an odd sense of regret.

Discreetly brushing the back of her hands against her burning cheeks in a futile effort to cool them, she turned back toward the wall and forced herself to once again concentrate on the Jungkind. However, it was with great reluctance that she returned to reality. She had never before been stirred to feel carnal passion and could hardly credit its existence. But if the lightheadedness, along with the strange tempest in the pit of her stomach, was the harbinger of the exquisite emotions she'd read about in *pfennig* novels, maybe she ought to welcome it because in the books everything always turned out so wonderfully.

"Shall we rejoin your father?" Dr. von Renz asked in the next instant as if the awkward moment had not passed between them. He offered his arm, which she gladly accepted because her legs felt like jelly and might not support her.

Had he been on the verge of kissing her? she wondered as they crossed the drawing room. No, he wouldn't have dared, not with her father looking on from the adjoining alcove. Then again, maybe he would? Instinct stronger than reason told her that neither her father nor anyone else could stop Johann von Renz from doing precisely as he pleased. With that thought came the realization that he had changed his mind, deciding not to kiss her.

Disappointment settled in hard and fast as Dorrit owned up to the fact that she would have liked to be kissed. Of course, a moment later she was ashamed of herself for such a hedonistic thought.

"Papa!" she cried later that evening on the way home, "how could you tell that man I'd be delighted to go to a dance?"

"That man?" Professor Zache frowned. "Surely a poor way to refer to a host who has just entertained us so lavishly and, moreover, insisted we be on a first name basis. I'd expect you to remember his name."

It was midnight and they were heading home through the center of the darkened city. It had snowed steadily for hours and the snorts of the horses laboring through the deep drifts could be heard inside the coach. By the same token, Schmidt riding in the driver's box might hear their conversation. Dorrit lowered her voice to a whisper.

"I do remember his name, Papa. But please tell me why you gave your consent when you know I can't dance. I can't distinguish a simple box step from a sarabande."

"Don't fret so, child. You can learn."

"Learn? By New Year's Eve? That's only a week away!"

"I've raised you to be clever. Your mind is sharp. Surely a few fancy steps won't overwhelm your feet."

"I am destined to die of shame! I just know it."

"Nonsense. Dancing will come naturally. It's in your blood. You'll see."

"In my blood? Please, Papa, make sense. You have admitted to having two left feet. Was my mother a Bolshoi ballerina?"

"No, she wasn't, my dear." Professor Zache sighed, closed his eyes and leaned into the corner of the coach as if he felt a headache coming on. It was clear that he did not wish to say any more.

She didn't press him. She was all too familiar with his stony silence whenever her mother was mentioned.

Chapter 36

Dorrit accepted her escort's arm and made her way along a gilded corridor of the Beckstein Schloss in Potsdam. At the brink of a wide staircase, Johann handed a card to a steward clad in white satin breeches, red coat, and powdered wig.

"The Baron von Renz and Fraulein Zache!" The man's sonorous voice reached to the far corners of the salon below, where two hundred of Berlin's most illustrious citizens now raised their eyes, some fumbling with monocles to get a better look at the newcomer on the arm of a very popular member of their crowd.

Surprised by the ceremonial announcement as well as Johann's title, Dorrit snatched a sideways glance and was again awed by her escort. Dressed in black formal attire, white cravat, and ruffled silk shirt with diamond studs in place of buttons, this baron was far too handsome for his own good—*her* own good, for God forbid, she falter this early in the evening. As she found footing on the marble stairs, beginning a slow descent, she was grateful for her father's largesse. The minute the stores reopened after Christmas, he'd fished into the well of the old pendulum clock and pulled out a fistful of money for a gown and a pair of dancing shoes. When she had questioned the prudence of squandering their savings on fancy clothes, he had simply said, "The time has come to invest."

Now swallowing nervously, Dorrit realized her father should have been concerned with things other than new finery; deportment, for example, because what was she supposed to do once she reached the salon? Was she expected to curtsy when presented to the host and hostess? Was a simple Happy New Year a proper greeting? She knew about painters, poets, and politicians, but her father had not thought to include ballroom manners in her education, and sooner or later this deficiency was bound to become apparent. Moreover, she had come to a ball not knowing how to dance. Miserable and tense, she turned cold with the scope of her predicament. She could fake a number of things, but her clumsy feet would fool no one. During the past week, she and Hannah had practiced various dance steps on the kitchen floor until the linoleum began to show bare spots; still, she knew her limitations and suddenly panicking, inadvertently dug her fingers into the fine fabric of Johann's sleeve.

"No one here scratches or bites," he whispered, placing his hand across hers and leaning so close she felt his warm breath on her face. "I'll personally vouch for their behavior."

"I wish you could vouch for mine," she said in a tight voice. "I haven't had much practice with formal balls." Anything formal, she would have liked to add but didn't want to confess too much all at once. Why ruin his good humor this early? He'd soon enough discover that he was saddled with a social illiterate. Besides, there was no time to explain. They had reached the reception line where she was now presented to the Count and Countess von Beckstein, tonight's hosts; their son, Wolfgang Reinhard, and their daughter, Monika Marie standing with her affianced, Baron Anton Jurgen Widermann. The aging Duke Henry Francis von Strelitz and his much younger Duchess were also part of the reception committee. With so many names to remember Dorrit neglected to curtsy, but since no one swooned perhaps it wasn't expected. And, having cleared this first hurdle, she hoped to now lose herself in the crowded salon to catch her bearings.

But that was not to be. Johann's friends were tripping over each other to make her acquaintance. However, these same individuals quickly lost interest when it became clear she had nothing to add to their banter. Of course, she knew that Ciro's was a supremely elegant nightclub in Berlin and that San Sebastian was a seaside resort in Spain, but insofar as she had never been to either place she could hardly sing their praises or lament their limitations. Forced to remain silent, she concentrated on the scenery.

Never before had she seen such magnificent gowns and such dazzling jewelry. And although she had never thought of herself as poor, she suddenly felt impoverished. One thing was clear, despite the fact that the material had been expensive and she'd worked for three days, sewing her gown, it didn't measure up. Initially, she'd believed the blue taffeta was stunning but in this sparkling salon it looked pale as water. Moreover, she was wearing no jewelry except the small pearl earrings her father had recently given her on her eighteenth birthday.

Her spirits in a downdraft, she realized that immersed in conversation and laughing uproariously with his friends, her escort was ignoring her. And who could blame him? Among these fine feathers, she was as nondescript as a patch of dry grass. Still, she tried her level best to look unconcerned, carefully molding an expression of bored amusement like she'd seen on the Duchess von Strelitz. But, unlike the Duchess, she couldn't sustain it for long and it vanished abruptly when a raven-haired female in an exquisite yellow gown approached. Wildly envious, she stared at her as the crowd parted, allowing this shimmering buttercup to elbow up to Johann, nudging Dorrit aside as she did so.

Biting her lips, she saw the girl laugh and toss her head, blinding Johann with the fiery diamonds in her ears, and it seemed a lifetime before he remembered that Dorrit ought to be introduced to this confection of satin and tulle. No sooner had he made the perfunctory introduction when Louisa von Tirpitz, bless her, pulled Dorrit aside for a private chitchat as if they were old friends. This so pleased her that she failed to see the malice in her eyes.

"So tell me . . ." Louisa said after a moment of inconsequential talk about the decorations in the ballroom, and now lowering her voice lest someone discover her obsessive curiosity, "how did you and Johann meet? Who introduced you?"

"No one. We met by chance."

"Really. When?"

"Last December."

"*Last* December?" Louisa's eyes narrowed in surprise. "A year ago? It's strange that we haven't seen you before tonight."

"Oh, not really. You see, we had a brief encounter at a country inn and immediately lost track . . ." Realizing her mistake, Dorrit snapped her lips together.

"An inn?" Louisa raised her eyebrows with an unspoken accusation. Dorrit's cheeks flushed a deep pink. Enjoying her mortification, Louisa prolonged the moment as she opened her reticule, found a small tin and popped a mint into her mouth. "Want one?" she asked as an afterthought, holding out the container. Dorrit shook her head. Louisa put the mints back and closed her purse. "Well, you obviously managed to track Johann down."

Recovering from her gaffe, Dorrit found her tongue. "No, as it happened, he became acquainted with my father."

"Well, that was convenient. What does your father do?"

"He's a professor at the university. In the medical school." Dorrit didn't think it was necessary to explain that he was only a part time lecturer.

"Hmm, that figures. Johann spends most of his free time experimenting on cadavers. Does your father do that too?"

"No. He limits himself to teaching."

"Which is much more sanitary of course. One can catch dreadful diseases, tinkering with the dead." Shuddering, Louisa changed the subject. "Where do you live?"

"On Niederlag." Although Louisa was nosy to the point of being rude, Dorrit decided that any conversation was better than none, and just in case someone was watching, she fashioned an expression of intense concentration as if they were discussing world-shattering events.

"Niederlag?" Again Louisa von Tirpitz raised her finely penciled eyebrows. "Is that in Charlottenburg?" she asked, knowing perfectly well that it wasn't.

"No. It is east of Unter den Linden."

Louisa's nose wrinkled imperceptibly; that part of the city was far from chic. She eyed Dorrit with a queer twist on her lips a moment before she seemed to remember her escort. Without a word, she turned on her heels, weaved through the crowd, and was soon smiling at a plain-faced but exquisitely dressed gentleman, who turned red to the roots of his blond hair with pleasure.

After Louisa's departure, when no one else picked up the slack, Dorrit felt more alone than before and toyed with the idea of seeking refuge in the ladies' lounge. Engaged in conversations, Johann had his back to her; she'd be able to slip away unnoticed. After visiting the lounge, she could strike up a conversation with one of the elderly guests seated in the various comfortable corners of the salon. As a rule, older people had poor eyesight, might not notice her lackluster appearance and although they usually liked to discuss the weather and their rheumatism, she might get lucky and find someone with an interest in politics. However, before she could melt away, Johann suddenly looked around as if he had misplaced something.

"Ah, there you are!" he said, slipping an arm around her waist, spoiling her vanishing act. "Enjoying yourself?" There was not a drop of penitence in his voice for having neglected her.

"Yes, very much," she lied.

"Wonderful." Switching into French, he asked if she would care to dance.

"I suppose we could make a gauche effort while waiting for the music," she quipped, her expression mocking him because the musicians in the adjoining ballroom were merely warming up their instruments.

"*Touché!*" He laughed. "I'm afraid you've exposed another weakness. I'm obviously deaf." Persisting in French, he tightened his grip on her waist. "Let's keep that just between us. I attend the opera regularly. It would be embarrassing if word got out."

The orchestra finally burst forth with the opening dance, a spirited Strauss waltz.

"Now may I have the pleasure?" Without waiting for an answer, Johann took her arm and walked through the doors among a flurry of people spilling into the ballroom.

Her heart sank to abysmal depths. Her kneecaps went rigid. The moment of truth had come; a moment she should have dreaded all along, and would have, except there had been too many other things to worry about. Perhaps she could fake a twisted ankle? After a few steps she'd falter anyway so an injury was bound to look convincing. But could she fool a doctor who would probably insist on examining her? No, it might be safer to claim a headache. Stomach cramps she already had, no pretense was needed, but it was too embarrassing to mention. In desperation, she finally chose the path of least resistance: candor. Forcing a smile and with a measure of grit inherited from some unknown ancestor, she came clean.

"I must warn you," she said in French, which Johann seemed to prefer tonight and she needed to stack the deck in her favor, "my footwork could prove a painful lesson in self-defense. Even for the most accomplished partner."

Johann threw back his head and laughed. "In that case, permit me to prove my courage," he said and bowed elegantly.

Dorrit allowed herself a moment to enjoy his wonderful gallantry; a fleeting pleasure because as she now found herself on the dance floor, she was no longer enjoying herself. Counting in her head, visualizing the diagram Hannah had sketched on the kitchen floor in chalk, she begged her feet to make the proper moves, all the while grateful that this first dance was a waltz. She and Hannah had practiced that more than any other, and she soon discovered it was much easier to follow Johann's steps than Hannah's. As she began to relax, she took stock of the glorious ballroom where a dozen crystal chandeliers sent flashes of light darting among the dancers. Garlands of colorful flowers were draped across the gold-leafed mirrors along the walls, and tall potted palms stood bunched together in the four corners like tropical forests. Dressed in eighteenth-century satins, the musicians played on a raised platform surrounded by miniature cherry trees forced into bloom. Mesmerized, it never occurred to Dorrit that she was fast becoming the subject of speculation among the other dancers.

Who is she, everyone wanted to know, and how could someone never before seen in their midst have snared one of Berlin's most sought after bachelors for this very important evening? Those who had been introduced could not recall her name from the Social Register. Of course, Louisa von Tirpitz repeatedly felt obliged to enlighten the curious, sibilating that Fraulein Zache came from an industrial part of town where her father taught school. But not everyone believed Louisa. Those of a more levelheaded nature reminded one another that no one here tonight consorted with individuals of no account. Certainly the Baron von Renz would not insult the Count and Countess von Beckstein by expecting them to entertain a person of common origins at this, the most prominent ball of the season.

By and by, people surmised that Fraulein Zache was a foreigner. Some declared they had heard her speak French. Others suggested she was Italian. Devoid of both lace and sequins, her gown was obviously Italian because no Berlin or Paris designer would sanction such a simple creation, which looked suspiciously akin to a Roman toga.

Chapter 37

The music stopped. Johann was leading Dorrit toward one of the champagne tables when he spotted Kurt Eckart arriving with Lillian; the two had been an item since meeting at the Chancellor's Ball back in April.

"Some friends of mine have just arrived," Johann said, changing course. "I'd like you to meet them."

Pretending she wanted to meet these people or die, and preparing herself for another frosty confrontation, Dorrit took a deep breath, pushed her shoulders back, and kept her head stoically erect as she walked through the crowd toward the newcomers, not realizing that her bearing made her look positively regal.

Kurt had a nose for quality and couldn't take his eyes off the astonishing beauty approaching with Johann, something the latter noticed with a measure of dry amusement as he now made the introductions, starting with Lillian Schindel who smiled warmly and offered Dorrit her hand.

Kurt couldn't contain himself. "Well . . . well . . . *well!*" he exclaimed with gusto. "So you're the little lady they're placing bets on in the card room." He took both her hands and put them to his lips with exaggerated ceremony.

"Bets?" Dorrit asked. "Whatever on?"

"The number of sutures needed to repair Kurt's jaw," Johann said tersely and issued his friend a withering look, one that would have sent a lesser man to his knees. Of course Johann was aware of this crowd's penchant for gambling; he was a gambler himself—mostly on horses—but it was galling to learn that players tonight were waging money on the shelf life of Dorrit's charms.

"Gambling is second nature to half the people here," Lillian said in an attempt to rescue the moment and neutralize Johann's remark. "I wouldn't give them a second thought. Some have been known to bet a small fortune on how many flies will land on a sugar cube. I can't imagine anything more droll." Without drawing breath, she changed subjects, now relating bubbly details from the

Christmas festivities at the Konauers. "We missed you this year." She slapped Johann's arm playfully with her fan.

"And *you* missed our announcement," Kurt added. "Lillian has agreed to marry me."

"Oh, Kurt! You've spoiled the surprise," Lillian cried and managed to convey exasperation although she was tickled pink that he had blurted it out, which indicated a delightful amount of eagerness on his part. "We're holding off making any official announcement," she now explained, "until the engagement party my parents are planning here in Berlin. You'll be invited."

"Well, let's have a toast to spoiled surprises." Johann smiled and waylaid a waiter carrying full champagne flutes. "When is the big day?"

"We haven't set a date yet," Lillian said a bit peevishly over the noise of clinking crystal before turning her back on the men and pulling Dorrit aside in order to share her tales of woe with another female; men rarely had the patience to listen. "Kurt and I can't agree on a wedding date," she told her. "He insists on being established first. He's got some absurd notion into his head about making do on his salary, which is perfectly silly, considering the pittance they pay resident doctors nowadays. We won't starve, mind you, but we can't live on it either. He stubbornly refuses to accept assistance from his family. Or mine."

"I think that's commendable," Dorrit said.

"Well, I don't. It's pig-headed! I'll be turning twenty-one in a couple of months. I'm practically an old maid."

Dorrit laughed. "If you were ten years older you'd never pass for one."

"Try telling that to my parents. They want grandchildren. I had a brother who died of scarlet fever at a very young age. My parents have never recovered and probably won't until I present them with a grandson. They have already expressed their wish that my firstborn be named Gerhardt in my brother's memory. A bit morbid, don't you think?"

"No, not really." Although the subject of a dead boy was not a cheerful one, Dorrit was enjoying Lillian's company. Every bit as glamorous as any female at the ball, she was not commensurately haughty, nor did she seem to notice Dorrit's lack of finery. A choker of perfectly matched diamonds glittered around Lillian's neck, and her pink *panne* velvet gown was so lustrous it reflected the light in the room. She had a soft, round face, a mouth like a rosebud, and curly blond hair, a striking contrast to her brown eyes. In a burst of gratitude for her friendly overtures, Dorrit decided that Lillian was the most attractive girl in the ballroom, demoting

Louisa to second place. She also concluded that Kurt, though not as tall and athletically lean as Johann, was every bit as handsome. His hair was jet black and his eyes the pale blue of a winter morning. Dorrit guessed that he had a sense of humor and laughed readily, evidenced by the small lines some called crow's-feet.

Chapter 38

She felt a hand on her elbow and, turning away from Lillian's pleasant chitchat, believed it to be Johann's. It wasn't.

"I've got your escort's permission to ask for a dance." Kurt grinned. "But only one, which should attest to the strength of our friendship."

"Just one?" Dorrit laughed, exhilarated with her sudden popularity. "Then we'll have to make it memorable."

"Not too memorable." Johann cocked an eyebrow and turned to Lillian, inviting her to the floor.

The dance was a polka and Dorrit was right about Kurt. He had a wonderful sense of humor, something he displayed each time she stepped on his feet.

When the music stopped, he returned her to Johann and reclaimed Lillian just as Count von Beckstein appeared to request a dance with Fraulein Zache. Surrendering her to their host, Johann now went in search of the countess to ensure that she was not idle while her husband danced. She was not. Philip von Brandt had finally arrived, solo as usual, and was delighting tonight's hostess with his suave dance steps. Johann smiled inwardly as he watched Philip. His blond hair was meticulously combed and there was not a crease on his black *recherché* attire. Philip banked on his neatness and chivalry with the countess to carry him through to the end of the evening when he would be in dire need of forgiveness. The distinguished Herr Doctor Philip von Brandt, member of one of Berlin's most celebrated families, religiously sober in the laboratories at Wirchow, did not remain temperate for very long at any social function.

As his eyes continued to roam the floor, Johann decided to cut in on Graf Zollern and dance with Louisa; he might as well get it over with because if he didn't, tongues would wag, which wouldn't be fair to her. However, while dancing with someone he had once considered marrying, he was craning his neck to catch sight of another wearing a French braid entwined with ribbons matching the blue of her simple taffeta dress.

"You seem distracted tonight, Johann," Louisa murmured when his distinct lack of attention became all too apparent. "You haven't once commented on my gown."

"Forgive me!" He smiled automatically. "It's lovely. Yellow becomes you."

"I'll wear it again at the Kaiser's Ball next month," she purred. "My father will be honored that evening. You are planning to attend, aren't you?"

"I'll be there." Johann looked at the beauty in his arms but felt no magnetic pull. "Is Wilhelm finally putting your father in charge of the fleet?"

"Yes. Isn't it exciting? But it's still very hush-hush. Don't breathe a word until it's official."

"My lips are sealed."

"Father will be ever so famous," Louisa gushed. "My mother dreams of the day when a city square is named after him."

"That'll be a great honor," Johann drawled, bored, but immediately juxtaposed his disinterest with an ameliorating smile because when she'd mentioned the Kaiser's Ball, he hadn't secured her for that important affair. However, any warmth he tried to project didn't keep Louisa from succumbing to an insane jealousy that had smoldered since arriving tonight and finding Johann with a newcomer.

"By the way, everyone's in a snit, wondering about the girl you're with this evening," she said in the hope that if Johann knew what people thought of his companion, he'd own up to his mistake.

"Is that so?"

"Yes. No one recognizes her. And she doesn't have a thing to say for herself. It's rather awkward for those of us who'd like to befriend her. I tried to be pleasant earlier but it got me nowhere. Is her family listed in the Register?"

"I don't believe so."

"Well, I hate to pass along gossip, but everyone agrees that she's rather odd. I heard someone call her introverted, or something like that. Suppose Kaiser Wilhelm makes an appearance tonight. It's rumored that he might stop in. I can't imagine what she'd say if she were presented to him."

"I'm sure she will make a good account of herself."

"I sincerely hope so. Of course, there's also the problem of her gown."

"A problem?"

"Well, it's rather plain." Louisa wrinkled her nose for effect. "Another thing, everyone knows that a French braid is not the appropriate coiffure for a ball. Especially where..."

"I get the picture."

"Yes, of course. Let me just say that it's a good thing..."

"It's a good thing," Johann interrupted again, "that fashion hasn't entered into any of my conversations tonight. I'd be pronounced a half-wit on the spot."

"Be serious, Johann! You're no such thing. Which only deepens the mystery."

"Mystery?"

"Yes, as to what you can possibly talk to Dorte ... ah, Doris about." Louisa was suddenly experiencing some difficulty with the name.

"Well, you can put your mind at ease." Johann adopted a grave expression rather than risk laughing out loud. "On the drive here tonight we I had a lively exchange about Fontane and Dehmel."

"Who? Who are they?"

"Poets."

"Oh ..." Louisa's lips fashioned a sour little moue; this conversation wasn't going as she'd hoped. "Well," she shrugged, "you're obviously temporarily ... What's it called?" When Johann didn't come to her aid, she lunged ahead. "Whatever it's called, people have placed some rather large bets. Graf Zollern wagered his finest racehorse."

"Pity."

"Pity?" Louisa looked confused.

"I hate to see the man lose a good steed."

There was a pause in the music. Johann returned the suddenly speechless Louisa to her escort, Graf Zollern, before seeking refuge at a champagne table from where he now saw Count von Beckstein keep Dorrit on the floor between dances.

"Now, as I was saying," Count von Beckstein was loath to relinquish Fraulein Zache because it was rare to find a young woman with an appreciation for the workings of government, "we must pray that the Kaiser can frustrate von Bulow into resigning. A full term under his chancellorship could spell trouble with our foreign neighbors. The man's too militant. Too aggressive."

"He's probably just getting all the unpleasant confrontations out of the way early in his term," Dorrit suggested.

"Yes, I suppose he could be putting Europe on notice, warning he's a chancellor to be reckoned with."

"Unlike his predecessor."

"Schillingfurst was an old fool," Count von Beckstein sputtered before realizing that the orchestra was again playing. "And so am I, it seems, not to have noticed the music. Please honor me with another dance."

"Of course." Dorrit smiled.

They fell into a box step that she was happily familiar with, but it was shortly interrupted when a steward, frantically winding his way through the dancers, came up to them. After first begging Dorrit a million pardons, he whispered something in Count von Beckstein's ear.

"Good God!" the count exclaimed. "Here? Now?" He looked around as if the sky was about to fall but that such a calamity would please him. "Forgive me, Fraulein Zache," he said, suddenly breathless. "It seems the Kaiser is about to grace our festivities with his presence. I'm told his coach has just pulled up. The Kaiserin has been ill with influenza, so although they are spending the holidays here in Potsdam at the Marble Palace, I didn't expect His Majesty tonight." The portly count pulled a handkerchief from his breast pocket, wiping it across a sudden sheen on his forehead as he pivoted around. "I must find my wife. Ah, there she is. Dancing with that rascal, Philip." Stuffing the handkerchief back into his pocket, Count von Beckstein took Dorrit's arm and plowed through the crowd, soon tapping Philip on the shoulder. "Philip, my good man! May I present Fraulein Zache?" Turning back to Dorrit, he said, "I leave you in excellent company. We'll finish our dance later." He kissed her hand, took his wife's arm, and sped from the ballroom.

Philip von Brandt grinned at Dorrit; he knew exactly who she was because Johann had told him about the gorgeous redhead he was bringing tonight. And although the room was full of beautiful women—some with red hair—none were this lovely. He bowed. "Philip von Brandt at your service. Let me guess. You're with Johann tonight."

Dorrit looked surprised. "How did you know?"

"I will tell you while we dance." And maybe, Philip thought to himself, maybe she will tell me why I have the feeling that we have already met.

As they fell into step with the music, Dorrit was thinking the very same thing until suddenly realizing that this was the doctor she'd talked to last March in the emergency ward at Wirchow. Of course she'd bite off her tongue before mentioning it because she'd been so wild-eyed and unkempt that the nurse who went home with her had avoided close contact; something Dorrit blamed on the old shawl from Herr Ziegler's shop.

Chapter 39

Kaiser Wilhelm and his entourage of distinguished aides entered the salon. "Eduard!" The Kaiser's eyes twinkled merrily; it was clear he enjoyed catching his subjects off guard.

"Your Majesty!" Count Eduard Hugo von Beckstein bowed. "You do us a wonderful honor."

"I trust our Kaiserin is convalescing," the Countess added, recovering from a deep curtsy.

"She has improved remarkably and would have liked to attend your festivities tonight," the Kaiser assured her. "But, alas, Dr. Renvers wouldn't allow it. So here I am. Quite alone!"

This declaration was a flagrant insult to the esteemed acolytes hovering at his side, but no one thought to correct the Kaiser, who without further ado strolled into the ballroom where the orchestra abruptly fell silent. The guests did as well the instant they realized Germany's exalted monarch was in their midst. Bowing, they parted like biblical waters to allow him to walk among them. Bejeweled fans fluttered as the emperor strolled about with the Count and Countess von Beckstein at his side, stopping now and again to exchange pleasantries with a chosen few.

When he came so close that Dorrit could see the blue of his eyes, she drew in her breath with awe at his persona and the splendor of his silk regalia. Dressed in white and gold with a colorful blue satin sash across his chest, heavy with medals and honors, he looked every inch a king.

"Would you like to meet him?" a voice on her right wanted to know.

"More than anything," she answered dreamily and without thinking, never guessing that Philip was serious.

"All right, come on then." He took her arm and pulled her forward.

"Oh, no!" Dorrit tried to plant her feet. "I didn't really mean it!" Her protest came too late. The Kaiser had recognized Philip von Brandt.

"Philip!" he exclaimed. "How nice to see you."

Philip executed a dandy bow from the waist. Following his lead, Dorrit curtsied, keeping her eyes on the floor.

"Tell me, how is the general?" Kaiser Wilhelm was evidently still addressing Philip. Dorrit didn't dare look up to confirm it.

"My father suffers the weight of his years but is otherwise quite fit."

"I'm glad to hear it. A great man. One Germany can be proud of. We wish him a long and comfortable retirement. Give him my best regards."

"I will. Thank you. May I present Fraulein Zache?"

In a state of panic, Dorrit sank further to the floor in what she hoped was a graceful show of reverence. She didn't know what else to do. Offering her hand seemed too plebeian.

"Fraulein Zache, I'm delighted!" When her head remained lowered, the Kaiser reached out and lifted her chin.

Dorrit snapped her head back. "Your Majesty, the pleasure is all mine," she said, a small nervous smile forming on her lips. Dear God, was she expected to say anything more? She cherished the hope that he would quickly move on.

He didn't. He continued to study her face before announcing, "I should like to dance." He turned to Count von Beckstein. "Why is the orchestra silent?"

Count von Beckstein motioned the musicians to earn their keep. "A waltz, Your Majesty?" he asked.

"Yes. A waltz to the New Year." Kaiser Wilhelm held out his hand. "Will you give me the pleasure, Fraulein Zache?"

"It would be a great honor," Dorrit heard herself say, her voice sounding foreign and strange in her ears. Months ago she had studied the Kaiser's picture in Herr Ziegler's shop, now she was about to dance with him. Surely, this couldn't be real.

The crowd fell back leaving an expanse of parquet that to Dorrit loomed as immense as Alexander Platz. The Kaiser put his good arm on her waist; she placed her left hand on his shoulder and with the other, held out her skirts. She had read about his lame arm and instinctively guessed that this was the way to manage the situation.

From across the ballroom, Johann watched her with quiet pride. In another corner of the room, Louisa's face took on a strange shade that didn't compliment the color of her gown.

Following the Kaiser's waltz—the grandest of endorsements—Dorrit was immensely popular. Every gentleman in the ballroom wanted a turn with her, and none minded her faulty steps when anything other than a box step was required. While reveling in her newfound prominence, she saw Johann at the champagne tables—glass in hand—talking with other men similarly occupied.

When supper was announced, he finally put his glass down and pried Dorrit away from a perspiring Austrian nobleman. They walked into the salon where they found Kurt and Lillian, the foursome securing seats at one of the many round tables set with white cloths, tall flickering candles, and red roses. A sumptuous dinner was served, and once the last piece of succulent lobster and lavish side dish had been enjoyed, coinciding with the countdown toward midnight, everyone went back to the ballroom where lights had been dimmed, the crowd now jostling for spots by the windows facing the lawns and the impending fireworks display.

Chapter 40

The sonorous clock in the great hall of the Beckstein Schloss struck the hour of midnight and the ballroom erupted with shouts of Happy New Year, drowning out the orchestra playing the national anthem, while one rocket after another exploded in the black heavens outside, sending showers of stars cascading down. Amid this noise, music, and merry-making, Johann turned to Dorrit and lifted her hand to his lips.

"Happy New Year, darling," he whispered.

Darling? Embracing his endearment, Dorrit felt pleasant shivers on her spine. Of course the magic began to dissipate the minute a number of women came up and threw their arms around him, including Louisa who pretended Dorrit didn't exist. But refusing to be cowed or shoved aside, she stood her ground, soon wishing she hadn't because she now heard Johann call every woman he kissed *darling*.

Hearing him use the word so cavalierly caused the stardust to settle like sediment at the bottom of her novice heart. She pushed out her chin and clenched her fists in a silent vow that no one, least of all her aristocratic escort, guess her foolishness in taking his affectionate moniker at face value; used so freely it obviously meant nothing. Becoming practical, she quickly tossed away all romantic illusions as well as her former popularity, when she realized that she was suddenly out of favor with the very same gentlemen who had walked through fire earlier for a dance. Popularity was evidently a fleeting thing in this crowd; not a single man kissed her. So far, only Count von Beckstein and Kurt came around to give her a peck on the cheek with their Happy New Year greeting. Philip meant to kiss her, but was now so drunk he missed his target. Others abruptly backed off after discerning something in Johann's face.

Was he telling them that she wasn't worth the trouble?

When the last dance was finally announced, Johann claimed it and as his arm went around her waist, his steps guiding her effortlessly across the parquet, Dorrit wondered how she could have enjoyed dancing with anyone else tonight.

However, she didn't dwell on her present luxury, and in order to keep her susceptible heart from intimidating her good sense, she offered a few political observations like those Count von Beckstein had enjoyed. Of course, when her comments were met by a peculiar disinterest, she realized champagne had dulled Johann's mind; something he confirmed when he suddenly pulled her so close that her breasts were pressed against the black satiny lapels of his jacket, stifling all dialogue. While inwardly questioning the propriety of such intimacy, she heard him whisper, "Dorrit . . . darling . . . I'm madly in love with you."

Her heart stopped with such a jolt she felt spasms of real pain. Her back became a picket fence, her steps so awkward that she tripped Johann to within inches of the floor. His shoulders shaking with muffled laughter, he regained his dignity and once their feet were again in sync with the music, repeated himself, adding, "You'll have to marry me or risk having a madman on your conscience."

This confirmed to Dorrit that he was hopelessly intoxicated. While she had danced with others, he had spent his time at the champagne tables and was now blithely toying with her, no longer in control of his faculties.

Chapter 41

Once Herr Baron and Fraulein Zache were comfortably settled inside the coach, Schmidt climbed up into the driver's box, pulled his hat down over his ears, clucked to the horses, and drove away from the Beckstein Schloss in a succession of sleek carriages moving along the dark, winding road from Potsdam to Berlin like a miniature train. Johann spread a fur blanket around Dorrit, for although the inside of the coach was warmed by hot bricks under the floorboards, a bitter cold pressed against the windows and would eventually gain the upper hand. The wintry landscape was one of frozen fields and darkened farmhouses. With little to see, Dorrit sank back against the soft leather cushions. Exhausted from hours of dancing, the unaccustomed rich food and champagne, she struggled to keep her eyes open.

As the carriage springs creaked and the wheels rattled across the uneven cobblestone streets on the outskirts of Berlin, she awoke with a start to discover that she was lying with her head in Johann's lap, his arms cradling her.

"Good morning," he said, grinning down at her and brushing some hair off her forehead with the back of his hand.

"Good mor . . . ? Oh!" Instantly awake, Dorrit sat up, mortified. She smoothed her hair, trying to throw off her drowsiness and more specifically, trying to avoid Johann's eyes; it was too embarrassing to look at the person whose lap she'd so brazenly occupied. She turned toward the window, pushed up the shade, and studied the dark streets. The coach was on a path that would take them through Tiergarten, exiting onto Pariser Platz.

Glancing out the window, noting the shortcut, Johann wished he'd told Schmidt to stay on the city streets to buy more time. He hadn't expected Dorrit to sleep during the entire trip from Potsdam. With time now growing short, he pulled her chin around so that she faced him.

"There's little to see in the park at night," he said. "Dare I hope that your studied silence means you're giving undivided attention to my proposal?" He groped under the fur blanket and found her hand, lacing his fingers with hers. "Or did you believe me drunk and disorderly and not to be taken seriously?"

Dorrit's lips twitched in a grin with his correct assessment.

"I thought so. Well, for the record, with the exception of an adventure with strong spirits at the age of fifteen, I generally don't disgrace myself in public. Admittedly, a marriage proposal on a crowded ballroom floor was somewhat out of character but it was extended under conditions of acceptable sobriety and with a great deal of forethought." When Dorrit slanted him a dubious look, he said, "I can prove it." He let go of her hand, leaned forward and opened the latch on a compartment under the seats facing theirs, now extracting a small box stashed among maps, gloves, and other paraphernalia. "There!" He handed it to her. "I saw this in the display window at Friedlander's days ago and decided it would suit you perfectly. I offer it as indisputable proof of forethought."

Friedlander's? Dorrit didn't trust herself to speak, her mind was in turmoil with the idea that Johann's proposal had been in earnest and was accompanied by a gift from the most expensive jeweler in Berlin. Her father had cautioned her never to accept anything other than chocolates or flowers, so how could she possibly accept a gift from Friedlander's? At a loss of what to do, she continued staring at the box without opening it. Except for Ivar Kozlowski many years ago in Bialystock, and a student at Warsaw University who'd sent her poems until her father discovered his identity and cooled his ardor, Dorrit had no experience with suitors.

"Go ahead!" Johann urged, smiling ruefully; in his experience women never needed pressure to accept his gifts. "Open it."

Thinking it couldn't hurt to take a look, Dorrit unfastened the gold filigree clasp. The lid fell back, revealing a large stone cut in the shape of a heart and attached to a gold chain. She gasped. She knew the gem was real because only a genuine emerald could sparkle so brilliantly in the dim light of the coach lamp. "It's . . . it's exquisite!" she said, not daring to touch it.

Believing she might never get around to trying it on before they reached Niederlag rapidly bearing down on them, Johann lifted the jewel off its velvet cushion and fastened it around her neck.

"There!" he said, looking pleased. "Just as I thought. It matches your eyes perfectly. Now we just need a dress to go with it. I believe it'll go particularly well with white." He reached out, cupped her chin in his hand, and looked at her with a penetrating mien. "White as in wedding gown. What do you say?"

The shiny heart around her neck and the one beating inside her rib cage were both reflected in her face. No other response was needed for the moment.

Johann's hands caressed her cheek a moment before his eyes traveled to her lips, lingering there.

Dorrit felt a strange craving; she knew she was about to be kissed and, unlike last Thursday evening in his home, was not about to discourage him. Her hands reached out, touching the smooth wool of his overcoat at the same time he found her mouth in a soft hesitant kiss testing the contours of her lips as if he were merely exploring a number of possibilities before proceeding.

The exquisite intimacy caused a sweet madness to rush over her, and as Johann's mouth grew more insistent, heat and fire fought for space inside her pounding heart. She wound her arms around his neck in an attempt to garner support from the very person who was undermining her balance.

Johann kissed her with an unhurried thoroughness, and when he pulled away to allow them both to draw breath, his fingers fanned into her hair, tousling the curls that had worked free from the French braid.

Dorrit felt she had reached the summit of happiness, and although her lips were bruised from the force of his, she ached for more, the silent request visible on her flushed face.

"I think you've had enough kissing for one night," he teased in an odd, choked voice. "Besides, I can no longer trust myself to behave. And I certainly can't bring you home like this. Your father will take one look at your untidy hair and throw me out the door before I can convince him of my honorable intentions."

Dorrit squelched a giggle at the vision of her less than robust father hauling this giant of a man out of the apartment. "He's a staunch believer in a good night's sleep," she said. "You have nothing to fear. He was planning to go to bed early and welcome in the New Year from beneath his eiderdown. He explicitly said that he was entrusting me into the company of gentleman and therefore saw no reason to wait up."

Johann laughed. "Your father is a clever man, but a poor judge of people. His faith in me is flattering. Pray he never learns of his misplaced trust. Let's suffice to say that I'm not worthy of his daughter, who tonight danced with the Emperor."

"Please, don't remind me!" Dorrit wailed. "Imagine how easily I could have tripped His Majesty!"

"He didn't look the least bit worried. On the contrary. He appeared to enjoy himself immensely. And not just the waltz."

"What else was there?"

"Your attention to his small talk. It's well known that in addition to raking a keen eye over the ladies, the Kaiser enjoys smothering them with gallant conversation."

"Gallant? Absurd is more like it. He claimed I had Romanov eyes. Can you imagine anything more ridiculous?"

Chapter 42

Hannah was visiting a sister who was ill, so Dorrit was in the kitchen, making soup a Friday afternoon in April when her father returned home from the university.

"Hi!" she called out. "Tea will be ready in a minute. How was your day?"

"Wonderful!" Dr. Zache hung his coat in the hall closet and retrieved the books and newspapers he'd balanced on the umbrella stand. "For once I was allowed to conduct my lecture in peace. Your fiancé wasn't there to baffle me with polemic abstractions."

"I know. Johann told me he'd be in surgery all afternoon and would miss your seminar."

Herman Zache came into the kitchen and gave his daughter a kiss. "That young doctor works awfully hard for someone who doesn't have to make a living."

"That's because he enjoys it, Papa."

"A man with inherited wealth who does not succumb to a life of leisure is quite refreshing," Professor Zache said, huddling his shoulder inside his tweed jacket as if he felt a chill. "Oh . . . and . . . uh, I'll take a spot of brandy with my tea."

"Brandy?" her eyebrows shot up.

"Without any moralizing, my dear."

Dorrit found the rarely used bottle in the back of a cupboard and put it on the tray she carried into the living room minutes later. Her father was already seated in the sofa, rubbing circulation into his hands. The newspapers were strewn about haphazardly, but his lecture notes and books were placed neatly on the table in front of him. The window in the room was small but let in enough daylight; it was not necessary to switch on any lamps.

The scene was tranquil and ordinary except for Herman Zache's silence as Dorrit set out cups and saucers. In the absence of his usual conversation, he was fixating on a peg in the floor as if planning to dissect it, and when he finally looked up and glanced around, it was with the expression of a stranger examining a room he was seeing for the first time. Having asked for brandy, a drink he used strictly for medicinal purposes and only in the dead of winter, Dorrit wondered if he was conscience-smitten and regretting his sudden indulgence. After all, it was mid April and the weather was pleasant; his lungs weren't troubling him, there was no reason at all for the liquor. But she kept quiet, poured the tea, added a spot of brandy and pushed a plate of *linzertorte* within his reach, before she settled into the wing chair with one of the newspapers and waited for him to relate details of his day; he always did, it was an afternoon ritual.

But he remained silent, sipping his tea and brandy without a word. Dorrit checked one of the more reliable clocks in the room. Not yet five. Good. She had plenty of time before Johann arrived. She had already fixed her father's supper, his favorite chicken soup with dumplings was simmering on the gas burner in the kitchen; all she needed to do was change into her navy blue suit. She and Johann were going to dinner and the theater tonight, and since Hannah wasn't here to help braid her hair or fashion a chignon, she'd wear it loose.

Reflecting on the wonderful evening ahead, Dorrit put down the newspaper and looked at her father, hoping for some conversation and growing uneasy with his continued silence. Steeped in thought, he seemed far away, his brow deeply furrowed, his hands clawing at his beard as if bothered by some inner demons. Moreover, he looked pale, something she hadn't noticed when he came home. Wasn't he feeling well? Always alert to any change in his appearance, Dorrit grew worried. Something was wrong. Maybe she ought to stay home with him tonight.

"Papa, are you feeling all right?" she asked at length.

"Yes, of course, *bubeleh*."

Bubeleh? Dorrit's heart felt a pleasant little lurch; he hadn't called her that since she was a little girl.

"You might be a bit less frugal with the brandy." He held out his cup between his palms like a mendicant monk and nodded toward the bottle. When she reached for the teapot first, he shook his head and said, "Just some brandy."

"Without tea?"

"Yes."

Dorrit hesitated.

"Come now. It can't possibly harm an old fellow like me."

Against her better judgment, Dorrit poured and watched as he put the cup to his lips. In order to engage him in conversation, for God forbid that he wanted more brandy, she began to describe her day, most of which was spent at the dressmaker for the final fitting of several gowns, including her wedding dress. It was hard to believe that a professional seamstress was making her entire trousseau, when sewing was something she could do perfectly well herself. But overriding her objections, Johann had hired the famous Madame Mimieux and given Dorrit *carte blanche*. She was just now telling her father about an imported bolt of green chiffon sprinkled with flecks of gold thread, when he stunned her by reaching for the brandy and topping-off his cup.

"That's enough, Papa!" she said. "Keep that, but you'll get no more."

Before he could drink himself into a coma, she took the bottle and brought it into the kitchen. She returned to see him shudder as the undiluted brandy cut a path down his unseasoned throat. Tears were springing to his eyes, and in the next instant his chest heaved with a sudden and frantic struggle for air before a convulsive cough wrenched his body.

"Dear God!" Dorrit flew to the sofa and beat her palms on his back. "Papa! Papa!" she cried.

"I'll thank you not to p . . . puncture m . . . my lungs," he sputtered when he had recovered enough to speak. "I'm fine. I just haven't learned to drink this infernal stuff like a gentleman." He realigned his shoulders inside his baggy tweed jacket, took off his glasses, and ran his sleeve across his watery eyes before reaching into his pocket for a handkerchief.

Dorrit watched as he wiped his glasses and put them back on. He sighed deeply and was once again staring into space with the detachment of a daydreamer, but his reverie did not appear to be pleasant.

A strange fear crept over Dorrit. There was something on his mind, something dreadful, the room was heavy with it. She was accustomed to his lachrymose moods; he had suffered them in the past but this was different, if only because he had never before drowned himself in brandy. She moved closer and put an arm around him. Now that her wedding day was approaching, perhaps he was lonely, already feeling the emptiness of the apartment once she was no longer living here.

"Won't you reconsider Johann's offer," she said in an attempt to dispel his moodiness, "and move with me to Lindenstrasse? Your bedchamber would be as spacious as this entire apartment. There'd be room for all your books and clocks."

"No, my dear." Herman Zache held up his hand to stop a sales pitch he'd heard a hundred times since January. "That place is entirely too big. I'd wander around lost half the time and never get any work done. Besides, how could I ever put my feet up without damaging all that fancy furniture?"

"Those are poor excuses, and you know it," she scolded sweetly.

"Yes, I suppose so. The truth is, I have moved too often. When you and I finally made it this far west, I promised myself that I'd never again budge. Berlin is my home now."

"Grunewald *is* Berlin."

The professor nodded. "Which means you'll be nearby. And that makes me very happy. Why spoil anything by asking an old man to adjust to new surroundings." He reached for his cup. Dorrit watched him drink and held her breath, expecting another attack. It didn't materialize. He was able to continue.

"But there's something else that might spoil . . ." his voice tapered off and his hands suddenly shook. He put his cup down. "Something that I must tell you." He cleared his throat noisily and again pulled the handkerchief from his pocket, only to fold and refold it as if he needed to occupy his hands.

"What, Papa? Have you had some bad news?" Dorrit was reminded of former times when bad news meant upheaval and a move to another town.

He shook his head. "No. Except for the fact that I'm a coward."

"You're no such thing!"

"Unfortunately, I am. It's something I've known for a long time. I've spent a lifetime being a coward and deluding myself. Or, more importantly, deluding you." Herman Zache picked up his cup and took a measured sip.

"I don't understand. What do you mean?"

"What I am trying to say is that I've been lying. It's an ugly word so I prefer to use delude. Still, it's all the same. The truth is that I've lived a lie, fabricating one cowardly story after another, convincing myself that each deception was justified because you were too young."

"Too young for what?"

"The truth. I found a thousand reasons to keep it from you, all the while promising myself that I would tell you when you were old enough to understand. And now, lo and behold, I discover you've grown up and are about to be married. Even so I still lack the courage and find that I need a . . . a crutch." Herman Zache emptied his cup in one gulp and set it down. "Fact is, I'm cowardly pinning my hopes on your present security to make it easier for me."

"My security?"

"Yes. You're about to step into the niche you were born to occupy."

"Niche? Papa, what are you talking about?"

"Johann. I'm talking about your fiancé."

139

Goose bumps were creeping up Dorrit's arms; her father never spoke in broken sentences or riddles. His speech was always concise and to the point. Was the brandy causing the mumbo jumbo?

"You see, I'm hoping that if you find hatred in your heart for me and think ill of your mother, Johann will help you bear it. You'll have a husband. You'll no longer need a father. A devious one, at that."

Devious? Dorrit sat perfectly still, trying to digest what he was saying. *Hatred for her father?* That was preposterous! And how could she possibly think ill of a mother she'd never known? "Does this have anything to do with Saint Petersburg?" she finally asked softly.

"Yes."

"Well, don't torture yourself, Papa. I know I was born there. I also know you changed our name after we left. I've known about it for years."

"You have?" The professor looked shocked. "But how?"

"I came across some papers once."

"What papers?"

"My birth certificate and some other documents. I found them in the bottom of a box during one of our moves."

"Why didn't you tell me?"

"Because I didn't care where I was born. And it certainly didn't matter to me that you'd shortened our name. I figured you had a good reason. Also, I didn't want to upset you. You always had so much on your mind and you were often sad."

"*Ach.*" The professor sighed and looked around for the brandy before he remembered that Dorrit had put it away. He steadied himself with a deep breath instead. He had far worse to tell her. Finding those papers was only the tip of the iceberg.

"I kept you in the dark . . ." he began slowly and reached for her hand, "to shield you from the drama surrounding your birth. You were completely innocent in a tragedy that touched us all. Touched your mother in particular. I was hoping to spare you for as long as possible. But more than that, I kept silent because I wanted to keep you for myself. It was very selfish of me."

Selfish? Tragedy? Drama? Dorrit flinched at the strong words and again when her father's grip on her hand tightened, plunging the diamonds in her engagement ring into her fingers.

"I loved your mother very much . . ."

"I've always known that, Papa. It was so obvious. I felt it. Tell me about her."

"I should have done so long ago. I regret my silence. But I kept quiet because to say anything meant saying too much. There was no halfway. It was all or nothing. And like I just said, I was afraid to lose you." Herman Zache leaned back, his shoulders sinking into the sofa cushions as if pushed there by an invisible weight. "Being selfish and a coward is a terrible thing."

"And you're neither!" Dorrit protested, recalling the many times her father had picked up and moved, facing an unknown destination fearlessly. "You are the bravest person in the world. And the most unselfish!"

The professor shook his head; he could take no comfort in her heated declaration. She had not yet heard his story.

Chapter 43

"*When you came* into the world," he said, uttering the words slowly as though each syllable caused him pain, "healthy and strong less than six months after my marriage to your mother, I knew you weren't mine."

What? Dorrit's mind railed in protest at such nonsense. Not his? Her wonderful father was not her father? It wasn't possible and she wanted to rail at him for saying something so ridiculous, but all she could do was stare in bewilderment, shock silencing her, because she realized that he would never say anything of the kind if it weren't true.

"Your sturdy condition," he went on, "confirmed what I had already suspected when your mother showed signs of pregnancy immediately after our marriage. But it didn't matter. I loved her desperately and loved the child she bore. I cried with profound happiness the first time I held you. I thanked God for the miracle of your birth and vowed to raise you with all the love in the world and all the earthly possessions I could provide. With regard to the latter, I fell short."

"No you didn't!" Dorrit's protests were muffled by a rubber band in her throat, strangling her. Hot tears blurred her vision. She blinked them away; he had more to tell her and she mustn't distract him with tears.

"It was not until many months after your birth that your mother told me about your father."

Dorrit sucked in her breath and held it.

"I never asked her. I didn't care. I was your father. Legally at any rate, and no man could love his child more than I did. But eventually she decided to tell me. I suppose she needed to clear her conscience and not play me for a fool any longer. I was a doctor and recognized a full term baby when I saw one. As her story poured forth, it became clear that she still loved the rascal who had violated her. Which didn't surprise me."

"Who was he? Is he . . . is he still alive?"

"No, he is dead, *bubeleh*. He preceded your mother into the grave."

Dorrit felt an odd stab in her heart.

"His name was Alexeyev Romanov. He was the only son of a Russian grand duke who enjoyed direct blood ties to the czar. And like most of his class, he was spoiled rotten. But he was a handsome devil. I often saw him riding through the streets of Saint Petersburg with his entourage of highborn friends. He sat well in the saddle. Girls swooned and old women twittered about his dashing looks. He was blond, and his eyes were a vivid green, peculiar to that branch of the Romanovs. You inherited those eyes, my dear, and his proud chin. But you have your mother's auburn hair and pretty smile. And, thankfully, you have your good old-fashioned common sense from me." The professor allowed himself a half-chuckle before continuing. "Your mother, rest her soul, was neither practical nor sensible. She was a hopeless romantic. She believed the prince loved her because for a long time he gave up all his other liaisons and only had eyes for her. It was not surprising. She was an enchanting creature. But she was young and naive. Alexeyev, an experienced rogue, filled her ears with pretty words, her heart with hope, and her hands with expensive trinkets, all of which she mistook for commitment. Had someone told her that a Russian aristocrat would never take a Jewish wife, she wouldn't have believed it. When she told him that she was expecting his child, he vanished on a grand tour, a lengthy world tour that included a visit to Denmark's Royal House, where his betrothal to a Danish princess was announced. The bride-to-be was only thirteen, so the wedding could not take place for another three years, but news of the eventual royal union was celebrated with much fanfare in Saint Petersburg.

"In her desperation, knowing the prince was lost to her, your mother turned to her parents, who, in turn, approached me. I was well known to the family. They had a number of children and I was frequently summoned when one of them fell ill. However, suddenly I was being invited to the house as a guest. I found myself at their supper table with the lovely Arina sitting next to me, smiling and listening to my didactic conversation with rapt attention. I was forty-one, she was only sixteen, and when her parents pulled me aside one evening and suggested that I marry her, I was quite frankly stunned. Of course, once I established that they were serious, I happily and immediately agreed. In my elation, in my incredible joy, I never stopped to question why this beautiful girl would consent to have me for a husband. I was neither handsome nor clever with sweet words. But I was dependable. As a surgeon I made a good living and under the circumstances, none of which I was aware of at that point, it was more than Arina's parents could hope for. Also, I had no living relatives who might raise bothersome questions or burden them with requests for a dowry. They had three additional daughters to marry off and no money for a matchmaker. As for myself, I felt that I was the luckiest man on earth. I'd never been one with the ladies, and now this dainty female was being thrust into my arms. I was infatuated. I never thought such happiness could be mine.

"Days into our marriage, when it became apparent that Arina was expecting, I knew I was not the one responsible. But I said nothing. I played the proud and happy father-to-be. I loved her unconditionally but it was not reciprocated. Her smile, her flirtation faded the day we took our vows. Still, I lived in the hope that some day she might look upon me differently. It was not to be. After you arrived, she grew even more distant and no matter what I did to cheer her, a strange sadness overwhelmed her. I realized it had nothing to do with me. If I'd been twenty years younger, a sight more handsome, she could no more love me than she could forget Alexeyev.

"When word spread that the prince had returned from his travels, a strange anticipation began to glow in her face. I saw signs of her former brightness. She took an interest in her surroundings, put flowers in the windows, and dressed herself and the baby each morning as if she were expecting a visitor. She must have believed that he would come to see her. And he did. But she never knew. I alone saw him.

"As fate would have it, I was home with bronchitis and your mother had taken you to her parents' house for a few days to avoid any contagion. He came on one of those afternoons while she was away. He came alone. No entourage. His horse neighed, and since I was expecting no visitors, certainly none on horseback, I got out of bed, went to the window, and peered out. I was not surprised to see who the caller was. I was only surprised that he had troubled himself to learn that Arina was married and where she lived. And, of course, I was angry. And jealous. Had I been fit, I would have opened the door and given him a piece of my mind, damned be the consequences.

"Being in poor health, I could only hover behind the curtains, watch his approach, and pretend that no one was at home. I saw him get off his horse. He walked up to the door, raised his hand and prepared to knock at the precise moment I suffered a terrible coughing spell. It shocked him. He had not expected to find a husband at home in the middle of the day. He turned on his elegant heel, got back on his horse, and rode off without a backward glance. I never told your mother that he had come. I still believed she would eventually forget him, that time would work its miracle. I was an enamored old fool.

"Weeks later all of Saint Petersburg was buzzing with terrible news. The prince had been killed in a duel. It was rumored that the duel had been with the irate husband of one of his new conquests. Arina became demented with grief. She shut herself off from everyone. Even from you. She grew listless, thin, and in her weakened state, contracted pneumonia. There was a dreadful epidemic that winter and it quickly claimed her tragic young life. But she died oddly happy. There was a smile on her feverish lips when she took her last breath. I think she went to her eternal rest believing Alexeyev was waiting for her in a better world and that death would grant them what life had denied."

Burning tears were streaming down Dorrit's face. But it didn't matter; her father was past the point of being distracted, and the flood from her eyes loosened the painful pressure in her throat.

Herman Zache went on with his story.

"Shortly after your mother's funeral, quite by chance while tending patients in the city hospital, I heard gossip that sent chills through me. Word was circulating that once the official mourning period for Prince Alexeyev ended, his family expected to find and raise a child they had reason to believe was his. I could only guess that as he lay mortally wounded, he must have told them about Arina.

"I became deathly afraid. I didn't know how much he had said. But I knew one thing. Armed with even the flimsiest of leads, his parents would soon enough find you and take you away from me. The power of the palace was at their disposal. I was a Jew. It'd be child's play for a Russian aristocrat to arrest me. My life and property was expendable. Any trumped-up charge would send me to Siberia or the gallows. Jews had taken part in the assassination of Alexander II, and it was well known that his son and present Czar, Alexander III, believed that an underground plot was being hatched to end the Russian monarchy. It was generally accepted that Jews were at the core of any conspiracy.

"I made desperate plans to flee. I told no one. Not even your mother's family. They were sure to be questioned. It was better for them if they knew nothing. I left everything behind except for important documents and whatever money I had.

"Carrying you in my arms, I walked out of the house in the middle of the night and made my way to the railway station on foot, leaving no hackney driver to bear witness. Likewise, I didn't buy tickets from the stationmaster. Hiding in the shadows behind a newspaper kiosk, I jumped aboard a westbound train just before it pulled away from the station.

"Several stops later, a tired conductor came around, and from him I bought tickets to Minsk. But even as the train lumbered toward daylight, putting comforting miles between Saint Petersburg and me, and I no longer needed fear immediate arrest, I was not to have any peace of mind. From that time forward, any curious look or comment from total strangers drove me into a panic. I dared not make friends because they might ask questions. Even after I changed our name I lived in constant fear of the long arm of the czar's police. I became paranoid. I stopped practicing medicine and became a teacher. I lied about our origins. I lied about your birthplace. I taught you German and French but never a word of Russian. We continually moved west. There were bloody *pogroms* throughout Eastern Europe. We had barely left Kiev when two thousand Jews were rounded up and murdered for no reason except their religion. Berlin was known as a haven for expatriates. It took years, but I slowly worked my way there."

Dr. Zache fell silent. His story finished, he loosened his grip on Dorrit's hand and looked at her with trepidation, afraid at what he might find. Knowing he had lived a lie, would she denounce him? Would she be angry that he had robbed her of a royal upbringing? But as he searched her tear-stained face, he found no bitterness on her brow, no condemnation fell from her lips, and her eyes remained soft and bright, soft with love, bright with tears. The love he recognized, the tears he understood, and when her arms fell around his neck, a profound happiness swelled in his chest.

"Popi," she cried. "I love you and I'm so sorry for your past fears and anguish. Sorry for all those years . . ."

His heart squeezed with joy. *Popi?* She hadn't used that term since she'd been a little slip of a thing. Smiling, he stroked her hair just as he'd done that night when he fled Saint Petersburg, carrying her onto the train, fear of discovery all but buckling his knees. Her sweet little face had been wide-eyed with wonder, the snow had swirled about them and she had clung to his neck, afraid of the huge belching locomotive, afraid to lose her Popi in the darkness.

"If I hadn't left Saint Petersburg," he now said, his voice thick with the memory, "you could have grown up in a royal family."

"I would not have wanted that. You're my family. I could never love anyone but you."

"Except that good-looking doctor, eh?"

146

"Yes." Dorrit smiled through her tears.

"Well, then you'd better go change your dress." Dr. Zache turned to consult a clock on a shelf above the sofa. "*Ach*, time is running away from us." He patted her hand. "You'd better wash your face. It won't do to let Johann know you've been crying. He might never forgive me for being the cause of it. I'd like to remain on good terms with my son-in-law."

"Should I tell him about Saint Petersburg?"

"By all means. When the moment is right, tell him everything." Dr. Zache suddenly grinned. "I dare say he'll be pleased to learn that half your blood is blue. I'm sure he has often wondered how a homely creature like myself came to have such a beautiful daughter."

Dorrit pinched his cheek playfully and got up, switching on the light as she left the room. Without either one of them having noticed, shadows from the adjacent building had crept across the window, creating an early dusk.

Chapter 44

The fifth day of May dawned to a cloudless blue sky. By afternoon it was as warm as August and, riding through the streets of Berlin to her wedding, Dorrit's heightened senses tingled with the rare beauty of the day.

Colorful petunias spilled from window boxes along Niederlag Strasse, giving the drab apartment buildings a whole new look, and at the foot of Unter den Linden, the chariot bearing the golden Goddess of Peace atop the Brandenburg Gate glistened in the sun. Beyond this impressive portal, Pariser Platz was alive with beds of red tulips bending their showy heads in the benign breeze fanning the fine mist around the dancing waters of the fountains in front of the Adlon Hotel. Sunday strollers sauntered leisurely across the square toward Tiergarten and its majestic groves of trees, where children chased each other across the grassy knolls. In the distance, church bells chimed the hour, one carillon right after another, in turn, so as not to compete for God's ear all at once.

Searching for reality Dorrit looked wistfully at her father, surely she was dreaming, surely she was back in Warsaw and would momentarily hear his voice calling: "Wake up, Dorrit! Wake up! It's time for school."

But she heard no such command. Her father sat silently next to her, an impish twinkle in his eye softening his stern deportment, while the constant smoothing of his gray beard bespoke of a touch of nerves. Schmidt was in the driver's box and the carriage was now heading west on Kurfurstendamm under the dappled shade of the ancient oaks in the center partition of the street.

"Oh, no!" Dorrit cried once Schmidt pulled into Lindenstrasse where, as far as her eye could see, elegant rigs were haphazardly parked on both sides of the street. "We're late! Everyone's here already."

"Well, I should hope so," the professor said, first to climb from the carriage so he could help her down. "Guests are supposed to arrive before the bride."

"Oh? Of course. How silly of me." Dorrit alighted and adjusted the voluminous folds in her sheer dotted Swiss gown that fell in a white cloud to her ankles. She stopped a moment to gaze at the magnificent house, recalling that frigid December day six months ago when she'd stood by these very same gates, wondering if she dared pass through them. The grand villa looked infinitely more approachable at this time of year. The windows facing the street reflected the golden glow of the setting sun, and the vines clinging to the wrought-iron fence drooped with heavy clusters of purple flowers. Lilacs bloomed along the south wall of the house and urns at the top of the walkway were filled with yellow primrose and pink Sweet William. Dorrit bit her lip, reached for her father's arm, and suddenly rushed him inside the gates and up the footpath in blind determination as though she feared the curtain would fall on this exquisite scene if she delayed another minute.

Chapter 45

The center hall was milling with guests making their way toward the salon where rows of folding chairs were set up for the ceremony, a civil ceremony in respect for the different religions of the bride and groom. Actually, Herman Zache would have agreed to a church service, had Johann insisted. Security for his precious daughter in a world where he himself had found none was first on his list of priorities. He would plead his case with his creator soon enough.

Gerlinde and Lillian were stationed just inside the door, watching for Dorrit and her father, and now quickly whisked them into the library before the guests took notice of their arrival.

Hans as flower bearer was sequestered in the library where his grandmother was bending over him, giving instructions and fretting over his sailor's suit complete with white piping and a brass whistle attached to a gold braid and placed in a pocket, where Ursula prayed it would remain. The minute she saw the bride, she straightened and greeted Dorrit and Dr. Zache effusively. They had met several times during the spring, and now with a look to Gerlinde that said *I've done my best with the boy,* Ursula excused herself and left for the salon where her husband was saving her a seat.

Smug at being included in the ceremony—his sisters were banished to an upstairs room with Fraulein Kruse—Hans was careful not to forget his instructions. No sooner was his *Oma* gone, when he dashed over to Uncle Johann's desk for a boutonniere of lilies of the valley, which he handed to the professor. Running back to the desk a second time, he grabbed a rainbow of roses tied with white silk streamers and proudly presented the bouquet, upside down, to Dorrit.

"Thank you, Hans," she exclaimed, carefully righting the delicate spray. "They're beautiful!"

Grinning from ear to ear, Hans shuffled back to the desk, this time to pick up the basket of rose petals he was to sprinkle along the aisle when he marched into the salon.

Gerlinde gave him a gentle shove in the direction of the closed French doors. "Time is drawing near," she said. "Be a good boy and stand guard. Alert us the minute the music starts." Hans happily skipped across the floor, kicking up a corner of a Persian Tabritz.

"He's so excited, one would think he was getting married." Gerlinde bent down to straighten the rug before turning back to Dorrit. "I hope to live to see the day. But now, let's have a proper look at you." She tilted her head and made Dorrit pivot full circle. "You look divine," she said, her eyes misting with emotion. "I often wondered why Johann didn't marry. When he telephoned New Year's Day with the surprise announcement, I thought he was rushing to the altar because . . . well, you know, because he was getting dreadfully old and beginning to worry about the lack of an heir. You know what I think now?"

Dorrit shook her head.

"I believe he was just waiting for perfection." Turning to Lillian, Gerlinde said, "Don't you agree?"

Lillian agreed, and Gerlinde threw her thin arms around both the bride and Lillian, hugging them fiercely. "Years ago, Johann became part of my family," she cried. "He and Karl-Heinz were like brothers and I took it for granted that he'd be mine well. In the same way, Dorrit, I hope you'll think of us as sisters from this day forward. You, Lillian, and me. The three of us . . . sisters! How about it?"

"There's nothing I'd like more," Dorrit said, almost brought to tears with Gerlinde's offer.

Keeping her emotions in check, Lillian looked askance at the two of them. "No more sniveling!" she admonished. "You're supposed to be nervous, not sad." She turned to Dorrit and stroked the frothy bridal gown gathered at the waist with a pearl encrusted sash. The neckline was softly scalloped, as were the elbow-length sleeves. Dorrit's hair was pulled back from her face and held in place by a band of tiny silk rosebuds sparkling with dewdrops. Real diamonds, Lillian guessed, figuring Johann would have insisted on that.

"I *am* nervous," Dorrit admitted as the hum of subdued conversation in the salon was replaced by a lively Mozart minuet. Flailing his arms by the French doors, Hans was jumping up and down to get his mother's attention.

"All right!" Gerlinde patted the air with her palms to calm him before turning to Dr. Zache, who'd been perusing the abundant bookshelves. "We've had our two minute warning," she said to him. "The next piece will be the Mendelssohn. That'll be our cue." She pulled a compact from her beaded purse and pushed her pale blond hair under the netting of her feathered hat before adjusting the layers of chiffon in her blue gown. Lillian was similarly dressed, but in a deeper shade of blue, and was so confident of her appearance that she didn't need to check the mirror.

The music changed. Gerlinde banded the small group together and left the library behind Hans sprinting ahead. She gave him the signal to proceed into the salon. In his excitement, he emptied the entire basket of petals on the floor just inside the doors. Tossing a look of apology toward the bride, Gerlinde motioned Lillian to ignore the spilled flowers and follow Hans. Then she, too, stepped around the pile of petals and disappeared into the salon.

Dorrit tightened her hold on her father's arm. He straightened his new silk vest under his new black suit and molded a proud expression such as she'd never before seen.

"We've traveled a winding and wobbly road you and I," he said softly. "But you've found solid ground. Now my heart can rest."

"I love you, Papa," she whispered, squeezing his arm.

Scores of Berlin's elite turned in their seats, cranking their heads to look at the bride entering the salon, their faces melting into a colorful kaleidoscope because Dorrit saw only Johann. Dressed in black attire as splendid as that he'd worn on New Year's Eve, he was standing at the far end of the large room, flanked by the solemn-faced officiating judge and a grinning Karl-Heinz. As she drew near, Johann's eyes dipped to below her throat where an emerald heart hung suspended on a gold chain. He smiled.

They were married.

Following the ceremony, and while the salon was being readied to accommodate a hundred people for dinner, the bride and groom mingled with their guests in the drawing room, champagne toasts continuing to delay a lavish six-course meal prepared by three renowned Berlin chefs under Frau Schmidt's auspices. Finally ordering her husband to ring the bell one last time, she told the staff to commence serving whether or not a single guest was seated. Food in the mouth was better than pretty speeches; besides, the first course, a light-as-air salmon mousse, could not wait another minute.

The evening remained delightfully warm and as supper drew to a close, the strolling violins in the salon joined other musicians on the terrace, their melodies pulling the guests outside. The trees throughout the garden were strung with colorful paper lanterns lending a festive ambience as shadows lengthened and darkness fell.

As he suspected, Johann managed only one dance with Dorrit, the first, because from that moment on his best-laid plans were sabotaged. Finally, he saw her in the arms of easy game, the inebriated Philip, and before anyone could invent additional duplicitous means of keeping him from his bride and delay his honeymoon, Johann cut in. Holding Dorrit's hand, he managed a beeline through the garden and out to the street; but not sufficiently swift to avoid a blizzard of confetti that fleet-footed guests staged by taking the shortcut through the house.

Schmidt was waiting at the curb. Tonight he would drive the baron and baroness to the Grand Hof Hotel in Potsdam. Tomorrow they would proceed by train to Paris and eventually to San Sebastian.

Chapter 46

It *was toward the* end of May when the honeymooners headed for San Sebastian, seaside retreat of wealthy Europeans and official summer residence of the Spanish Court. Arriving from Paris by train in the late afternoon, they were met by a driver with a two-seater rig where their luggage was loaded into a net hanging behind the backrest.

"Our hotel is off the beaten track," Johann explained as Dorrit registered surprise when their driver left the main road from the station and instead of continuing into San Sebastian, cracked the whip over the horses, guiding them onto a steep, narrow lane and into the foothills of the Urgull Mountains. "The Villa Solana does not attract your typical tourist."

"I can see why," Dorrit gulped, eying the sheer drop-off on one side of the road. Waves were crashing onto the rocks below, but she dared not lean over and look down, it might tilt the precarious balance the carriage held on the small strip of dirt. Keeping her eyes straight ahead, she concentrated on the pleasant, tangy smell of kelp and seawater, all the while worrying about how the driver would manage any on-coming traffic.

"In fact," Johann continued, "it is so inaccessible that it appeals only to a very select clientele."

"Such as?"

"Disgraced royals sent into exile. An occasional ambassador with his paramour. International jewel thieves on the lam, and a couple of ordinary citizens from Berlin who have their own reasons for wanting seclusion." He draped his arm across her shoulder and looked devilishly smug. "To ensure our complete privacy and to avoid being badgered with invitations from those of social rank who might wish to investigate ours, I reserved our accommodations simply as Doctor and Frau von Renz."

"Oh." Dorrit contrived a piqued look. "Just when I had my heart set on meeting a Spanish duke."

"I'm afraid you'll have to settle for a Spanish chef. But I guarantee he'll be top drawer. The hotel offers haute cuisine, an excellent library, marvelous gardens, and beautiful beaches."

"Well, I supposed that takes the edge off my disappointment," she laughed, incredibly happy. In the next instant she felt a strange icy sensation on her spine. Her fingertips tingled. Someone was walking on her grave. She sobered, wondering if it was bad karma to wallow in such utter contentment.

Chapter 47

On *their first* evening at the Villa Solana and as if God was in collusion with the Spanish Ministry of Tourism, the honeymooners were treated to a sunset of such glory that it was a while before they could turn their backs on it and go downstairs for dinner. Lingering on the balcony outside their suite, they stood gazing at the broad strokes of orange and pink brushed across the endless purple sky above a tranquil silvery sea.

However, just as the last rays of the sun sank into the bay, drawing the brilliant hues from the sky, enormous waves began crashing against the rocky shore as though determined to devour it. Sea gulls roosting peacefully on the breakwater only moments earlier, shrieked and swooped into the air, gliding and diving over the now churning sea.

"How odd," Dorrit reflected, leaning over the vine-covered balustrade, fully expecting to see waves lap up against the road and the flowerbeds below. "What happened?"

"A sudden change in the wind," Johann said. "This bay is notorious for unpredictable crosswinds and treacherous currents. Which reminds me . . ." his voice became dead serious, "there's to be no swimming on your own. When I came here years ago, my parents never allowed me near the beach without a male escort. An expert swimmer. I suffered in embarrassed silence till I was seventeen."

"By that yardstick, I'm too old for an escort," Dorrit quipped.

"The order still stands. Each season a number of bathers drown along this coast. In fact, I forbid you to walk on the beach alone."

"That'll be easy to remember. On the Champs Elysees where ornamental fountains were the only source of water, you never once allowed me to walk alone. You even tagged along the morning I went shopping for a clock for my father. This after you'd repeatedly claimed souvenir hunting was a tedious tourist amusement to be avoided at all costs."

"There were other hazards in Paris."

"Such as?"

"Frenchmen."

"Oh, come now!" Dorrit sputtered.

Turning her toward him, Johann's hands cradled her face. "Haven't you noticed I'm incurably possessive?" He kissed the tip of her nose. "And jealous."

"Be serious, please!"

"I am serious."

"If I have attracted unwanted attention, blame yourself. I tried to tell you Madame Mimieux was too expensive. Now you're telling me her styles are too risqué as well?"

"Perhaps," Johann mumbled, drawing her up against him. The breeze sent her fragrant hair tumbling into his face and he was ready to ignore his stomach and cater to that other more powerful need, when somewhere in the interior of the hotel the final dinner bell sounded. He became practical. "I guess we'd better go down and introduce you to that celebrated Spanish chef."

Chapter 48

It was a few days later, after strolling along the beach and coming upon some rock formations offering a good place to rest, that Dorrit told Johann about her mother's tragic love affair resulting in her unconventional birth.

"Just goes to show that I was right," Johann said when she had finished the story.

"Right about what?"

"You. I always suspected that you were a princess. From the very first time I saw you in Ladeburg."

"Ladeburg?" Dorrit laughed. "What gave me away? The secondhand coat?"

"Yes. Only one of noble birth could carry herself so regally in a simple garment."

"Then why all the fuss outfitting me in haute couture?" Dorrit brushed at the sand clinging to her white pleated skirt, its hem trimmed with rows of blue piping. Her blouse was blue with white piping on the collar. "To justify the cost, Madame Mimieux never tired of telling me that every stitch was zee rage! Zee pinnacle of zee high fashion!" Dorrit managed Madame's accent with flair. "At such heights, I questioned if her *mode et parure* might fall from favor before I had a chance to wear everything."

Johann laughed, his white teeth gleaming against his deeply tanned face.

Watching him, Dorrit's heart skipped a beat. The Spanish sun had done a job on him. The neck of his blue shirt was open, showing a patch of bronze as dark as his face. His brown hair was windblown and his white linen jacket hung negligently on his broad shoulders. Without any conscious thought, she snuggled up against him.

His arms immediately closed about her.

She tilted her face up, reached out her hand and traced the outline of his mouth with her forefinger.

"Stop that!" he grinned. "Stop tempting me in broad daylight unless you want your shapely little bottom in the sand and a public display of our intimacy."

Dorrit pivoted her head and peered across their rock fortress. "Public?" she murmured. "We're too far from the hotel. There's no one here but us."

"That observation . . ." Johann lowered his mouth toward hers, speaking against her lips with feather-light kisses, "could get you in a lot of trouble." His hand slid under her blouse at the same time his mouth began exploring hers with sweet and scorching madness. Of course, he would stop before it went too far, he told himself; he was not going to make love to his wife on the beach, even if they were alone. Still, it was an enticing idea, one that was suddenly shattered by a hair-raising scream, which he took to be the battle cry of a sea gull. However, when another high-pitched shriek was again carried on the wind, it sounded remarkably human. Instantly alert, he stood up, scanning the beach in both directions.

"What is it?" Dorrit picked up her straw hat, beating it against her knees to shake off the sand.

"I'm not sure." Johann took her arm and helped her climb over the rocks, his other hand shielding his eyes from the sun as he looked around, now spotting a couple of women silhouetted a distance away at the water's edge. Their presence, in and of itself, was no surprise because the beach directly in front of the Villa Solana was rocky and many bathers chose to walk down shore where there was more sand. Johann noticed the wind had shifted and that the bay was seething with frothy white foam topping the waves; not optimum swimming conditions by any stretch of the imagination. When one of the women suddenly plunged into the surf, fully dressed, while the other began running back and forth, tearing at her hair, the scene took on an ominous suggestion.

"Good God!" Believing he was about to witness a suicide, Johann shook off his jacket, tossing it negligently on the rocks and leaving Dorrit to follow at her own pace. Racing across the sand, he reached the frantic woman running in circles, her uniform identifying her as a maid. When he grabbed her arm, she stopped running, now gasping incoherently.

"*Mon . . . Madame . . . noyer! Mon Madame . . . noyer!*"

Johann didn't need to be told in French or in any other language that the woman in the surf might drown. Swirling waves were crashing all around her, even so she continued heading out to sea. Turning his back on the hysterical maid, Johann ripped off his shirt, kicked off his sandals, and dove in.

After a few determined strokes, he reached the spot where the woman was floundering, hopelessly trapped in the heavy wet folds of her skirts. As he lunged for her, she threw herself further out to sea, but not before he grabbed her arm. She began a desperate struggle to free herself; her fists beating against his chest, her face distorted in the harsh contours of wild-eyed panic. Dodging her assaults as best he could, Johann dragged his uncooperative catch back toward shore.

Once they reached shallow water, she stopped resisting and looked at her savior, sanity softening her features for an instant before she slumped to her knees in the foam of a retreating wave.

"Please . . . let me go! Please . . ." she cried in French between heart-wrenching sobs as she pounded the wet sand. "My son is out there. Oh, God!" she moaned. "My little boy." She faced the churning surf, now screaming, "Marcel!"

Marcel? Stunned, Johann's eyes searched the hostile sea. He saw no little boy. There was no one in the breakers.

"It's true, monsieur. It's true!" The maid, hitching up her skirts, had rushed to her mistress's side. "We let him go swimming with his cork float. We were watching him carefully but a large wave caught him and swept him out. We saw him lose hold on the float." She wrung her hands. "*S'il vous plait*, can you help us? It's a long way back to the hotel. I would have run for help, except I was afraid to leave. I was afraid Madame de Loncourt would drown herself."

Johann was about to berate both women for letting a boy go swimming with or without a cork float, but this was not the time for conversation. He turned back toward the surf, narrowed his eyes and searched the top of the swells. Sure enough, a small head and one thin flailing arm suddenly popped up well beyond the breakers. How had the boy gotten himself out that far? Well, there was only one thing to do. It was time for a swim.

Chapter 49

"*Keep your mistress* out of the water!" Johann ordered the maid clinging to the hysterical woman. "My wife will help you." He waved at Dorrit standing on dry sand, clutching his jacket, her frightened eyes pleading with him not to go in. But of course she knew that he would.

Johann again dove into the pounding surf, his body slicing through the water with great speed. However, when he reached the spot where he'd seen the boy, there was no sign of him. Only the slab of cork was visible, bobbing further out at sea beyond reach.

Diving repeatedly, Johann searched under the water. There was no telling how long the boy had struggled so time was critical. He noted that it was surprisingly deep in this area and when he spotted a steep drop-off on the sandy floor, he felt uneasy. It was unusual to have a trench so close to shore.

Close to shore?

Surfacing for air, a quick glance told Johann that he was no longer close to land. But how could that be? He was diving and crisscrossing the water just beyond the breakers. Suddenly a sick feeling came over him. *Riptide!* That would explain the boy's distance from the beach when first spotted. After being caught by the wave, the lad had not venture further out. He'd been pulled!

A cold fear such as Johann had never before experienced, rushed over him as he realized that he, too, was being pulled out to sea by an invisible force of a terrifying strength. And although he was an accomplished swimmer, he was as helpless as Marcel against the savage tow.

Don't panic. Find Marcel, he told himself, then worry about the current. Diving again and again, he finally caught sight of the boy submerged some ten meters away, hanging suspended in the water, not struggling, not attempting to swim. The first stage of drowning!

Johann raced forward. A heartbeat later, his own lungs bursting, he surfaced with the limp child. Holding Marcel's head above water, he applied upward thrusts of pressure on his diaphragm until the boy began vomiting and spewing seawater. Once his stomach and lungs cleared, Johann gave a victory sign toward the women on the beach and, holding Marcel against his chest, began the arduous journey toward shore, using the backstroke.

Marcel, who appeared to be eight or nine years old, was in shock and did not fight the rescue as victims of the sea frequently do. A small blessing because Johann knew he would need total concentration if he was to reach dry land, a goal that was fast slipping through his fingers. Using every ounce of strength to swim in one direction, the current was pulling him in the opposite. Alternating between every stroke he knew, he soon realized he was gaining no ground and only exhausting himself. At odds with a powerful element, simply staying afloat was a major victory, hard won and not guaranteed to last. But he persevered, keeping his strokes even to conserve energy.

Turning his head, glancing over the top of the choppy water breaking against his face, Johann again waved to the three women, wondering if they could actually see him. The distance had grown so great they looked like small dots on the beach. He couldn't even make out which one was Dorrit.

Dorrit! A sudden surge of renewed energy launched him forward but any gain was immediately lost to the deadly tow. He swore out loud. He was no marathoner. The summers he and Karl-Heinz had swum the river in Bernau, and his former visits to these shores, were no preparation for this inequitable test against an ill-tempered sea. Hands down, the current held the advantage.

He continued swimming, his legs like lead weights, his shoulders aching with a remorseless pain; breathing was a labor in itself. Chilled to the bone, his teeth began to rattle like ill-fitting dentures. He stopped a moment to rest and to shift the weight of the semiconscious boy. He couldn't tell which arm hurt the most; the one holding Marcel or the one he used for swimming.

By and by his rests grew more frequent. A numbing weariness was creeping over him. His mind became as battered as his body and he was growing tired of a battle he wasn't winning. His energy was spent, his reserves drained, what little remained was imprisoned in rigid muscles rendered useless by the cold. Crazy thoughts of yielding to the pull and welcoming the soft underwater environment began to seduce him.

It seemed an eternity since he'd gone into the surf. The shoreline was still slipping further and further away; his situation was growing desperate. Even if the icy tentacles of the tide were to let go of him, he was too spent to swim using one arm and dragging the boy with the other.

When a swell lifted him up long enough to look over a cresting wave, he searched the beach for the women. There were only two in his line of vision; a third was running along the shore in the direction of the hotel. Was one of them going for help? Had they finally decided he was in trouble and couldn't make it on his own? Too exhausted to worry about his pride, he hoped so. Of course the hotel was some distance away, the sand was a slow track to run on, and it was doubtful that any meaningful help could be mobilized. No local familiar with this ornery sea was fool enough to dive in, and it was highly unlikely that the small dinghy the hotel kept on quaint display could be launched in these high seas. It'd be swamped and there'd be more bodies needing rescue.

Johann could no longer swim. It was no use kidding himself. He was barely staying afloat and was swallowing large amounts of water. He didn't care. It didn't matter somehow. The numbness in his muscles was spreading to every part of his body, bringing blessed relief from the burning pain. He was no longer cold. This anesthetized state was almost pleasant.

Again a large wave hoisted him above the surface of the water. He scanned the coastline and the mountains rising in the distance. It was a ruggedly beautiful sight. Dorrit loved being here; he suspected she loved it far more than Paris. Too bad he had to spoil it for her. She was awfully young to be widowed.

He strained to see the beach and the two women. Which one was Dorrit? He couldn't tell, but as long as he could see someone walking along the water's edge, he knew he was still in the game. Walking? Actually, the women appeared to be running. They stopped and repeatedly pointed. Pointed at *what*?

The shoreline had changed, Johann noted, less rock formations and longer stretches of sand. He must have been dragged quite some distance down the beach. Renewed hope suddenly surged through him. Perhaps all was not lost? If the current had changed direction and was no longer pulling him out to sea, instead pulling him parallel to the shore, he might eventually be deposited on a spit of dry land like a piece of driftwood. If he could just stay afloat long enough, then maybe, just maybe . . .

He caught sight of an old sea wall jutting out into the water. Was that what the women were pointing at? Were they signaling that he ought to try reaching it? Yes, that was precisely what they were doing. If he could tread water and hang onto the boy, the current would do the rest. Again he looked toward the beach. He could now distinguish Dorrit from Madame de Loncourt. In fact, he could see her quite clearly. She was still clutching his jacket.

Dorrit and the seawall!

He forced his mind to think of nothing else.

Chapter 50

Johann fell into a coma-like sleep early that evening. The following morning after a breakfast of three boiled eggs and buttered buns, along with gallons of coffee, he was himself again as if yesterday's ordeal had never taken place.

"How about a swim?" he said, putting his napkin down and standing up to help Dorrit from her chair.

"Sure, but only if there's a nice strong undertow," she shot back.

Laughing, they left the dining room to a sedate dilatory crowd lingering over the morning papers. Crossing the courtyard behind the main building, they continued through an arch of purple bougainvillea leading to the hotel gardens, a pleasant stroll that was part of their regular morning routine.

"All kidding aside, solid ground feels pretty good," Johann said. "I suggest we stay on dry land today."

"We could try painting?" Dorrit nodded toward an elderly couple sitting in the shade of a gazebo, sketching the rosebushes growing in a semicircle around the dolphin fountain at the entrance to their sanctuary, the gentle splash of water mingling pleasantly with the buzz of bees working the flowerbeds.

Johann grimaced. "Let's save that activity for . . . hmm, thirty years from now?"

"That should give me time to perfect my technique," Dorrit laughed.

"Actually, I've got an idea," Johann said. "How about we go into town and pretend to be tourists shopping for souvenirs?"

"You're that eager to avoid the beach?" Dorrit teased.

"I was thinking of Professor Zache." Johann stopped to nip some white gardenias from a prolific shrub.

"My father?" Dorrit stood still while Johann fastened the flowers into the barrettes keeping her hair in place.

"Yes. You bought him a clock in Paris. I figure I ought to bring him one from here. He collects them, doesn't he?"

"Passionately."

"Then it's decided." Johann stepped back to admire his handiwork. "You look wonderful," he smiled. "Only one of us will pass for a tourist. You, darling, look like a local senorita at the market."

"Or at a wake," Dorrit said, inhaling the gardenias' heady perfume. "I smell like a funeral parlor."

"I don't like that reference," Johann grinned as they continued through the magnificent gardens toward the guest bungalows. There had been a great to-do in this part of the hotel compound yesterday when a semiconscious boy was carried home. Dorrit guessed Johann's intentions before he spoke.

"Would you mind stopping for a brief visit with Madame de Loncourt before we head off to town?" he asked. "I'd like to check on Marcel to make sure he's experiencing no ill effects from his exposure."

Although she had zero enthusiasm for a visit with a boy who had almost cost Johann his life, Dorrit agreed, telling herself that she mustn't blame Marcel for the near tragedy. It was the foolish Madame de Loncourt whom she ought to be angry with. And had she not been paralyzed with fear yesterday, she would have strangled the woman for being so incredibly naive to think that a piece of cork would keep the boy safe.

The door to Madame de Loncourt's bungalow was opened by a fully restored maid smiling broadly as she ushered the visitors in, one of whom she equated with the Second Coming of Christ.

Marcel was lying prostrate and penitent on the sofa in the large airy living room. A breakfast tray on the table next to him had been picked clean. A good sign, Johann noted, and his subsequent examination of the little fellow established that Marcel was suffering nothing more serious than a case of remorse for having caused such a drama.

"Promise me," Johann spoke gently in French to the boy, "that you'll never again venture out in rough seas." The boy nodded solemnly. "And don't rely on a float to keep you safe. Even when the water is calm."

"Oh, I won't! Cross my heart."

"Good." Johann smiled and tousled the boy's dark hair. "Actually, I was very pleased with the way you cooperated while we were swimming toward shore."

"Really?" Curious, Marcel pushed himself up on his elbows.

"Had you thrashed about, we might have had a much worse time of it."

Grinning, Marcel glanced toward his mother to see if she had heard him being praised.

She had and she looked pleased.

When Dorrit and Johann were ready to leave, Madame de Loncourt walked them to the door. Once out in the garden, out of sight of her son, tears welled up in her eyes.

"We will forever be in your debt," she cried softly. "Words can not express our *remerciement*. Had you not happened along and been willing to risk your life, my little Marcel would be dead. I would have drowned as well. I know I would have wanted to."

"Everything turned out fine. Don't dwell on it," Johann said. "If anything, be grateful to that old pile of rocks. It was obviously waiting to do one more good deed before crumbling."

His flippancy brought a smile to Madame de Loncourt's lips. She dried her tears, saying, "My husband is attending to some business in Madrid. He's due back here tonight. We're supposed to stay for another week but, lovely as this resort is, I'm suddenly eager to get home."

"I understand," Johann said.

"We'll probably return to Paris tomorrow. Still, I do hope my husband will have a chance to meet you both before then."

"It'd be our pleasure."

After Madame de Loncourt and Dorrit exchanged a few words about the charms of San Sebastian, the visitors left.

Chapter 51

In *addition to* the main dining room, the Villa Solana served meals in an enclosed courtyard where discriminating guests—those who wished for complete solitude—could dine alfresco at tables discreetly separated from one another by decorative trellises supporting canopies of lush greenery. A lone guitarist strumming Spanish ballads in a shadowy corner added to the ambiance.

Dorrit and Johann, regulars in the courtyard, had just been served their main course and were discussing plans to go into town after dinner to see a Barcelona flamenco troupe at the Casa Verde nightclub, when an impeccably dressed gentleman entered their sanctuary, disregarding their obvious wish for privacy.

After bowing to Dorrit, he turned to Johann, inquiring if he was addressing the physician from Berlin. Believing a hotel guest had taken ill and that the inevitable call: is there a doctor in the house? summoned him, Johann rose and acknowledged with a slight nod, only to suddenly find himself imprisoned in a masculine hug, his cheeks suffering the ardor of a madman. Astonished, he stared at the individual assaulting his person but, of course, quickly realized who it was even before Monsieur de Loncourt began his fervent speech.

Johann attempted to minimize the rescue, saying, "It was a small matter..."

"*Non!*" Monsieur de Loncourt held up his hands to silence him. "Small matter? *Non!* My family means everything in the world to me. Everything I live for. Without my wife and son I would have no reason to exist." His eyes bright with emotion, Monsieur de Loncourt articulated his gratitude a moment longer before he turned back to Dorrit, placed a gallant kiss on her hand, then left the courtyard as abruptly as he had arrived.

Johann remained standing and watched him go.

"The French are a demonstrative lot," he shrugged and sat back down to attend to the delicious stone crabs.

Chapter 52

Two weeks later in preparation for returning to Berlin, a maid and a valet came the von Renz suite to assist with the packing. While Dorrit supervised, Johann went downstairs to settle the bill.

"What? *What* did you say?" he sputtered at the hotel manager a moment later.

"I said that your bill has already been settled," the man repeated himself.

"How? I mean . . . *who?* Who settled it?"

"I can't say."

"I demand to know!"

The hotel manager spread his hands and drew his shoulders clear to his earlobes—forcing three double chins – all the while remaining disdainfully silent. This resort catered to a titled clientele; how had this Berlin doctor and his wife managed to secure reservations in the first place? Furthermore, he was baffled why a guest saw fit to complain about an account being settled by some philanthropic soul who wished to remain anonymous.

Johann left the man and stormed up to the suite, taking the stairs rather than the elevator to vent some of his fury. Loncourt? De Loncourt! The manager's lips had been sealed, but of course Johann figured it was that emotional Frenchman who had paid the bill! *Damn!* What was Loncourt's first name? There were probably a hundred de Loncourts in Paris. It'd be a job to try to locate the right one.

By the time Johann reached the second landing, he realized that even if he found Monsieur de Loncourt, he could not reimburse him. The man's pride would be damaged, and to shred another man's vanity for the sake of his own was not his style. He would have to let it go. *Damn!* Still scowling with impotent indignation, he walked into the suite, tersely dismissing the maid and the valet, handing each a generous sum. Shock and delight mingled on their faces; first at being so roughly discharged, secondly at being so handsomely paid.

"That bloody Frenchman covered my account!" Johann muttered under his breath as he snapped the suitcases closed and opened the door for the porter who had come to take the luggage downstairs. "It's an outrage! I can't imagine how the hotel can allow such a thing!"

The old porter took charge of the valises, placing them on a cart in the hall. He turned to the still-fuming guest, touched his cap and smiled, displaying the unfortunate space of missing teeth. He didn't understand German, but the timbre of this tall gentleman's voice was decipherable in any language. "The coach is at the curb," he announced in Spanish, pushing the cart toward the elevator. "I'll load these suitcases right away." He left, believing he had intruded on a marital tiff.

While Johann made a quick visual check of the rooms and gathered the morning papers together for reading on the train, Dorrit walked out on the balcony for one last look. The blue bay stretched as far as the eye could see, and iridescent hummingbirds buzzed around the colorful blooms on the vines clinging to the stucco railing, the flowers' scent mixing pleasantly with that of drying kelp on the beach. She would treasure the memory of the Villa Solana for the rest of her life; every minute was wonderful except for that dreadful day when this beautiful bay almost took Johann from her. She shivered. Thankfully no harm had come to anyone, no harm until today when Johann's pride suffered a blow at being the recipient of charity.

Inhaling deeply, she leaned over the balustrade. The old porter had reached the sidewalk in front of the hotel and was loading the suitcases into the coach that stood ready for the drive to the station. She saw him fish some carrot bits from his pockets and feed the harnessed horses. Enjoying the balmy scene and heedless of her complexion, Dorrit aimed her face to the sun, letting its tingling heat turn her cheeks pink. Johann would be furious if he caught her ruining her skin, but since he was already angry, a sunburn wouldn't make much difference. A moment later, she was distracted by a sharp voice from below. She glanced over the railing and heard the hotel manager give the porter a tongue-lashing. She didn't understand his rapid Spanish but his tone was cruel and if the porter's only crime was to feed the horses, totally uncalled for.

She felt bad for the old porter. He did not deserve a dressing down. No one around the place worked harder or more cheerfully. He was always on hand, opening doors, carrying packages and luggage larger than himself. On the day of the near drowning, he'd been first on the scene. With the agility of a cat, and with no concern for the distinct possibility that he might break his neck, he had scampered out on the rocky pier with warm blankets for the two human forms the sea had spared.

"Ah, there you are!" Johann joined Dorrit on the balcony. "Sorry to be leaving?"

"Yes and no," she smiled and ran her hand through her loose hair that gleamed like fire in the sun.

"Make up your mind, *Liebchen*."

"I can't. The view is completely intoxicating. It inhibits all rational thought."

"In that case, I guess I'll be stuck with a tipsy wife from now on," Johann grinned.

"What do you mean?"

"You'll have this view when we get home."

"That's silly, Johann. How?"

"Remember the painting we saw in town the day we bought the clock for your father? The painting you didn't want because your sense of thrift got in the way of your excellent eye for art."

"The Georges Seurat?" Dorrit said, surprised. "The picture of this bay . . . the beach . . . the breakwater . . . the gulls?"

"That's the one."

"You . . . you didn't!"

"It's on its way to Berlin."

"Oh, Johann!" She flew into his arms. "It's so beautiful but so . . . so large! Where will we put it? There's no room on the walls."

"I'm sure we can find a spot in Bernau."

A malicious bark from the curb below intruded on Dorrit's happiness. She slipped out of Johann's embrace and leaned over the balustrade.

"Not again!" she sighed, exasperated. "I don't understand why that trite manager keeps picking on the porter. He gave him a terrible public humiliation a minute ago. I guess he knows that a menial worker with a large family to support won't dare talk back or defend himself."

Moments later, while riding down in the elevator, it occurred to Johann that Dorrit had been mighty quick to stir-up compassion for an old hotel lackey, as well as remind him of the tiresome manager. Was she suggesting an opportunity to rid himself of Monsieur de Loncourt's handout?

Before the carriage pulled away from the curb, Johann did precisely that, pressing the amount of a month's stay at the most expensive hotel in San Sebastian into the porter's bony fingers.

Dorrit noticed the exchange out of the corner of her eye and smiled. But her smile did not match the one spreading on the porter's furrowed face as he looked at the fortune he was holding.

"Sir . . ." he stammered, bewildered. "This must be a mistake."

"No mistake," Johann assured him.

"May God be good to you," the old man whispered as the carriage drove off. Standing on the curb, he removed his cap in reverence of such bounty. He was not sure whether to laugh, cry, or kick up his heels and whistle.

He went back to work.

Chapter 53

The house in Bernau was so enormous it took several days before Dorrit found her way around. From the center hall, a wide staircase rose to a landing where it continued in opposite directions to a second floor gallery that led to the bedroom suites, guestrooms, and various other chambers. On the ground floor was a drawing room—twice the size of its counterpart in Berlin—a ballroom, a library, and dining room with two sets of French doors opening onto a flagstone terrace surrounded by flower gardens. Kitchen, pantry, and servants' wing completed the downstairs.

Dorrit made it her business to learn the names of everyone employed on the estate from the adipose housekeeper, Frau Erdmann, to the most menial maid. It was the least she could do in view of their obeisance when they curtsied and addressed her as *Mein Baroness*. As she slowly adjusted to this formality, she discovered there was something else she had to adjust to: Johann's absence. She now saw him mainly in the evenings and as wonderful as that was she missed his company during the day. But it appeared he preferred to spend his time with the horses, and how could she compete with forty magnificent animals? Truth be known, with the exception of the old bays that pulled public coaches, she was terrified of them. Even the well-tempered gelding that Johann bought at auction only days after arriving in Bernau scared her silly.

"For you, darling!" he announced proudly when the horse was delivered to the front steps of the house so she could admire him as he was led from the transport cart.

"For me?"

"Surprised?"

"Y . . . yes."

Johann winked. "He comes with strings attached."

"Strings?"

"Riding lessons. Something I'll attend to *personally*."

Dorrit smiled to cover her horror. She had no desire to ride this animal or any other, but was careful not to let Johann see the dismal impact of his gift and managed a cheerful, "He's beautiful."

"Do you want to try him now?" Johann checked the straps on the saddle and bent down to tighten the girth.

"No! I mean . . . I'm not dressed for riding." She wondered why Johann hadn't noticed she was wearing a delicate yellow morning dress with white roses appliquéd at the hem, hardly riding garb.

"Oh? Yes, I see." He gave her pretty frock an appreciative look. "Well, it can wait. Now that you've seen him, decide on a name and tell Otto so he can make a sign for his stall." Johann turned and led the animal down toward the stables, leaving Dorrit to ponder how terrific her husband looked in jodhpurs and long, sleek boots. She also realized that she would have to visit the stables and at least pretend an interest in the gelding. She watched as he crossed the graveled courtyard, swishing his tail with self-important affectation. His coat was a mottled gray like the sky in advance of a terrible cloudburst. She could think of a number of fitting names for him. Foul Weather being the most benign.

Once Johann and the gelding were out of sight, Dorrit went back inside to change into a sensible cotton dress, but not so sensible it could be construed as riding attire. Minutes later on her way out the door she grabbed a straw hat for protection against the sun and a handful of sugar cubes from the bowl on the sideboard in the dining room. The sugar was a bribe for Foul Weather.

As she rounded the corner of the corrals, she spotted Johann at the timing track, sitting astride the fence, stopwatch in hand. He and the trainer were cheering a horse running the oval, apparently to their satisfaction, including Dorrit's, because she could pass unseen and avoid riding lessons. She had no plans to get close to any of the animals. If the new gelding was securely restrained, she'd offer him the sugar. Ride him? Never! That would scare her unconscious.

"Good morning!" Otto smiled and removed his cap, sizing up the young baroness as she stepped gingerly through the stable doors. "Did you come to see your new gelding?" He pursed his lips knowingly. He'd been a groom for over thirty years and could smell fear from any distance.

"Good morning. Yes, I brought some sugar." Dorrit was careful not to speak too loudly or make any sudden movements that might incite the horses. "Would it be all right to give him some?"

"Of course. Come on in. He's a mighty fine horse. You'll have to give him a special name."

"Winter's Sky," she suddenly said, inspired. Besides, she didn't think the groom would approve of Foul Weather.

"Well, now that's a right and proper name." A smile spread on Otto's leathery face; he was pleased that the name had a vigorous quality, not effeminate like Velvet or Pearl. "Come, I'll show you the way."

Dorrit was glad of Otto's company because if any of the animals became riotous, he would know how to handle it. Furthermore, he walked next to the stalls, shielding her from several beasts poking their heads over the portals. And when they came to the new gelding, he stepped inside the stall and held the halter as she put her hand out and offered the sugar cubes.

When Dorrit left the stables, it was with the sensation that Otto was watching her departure with an odd expression. Once clear of the compound, a quick glance over her shoulder confirmed that Johann was still at the timing track. She hurried up the path toward the house before he could spot her. The midmorning sun was warm, another scorcher was on tap, Berlin would be particularly stifling on a day like this, and she again became determined to pressure her father to come out for a visit. He was obstinate about leaving his apartment for any overnight excursion.

Chapter 54

Halfway up the hill, she decided to go cut some flowers and left the graveled path, taking a shortcut toward the greenhouse near the kitchen where gloves, sheers, and baskets were kept. Jens, the gardener, would probably spot her and follow on her heels like an alert watchdog. Yesterday, he'd all but gnashed his teeth while she pruned some hollyhocks. He clearly did not want any meddling in his domain, but she had little with which to occupy her time and enjoyed arranging flowers in the vases throughout the house. As she picked up her steps, she decided on pink roses for the mantle in the library, while a mixture of white and red peonies would look spectacular in the vase under the mirror in the hall.

The ground behind her suddenly shook. Without turning, Dorrit knew that Johann was approaching; no one else dared ride so recklessly on this narrow strip. She experienced an overpowering impulse to run, but only managed to coax her legs off the path and into the tall grasses. Discreetly wiping her moist palms in the folds of her plaid cotton dress, she had no choice but to face the huge black beast Johann brought to stop only inches away. The horse turned his head toward her, laid his ears back, and snorted.

Dorrit jumped.

"Don't be afraid." Johann laughed and then lowered his voice as if he were concerned about insulting the animal. "Asmodeus is the gentlest of creatures. He's practically a house cat. A de-clawed house cat."

"Well, he could have fooled me," Dorrit said with a short nervous laugh. In Jewish demonology, Asmodeus meant evil spirit. She decided the name fit perfectly.

"He's particularly fond of sugar cubes."

"Oh!" Dorrit realized Otto must have told Johann about her visit, and as her hand now dove into her pocket she was glad to discover there were a few pieces left. She dropped them on the path in front of Asmodeus. She was not about to tempt fate by letting this horse near her hand. While she was momentarily preoccupied watching him nuzzle the dirt, Johann leaned down and—quick as a wink—grabbed her around the waist, depositing her into the saddle in front of him.

"Let's go beg some lunch from Gerlinde," he said, and turned the stallion—which didn't balk at the additional weight—toward the village road.

Lightheaded with terror, convinced the horse would toss her off, Dorrit wished she'd had more sugar; those measly few clumps couldn't have bought much consideration from this brute. Clenching her teeth, and gulping down her fear, she kept her head pointed forward, glad Johann couldn't see her face; it had drained of all color and would give her away. Ironically, she had wanted to spend more time with him, but this was not what she'd had in mind.

"You'll be riding the gray gelding within a week," Johann declared once they reached the road. He kissed the back of her neck, brushing her hair aside to do so. "I like the name you gave him."

"Thank you." As pleasant as his kisses were, Dorrit wished he'd stop and instead concentrate on Asmodeus, who might be waiting for precisely this kind of inattentiveness to bolt.

"You will make a fine equestrienne," Johann said after a while when Dorrit remained silent. "You show tremendous endurance."

"Endurance?"

He chuckled. "Yes. For holding your breath."

"Your arm's so tight it makes breathing impossible." Considering the state of her nerves, her repartee came quickly, but her voice shook, something she hoped Johann would assume was due to the movement of the horse.

"What's this?" Karl-Heinz cried in sham outrage when he saw Asmodeus approach with two riders. He was in the courtyard, coaxing a stud stallion into a horse cart for the trip to a neighboring farm. However, the minute he spotted visitors he threw the reins to a groom, letting him deal with the skittish animal. Hands on hips, Karl-Heinz cocked his head. "Don't tell me your overrated stables succumbed to neglect and disease while you were away, stranding you with a lone survivor."

"Can't say I'd ride all the way over here to give you the satisfaction of that kind of news," Johann said. "We came to have lunch."

"Lunch?" Karl-Heinz caught Dorrit around the waist as Johann swung her down. "Frau Erdmann finally quit?"

From inside the house Gerlinde heard the familiar banter. She tucked her hair into a coiffure net and, glad she happened to be wearing a pretty blue linen dress, rushed out the door and down the steps.

"Of course you're having lunch," she said, hugging Dorrit, noting the poor thing was pale as a ghost, which was why when she turned to Johann, her kiss was accompanied by a stern look blaming him for Dorrit's pallor. "But before we eat and get lazy I want to give Dorrit the grand tour. I've been dying to show off my new house. And of course we want to hear all about Paris and San Sebastian." She linked arms with Dorrit. "When did you get back? I've been so eager to see you and would have come over, except Karl-Heinz insisted we give you time to settle in." The two women went inside, leaving the men with the obstinate stallion.

Karl-Heinz reclaimed the reins from the groom and tried to sweet-talk the horse up the ramp. When that didn't work, he tugged on the bit. The animal reared up and nickered.

"Whoa!" Johann slapped its flanks and, pushing at its hindquarters, while Karl-Heinz and the groom pulled, the men finally got the stallion into the cart. Once the groom drove off, the two friends went across the courtyard to a water pump to wash the smell of horse sweat from their hands.

Chapter 55

After a full year of construction, Gerlinde's house was nearly completed. Built of yellow masonry with over-sized windows and ornamental wooden slats decorating the upper story, the roof was laid with red tiles. Only a few inside touches, such as ceiling moldings being carved in Italy still needed to be installed. But the family had taken occupancy, furnishing the rooms in light Biedermeier, except for the library, which had traditional wood paneling, hunter-green leather sofas, and antique side tables.

Lunch at the Konauers' was a relaxed affair served on the unfinished terrace. As the four friends sat down around the wrought iron table, Gerlinde apologized for the building materials strewn around, explaining that since the weather was so beautiful today it'd be a shame to eat indoors.

Dorrit commented on the treillage against the back wall of the house, saying she could visualize magenta bougainvillea climbing onto the roof such as she'd seen in San Sebastian. "But I doubt it'd survive our winters."

"Bougainvillea might be a bit optimistic," Gerlinde agreed. "I'm thinking about planting some hardy climbing roses. By next summer in time for a garden party I'm already organizing, I see this entire wall covered from end to end in pink blooms."

"That'll require a miracle," Karl-Heinz sniped under his breath, thinking that women were often unrealistic.

The four friends put away a meal of weisswurst steamed in home-brewed beer, with side dishes of apple fritters and cucumber salad and baskets of crusty Bavarian bread. Plates were being pushed aside just as Ursula and Karl Konauer were spotted, trudging arm-in-arm down the hill from the old mansion, Karl's predictable cigar smoke signaling their arrival.

"You missed lunch!" Gerlinde called out as her in-laws rounded the corner, stepping cautiously across boards of lumber serving as makeshift walkways over dirt and patches of old grass. "How about some dessert?" Without waiting for an answer, she told the maid clearing dishes to set two more places.

"We didn't come to eat, my dear," Karl Konauer declared, winded from the hike. "We came to see you and the grandchildren. And your company."

"Yes, what a pleasant surprise!" Ursula cried as she greeted the honeymooners warmly.

"Finally home from your trip, eh?" Karl embraced Dorrit before pumping Johann's hand.

Hans, who was eating lunch in the kitchen with Fraulein Kruse and his twin sisters, heard his grandfather's booming voice through the open windows and immediately came running, for although he knew that he was not allowed to intrude on the adults' meal, his grandparents' arrival changed all the rules.

"*Opa! Oma!* You wanna watch me ride?" he yelled and in his rush across the terrace tripped over a box of tools. Picking himself up without a whimper, he looked around, grinning at Uncle Johann and *Tante* Dorrit. "Hi!" he said, remembering his manners before getting back to business. "Who wants to come see me ride?"

Karl Konauer dropped down into a chair. "We were about to have some coffee, Hans. How about if you run down to the stables and bring your pony here? Then we can all watch you."

Hans liked that idea, looked toward his father for permission, and getting it, ran off like a bullet toward the stables.

"At least we don't have a lawn yet that the pony can ruin," Gerlinde smiled as she watched her son disappear around the side of the house.

Accompanied by a stable hand, Hans returned shortly, riding a show-quality miniature Russian pony, a gift from his grandparents.

"Watch me! Watch me!" he hollered as he now rode in proud circles around the large open field next to the terrace. He didn't try to race the animal, Johann noticed. Apparently, his concern for birds in winter extended to horses laboring under a hot summer sun.

Chapter 56

During the latter part of August, with Dorrit's constant urging, Herman Zache finally agreed that a short trip to Bernau would not set him back immeasurably if he took some work along.

Dorrit was gripped by anxiety the day he arrived. He looked awful, much thinner and more stooped than she remembered. A pang of guilt for her neglect put a damper on her initial elation with his visit, and as she helped him settle into the loveliest guest room on the second floor – a room she'd filled with fresh dahlias this morning—she decided to speak to Hannah the minute she returned to Berlin. Herman Zache was a man who never complained and she suspected it was easy for Hannah to become careless if no demands were made of her. But for now, Dorrit would indulge him iniquitously and instruct Frau Erdmann to keep a pot of fresh fruit soup on the stove at all times. Elderberry soup with a dab of sour cream was her father's favorite summer meal, something Hannah had probably forgotten.

Indeed, Dr. Zache's appearance improved with Dorrit's pampering, the languid country life, and the stimulating nights when assorted neighbors came for dinner. He strutted around proud as a peacock the day following a dinner party where he'd been seated next to a dowager duchess.

However, far better than anything else were the quiet evenings spent in the library with his son-in-law, tackling contemplative medical topics and watching Dorrit—content in her reading—curled up on the sofa. Herman Zache noticed that Johann couldn't keep his eyes off her, which was far more beneficial for a father's wellbeing than any amount of fruit soup.

Chapter 57

In *September, once* back in Berlin, Johann resumed his work at Wirchow where, except for an occasional emergency, he now kept daytime hours. Dorrit entertained callers at home, met Lillian in town, and visited with her father. Of course she was always back by five o'clock in the afternoon and before the front door groaned on its heavy brass hinges, signaling that Johann was home.

"Missed me, *Liebchen*?" he invariably asked, catching her in a tight embrace as she ran into the hall to greet him. Wrinkling her nose at the strong smell of hospital antiseptics that clung to his clothes, she nonetheless tipped her face up for a kiss and without caring if the servants were watching.

On a day in October Johann came home, carrying a box under his arm, which he proceeded to bring upstairs, motioning for Dorrit to follow him.

"This," he said, strolling into her dressing room and putting the tortoise and ebony-inlaid chest down on a table, "has been in the bank vault since my mother died. There's an awful lot to sort through. Some of it may not suit you. But if you like the stones, Friedlander's can reset them in new styles that appeal to you."

Like the stones? Dorrit could scarcely contain her curiosity as she eyed the miniature chiffonier, a work of beauty in itself. She opened the first drawer and, lifting layers of protective velvet, drew back in surprise, her eyes fairly bulging at the sight of several exquisite diamond necklaces paired with bracelets and earrings. Other drawers held matching emerald sets, rubies and sapphires in all sizes and shapes. There were amethyst and topaz chokers, lavalieres, elaborate glittering pins, an enormous brooch with a piece of carved jade the size of a door knocker; one entire drawer held strings of pearls. On the periphery of this Arabian Nights' fantasy, she heard Johann explain that his ancestry had not been a prolific one.

"Generally, no more than one offspring survived to a marriageable age," he was saying. "My father had two brothers who died in infancy and my mother was an only child. So these trinkets have accumulated instead of being divided among female heirs. Of course if you and I have better luck . . ." he grabbed her around the waist and kissed her neck, scraping his teeth on a row of diamonds she had playfully draped around her throat, "then maybe all this stuff will finally be distributed democratically among daughters and daughters-in-law and not be a burden for any one woman."

"Burden?" Dorrit giggled and, pushing him away, tried on another piece of jewelry. She bent toward the mirror and was almost blinded by her own reflection. Unfastening the necklace and letting it slip through her fingers, she reached into a drawer of rubies, marveling at the sparkling red stones. "These will do wonders for my white velvet gown," she said dreamily before picking up a collar of opals. "And this," she looked at the fabulous choker in her hand, "will enhance my strapless blue satin. Oh, and just look at these emeralds!" She rummaged through a velvet pouch. "They will go well with . . ."

"Your greedy green eyes!" Johann laughed. "My sweet and unassuming wife is turning gluttonous. But let's make one thing clear. With or without the opals, you're not to wear the blue strapless gown in public. It's . . . it's indecent to say the least."

"Madame Mimieux called it *zee rage*."

"Outrage is more like it," Johann corrected, cupping Dorrit's chin in his hand. "You can wear it when we're alone at home. In fact, it might behoove us to spend some evenings at home this season in the pleasant pursuit of enriching the family tree."

Dorrit looked up into her husband's jaunty gray eyes, dropped a strand of olive-sized pearls into the chest, and threw her arms around his neck, all the while wondering why after six months of marriage she was not expecting a child. Last week at a dinner party, the Count and Countess von Beckstein had proudly announced that they were going to be grandparents, news that had stung Dorrit because Monika Marie's wedding had taken place two months after hers. In the days following the Beckstein's announcement, she had seriously begun to worry that there was something wrong with her, but couldn't bring herself to consult her father. They had never discussed subjects pertaining to female anatomy and if she were to suddenly start now, he'd wonder why she didn't just ask Johann—her husband—a practicing physician. However, to bring her fears to Johann was even more unthinkable because she couldn't bear his disappointment if it was discovered that she was barren.

Chapter 58

Along with ringing in the New Year, Berliners would have welcomed a blinding blizzard; anything was preferable to the cold and steady rain that sent shooting pains through their bones and put many a fine wine cellar under water.

Increasingly bothered by shortness of breath, Professor Zache found little stamina for even simple tasks, and the three flights of stairs to his apartment might as well have been the sheer face of the Zugspitze. He cut back on his teaching schedule, soon stopping altogether.

The weather dried out in February but Herman Zache's lungs did not, and Dorrit was immensely relieved when Johann threatened him with a hospital stay unless he agreed to move in with them and submit to their care.

Herman Zache swallowed his stubborn pride and moved into the guest suite on the ground floor on Lindenstrasse, where no stairs taxed his strength and where the fireplace would be stoked around the clock. Frau Schmidt made gallons of hot soup, Johann attended to his medication, and Dorrit provided him with the cheer of her company. All assumed their duties with faithfulness and prayed for his convalescence. However, by the middle of March, Johann knew the end was near. Nurses were hired in eight-hour shifts while everyone waited for a miracle.

The miracle never came. In April Herman Zache died after days of convulsive coughing.

Dorrit was slow to recover from his death. In June, just when she was beginning to again take an interest in her surroundings and was looking forward to spending the summer in the country, she suffered a terrible setback. Arriving in Bernau, her mood plummeted to new depths. Everything reminded her of her father's visit last year. He had loved being here and realizing that he would never again enjoy this beautiful countryside, it lost its allure. Dorrit felt ill and dispirited, and Johann's attempts to restore her humor only irritated her. She found herself snapping at him. Although she was immediately remorseful, she was unable to control herself. Prudently, she began to stay out of his way. Unlike last summer, she was now glad that he was busy with the horses; so busy, in fact, that he forgot to mention riding lessons. She cloistered herself in her rooms, reading and sleeping; mostly sleeping because it was an escape from her sorrow.

Occasionally she sought refuge in the rose gardens where she puttered around, fully determined to vent her black mood if Jens appeared with a scowl on his face. She had enjoyed working in the flowerbeds last year; this summer, however, the perfume of the exquisite blooms made her feel wretched. After a few minutes of pruning, she felt faint and was forced to retreat to a shady bench; a retreat she suspected pleased the groundskeeper no end, but depressed her to such a point that she often started to cry. She'd sit on the bench and sob without caring a speck if anyone saw her, as long as it wasn't Johann.

Dorrit blamed herself for her father's death. She had not been diligent in attending to his welfare. She should have known better than to marry and leave him. It had killed him, same as if she'd put a knife in his heart. And although Johann had carefully explained the ravages of pulmonary consumption, which led to Herman Zache's death, she allowed a terrible guilt to gnaw at her innards, dulling her. Listless and despondent, she stayed in bed till noon without reaping any benefit, because by supper and no matter who graced their dinner table she had to fight a constant need to yawn.

Friends sent her pitying glances. The glances hurt, but not nearly as much as Johann's grim looks from the far end of the vast table. There were evenings when she was grateful for the distance because she feared he'd like to kick her. It was all he could do to look civil in the face of her colorless conversation, which did nothing to help him entertain their dinner guests.

To make matters worse, Dorrit suspected that she looked awful. For weeks after her father's funeral, she had been too distraught to take an interest in her appearance and now she was too tired to bother. Tonight she made the mistake of wearing a mauve gown, which didn't suit her at all, something she'd discovered at a reception in Berlin during the spring when Louisa von Tirpitz had gone to great lengths to gush about its color. Like so much about Louisa, her flattery was not genuine. Still, Dorrit had worn the gown tonight because it was the first thing to fall from her closets when she was dressing for dinner. It was a wonder Johann didn't said anything; he was usually very opinionated. Didn't he care? Was his marriage not wearing well? Now that she exhibited such lackluster qualities was he tolerating her because he was stuck with her, and was he looking for pleasant diversion elsewhere? Johann was the kind of man women couldn't keep their eyes or hands off. She'd seen that often enough. Tonight, no less than three ladies at the table were squirming for his attention. He seemed particularly charmed by Countess von Richthofen, whose husband was drinking a great deal and didn't seem to notice what was going on between his wife and Johann. But Dorrit noticed. She saw Johann laugh at every snippet of conversation that fell from the countess's pretty lips. Perhaps the two of them were already making plans for a tryst, which—rumors suggested—was accepted among the *haute monde*. Johann had once told her that Karl-Heinz was occasionally unfaithful because another pregnancy would put Gerlinde in the grave. But Johann didn't need to take such precautions. Dorrit would welcome a baby . . . if it killed her. Dear God! Johann? Unfaithful? She could stand a lot of things but not that. She'd rather he beat her than ignore her. When had he stopped loving her? And why? Actually she knew why. Her hair was limp, her complexion sallow, and tonight her personality was so flat it earned weird looks from everyone at the table; even Gerlinde eyed her with a strange expression. In fact, Dorrit felt as though everyone was humoring her like a senile aunt, appeasing her with a bland comment now and again until even those tapered off. It didn't take long for a pall to settle over her end of the table, a pall that didn't involve the effervescent Countess von Richthofen, who remained in a festive mood in her bid to engage Johann's attention.

Dorrit grew increasingly miserable. Things came to a head when during dessert she saw the gorgeous countess reach over and put her hand across Johann's in a lover's caress. How dared that woman? Right here for all to see! Anger boiled over in Dorrit's chest, sending bile into her throat, strangling her. She couldn't breathe. The room swayed. Her stomach lurching, she rose in defiant desperation, committing a hostess' most unforgivable act when, without a word, she left the table.

Behind her, she heard a chair scrape violently against the floor. In the next instant, Johann was at her side; she braced herself for a public reprimand. But though his brows were snapped together he was displaying no visible spleen. Of course, he would never compound her rude behavior and give their guests further indigestion by parading his own ill temper. On the contrary, he clearly meant to mitigate everyone by playing the role of attentive husband, something he confirmed when he addressed those present.

"Dorrit appears to be ill," he said with his flair for correctness. "She needs to lie down. Carry on. I'll be right back."

Dorrit's knees buckled in shame.

Gerlinde rushed from her seat and came to hug her. The gesture brought tears to Dorrit's eyes, but thankfully no one saw because Johann was already marching her into the hall and up the stairs, summoning a maid as he went.

"Help my wife undress!" he ordered once they reached Dorrit's rooms. "And ring for some tea. Under no circumstance leave my wife alone until she's in bed. Is that clear?" His tone was so blunt he could have used Latin and the maid would have understood.

Dorrit wondered why he was taking out his anger on the poor girl who had done nothing wrong. Had she dared, she would have intervened. However, she was hardly in a position to question her husband's tone when it was her own conduct that had pushed him to be short-tempered.

Satisfied that his orders would be carried out, Johann returned to the guests.

Dorrit had barely undressed, finished a cup of chamomile tea and sunk into her soft feather bed when he reappeared, claiming everyone had shown the good sense to leave early. Oddly, she discerned no irritation in his voice, although she knew perfectly well that he enjoyed high-staked card games in the library after dinner. Puzzled, she was too weary to figure it out. She could not keep her eyes open. Her head felt heavy as a boulder. She was asleep before Johann left her rooms, closing the connecting door to his bedchamber behind him.

In her semiconscious state, and before oblivion claimed her, Dorrit sensed he had stood by her bed for some long moments, brooding dangerously. Had he contemplated strangling her?

Chapter 59

Gerlinde walked cheerfully into Dorrit's bedroom the following morning, uninvited and unexpected. Dorrit felt horrible and wished to see no one, least of all a perky neighbor who might inform the entire county of her wretchedness and describe to the curious how her room smelled. She had vomited in a chamber pot that had not yet been removed because she was too feeble to tug at the bell pull. Her satin sheets were stained and the yards of Valenciennes draped from the canopy of her bed hung lopsided; she must have yanked on the lace in her sleep instead of the bell rope. Withal, she wished she were dead and hated Gerlinde for seeing her like this, hated her smug smile and cheerful greeting, which she returned with a glare as harsh as she could manage, given her illness.

But the cold reception did not deter Gerlinde. "Your sickness is quite typical," she said, walking briskly across the soft carpet to draw back the pink striped curtains on the dormers, instantly spreading cheer in the room. Turning toward the bed, she asked, "Mind if I open a window?"

"Please do."

Throwing both dormers wide open, Gerlinde leaned out to fill her lungs with the fresh summer air, silencing the chirping birds flitting about in the ivy clinging to the brick walls. As the room aired out, she came back and sat down on the edge of Dorrit's bed.

"As I was saying," her small frame fairly bristled with self-importance at the wealth of information she carried in her sparse bosom, "your sickness . . . the reason you're queasy and only want to sleep . . ."

"Oh, I know!" Dorrit interrupted.

"You do?"

"Of course. I have a stomach ailment. A nasty strain that won't go away. Please," Dorrit pointed to the bell rope, "I need to get rid of the chamber pot. The . . . the smell is nauseating." Having to admit to the mess under the bed was mortifying. She turned into the pillow so she wouldn't have to meet Gerlinde's eyes.

Forgoing the bell, Gerlinde walked over to the door, stuck her head out into the hall and called for a maid; at her own house that usually got quicker results. Once the offending chamber pot was removed and replaced with a clean one, she sat back down and looked as if she'd burst if she didn't speak soon.

"Dorrit," she said, "Turn around and look at me." Reluctantly, Dorrit obeyed. "I know you're nauseous but you don't have a stomach ailment."

"I don't?" Dorrit wondered how Gerlinde could so cavalierly dismiss the foul chamber pot.

"That's right. Certain foods turn your stomach. Particularly that custard cobbler Frau Erdmann served last night. But for the most part, you're only ill in the mornings, right?" Dorrit nodded. "And lately you've had none of that monthly stuff. Am I right?"

A spot of scarlet crept into Dorrit's cheeks with acute embarrassment at such frank talk. She averted her eyes, realizing she had completely forgotten about that.

"I thought so." Gerlinde folded her arms across her chest like a teacher about to give a lecture. Admittedly, a few years ago she'd been just as uninformed as Dorrit and a hundred times more shy, but at the age of twenty-three with three children to her credit she now owned a world of knowledge that she was happy to share.

Remaining mute as a stone, Dorrit sank into the bedding, drawing the sheets clear up to her neck while Gerlinde spoke, ending her lecture with a dramatic statement. "All your symptoms point to the fact that you are pregnant!"

"What?"

"You heard me. You are going to have a baby!"

The corner of the sheet was in Dorrit's mouth; she didn't know how it had gotten there, but all at once she was chewing on it while her heart made squishy sounds in her chest. She was suddenly overwhelmed by a great need to laugh—or cry—she didn't know which, except she was so happy that laughter seemed the more appropriate of the two. "Are you sure?" she said, her voice bubbling with giggles. "Are you sure that's all that's wrong with me?"

"Positive. But if you want a second opinion," Gerlinde managed a sly look, "Johann can examine you."

"No!" Dorrit said, horrified. "I mean . . . uh, I don't think he wants to come near me unless it's to wring my neck." She didn't go so far as to elaborate on his absence in her bed during the past weeks.

"Wring your neck? Why on earth would he want to do that?"

"Because I . . . I deserve it." Dorrit had grown up without any friends and it suddenly felt so good to confide in someone.

"You what?"

"I deserve it. I've been a monster lately. I haven't been myself since my father died. And since arriving in Bernau I've gone from bad to worse. Yesterday, as you saw, I hit rock bottom. Johann was angry. I can't say that I blame him. I behaved miserably in front of his friends. On God, I actually walked out on them."

"Wait a minute! What do you mean *his* friends? We're just as much your friends. Most of us anyway." Gerlinde's small heart-shaped face was an open book; it was obvious that she had seen the Countess von Richthofen trifle with Johann at the dinner table. "Now listen! Let me tell you something. Johann is not angry with you. Far from it. He is worried. Worried to death about you. Particularly about your condition."

"My condition? You think he has guessed?" Dorrit's spine tingled with the idea that Johann might know.

"Guessed?" Gerlinde snorted as if his intelligence had come into question. "Of course, he has guessed. He's a doctor. The best! My daughters and I are living testimony to that. He is only dumbfounded that you haven't wanted to share your good news with him. Being an impatient man, he has shown remarkable patience waiting for you to mention the fact that he's going to be a father. Men get quite excited about that sort of thing."

"But how could I tell him? I didn't know."

"That's precisely what he began to suspect and why he felt obliged to enlist my services. He looked pretty sheepish last night after you went to bed and he threw the rest of us out. But before Karl-Heinz and I got the boot, Johann ordered me to come back here this morning. He figured a heart-to-heart talk with a woman might do you a world of good. Exasperated, he was stammering about the fact that you had grown up without a mother and therefore might not know certain things."

Dorrit grinned. Johann never looked sheepish, nor did he stammer.

"Besides, haven't you wondered why he hasn't pestered you to ride? For years he's been ribbing Karl-Heinz for failing to get me up on a horse. Karl-Heinz was getting ready to dish out some crow. You're saving Johann the trouble of eating it."

"Please don't mention eating," Dorrit moaned.

"Sorry." Gerlinde laughed and got off the bed. "Anyway, I'll be going now. Johann is waiting downstairs. He hasn't gone out to the stables yet, which proves how anxious he is about our little chat. So do get dressed. Go down and put him out of his misery." She went the door, waved, and was gone.

Dorrit had barely put her feet on the floor before Johann burst into her room. For a moment, he just stood there, grinning broadly, looking at his disheveled wife as if she were the eighth wonder of the world. Then he crossed the floor, ignored the traces of vomit on her nightgown, and gathered her into his arms.

Chapter 60

In *August Lillian Schindel* and Kurt Eckart came to Bernau for a week's visit. Inasmuch as they were not married propriety required that they maintain separate roofs, so Lillian stayed with the Konauers—relatives were the most exemplary chaperones—while Kurt stayed at the barony, where Dorrit and Johann hosted a party on the first night of the visit.

Desperately wanting to look her best, Dorrit perused her closets carefully before settling on a green organdy, although she would have to wear it minus its pretty sash or risk fainting from being cinched too tightly. Her figure was thickening and she would soon have to let out the seams in her dresses to accommodate her expanding midriff. However, she had never been particularly vain, losing her waistline was of no account and, admiring her swelling figure in the full length mirror, she smiled, went over to her dressing table and gave her hair a few good strokes with a brush before twisting it into a chic knot at the nape, the latest in Berlin fashion. To soften the severity of the style, she pulled a few springy curls loose around her forehead, chose dainty clusters of seed pearls for her ears and fastened the emerald heart around her neck. It went well with the dress and Johann was always pleased when she wore it.

Satisfied with her appearance, she took a deep breath and realized she was feeling rather well tonight and was actually looking forward to the evening ahead. At least she was sure her stomach wouldn't riot at the mere sight of spinach soufflé or cream cakes. Twenty people were expected for dinner, but as Johann had commented earlier when he walked through her rooms, buttoning his white evening jacket before going downstairs, they could never be quite sure about Philip von Brandt. It was common knowledge that the fair-haired Philip might stop at a tavern along the way to indulge in various sins, in which case he would arrive in Bernau the following day. Summer parties in the country easily lasted a week, so it was generally no disaster to miss the first night.

Making her way downstairs, crossing the enormous hall, Dorrit blew a whimsical kiss to the George Seurat seascape from San Sebastian, hanging in a prominent spot. The double doors to the terrace at the far end of the hallway were open and gales of merriment wafted in from the group gathered outside. Dorrit realized she was late, but Johann had promised to make her excuses. She quickened her steps, ready to carry out her role as hostess.

Johann extricated himself from a conversation cluster and came to her side the minute she stepped out on the terrace. Taking her arm, he led her across the flagstones. "Twenty minutes on your feet, and I'll scowl like a black devil if I don't see you sitting in a chair," he whispered as they went.

"But I feel terrific tonight, Johann."

"That's wonderful. Still, I expect you to be obedient. If not, I'll put a bug in Anna's ear about how you are dying to hear about her and Enno's Mediterranean cruise. That ought to keep you nicely pinned in a seat till dinner."

"You are assuming I won't be delighted to hear about their trip."

"That's right. They encountered rough seas and her details are quite graphic."

Dorrit laughed and was about to explain that her stomach had called a truce, when Enno's new wife rushed over.

Enno von Steigert had been Johann's friend in Grunewald since the time when the two small boys had first studied each other through a hole in the hedge separating their families' properties on Lindenstrasse. The opening was eventually expanded to allow easy access, and the boys became inseparable whenever Johann and his parents were in residence. Many years later, when Enno's parents left the villa to his older sister and left him the money to build a home of similar grandeur, he did so in neighboring Wannsee. However, he used the house infrequently because his diplomatic work necessitated living abroad. There had been only one exception, a tragic one, when his first wife suffered a snakebite and died during their honeymoon in Kenya. Nearly losing his mind over the incident, Enno was sedated and housebound in Wannsee for many months.

Once he emerged from his depression and returned to work, and while on a visit to Hamburg, he met the blond and vivacious Anna Schellenberg, who convinced him in a remarkably short period of time that her dearest wish was to move in diplomatic circles. Not one to let a lady's wish go begging, Enno married her and Anna immediately proved her veracity as well as her ability to live abroad. She packed and unpacked her suitcases with scientific precision and no matter the foreign language made life-long friends on the spot.

As the party on this balmy evening in August drew to a close and the wise went home or retired to the guest rooms, stalwarts like Kurt and Johann were left alone to polish off a bottle of 1880 English bourbon along with a highly wagered card game.

It was long past midnight when Johann staggered upstairs, noticed Dorrit's lights were still on and, figuring she had fallen asleep, walked in to turn them off. He was surprised to find her awake, reading. Realizing he looked like hell's picnic, he raked a hand self-consciously through his hair. His collar was open, a crumpled tie was slung negligently over his shoulder, and the red fissures in his eyes could only be repaired with a good night's sleep.

"I wore Kurt down and sent him to bed broke," he grinned, bending down to kiss Dorrit goodnight.

"In that case you had better lay low tomorrow or prepare yourself for Lillian's wrath. She has finally convinced him that he's financially solvent and able to set a wedding date."

"I'll forgive his debt first thing in the morning," Johann laughed and Dorrit reached for his hand. It only required a slight tug to make him sit down on her bed. She put her book away, pushed an extra pillow behind her back and played with the lapels of his evening jacket, all the while thinking how extraordinarily handsome he was despite his rumpled appearance.

Johann took her hands, kissed the inside of her wrists, silently reminding himself of her *enceinte* condition. However, the lateness of the hour was impinging upon his good judgment and it was proving a struggle to get off her bed, especially in the wake of her next words.

"Aren't you going to keep me company?" She slipped her hands inside his open jacket.

"No, darling." He soothed the piqued frown off her forehead with his lips. "We have to be careful a little while longer. Until you feel better. The first few months are the most critical."

"I do feel better," she whispered against his face. "Only the mornings are dreadful. But that's a long way off."

"It's later than you think. You need sleep and definitely no exertion. Doctor's orders!"

"Perhaps we ought to get a second opinion." Dorrit managed a look as sly as Gerlinde's the morning she'd suggested the same thing. "Not that I question your professional competence, of course, but since Kurt . . ."

"Kurt?"

"He's conveniently on the premises."

"Why, you little . . ." Johann's words died away as her arms locked around his neck and he felt her breasts; enlarged by pregnancy, press against his silk shirt. His starved body could stand only so much stimulation and every fiber of his being went AWOL with her pleasant invitation. A heartbeat later, his good intentions disintegrated altogether as she moved over to make room for him, displaying her shapely legs in the process.

Chapter 61

In *February—a day* when Berlin was buffeted by an ice storm that snapped trees and brought down power lines—Johann finished his shift at Wirchow and arrived home to find Dorrit in labor. He immediately put her into the coach and returned to the hospital, along the way cursing Schmidt for attacking the icy roads with sound caution.

Nature was rarely kind to first-time mothers. Dorrit's labor was long, and after midnight when Johann's own exhaustion made him ineffectual, he turned to a trusted colleague, Dr. Benjamin Tarnoff, who had just come on duty. Secure in the knowledge that Dorrit was in good hands, Johann dropped down on a cot in the physicians' lounge, intending to take a short nap. But, clamping his eyelids shut—numb to the hard mattress and deaf to the scraping noise of sleet blowing against the window—he was unable to sleep. His brain was racing with timeworn gossip concerning the birth of Kaiser Wilhelm in 1859; an event known in professional circles as the great insult to German medicine because Britain's Queen Victoria had sent her own physician to Berlin, telling him that if it came to a decision, he was to save the life of her daughter over that of the child. In his eagerness to obey the royal command, the English doctor pulled on the baby with such force that one arm became separated from its shoulder socket. Keeping his attention on the mother, the baby was tended by a tired nurse and the damage was ignored during the critical hours when it could have been corrected. This bungling condemned Wilhelm II to carry a lame arm. Until today, Johann had frequently wondered at the mindset of those involved. Today, however, when all his concern was for Dorrit, he understood Queen Victoria. Nothing on earth mattered to him except Dorrit.

And if it came to a decision . . . ?

He jumped off the cot, left the physicians' lounge and with his white surgeon's coat flying behind him, ran down the narrow corridor, sending hospital personnel diving into doorways.

He had neglected to instruct Dr. Tarnoff that if it came to a decision . . .

Johann barged into the delivery room just in time to have a nurse place his son, squealing lustily, into his arms.

They named him Maximilian Johannes, soon shortening it to Max.

Chapter 62

Kaiser Wilhelm's personal doctor, Theodor Renvers, had on numerous occasions been an observer in Wirchow's operating rooms, where the ability of a certain surgeon had come to his attention. Therefore, it was not surprising that this particular physician was on Dr. Renvers' mind one morning in early June of 1905 as he accompanied the Kaiser on his regular constitutional through the palace gardens on Unter den Linden. Wilhelm II was an early riser, fond of fresh air and exercise, which included beating his chest with his good arm while he inhaled and exhaled; a ritual Dr. Renvers had not prescribed and which invariably caused a smirk to form on his lips; something he was careful not to let the Kaiser see. Wilhelm took great pride in perfect health, ignored his deformity, and people who wished to serve him learned never to cast a glance toward his withered arm.

Lately, however, he'd been bothered by painful growths in his throat that could not be ignored. His father, Emperor Frederick III, had died shortly after being diagnosed with throat cancer, and the possibility of suffering the same fate disturbed the forty-five year old Kaiser. He and Dr. Renvers had discussed various medical options, all pointing to surgery, but Theodor Renvers, a physician entrusted with the health of the entire imperial household, was a man of some sixty-plus years and past his prime as a surgeon; especially for something as delicate as the sovereign trachea, which was why he today sang the praises of a much younger man.

"There's not a steadier pair of hands in all of Germany," he avowed once the Kaiser had finished his chest-pounding exercise. "The man has nerves of steel."

"I see." Wilhelm started to walk again, the gravel crunching beneath his mirror-polished boots as he strolled along a path through a sea of pink and white azaleas. He stopped to pull a dandelion out of the ground. How on earth had thirty gardeners missed such a large weed? Holding the offending plant pinched between two fingers, he resumed walking. "Nerves of steel and good hands, you say." He looked at Dr. Renvers. "But can he be trusted to be discreet?"

"Absolutely." Renvers was forced to pick up his steps to keep abreast of the monarch, exertion that left him short of breath. "He's a very private individual who shuns personal acclaim. A baron with a large estate in Bernau, he's not out to make a name for himself."

"A baron toils at Wirchow?"

"Not to make a living, I assure Your Majesty. Something else drives him. The challenge of the profession, I imagine. Some call him an eccentric. Others say he's a dreamer. He talks of spare parts for humans and the possibility of reattaching severed limbs." Renvers allowed himself a hearty chuckle. "His outlandish theories provide us with provocative entertainment now and again. As for his own amusement, I'm told he experiments on cadavers."

Pursing his lips, Wilhelm gazed skyward. Dr. Renvers waited for him to speak. If this surgeon was not acceptable, whom could he possibly recommend? There were so many butchers and gifted doctors were ambitious and might threaten his position with the royal family. He did not want to be sent out to pasture yet, which was why Dr. von Renz was so perfect. He was too talented to aspire to playing nursemaid to the Kaiser's household, retreated to his estate each summer, and would therefore not be at the beck and call whenever someone sneezed at the palace. But it was safe to assume that he'd consider it his patriotic duty to help out in a pinch, which this was, because a slight and hopefully a temporary trembling bedeviled Dr. Renvers' right hand, preventing him from attempting the precarious incisions of the Kaiser's throat.

"A baron who derives pleasure from evisceration of the dead." Wilhelm found an appropriate receptacle for the dandelion and wiped the sharp smell of the weed from his fingers with a handkerchief. "Sounds like an intriguing individual. What did you say his name was?"

"Forgive me. I don't believe I mentioned it. His name is Baron Johann Maximilian von Renz."

"Oh!" Wilhelm's eyes widened with surprise. "I know the man and his charming baroness. Send for him at once!"

Chapter 63

That very afternoon, summoned by a vague but urgent message, Johann was shown into a private chamber in the Imperial Palace on Unter den Linden. Clasping his hands behind his back, he wondered about the ambiguous summons as he strolled the floor and studied a number of royal portraits hanging in heavy gold frames along the walls. The entire room was gilded; walls, ceiling, every piece of furniture was clad in an aurous finish, including the upholstery on the chairs and settees, making the blue porcelain *Kamin* in the corner look completely out of place.

A door opened at the far end of the room, and Johann instantly recognized Dr. Renvers as he crossed the expanse of shiny parquet, his shoes clicking noisily as he approached.

"*Ach!* Herr Baron! I am delighted to see you!" Renvers pumped Johann's hand, then motioned for him to sit down on a gilded satin chair. After glancing around to assure himself that they were quite alone, he pulled up a similar national treasure and sat down opposite his colleague. Servants were known to have extraordinary hearing and, taking no chances, Dr. Renvers spoke in a whisper as he came right to the point, explaining how Johann could be of immeasurable service to the Crown.

"If you accept this assignment," he said after he finished detailing the Kaiser's complaint, "you must perform the surgery forthwith. Our Kaiser has suffered many sleepless nights and wishes to have it over with. I must stress that word of it cannot leave your lips. It's crucial the population at large not suspect any illness. We're living in a volatile time of soaring unemployment. Young people are leaving the land for the cities and I don't need to tell you that it's straining the job market. We increasingly have to put down street riots, each a crisis. I don't know where it'll end, but I do know that in times of turmoil, there must be no hint of vulnerability at the top." Renvers looked grim. "Not even our dear Kaiserin has been told of her husband's ailment. I've taken the liberty of assuring His Majesty that I can count on your complete discretion." Johann nodded and Dr. Renvers continued. "If, *Gott bewahre*, a malignancy is found, we shall of course be forced to make an official statement regardless of any civic unrest."

Nodding, Johann was aware of the tension among workers and the jobless alike; casualties from riots and street fights were regularly admitted to Wirchow. He rose, indicating the interview was over.

Ignoring the snub to his position, Dr. Renvers led the haughty aristocrat through the interior maze of the royal residence, arriving at his private office next to a state-of-the-art hospital facility.

Walking in, Johann looked around and took some mental notes. He had toyed with the idea of establishing a medical clinic of his own and this was precisely what he'd envisioned. A house on the corner of Lindenstrasse and the well-traveled Halensee had recently come on the market and here on the spot, he decided to buy it and put his architects to work designing its conversion, a project that was sure to please Dorrit. She was not always reconciled with his long hours at Wirchow, especially when an emergency caused him to arrive home too late to see Max before the boy's bedtime.

While both doctors scrubbed, Dr. Renvers elaborated on the Kaiser's health history, underscoring his tolerance for pain. "He's hard as nails," he said, smiling with apology at his choice of words and eying Johann's hands with envy, hands that would momentarily be entrusted with the life of the most powerful man in all of Europe. One slip of the scalpel and the Kaiser might drown in his own blood. Watching the younger surgeon scrub, Dr. Renvers began to worry that he was perhaps too calm in the face of his paramount assignment.

The patient, who had gone to great lengths to arrive without being spotted by family or servants who might wonder why he was heading for the infirmary, strolled in moments later, having taken pleasure in outwitting one and all. Giving no clue to his fear of cancer, he greeted Johann warmly and engaged him in small talk. However, when it seemed that the Kaiser might have forgotten the urgency that existed, Dr. Renvers put a stop to the tête-à-tête, cleared his throat and discreetly reminded both men about the consequential situation that had brought them together.

Kaiser Wilhelm proved to be an excellent patient, required a minimum amount of sedation, and Johann removed the growths and cauterized the incisions with routine perfection. While the patient remained recumbent, Dr. Renvers hovered at his side, checking the royal throat for any unusual bleeding and congratulating himself for choosing Dr. von Renz for this assignment. In all his years in the medical profession, he had never seen such quick and neat work. Wilhelm might well be on his feet in an hour. Tonight he could claim a touch of laryngitis, insist on broth for dinner and a liquid diet for the next few days.

After carefully examining the removed tissue under a microscope, Johann announced that although the specimens were large, they were harmless polyps. No cancer was found.

That verdict did much to revive the monarch. He clasped Johann's hand warmly. "I'm in your debt," he whispered in a raw postoperative voice.

"Not at all," Johann said.

The Kaiser wanted to say more, but both doctors cautioned him not to speak because there was still a danger of hemorrhaging. After assuring himself that the patient was resting comfortably, Johann left him in Dr. Renvers' care.

He was never to speak of this surgery and as he now made his way back to Wirchow, he had no way of knowing that this service to the Crown would someday impact a tragedy of such proportions he couldn't possibly imagine its scope on this benign June day.

Chapter 64

From the day it opened its door, Johann's clinic on Halensee Strasse met with tremendous success. Specializing in reconstructive surgery—a new field few physicians ventured into—the clinic attracted a discriminating clientele, those who wished for the privacy that large city hospitals couldn't offer. Patients were also occasionally transferred from Wirchow or from Charite when an industrial accident taxed their resources. Dr. von Renz never turned away a charity case. He had two full-time assistants but personally handled all trauma and burn victims which meant that, following a civic disaster, those who endured the additional ride in the ambulance to the Halensee Strasse Clinic were the lucky ones.

In the years following Max's birth, Dorrit suffered a miscarriage, but in 1908 she gave birth to another son. They named him Frederick Alexander and called him Fritz. With the arrival of a second child, Johann lessened his professional duties. Max had already turned four, and he didn't want to miss out on his sons' tender years altogether. He approached his colleague at Wirchow with an offer of partnership.

Dr. Benjamin Tarnoff accepted the position and with his wife, Gertrude, moved into the spacious quarters on the top floor of the Halensee Strasse Clinic. In addition to the convenience of residing on the premises, the move was a pleasant one. The apartment was larger than the flat they had occupied near Wirchow and came with a garden. Having reached middle age childless and resigned, Gertrude Tarnoff was soon directing all her untapped maternal instincts to the rebirth of this wonderful green spot behind the clinic where, in defiance of neglect, several apple trees thrived; a good pruning encouraged them further. She weeded and trimmed; indeed, the only greenery that didn't suffer her clippers was some gnarled grapevines clinging to an ancient trellis along the sunny side of the brick terrace. They were spared because after a thorough inspection Gertrude couldn't decide if the trellis was supporting the grapes or if it was the other way around. However, if left disturbed, she figured their collaboration might outlast her expectations.

Despite a twenty-year age difference, Dorrit and Gertrude became fast friends, their similar backgrounds forging a bond. Both Ben and Gertrude were Russian-Jewish expatriates. He a doctor, she a nurse, they had met and married in Moscow in 1887, months before a sudden roundup of Jews. Tipped off by a colleague only hours before the hospital was under siege by the czar's police, they managed to escape and from that day forward fled steadily west, eventually settling in Berlin.

"Germany has been good to us," Gertrude was telling Dorrit one afternoon while they were sitting on her terrace, enjoying a cup of tea. Her face permanently creased with sad memories, she wore her dark hair in a severe bun that along with a square build and slightly swollen ankles spoke to her years. Only her brown eyes remained bright and ageless. "Neither Ben nor I felt truly safe until we reached Berlin."

Dorrit nodded and told her why Herman Zache had felt precisely the same way.

Chapter 65

At the age of twenty-seven, Dorrit was without question one of the most glamorous of Berlin's elite, and on an evening in 1909, when she and Johann attended a palace ball in honor of Germany's new chancellor, Theobald von Bethmann-Hollweg, she turned the most jaded heads. A king's ransom in diamonds was draped around her throat, enhancing a low-cut shimmering chartreuse gown flaring with pearl-studded lace at the wrists and flounced hem.

The former chancellor, Furts von Bulow, had resigned earlier in the year when he lost the support of both the Reichstag and the Kaiser. But though his tenure had been difficult and his departure bitter, he and his wife, Princess Maria, showed no battle scars during the celebratory night for his successor.

"He has fallen from power but I've never seen him look more pleased," Dorrit whispered to Johann after passing through the receiving line and strolling into the salon.

"I suppose he's relieved not to be involved in the daily turmoil."

"Most of which he created. His foreign policy was a disaster."

"Yes, the French are still angry with our interference in Morocco and it doesn't look like the Russians are going to let the Bosnian crisis pass." Johann made a wry face. "Now the British are seething."

"Why?"

"They don't like rivalry. Our plan for a Baghdad railway irritates them."

"Well, let's see them build it." Dorrit was swift to come to Germany's defense. "They're free to compete."

"They'd rather stop us. And Wilhelm's talk of German superiority hardens their resolve."

"You sound like Count von Beckstein."

"He and I occasionally see eye to eye." Johann stopped at a champagne table and, handing Dorrit a glass before taking one for himself, they stayed long enough to exchange a few pleasantries with the group gathered there.

"At a tea last week, Countess von Beckstein told me her husband likes our new chancellor," Dorrit told Johann as they walked away.

"If he can soothe our troubles abroad, ease economic tension at home, and retain the Kaiser's support, I'll like him as a well."

"That's a tall order."

"I'm merely quoting his own campaign promises."

"What about his promise to expand the army? He claims to be a dove, yet he wants to build-up the military. I don't like that."

"He's hoping it'll ease unemployment. Joblessness has to be brought under control before escalating beyond the street riots we're familiar with."

"You mean revolution?"

"Worse."

"Now you're depressing me!"

"That's the last thing I want to do, darling." Johann deposited his empty glass on the tray of a passing waiter. He nodded toward her champagne. "Do you want to finish that?"

"Not really."

Johann placed it on a wide mezzanine ledge where it'd be safe until it could be collected. "Now, on a totally different subject," he said as they walked into the ballroom, "since leaving the house this evening, I've been wondering what possessed my virtuous wife to display herself so immodestly." He bent down and kissed her bare shoulders, attracting a number of disapproving looks from Berlin's *prominente* matrons. The Kaiserin sitting on a raised platform among her ladies-in-waiting also took note of it and pursed her lips with disapproval.

"What do you mean?"

"Don't play innocent with me. You know perfectly well that you're encouraging half the men here tonight to commit mental adultery."

"Only half?" Dorrit said, a sly lilt in her voice.

"The other half, *Liebchen,* are foreigners seething with envy because not only are our railroads superior, our women are as well."

Dorrit was still laughing when they joined others on the floor. However, it wasn't long before their dance was interrupted by a tap on Johann's shoulder, obliging him to relinquish her to none other than Germany's devil or savior, depending on how one perceived Chancellor Theobald von Bethmann-Hollweg this early in his administration.

When Dorrit's next partner turned out to be Kaiser Wilhelm, who astonished one and all by keeping the Baroness von Renz in his company for the length of two complete waltzes—generating a buzz of whispering—Johann danced with the Kaiserin, then with Louisa who had married Graf Zollern, given birth to twins and grown so plump that ball gowns were no longer flattering.

"So, did you enjoy the evening?" Johann asked on the way home, putting his arm around Dorrit, drawing her close in the back seat of the car.

"Yes, except for some remarks that came to my attention."

"Remarks? About what?"

"Not what. You! The gossipmongers said you must behave with more dignity. No public kissing. Apparently, the Kaiserin frowns on anything other than a chaste waltz."

"Good Lord!" Johann sputtered. "Her Majesty has had seven children with a one-armed husband. I suppose she'd like us to pretend we're in the presence of a blushing virgin. Under that haughty exterior, I bet she's as promiscuous as a courtesan."

"What a thing to say," Dorrit giggled. "Have you no respect?"

"None for hypocrisy. Also, I'm still trying to decide whether to blame you or Madame Mimieux for the gown you're wearing."

"Pardon?"

"You heard me. What compelled a matronly mother of two to display herself so immodestly?"

"Promiscuity." Dorrit gave him a slanted look.

Grinning, Johann bent down to kiss her but was rewarded with a painful bite for the ill-chosen word *matronly*.

Schmidt kept his eyes on the dark road ahead, concentrating on managing the motorcar. The horse-drawn carriages were retired several months ago when the baron purchased two Daimler-Benz automobiles, a seven-liter Mercedes touring car for summer driving and a heavier sedan for the winter months.

Chapter 66

Five years later . . .

After years of simmering trouble across Europe, spring of 1914 saw it reach the boiling point. Ignoring old friendships, crowned heads eyed each other with suspicion, increased their military strength, and rushed to line up with their allies.

Kaiser Wilhelm joined ranks with Austria-Hungary and Turkey and sent urgent messages to the Court of St. Petersburg, hoping for assurances of a friendly alliance with Russia. Generally speaking, he and his cousin, Czar Nicholas, enjoyed a pleasant relationship. Years ago when Nicholas had been too shy to ask for the hand of a mutual cousin, Princess Alix of Hesse, in marriage, Wilhelm came to his aid during a family holiday. Thrusting some roses into Nicholas' hand, he took him by the arm and marched him to her door. When Princess Alix became Empress Alexandra of Russia, Wilhelm took some credit for the happy union.

However, when his ambassador returned to Berlin in May of 1914 with stories of dangerous unrest inside Russia which slowly weakened Czar Nicholas, Wilhelm decided that the giant country to the east might not be trusted and would fare better under German rule. A turbulent Russia with a vulnerable ruler was bound to fall quickly. Wilhelm summoned his generals to discuss an invasion of Russia along with his planned assault on France, and would hear none of it when they warned him about fighting on two fronts.

While talk of war reached fever-pitch proportions, the fuse was lit when a Serbian nationalist hoping for Slavic freedom mixed with hatred for Austria-Hungary, assassinated Austria's Archduke Ferdinand at Sarajevo on June 28, 1914.

At the time of this shattering event, Dorrit and Johann were spending a pleasant summer in Bernau with their two sons. Max, at eleven years of age, was a handsome boy with the blond hair of his Romanov grandfather and eyes as startling green as Dorrit's. Long in the legs like his father, the boy sat well in the saddle and was this summer allowed to choose a full-sized thoroughbred for his own. Without hesitation, he picked the most spirited two-year-old in the stables and set about training the animal with a firm voice and grip, triumphing in record time, which came as no surprise to anyone. Once Max's mind was made up, he usually prevailed, no matter the obstacle.

His younger brother, Fritz, preferred to spend long hours in the quiet pursuit of some solitary activity. He would soon celebrate his sixth birthday and was perfectly content to ride his small Welsh pony around the confines of the paddocks, occasionally venturing up to the back of the house when his mother entertained her lady friends on the terrace. Trotting around on the lawns, he could show-off his riding skill and bask in the limelight because Max could be depended on to be nowhere in sight. Fritz bore a strong resemblance to his father. He had his gray eyes, the square jaw, and the dark brown hair. Although he was inclined to be reserved and quiet, his face shone with curiosity and, timid or not, Dorrit and Johann agreed the boy was intelligent beyond his years.

It was noon on a day in early July when Johann and Max returned from their regular morning ride. While Max remained in the stables to scrub down his horse, Johann left his to the grooms and walked up to the house, where he knew he would find Dorrit on the terrace. The minute she spotted him cutting across the lawns, she quickly put down the book she was reading and unfolded a parasol so he wouldn't scold her for sitting unprotected in the sun.

"Is that bumbershoot for my benefit or yours?" Johann hadn't missed the umbrella's sudden release and cocked a censorious eyebrow as he bent down to kiss her. Dorrit managed to look as though she didn't know what on earth he was talking about.

"Please!" she laughed, pushing him away. "You smell like a stable rat!" She wrinkled her nose and pretended to be offended when, in fact, she didn't mind the redolence of leather and horse sweat that clung to his clothes. "In a minute we'll be bothered by flies."

"Sorry." Johann grinned, raking a hand through his hair as he pulled out a chair and fell into it. He was forty-two but not a strand of gray was visible on his head. His damp shirt was partially unbuttoned, the sleeves negligently rolled up, and he hadn't shaved before setting out this morning. "Do you want me to clean up before lunch?" he asked in all seriousness, realizing his present condition might, indeed, offend.

"Not so long as we're eating outside and the wind doesn't shift," Dorrit teased.

"Where's Fritz?" Johann pointed to a pile of coloring books and pencils strewn on the flagstones.

"He went inside to have Frau Erdmann fix him something to eat. He couldn't wait till lunch."

"I've never known a boy to eat so much and remain so skinny." Johann smiled indulgently before being distracted by the revving of an engine in the courtyard; the familiar announcement that Hans Konauer had arrived in the Duesenberg. Johann squinted as he turned to watch the young man coming into view, strolling around the side of the house and jumping a boxwood hedge before cutting through the rose garden.

"Hi, there!" Hans swung his arm in a sweeping greeting. "Rolf told me I'd find you out here but he wouldn't let me take the shortcut through the house. I suppose he figured I'd drag engine oil across the floors. The old fellow must be a hundred. Isn't it time he retired?" Taking the steps up to the terrace in a single leap, Hans sauntered over to the glass-topped patio table and kissed Dorrit. "You look ravishing as always, *Tante* Dorrit. How are you?"

"Fine, Hans. And yourself?"

"Never felt better." He walked over and boxed Johann's shoulders before plunking down on a chair, propping a foot up on an empty one.

Although there'd be wheel ruts in the driveway to tend to after Hans' visit, Johann was enormously pleased to see him and signaled Rolf hovering behind the terrace doors. The butler disappeared, returning moments later, carrying tankards of beer.

"Thanks Rolf!" Without waiting for formalities, Hans blew at the foam, slouched back in his chair and took a thirst-quenching gulp. He was as comfortable here as at home on a kitchen stool and, ignoring the fine linen napkins Rolf placed on the table, wiped his mouth on the back of his hand.

Hans Konauer had grown into a good-looking eighteen-year-old. Of medium build, his hair was as pale as Gerlinde's, while his complexion was tan like his father's; he had his deep blue eyes as well. Johann didn't doubt that the local *Frauleins* were charmed when he came calling.

After an initial round of pleasantries about nothing more consequential than the perfect July weather, Hans put down his glass and sat up straight as if he were bursting with news that couldn't wait. He pushed the center bowl of dahlias aside, flicking at the small insects dropping from the showy blooms and, having now established a clear line of vision across the tabletop, came right to the point of his visit.

"If this nasty business," he began, "you know . . . last week's assassination of the archduke blows the lid off Europe, I have decided to enlist in the Kaiser's army."

Dorrit's mouth dropped open. She looked at Johann and saw his eyes narrow as he put the beer down. Leaning forward in his chair, he was paying rapt attention as Hans went on.

"I haven't told my parents yet. I expect they'll be dead set against it. But that's where you come in, Uncle Johann." Idly rotating the cold tankard between his palms, Hans failed to discern the terrible effect his words were having on the very person he was trying to impress. "The way I see it, if I sign up early I stand an excellent chance of getting a commission. I'd like to go to the front as an officer. If I wait to be inducted, I'll have to go as an infantryman. What do you think?"

A stony silence greeted his question; a pall had fallen over the table and as Hans glanced around, he finally noticed the distinct lack of enthusiasm on the part of his listeners. However, that didn't deter him.

"Grandfather agrees with me about being an officer," he quickly went on. "I've discussed it with him at length. As you know, he was in the Franco-Prussian War. Of course military tradition won't sway my parents. Nothing *Opa* says has any impact on them. Father simply humors him when he talks about his glory days as a colonel. And mother? Well, you know, she makes dour faces at the slightest mention of war." As Hans continued to press his point, he rested his elbows on the table and looked directly at Johann. "But I know they'll listen to you. Mother thinks the sun rises and sets on your shoulders. Sentiment I plan to take advantage of. That's why I'm here. I've come to ask you to speak to her. Perhaps tomorrow during her garden party? It's an all day affair so you'll have plenty of time to casually bring up the subject. You know, help prepare her to accept my decision. I'm of age. I don't need parental consent but I'd like to have it. And I want to get in on the action before it's over. The papers say that if war breaks out, it'll be a short one. A few months at the most."

"Yes, I've heard that." Johann sighed; he had read the reports. "But let's hope war can still be avoided." He looked long and hard at the young man, a boy he loved as his own, a sturdy lad with a soft heart; to this day Hans manned elaborate feeding stations for the birds that wintered in Bernau. Of course, at the moment, he was restless and like most young men harbored a romanticized view of war.

Having grown up in the quiet countryside, he craved adventure. Johann remembered all too well the boredom that had propelled him to move to Berlin years ago. "How about the university?" he now recommended as an alternative.

"I'll consider it," Hans nodded. "But after the war when we'll be in control of twice the geography we have now. There'll be all the more to learn." He grinned. It was obvious he had already measured himself for a uniform.

Deep in troubled thought, Johann finished his beer without speaking and did not mince words when he broke his silence.

"Hans," he said, "I can't possibly try to influence your parents. My heart isn't in it. Truthfully, I'd like nothing better than to dissuade you from enlisting. War is a serious and dangerous business. The Kaiser has a large professional army. Tough and well-trained men. Let them prove themselves. You are the only male heir. Consider your responsibilities to your family." Suddenly Johann looked downright grim. "If you volunteer it might kill your mother. She's not a robust woman."

"Uncle Johann, with all due respect, you're missing the point." Not daunted by sobering statements, Hans forged ahead. "Once the war starts the Kaiser's army won't be enough. If I don't sign up I'll be drafted. The newspapers are already talking about mass inductions. Mother reads the papers. She knows that anyone between the age of eighteen and thirty can expect to be called up. And, like I just said, I want to get a jump on the rest of them and be trained as an officer. I don't believe Mother would want me to go to the front as a foot soldier."

"Officers are the first the enemy try to pick off," Johann said morosely. "Because once the leaders fall, the men lose their focus." He argued his point a while longer, putting war in its worst possible light; in other words, sticking to the facts as best he knew them.

Hans enjoyed the debate. Uncle Johann didn't lose his temper or pound the table. How differently this scene would have played out at home. Karl-Heinz hated to be contradicted, would immediately take offense and roar like a bear.

Fritz came out on the terrace, chewing on a chunk of black bread spread with butter. Johann patted his knee and the boy immediately came running over. As Johann's arms closed around him he thanked God that Max and Fritz were too young for the army. A while later, Max came up from the stables and Hans stayed for the midday meal.

Frau Erdmann brought baked Brie out to the patio table, followed by chilled buttermilk soup and poached cod in parsley sauce with small round potatoes. She was long past retirement age but clung to her job with sanguine pride, keeping the maids in the kitchen and personally serving the food. Heaven forbid she be found lacking and pensioned off. She had no intention of leaving the baron's employ—or the comfort of living under his roof—until the Lord saw fit to take her like He had taken Otto. Without suffering a day's sickness, the old groom was found one morning in the tack room in a peaceful natural death, his weather-beaten face strangely free of lines.

Chapter 67

On *August the third*, only days after declaring war on Russia, the Kaiser sent his army on the march toward Paris. When England did not remain neutral, as he had hoped, Wilhelm sent his navy into combat against the British fleet rushing to the aid of France. At about the same time, and much to Wilhelm's surprise, Russia went on the offensive with unanticipated strength, forcing Germany into battles on two fronts. Privately, the Kaiser's generals shook their heads. They had warned Wilhelm about inciting Russia, but they kept a stiff upper lip and threw their resources into a two-fronted war, not yet aware that they had underestimated the power of their enemies.

In September Hans left for the eastern front but only his grandfather watched his departure with pride. Gerlinde and Ursula sobbed uncontrollably, and since Karl-Heinz's emotions were teetering on the brink, he did not trust himself to console the women and ordered the twins to comfort their mother and grandmother. Then he went down to the stables and mucked out the stalls with such determination that embarrassed grooms began attacking the place with spit and polish, giving the entire compound the appearance of being brand new within an hour.

Karl-Heinz was at a loss as to why this war was being waged and hoped the Kaiser was being candid when he promised it'd be short with swift victories. Conceivably, this whole bacchanalian farce might be over with before Hans saw combat. Karl-Heinz hoped so. He did more than hope. He prayed. He prayed for his son's safety and he prayed for Germany, no minor task because he'd never been a praying man.

The war spread. Where was God? Karl-Heinz doubled-up on prayers, but his pleas fell on deaf ears. New countries entered the conflict and it soon became a world venture of untold death and destruction.

Chapter 68

In December the Konauers came to Lindenstrasse for a visit and to indulge in some Christmas shopping at the fabulous Berlin stores. However, while her teenaged daughters, Klara and Leni, were giddy with excitement, it was impossible for Gerlinde to feel any enthusiasm for the upcoming holidays, knowing they would be spent without Hans. On the first afternoon of the visit, she walked mechanically with Dorrit and the twins along the festively decorated storefronts on Tauentzienstrasse. She had no interest in shopping, nor was she in the mood to satisfy her sweet tooth at Kranzler's Konditorei when they stopped for refreshments. Only when she spotted a handsome sweater in the windows at Kaufhaus des Westens did she brighten.

"It'll be perfect for Hans!" she cried, rushing inside to buy it. "I'll mail it right away." Although the purchase cheered her, it had no staying power and was gone before evening when Johann came home from the clinic and immediately inquired about Hans.

"We've had no word in three weeks," she reported morosely as everyone went into the dining room.

"Where was his last letter mailed from?" Johann asked, pulling out a chair for her.

"Grodno. His unit was pushing into Russia the following morning. It scares me to think that he's now inside enemy territory." With a look more pitiful than tears, Gerlinde sat down, taking only small portions when the maids came around with patters of sliced duck and sugar-braised potatoes; she had no appetite. "I'm . . . I'm praying for another letter," she said softly, her slim shoulders collapsing under the weight of her worry, making the padded sleeves of her blue velvet dress look like bat wings.

Johann reached over to squeeze her hand, saying, "Even if Hans is now a hundred kilometers east of Grodno he's still behind the furthest German advance and surrounded by more Germans than Russians. I hear conditions are not too bad on the eastern front. The Russians are ill equipped. Their armies are undisciplined and depleted by an inordinate number of deserters. Since their initial strikes, which caught us by surprise, they've enjoyed no victories. Be glad Hans is not in France where we're using yellow cross."

"What's that?" Gerlinde asked.

"Mustard gas." Johann said with a grim twist on his lips. "A god-awful ground-seeking toxic mist with the unfortunate tendency to drift back over our own troops at the slightest change in the wind and once it seeps into the trenches there's no escaping it. It dissolves exposed skin on contact. Obviously, it is terribly disfiguring. Our men are issued masks but some are careless about using them."

Listening, Klara stiffened. She had a beau fighting the French. Their neighbors in Bernau, the Borsts, had four sons. The oldest was exceedingly handsome and had regularly sought her out at parties. He was a divine dancer and had promised to write once he went to war. She had already received three wonderful letters, which she kept in a heart-shaped box on her dresser. So although adult conversation usually bored her, she paid rapt attention as Uncle Johann continued.

"A small dose of this gas is so excruciatingly painful that afflicted soldiers shoot themselves to end the torment."

Klara paled and sent a look of panic toward her sister, the only one at the table who knew about her beau. Leni shrugged negligently; she had not yet developed a fondness for boys, preferred horses, and thought Klara's love interest was sappy. Although they were twins, the two girls were as different as night and day.

"Those who survive the gas are often blinded, hideously deformed and . . ."

"And that's enough!" Dorrit said with a quelling look from the far end of the table. "Please, Johann, spare us the details. Hans is not in France and your lecture on chemical warfare is not cheering Gerlinde. Or anyone else, for that matter." She glanced toward Max and Fritz. Both had vivid imaginations and this kind of talk might give them nightmares.

"You're right, darling. I'm sorry." Johann winked at the boys, making light of his comments before turning back to Gerlinde. "How about a game of bridge after dinner? Will you be my partner?"

"Losing at cards won't cheer my wife either," Karl-Heinz muttered, his stab at humor conspicuously bland; the jovial bite was gone from his jaw. He missed Hans and, mustard gas or not, was plenty worried.

Over the course of the next few days, the normal atmosphere in Berlin served as a tonic for all concerned. Festive lights and holiday decorations were strung throughout the city, an early snowfall added to the ambience, and it was at times possible to forget that war raged across Europe. Germany was not fighting on her own soil and the Berlin papers reported splendid victories, particularly on the eastern front. Moreover, Dorrit made sure the Konauers had little time to brood. She had secured tickets to a popular play and, of course, everyone was attending the Eckarts' annual holiday party.

Chapter 69

The Eckarts' marriage had produced only one child, a girl two years younger than Fritz, which left Lillian and Kurt the pleasure of squandering any excess known to man on their little Elsie.

Philip von Brandt had remained a bachelor, which surprised no one because the coarse and painted women who caught his fancy were not the kind he could marry. However, on the occasion of the Eckarts' Christmas party he surprised one and all when he arrived with a lovely brunette socialite from Dusseldorf. Isabel Thimm was a widow in her thirties with two daughters, delightful girls, as poised as their mother. Of course they were not above giggling with the Konauer twins when the four of them quickly found each other at the party and just as quickly disappeared upstairs, where they could talk their hearts out and squeal without bothering any of the adults. Klara told her newfound friends about her beau who faced mustard gas daily without flinching because she was sure he was as brave as he was handsome.

Because of the war, Enno von Steigert was temporarily recalled from his diplomatic post in Lisbon. He and Anna were now enjoying their Wannsee villa, and when Anna cornered Gerlinde during the early part of the evening at the Eckarts, she discovered her to be all ears. In view of Hans' role as a soldier, others at the party hesitated to discuss the war within Gerlinde's hearing. But being childless, Anna did not know the pain carried in a mother's heart at a time like this and rambled on without whitewashing the stories her brother, Georg Schellenberg, sent home from his post along the River Marne.

"Georg is thirty-six," she told Gerlinde. "Past the optimum age for the military. Still, he volunteered the minute war broke out. Did I tell you he's a graduate of the Krampnitz Academy?" Gerlinde shook her head but knew of the elite officer training school on the outskirts of Berlin and was duly impressed. "That's why he didn't hesitate when it came to serving the Kaiser," Anna went on.

"He left his wife and children in Hamburg and joined the onslaught into France. He's now a front-line *Korvettenkapitan!*"

"I see." Gerlinde was again impressed.

"Of course rank doesn't preclude him being up to his waist in mud and up to his neck in danger. Living in vermin infested trenches with bullets flying can't be much of a picnic." Gerlinde shuddered, suddenly glad Hans was on the march in Russia, not in the trenches. "Last week Georg wrote that he and his men had to peel some French soldiers from the barbed wire. Apparently, they left their dugouts before daybreak and didn't see the coils until it was too late. Their skin torn to shreds, they were put into our medical tents where they died of blood poisoning before they could be traded for some of our own. Imagine? Getting stuck in wire. Rather clumsy of the elegant French. Of course our traps are clever and we are superbly equipped. Far better than the French and the British combined." Anna patted her blond coiffure, but might as well have patted herself on the back; the message was the same.

"Naturally, we lose a few of our own men now and again," she went on. "Georg says some of his troops are such greenhorns they freeze the first time they come face to face with the enemy. They make the mistake of looking him in the eye and, finding a boy no older than themselves, hesitate to kill him. That split second allows the enemy to ram a bayonet into their ribs. It bothers Georg terribly. He's responsible for these young men. Some were so eager to go to war that they lied about their age and signed up at sixteen, only to suddenly look around shocked, clutching at the hole in their chests, wondering what happened. They invariably cry out for their mothers as they die."

Gerlinde turned ashen. "Do . . . do you think the Russians use bayonets?"

"I doubt it. They have little in the way of weaponry. Their ranks are full of peasants who'd rather farm than fight. Most have no allegiance to Czar Nicholas. I've been told the Russian army is hopelessly divided."

"Still, I'm awfully worried about Hans."

"Well, certainly. But at least he's not in those dreadful trenches facing two armies. French and British."

"I suppose I should be grateful for that."

"Sure. Besides, the war will end first thing in the New Year. And it'll end sooner in the east because the Russians are going to collapse from starvation. Everyone was put in uniform this past summer. No one was left behind to bring in the harvest. Soon there'll be nothing to eat." Anna took Gerlinde's arm and moved through the Eckarts' delightful crowd. "You'll see. Hans will be home within a few weeks. So will my brother. In fact, before Enno and I go back to Lisbon, we'll host a party celebrating the end of the war." Anna craned her neck. "Oh, look! There's Philip. Come let's go meet his new lady friend. If she can keep him sober tonight, she'll have Lillian's undying gratitude."

Chapter 70

Spring came with nothing to celebrate and the mood in Berlin grew increasingly caustic, everyone grousing that the successes Kaiser Wilhelm had promised were long overdue. The war was dragging on. Germany had not yet taken France and naval battles with the British were at a stalemate. Along the eastern front the Russians were regrouping; they had not been starved into submission and were showing sporadic signs of strength.

Dorrit was both surprised and delighted on the first day of April when Johann came home from the clinic much earlier than usual. However, her pleasure was short-lived because she immediately sensed that something was wrong. He seemed preoccupied and averted his eyes when he saw her in the hall. Handing his coat to Schmidt, he kissed her, same as always, but then abruptly walked into the library without his usual questions as to Max's and Fritz's whereabouts. Dorrit wondered if a surgical procedure gone wrong. Had a patient died? Or, dear God, had Karl-Heinz telephoned him at the clinic? Was Hans wounded? Missing?

"Johann, what's wrong?" She followed him into the library, bracing herself for the worst. "Tell me!"

"Wrong? Nothing's wrong."

"But you're home so early," she said, plucking at his sleeve as he poured some sherry from the cart behind his desk.

"I can't come home early without something being wrong?" Johann held out the decanter questioningly. "Want some?"

She shook her head. "Of course you can come home early. It's just that you look like you're carrying a ton of bad news. Have you heard from Karl-Heinz?"

"No."

"Well, thank God for that." Dorrit exhaled, relieved. "No news is good news nowadays."

"Yes." Johann nodded. "As far as I know, Hans is fine." He put his glass down on the green blotter on his desk and walked over to close the doors to the hall.

Dorrit tensed. He never closed those doors. Something was wrong. "Come here," he said, leaning against them.

She ran into his embrace, felt the smooth gabardine of his gray jacket against her cheek and heard his heart beating rhythmically. Some of her apprehension left her because if something was truly amiss how could his heart beat so calmly?

"So tell me . . ." he asked against her hair, "what have the boys been doing today?"

"The usual. School . . . sports, and since the weather's so agreeable, Fraulein Werner took them bicycling in the park. They should be back shortly."

"So she's still in our employ?"

"Of course."

"Then the boys must have done something *unusual.*"

Dorrit laughed. "No. Fraulein Werner has merely abdicated her position as governess and, befitting the times, become a drill sergeant."

Johann grinned. "Remind me to raise her salary proportionately." He released Dorrit, went back to pick up his drink and stood for a moment by the windows near the fireplace where a small heap of ashes reminded one that winter was just a memory. It was a beautiful day. Spring was fooling around in Grunewald Park, waking everything up, the ancient trees once again preening themselves in lush new greenery. On a glorious day like this it was hard to believe that there was so much wrong in the world.

"I really don't know why Max and Fritz insist on waging war with each other," Dorrit said, sitting down in one of the comfortable red leather chairs. "Of course they come home from school with reports of exciting battles, so I suppose it's only natural that they act out a few skirmishes of their own. I'm only afraid someone will get hurt. Fraulein Werner, dear soul, gets in the middle and tries to restore order when she ought to stay clear of it. As the intervening party, the boys occasionally forget their own fight, join forces, and gang up on her."

"I'll speak to Max."

"And to Fritz. They are equally guilty."

"All right. I'll take them both by the scruff of the neck and . . ." Johann's voice faded away, his expression darkening with something he needed to tell Dorrit before the boys returned home. It was no use stalling any longer. He turned away from the window, faced her squarely, and came out with it. "As you suspected, I came home early today for a reason. I *do* have some news. Nothing tragic. Still, I don't expect you to applaud it. But in view of our sons' newfound lust for war I suppose they'll find it interesting." Johann put his glass down on the mantelpiece, saying quietly, "I have volunteered . . ."

"What?" Dorrit jumped up from the chair to face him. She had seen the posters plastered all around town, asking for volunteers. Men from all walks of life were signing up. "You must be kidding!" She remembered today was April 1st. "If this is your idea of an April Fools' joke, it's not the least bit amusing."

"It's no joke, darling. I have volunteered . . ."

"Stop it!" she demanded hotly, interrupting him and wanting to scold him good for scaring her. But in the next instant her throat tightened with the realization that although Johann occasionally enjoyed playing a practical joke this was not such a time. He would never make sport of anything having to do with the war. "You *can't* volunteer," she said. "You're . . . you're too old to be a soldier."

"A soldier? Good Lord, Dorrit!" Johann smiled with her wrong conclusion. "Of course I'm too old. Much as I hate to admit it." He took her face between his hands. "Darling, I'm not going to be a soldier. Our Kaiser is not that desperate yet."

"What then?"

"I've volunteered as an army surgeon."

"Oh . . ." Dorrit felt better and now listened without interrupting as Johann explained.

"Urgent calls have been going out to the medical community for the past few months, asking for experienced surgeons. When a lottery was introduced a few weeks ago, I put my name in the hopper. This morning my number was drawn and I received my orders. I've been assigned to a field hospital on the outskirts of Kapsukas in Lithuania."

"Is that near the front?"

"I'm not sure. Battle lines are constantly changing. But I suppose it would have to be, because field hospitals are crucial for treating the wounded who can't be moved back into larger urban hospital centers. Medics in the trenches are doing a heroic job. But for the most part they are not surgeons."

As she listened, Dorrit was absently twisting the long strand of pearls around her neck. *Battle lines!* When Johann initially said army surgeon, she was relieved; now she didn't know what to think because she couldn't imagine that a physician at the front was any better off than a soldier. Enemy artillery couldn't possibly distinguish between a man in uniform versus one in a white coat. In fact, the latter might attract more attention. Her heart cringed. The string that held the pearls snapped.

"The situation is getting more and more desperate," Johann continued as he calmly bent down to retrieve the luminous spheres rolling on the carpet. "Interns fresh out of medical school are being sent out on a rotation system. They are dedicated but have little or no surgery experience and shy away from amputations. I'm told the wounded die needlessly from gangrene left to spread. I can't sit by and listen to the reports, shake my head in commiseration, then do nothing. You do understand, don't you?" Johann placed a fistful of olive-sized pearls in a crystal dish on the Queen Anne desk.

Dorrit nodded reluctantly. "How . . . how long will you be gone?" she asked, her eyes on the floor, pretending to look for more pearls, because she didn't want Johann to see the disappointment and anger in her face, anger with the war and disappointment that he had not asked her opinion before committing himself.

"I don't know. Probably a year. Of course, the war may be over long before then. If not, I'll be replaced by another volunteer in twelve months."

Twelve months! Dorrit almost sank to the floor, the shock of the verdict slowing her mind like a clock running down, giving anger the upper hand. "When you volunteered," she said, her voice harsher than she intended, "did you know that it'd be for an *entire* year?"

"Yes."

"Then how could you? How could you when you knew it would be for so long? Couldn't you have promised the army a couple of months? Did it have to be a whole year? What about Max and Fritz? Did you stop to consider them? They need you. They need their father. And . . . and I need you . . . I . . ." Bitter words raced to her lips but were quelled by sudden sobs strangling her. She dropped her head in her hands.

"Darling, please don't cry." Johann had not expected such an outburst. Dorrit was usually so levelheaded. He dug a handkerchief from his pocket and offered it to her. "Darling, please get hold of yourself." She snatched the handkerchief and blew her nose. "Try to understand," he implored. "I have no choice. This war is a catastrophe in terms of maimed bodies and lost lives. If I can do something, however little, I'm willing to make a personal sacrifice."

"Such as your life?"

"I don't believe it'll come to that. Besides, if I didn't go, I couldn't live with myself. How can I sit idly by while boys are dying? For God's sake Dorrit, think of

Hans! He's out there somewhere. Suppose he's hurt. Suppose there's no doctor to tend his wounds. Please try to understand."

"I . . . I do understand. I think of Hans all the time." Dorrit pocketed the handkerchief. "It's just that you surprised me. This is so sudden. For months I've been grateful that you're too old for the war and that Max and Fritz are too young. Every time I talk to poor Gerlinde, I feel awful and . . . and glad at the same time. Glad that I don't have a loved one at the front. She's dying a slow death worrying about Hans. But now, oh God! Now what? I'll be so afraid for you. Gerlinde has Karl-Heinz. I'll be alone. I don't know if I can stand it."

"Darling, you have the boys. A house full of servants. And friends. You will not be alone for a minute."

Friends? Dorrit hit upon an idea. "How about Philip?" she said. "Can't he go instead of you? He has no wife. If he hasn't decided that Isabel Thimm is perfect, he never will. All he does is sit and tinker in that old laboratory. He's not seeing patients. If he left for twelve months no one would miss him."

"His lab work is precisely why he's not suited for the front. He has never done any surgery."

"Oh, I forgot." Dorrit sighed. "It's ironic."

"What's ironic?"

"That I've always been so proud of your work, practically bursting at the seams whenever I heard people talk about the wonders you perform at the clinic. But right now I wish you were a . . . a . . . chimney sweep."

Johann took her into his arms.

"When do you leave?" she asked him.

"In a week."

"So soon?" She had hoped for more time but made no mention of it. "What about your patients?"

"Ben Tarnoff has assured me that he can manage the clinic. Our associates have volunteered as well and will be called up in due time."

"Has Ben volunteered?" Dorrit asked. "Maybe he could go first? He and Gert have no children. It would only be fair if he went first."

"Ben has not volunteered. Doctors are primarily being sent east and he doesn't want to set foot on Russian soil again. Have you forgotten his and Gertrude's stories?"

"No, of course not. I spoke without thinking." In the next instant she heard herself ask, "What about Kurt?"

"I don't expect him to volunteer. He's been distancing himself from the medical profession. He's been keen on politics for years. It wouldn't surprise me if he changed careers altogether."

Chapter 71

A *week to the day* of this conversation, Johann joined an eastbound regiment and boarded a troop train moments before it departed from Potsdam Platz Station in rainy predawn darkness.

Hours into the journey, as sunlight eventually brightened the sky the transport chugged through East Prussia, where as far as the eye could see the black earth was dotted with green seedlings. Farmers in the fields stopped their labors, wiped brows as furrowed as the soil they tilled, and saluted the passing train. Waving paper flags, children gathered at village railroad crossings while boys—a few years short of enlistment age—raced along the tracks, shouting encouragement to the soldiers leaning from the windows. When the train stopped to take on coal and water, it was welcomed by groups of local ladies and their nubile daughters, the women handing pastries through the open windows while the girls blew kisses. The soldiers, to the man, made solemn vows to quickly rout the enemy and return.

By nightfall the train lumbered into Tannenberg where it was met by Red Cross sisters dispensing food packets to the disembarking troops bunking down for the night on the station floor. The space vacated on the train was promptly filled with furloughed soldiers. Come morning, they'd be back in Germany on home leave while the newcomers continued east to the battlefields. Yet this latter group was a sight more cheerful, joking with the veterans, calling them shirkers and promising them they needn't come back because real men had come to finish the job. Of course the joking stopped abruptly when the last to board the homebound train did so on stretchers. Even carefully tucked sheets couldn't hide the fact that each of these shirkers had left a limb at the front.

Aroused before daybreak, the troops in the Tannenberg station were given ten minutes to collect their gear and eat a bowl of oatmeal washed down with a cup of coffee without cream or sugar, but no one grumbled. It was common knowledge that luxuries were scarce at the front and all stood ready to make concessions for the Kaiser.

On account of his peerage, Johann had the rank of major and wore the appropriate uniform with the required pistol. His medical armband was the only thing that distinguished him from a frontline commanding officer, and although he'd been obliged to sleep on a threadbare rug in a drafty station cubicle last night, this morning he would enjoy his rank and travel up front with the driver. It turned out to be a distinct privilege because the rest of the journey was over bumpy dirt roads, where the men in the open trucks had to contend with clouds of dust and exhaust fumes that tested the strongest stomach and put a green tinge on the healthiest complexion.

By mid afternoon, choking and bruised, the convoy sputtered into Kapsukas. Five hundred troops alighted from the trucks and fell into formation, every pair of knees uniformly slow to snap to attention. After a short rest they were on the march toward the front lines.

Kapsukas was Johann's final destination. After reporting in at headquarters, he was given a brief tour of the amenities available to officers, such as the canteen, bath, and barbershop, before getting a ride to his assigned medical facility on the outskirts of town. His driver, a young sergeant who reminded him achingly of Hans, saluted smartly before throwing Johann's personal effects into the rear seats of a battered lorry, which suffered internal injuries as well when he stripped the gears, backing out of a tight spot.

The center of town was teeming with German militia. Local citizens venturing about had to jump for their lives as army trucks barreled through the narrow streets with little concern for pedestrians, a situation the Lithuanians accepted good-naturedly because the Germans had liberated them from the Russians who had occupied their city with no concern at all.

"We secured Kapsukas only recently," the driver explained when his passenger commented on some scorched buildings they passed. "The czar's troops weren't keen on leaving. We had to persuade them with flame-throwers. Taking Kapsukas was an important victory. We now control the main roads going north and east and can supply a critical line of trenches."

"The Memel Line?"

"Yes, the two-hundred-kilometers that run parallel with the Niemen River. The Russians are mobilizing on the other side, but we've got the bridges covered and plenty of coal boxes to launch. Daisy-cutters too. Let me tell you, just the whistle of a flying d-cutter scares the living daylights out of them." Grinning, the sergeant looked sideways at his passenger. "They run like rabbits."

Daisy-cutters? Johann shuddered. An insanely pleasant name for an explosive shell scattering shrapnel close to the ground, mowing down men and shrubs alike.

"Damn!" The driver stood on the brakes to avoid two women carrying bundles of firewood across the road. Screeching to a halt against the curb in a cloud of dust, he doffed his hat to the ladies, smiled, gunned the lorry and drove on, cursing them soundly.

Chapter 72

No rumor circulating in Berlin could have prepared Johann for what he encountered once the driver dropped him off, made a U-turn and sped back toward Kapsukas as if he feared that his passenger having seen the place, would trouble him with a return trip. Bags under his arms, Johann stood silent and alone, studying a sagging brick structure, where a crudely painted medical cross covered the faded sign of its former use as a roadside inn. In addition to being enveloped in depressing neglect, the pine forest at the back of the building cast long shadows denying it any sun. A cast-iron pump stood in a puddle in the front yard, indicating it was very much in use, and although the red tiled roof seemed in adequate repair, Johann figured any scorched building in town could have served the purpose better. Of course, being closer to the front could determine life or death for the wounded.

Perusing the dismal environs, Johann's ears suddenly pricked. The boom of howitzers could be heard in the distance where a battle was heating up, giving proof that location alone was the reason this property had been resurrected as a hospital. Shivering involuntarily, he lifted his eyes skyward; white puffy clouds overhead were smudged with black smoke turning the sky yellow. Taking a deep breath, he reminded himself why he'd come, put both bags under one arm, and pulled resolutely on the door. It creaked open on a rusty hinge, swung back by its own weight, and banged against the outside wall.

Johann stepped into a narrow hall, where from the general looks of things, he guessed there'd be no reception committee. Doors opposite the center staircase were closed, and while the hum of voices could be heard behind one, behind the other there was nothing but an eerie silence broken by an occasional moan. He was wondering how best to make his presence known, when the door to the silent room opened and an orderly wearing an oilcloth apron limped into the hall, balancing a stack of bedpans. The door shut behind him.

"Excuse me!" Johann waylaid the man, guessing he had suffered a leg wound and was now making himself useful as an orderly. "I'm Dr. von Renz. Can you tell me where I might find Dr. Bergen?"

"You're our new man from Berlin?"

"Yes."

"Welcome! Herr Director Bergen will be glad to know you've arrived. He's right down this corridor. Second door on the left." Clutching his indelicate cargo, the orderly pointed with his chin and eyed the luggage under Johann's arm. "Doctors' quarters are upstairs," he said. "Just leave your gear here in the hall. I'll bring everything up the minute I take care of this." Without further ado, the man hobbled through the front door.

Removing his hat and depositing his bags against the wall, Johann found the designated door, knocked and entered when bid to do so by what could only be interpreted as an angry grunt. Once inside the small room, the tenor didn't improve. Herr Director, a graying, balding man in his sixties, was standing with his back to the door and was far too preoccupied working on a sedated soldier to turn and acknowledge the newcomer.

"Good afternoon," Johann said, circling the gurney, inadvertently blocking the light from the window as he introduced himself. "I'm Dr. Von Renz."

"I know." Dr. Bergen glanced up briefly. "Glad to see you finally made it." He waved Johann away from the window and once he again had a beam of light continued tugging on a bomb fragment embedded in the man's shoulder. "One of our wards have been without a physician for two weeks," he said as if it was Johann's fault. "We're short of chloroform as well. This patient will get no more. I'm sure you can appreciate the fact that I have to be done with him before he comes around. So, if you'll excuse me."

"Certainly." Johann turned, glad to leave this testy individual. "I'll go unpack."

"Unpack?" Herr Director snorted. "That can wait. Time is at a premium around here. We have to take advantage of every minute of daylight. There's no guarantee we'll have electricity or kerosene tonight."

"All right. I'll start with some rounds."

"Good. You will be in charge of Ward B. First door on the right where you entered the building. Most of the men in that ward are terminal. At best, they'll go home with only half the limbs they came with. I trust you have no qualms about amputations?" Dr. Bergen peered over his horn-rimmed spectacles splattered with dried blood, the look he gave Johann skeptical.

"Amputations?" Johann shrugged. "Shouldn't be a problem."

"Glad to hear that. Dr. Reymann has yet to show the stomach for it."

"Dr. Reymann?"

"Our esteemed colleague," Dr. Bergen said with another snort. "He arrived straight from medical school, *summa cum laude*, but he's not cut out for the profession. I put him in charge of Ward A where most of the patients are expected to survive unless Dr. Reymann slips up." Dr. Bergen consulted a clipboard on the instrument tray. "All right. Where were we? Oh, yes. Ward B. Cot number ten. Leg amputation. Advanced gangrene. You'll have to operate immediately. Use the room next to this one. It's got running water. And, mind you, ether is to be administered only during amputations. Under no circumstances are you to waste it on any other procedure no matter how loudly a man hollers. The way I figure it, if a soldier can yell, he's strong enough to stand the pain."

"I'll examine the patient immediately," Johann said.

"I've already done that. Take the leg off. Mid femur."

"I'll determine the extent of the surgery once I've seen the patient," Johann said in a deceptively conciliatory tone. He was not accustomed to taking orders.

Shrugging, Dr. Bergen bent over the comatose man. "Rule of thumb," he said and went back to work, "start with the worst cases and pray the others don't deteriorate before you can get to them. Occasionally some wounded Russians are brought in. Treat everyone equally. Prisoners-of-war are worth more in trade if they're alive."

The large piece of shrapnel finally loosened and slipped out of the soldier's arm. Dr. Bergen reached for the sutures with one hand while he groped the wound for small fragments with the other. Finding it clean, he wiped his fingers negligently on his surgeon's coat and, using a wad of gauze, swabbed at the blood oozing from the gaping hole. "A word of caution. Never turn your back on a POW," he said, plunging a bow-shaped needle into the flesh, sewing flaps of tissue and skin together. "Crippled or unconscious, they've been known to make weapons from a mess tin. You're replacing the doctor we lost two weeks ago to a Russian patient believed to be comatose. The scoundrel had fashioned a sharp instrument from a bedspring and when Dr. Buhler bent down to examine him, he sunk it into his heart."

"Good God!" Johann exclaimed.

"Don't waste your time calling on The Almighty. He can't hear you over the mortar shells." Dr. Bergen flicked his eyes over his new colleague, wondering how this clean-shaven individual would fare in this hellhole. He appeared much too sanitized for this sorry duty. Of course, he'd soon enough get dirty. *If* he lasted a week. "Be on guard at all times."

Johann nodded and turned toward the door. "Is a surgery nurse available?" he asked in reference to the impending amputation.

Herr Director jerked his head around, scarcely able to contain his scorn. If Dr. von Renz was expecting assistance, forget a week; he wouldn't last the day and it was already three o'clock. Why did Berlin persist in sending prima donnas and neophytes out here? Didn't the idiots at the war ministry realize professionals were needed, surgeons who'd clamp an artery with their teeth, if necessary. Dr. Bergen was moving his lips, preparing to vent his spleen, when some scuffling outside in the hall distracted him. Someone was leaning against the door, trying to push it open. Johann, about to exit, turned the knob.

"Ah, Hofmeyer!" Dr. Bergen's face softened imperceptibly at the sight of the woman coming in with a basin of clean instruments.

Johann stepped forward and took the heavy tray from her, placing it on an empty table in a corner.

"Thanks!" she smiled; a pleasant contrast to the caustic demeanor of Herr Director.

"Nurse Hofmeyer, this is our new surgeon from Berlin. Dr. von Renz." Herr Director accomplished the necessary introductions with a distinct frugality of words. "I have put him in charge of Ward B."

Olivia Hofmeyer offered her hand. "Welcome to the front," she said, still smiling.

"Thank you."

Dr. Bergen waved his arm in a pointed dismissal. "I suppose it won't hurt to take a few minutes to show Dr. von Renz around," he told the nurse. "Go ahead and introduce him to the staff. But step lively. There's work to be done."

Chapter 73

Once out in the hall, Olivia Hofmeyer looked at the newcomer, guessing his thoughts. "No time for pleasantries around here," she said in reference to the contumelious Dr. Bergen.

"It doesn't matter. I'm not here on a social call."

"Far from it," she laughed, her lively blue eyes playing on his face. "In these godforsaken parts, a good time means getting two hours of sleep. Have you seen your quarters?"

"Not yet."

"Just as well. By tonight you'll be too tired to care. It'll be less of a shock that way. At least your accommodations are private. Nurses sleep dormitory style at the rear of the building and the nuns go back to the cloister in Kapsukas right before dinner so the army won't have to feed them."

Smiling at her candor, Johann studied Olivia Hofmeyer as she walked next door and stepped into a room that appeared to have been a laundry facility at one time. He guessed she was in her early forties. Her short blond hair was streaked with silver and various shades of dye, indicating a valiant attempt to stave off middle age. It worked, helped by the fact that her figure was trim and her face had a pixie quality about it, round and soft, the kind that's slow to age. She was a very attractive woman.

"This is where you'll do amputations," she said, walking over to a cast iron sink standing under a cracked window. Turning the tap, she bled rust from the line before getting a trickle of clean water. Shrugging in resignation, she quipped, "At least this room is removed from the wards so screams won't carry the distance."

Frowning at her unprofessional talk, Johann's frown deepened when he realized that a tavern table, mottled with accumulated wine and food stains, served as an operating platform. Moreover, sheets stained with blood and other body fluids were folded and ready for the next patient, the pile attracting flies.

"Linens have to be washed and changed with each patient," he said sharply, attesting to his level of outrage.

"Sure," Nurse Hofmeyer agreed. "And they would be if we had enough of them. This two-fronted war is overwhelming us. There aren't enough doctors, supplies, or linens to go around. While we wait for headquarters to fill our requisitions, we have to conclude that clean sheets won't save our patients and dirty sheets won't kill them. The nuns wash every day, bless them, but they can't keep up with the demand." She leveled her gaze on Johann, bluntly challenging him. "Have you done many amputations?"

"Only on cadavers."

Cadavers? It was Nurse Hofmeyer's turn to frown. According to Berlin, this new surgeon was experienced. And if not, why on earth had Dr. Bergen put him in charge of Ward B? Concealing her dismay, she walked quickly from the room.

"I meant no personal offense about the linens," Johann mumbled, somewhat chastened, as he followed her out.

"I didn't take any," she said and looked up at him, all the while deciding that, experienced or not, at least this newcomer was more likeable than Dr. Bergen.

Walking back along the corridor toward the wards, she glanced at his left hand, not surprised to see that he was married. She sighed. It was the story of her life; she invariably fell for men she couldn't have. A disastrous affair with a married man back home in Paderborn was the main reason she had volunteered for war duty and had, like Herr Director Bergen, committed herself for the duration of the conflict.

Olivia Hofmeyer took Dr. von Renz into Ward A and introduced him to the nurses and to Dr. Reymann, the intern Herr Director had all but crucified. Indeed, the young man looked pathetically relieved when Johann told him he'd handle the cases in Ward B.

"I saved the worst for last," Nurse Hofmeyer whispered as she now led Johann into the silent ward occupied by men long past making conversation. Following her in and although he had smelled death before, his breath caught in his throat with the fetid stench hanging over the entire room. He immediately made a beeline for the windows to open them. They wouldn't budge. They'd been painted shut decades ago. He turned on the two nuns in the ward and ordered that the door into the hall remain open at all times to ensure some ventilation.

"Herr Doctor," one of the nuns spoke up, "we have to keep the door closed so the . . . uh," she lowered her voice, "so the cries won't disturb the patients in the other ward."

"I see." Johann glowered at the woman. "I suppose you haven't considered the fact that the lack of air might disturb these patients?" He looked around at the broken and bandaged bodies. "Are we making a conscious choice here?"

"No . . . no, of course not." The nun shook her wimpled head and ran from the room.

As Johann watched her go, he realized it had taken him exactly five minutes to become as petulant as Dr. Bergen. He smiled at the remaining nun. "I'm sorry," he said. "I was rude." Then without wasting another moment, he began to walk among the patients, aware that Nurse Hofmeyer stayed at his side. It pleased him.

There were some twenty beds in this infirmary and, reading individual charts as he went, Johann spoke to every man who was not comatose. Olivia Hofmeyer added personal particulars and warned him well ahead of time that the two men in the far corner were Russians.

"They're not expected to last long," she whispered as Johann approached them.

Remembering Dr. Bergen's story about the sharpened bedspring, Johann studied their pale yellow skin and tested their rigid limbs without bending down too far. Both men were suffering from advanced tetanus; nothing could be done for them at this point and while he jotted notes on their charts, he felt their eyes on him. He tried a few Russian words from his sparse vocabulary. One of the men smiled, the other—still fighting the war—turned angry eyes away. But he didn't have long to hold a grudge. Death was on the march in his body and would defeat him by morning.

Crossing the center aisle, Johann made his way to the cot of the soldier whose chart carried the code for amputation. He approached the young man's bed slowly as if no emergency existed, no sense setting off alarm bells.

A wisp of a girl, a local Lithuanian volunteer, was bent over him, holding a cup and helping him drink. Seeing the new doctor, she put the water down, straightened, and introduced herself. Her name was Marja. She had a fresh-scrubbed face, a smile that lit up the room, and whatever she lacked in age and nursing experience was compensated for by her eye-appealing presence, which was probably as beneficial in this pitiful ward as a shot of morphine.

"So, how are we doing today?" Johann asked the fellow and peeled back the sheet covering his legs, one of which was mangled below the knee, red lines of gangrene spreading upward into healthy tissue. Dr. Bergen's diagnosis had been right on the mark. Amputation could not wait.

The lieutenant mumbled something unintelligible. Johann studied his chart. He'd been given a dose of medication an hour ago and was groggy. Just as well, in view of what was in store for him.

"Don't give this patient any more to drink," Johann said to Marja and replaced the sheet over the man's legs to keep the flies off. "Stay with him till I come back."

"Why . . . why are you coming back?"

"Pardon?" Johann spun around. The lieutenant was boosting himself up on one elbow, apparently not as dazed as first believed. However, before Johann could respond, he fell back down on the pillow and closed his eyes, again falling into a semi-conscience state.

Johann left the ward. "Show me the supply room," he said urgently once he and Olivia Hofmeyer were out in the hall; he hoped to God there was plenty of ether. "And tell me what you know about the circumstances surrounding the lieutenant. Has he been told anything yet?"

"No. He was admitted about an hour ago, shouting at the top of his lungs that we'd better not take off his leg. We gathered from the medics who brought him in that he'd stepped on a mine and spent hours in a field, ducking bullets from both sides before they could rescue him. The pain must have been horrible, as horrible as wondering who would get to him first. The enemy or his own men. While pinned down, he had enough wherewithal to apply a tourniquet with a sleeve he tore from his shirt. That saved his life. He arrived here, realizing his leg was in bad shape, but flung his arms wildly at anyone who tried to touch him. Dr. Bergen couldn't work on him while he was in such a state and gave him a sedative. You'll need two orderlies to hold him down. Ether is not always a hundred percent effective. I suspect our supplies are diluted."

Chapter 74

April slipped by. May came and went. It was June . . . then July. Daylight lingered past ten in the evening and returned a couple of hours after midnight, melting the days together. Weeks became months and Johann lost track of time, dates were important only when a soldier died and the particulars had to be reported to headquarters so a telegram could be sent to the man's family. A short and standard one; there were too many deaths and not enough time to be original.

Death happened so frequently Johann felt numbed by it, numbness he fought because it would breed indifference, dull his judgment, and slow his hands. There could be no lax surgeons at a hospital where men came in, trailing their intestines behind them. Some arrived with mud-impacted faces, then no face at all once the mud was cleaned away. A seventeen-year-old had hobbled in on a bloody and clumsily wrapped stump, all that remained of his right foot. He had supported himself on a homemade crutch on the long trek from the hinterlands because those with worse injuries than his needed the space on the lorries. His desperate effort was for naught. He died of blood poisoning.

Feverish men staggered in with burns and lacerations treated in the field, but which refused to heal and smelled abominably of ham gone bad. Some came with wounds impacted with maggots, others with once-mended scabs ripped open by yet another volley of enemy fire. They came with typhoid and lockjaw, came to have anti-tetanus needles plunged into their chests in the frantic hope that it wasn't too late. Some, blinded by shrapnel, arrived tied to the walking wounded. Some simply came to draw their last breath in a bed, friends carrying in their mortally wounded comrades for this final bit of dignity, which would afford them a proper burial. To die in the battlefields meant to rot in the open.

After his initial harsh assessment of the Berlin surgeon, who upon arrival had looked much too elegant to be of any practical use at the front, Dr. Bergen soon realized his error. Men pulled through against all odds because Dr. von Renz refused to give up on them. Operating through the night by the light of a kerosene lamp, he performed impossible feats, which included repairing facial wounds so a soldier could look in the mirror without begging for a *coup de grace*. Intrigued by his colleague, Dr. Bergen began to seek out his company during meals, the only lull in their hectic routine for any kind of socializing. Besides, conversation helped flavor the bland rations sent down from headquarters for staff and patients alike. The food was even more palatable when one or two of the nurses joined the men at supper. Female company was invariably pleasant and both doctors found Olivia Hofmeyer's particularly so. Johann couldn't help notice that Herr Director's mood always improved when she was around. Her smile was contagious. The strenuous work and long hours had yet to harden her face. She laughed readily and without the brittle, discordant sound of some of the other nurses. During the worst of times, when a patient screamed in agony and she all but tripped over amputated limbs in the operating rooms, Olivia Hofmeyer remained calm, her expression beatific like the nuns at prayer. Soldiers in the throes of dying poured out their hearts to her, she stroked their feverish brows, and painstakingly wrote down last messages for mothers, wives or sweethearts back home.

Each morning before starting his duties, Johann glanced around, hoping to catch her eye and a smile, which helped chase some of the gloom from the ward. He enjoyed the very sight of her, enjoyed the way her uniform hugged her slender hips and the way her full breasts strained against the bib of her apron. She looked incredibly good. Of course, with the passing of time, even the nuns in their black habits looked good, and Johann occasionally wondered if he was becoming some sort of a pervert. Although he kept all contact with any female staff member on a professional level, he soon discovered it was becoming increasingly difficult to remain impartial to Nurse Hofmeyer.

She didn't talk much about herself, but he learned that she'd been widowed years ago when she'd lost both her husband and a small child to a pneumonia epidemic. She had never remarried, had volunteered the day the war broke out and, for reasons she kept to herself, never requested the home furloughs nurses were entitled to.

Chapter 75

An evening in September when, in lieu of their dinner break, the nurses went to headquarters for that once-a-week privilege of a hot bath, and Dr. Reymann remained on duty in the wards with Marja, Johann and Dr. Bergen were left to eat supper alone.

The weather on this late summer evening was balmy and taking full advantage of it, the two doctors took their trays out to the back steps of the hospital and sat down in separate corners, leaning into the same rotting banister and listening to the rumbles of a skirmish somewhere in the woods. Both doctors half expected to hear a stray shell whistling overhead. Last week, one had made a deep crater a stone's throw from where they now sat, the percussion breaking several of the hospital's windows.

By and by, the noise of the big guns silenced as the battle lost steam along with daylight. The long shadows of dusk crept through the pine forest towering behind the hospital, the encroaching darkness obscuring the rows of graves rippling the ground along the perimeter of the woods; a foreboding sight, and the only thing that interfered with the pleasure of eating in the out-of-doors where a favorable breeze kept the carbolic odors of the wards at bay.

"I wonder if headquarters have retained a cook with allegiance to the enemy." Dr. Bergen was eying his tray suspiciously; the fare was particularly unappetizing tonight. "How in God's name can we hope to win the war on these putrid provisions?"

Johann dunked a rock-hard biscuit into the watery soup in front of him. "I'd like to think we're getting the scraps so there'll be more for our men out there," he said, pointing toward the woods with the biscuit before clamping his teeth into it.

"If not, starvation will claim them before Russian bullets." Dr. Bergen submerged a utensil into his bowl, exploring the depths like a submarine hunting unfriendly objects.

Leaving the rest of his biscuit to soak in the broth, Johann ate a piece of cheese and watched his older colleague sample the cloudy soup.

Dr. Bergen made a terrible face and threw his spoon down. "These weeds came from a stagnant swamp," he sputtered, plowing a hand through his thinning hair. "And to think what I have refused to eat in the past!"

Johann chuckled.

"Go ahead and laugh! But when you're through, I'd suggest you check the cheese on your tray." Dr. Bergen jabbed at his piece with his fork. "Look at this! Mine is so inhabited by vile organisms, it's trying to walk off the plate."

Johann felt himself go pale. He had just swallowed a large chunk without examining it for worms.

Chapter 76

In *November after* a year of service, another intern, Dr. Stocker from Bonn, replaced Dr. Reymann. Before embarking on the trip home, Dr. Reymann made a surprise announcement. He and Marja, the pretty volunteer from town, were getting married. However, since her parents were not pleased about losing her to Germany, they were also not motivated to step forward and host a wedding. Hence, the celebration was held in the officers' canteen at headquarters, courtesy of the army.

Leaving the new man, Dr. Stocker, in charge of the wards, the hospital staff crammed into the one vehicle at their disposal and drove to the nuptials. Olivia Hofmeyer slipped into the seat next to Johann, who'd been elected to drive the overloaded motor lorry to town; a trip made pleasant by the feel of her body pressed against his when everyone squeezed together to make room. As he put the car in gear, his hand brushed against her thigh, sending a schoolboy's rush of pleasure through him. Chagrined, he forced himself to concentrate on the road ahead, but found himself wondering how Olivia managed to smell so nice. The staff was allowed the one weekly bath at headquarters; the rest of the time the small trickle of water in a common shower rigged next to the laundry room, was supposed to suffice. Johann occasionally questioned if his own lack of hygiene offended anyone.

At the conclusion of the wedding festivities, Dr. Reymann and his bride stayed in Kapsukas for their morning departure to Germany. Everyone else returned to the hospital and tended patients until midnight. It was past two o'clock in the morning before Johann finally left the wards and staggered upstairs long after everyone else had gone to bed.

Once in his room, he shrugged out of his blood-smeared surgeon's coat, hanging it on a hook behind the door. It slipped off. He let it be. Already dirty, it would be none the worse for spending the night on the floor. It was expected to last a week between washings and he could only imagined what they'd say about that back in Berlin. But he didn't dwell on it. Wirchow's fastidious wards and his own pristine clinic were far, far away, both a fading memory. Peace, civilian life, were all but forgotten out here, existing only at night in short, sweet dreams that were quickly dispersed in the harsh reality each morning when new casualties were brought in.

His body throbbing with fatigue, Johann threw his military jacket over a chair and unbuckled his belt holding the required pistol. Loosening his collar, he glanced longingly in the direction of his bed, only to suddenly stiffen. He blinked and looked again. There was no light in the room except what the moon let in through a small slanted attic window. But narrowing his eyes, he could see well enough to make out a curve under the sheets. As he leaned closer and bent over the bed, his gaze fell on a head of short blond hair on the pillow.

"Nurse Hofmeyer!" he exclaimed, his gray eyes impaling the streamlined female form under the covers. For an instant, he believed he'd mistakenly walked into the wrong room, until he remembered that the nurses slept downstairs in only slightly more comfortable quarters than the orderlies enjoyed.

"Um . . ." she stirred, turned over, her eyes heavy with sleep; even so, Johann thought he'd never seen anyone look more appealing.

"Nurse Hofmeyer?" he repeated, his heart beating irregularly with this surprising windfall if, indeed, it was, because it was entirely possible that she had come into his room by mistake. The cheap wine served at the wedding celebration might have confused her.

She rose up on her elbows and as the blanket fell away, Johann sucked in his breath. The sight drugged his senses. He swallowed clumsily like a man wandering in the desert and finally coming upon a pool of fresh water.

"Nurse Hofmeyer," he uttered again and reached out to touch her bare shoulder to convince himself that she was not a mirage.

"Hush, Herr Doctor," she whispered, her soft mouth curving in a smile, his touch made something leap inside her. "There's no need to alert the entire hospital to my whereabouts."

Johann grinned at her, still grabbling with her unexpected presence in his room. He continued undressing. All at once, he wasn't the least bit tired.

Watching his every move, Olivia's pulse quickening at the sight of his hard and lean male body. She grinned. "Why don't we drop the Nurse Hofmeyer bit," she suggested coyly. "It's much too formal under these circumstances."

"I agree." Johann lifted the covers and slipped into the bed. "Except Olivia is much too melodic a name in this noisy place."

"Nights are quiet. Use it at night when we're alone." Her arms wrapped around him.

When we're alone? Her promise reverberated pleasantly in his mind and acted like an exquisite massage on his weary soul. His pledge to a year of celibacy took a battering as his body responded to her delightful invitation. He had no interest in resisting this alluring woman. His heart rate accelerated dangerously. He cursed middle age, the long dry spell, and although he was about to break his marriage vows, it caused him no qualm of conscience. His past life, Berlin, his family, were so far away that they seemed in another world, and his future in this one was not at all assured. Battle lines changed daily. A mortar shell could hit the hospital at any time, while any number of contagious diseases, for which there were no cures, could strike with similar results.

Johann concentrated on the present. Olivia was the present and she was offering him a lifeline to *mens sana* on this bleak and godless front where nothing mattered but the moment at hand because there might not be another.

Chapter 77

In December, in one of her weekly letters, Dorrit wrote that she had seen Hans while he was home on furlough. He was thin but otherwise well, had distinguished himself in battle and been promoted to first lieutenant. The remainder of her letter was dedicated to glowing reports about Max's and Fritz's exemplary behavior; reports Johann didn't believe. He suspected Dorrit embellished her accounts so as not to worry him. Especially since Max's letters were invariably full of complaints about his younger brother, while Fritz sent drawings of a violent nature.

In their Christmas correspondence to Johann, both Gerlinde and Karl-Heinz essentially repeated what Dorrit had already told him about Hans. In fact, their letters were so full of their son's wonderful home leave that they neglected to mention the twins. At the bottom of the page, Gerlinde added a poignant postscript: *Come January, Hans' battalion will be assigned to the Memel offensive along the Niemen River,* she wrote in her neat cramped hand. *I'm comforted knowing that you are nearby. Dearest Johann, please look out for him!*

Johann smiled wryly at Gerlinde's naive words. The front was enormous and the Niemen River was a thousand kilometers long. How could he possibly look out for Hans? Indeed, he hoped that he would never come across him out here because if he did, it would mean that Hans had been wounded.

Gerlinde's plea haunted Johann all that winter and whenever new casualties were carried in and he spotted a tuft of blond hair from beneath the spiked helmet, he felt an icy draft race through his heart until he removed the *Pickelhaube*, cleaned the grime from the face, and confirmed that the wounded man was, *Gott sei Dank*, not Hans.

Chapter 78

The war had passed the point of being a short war. Victory was not at hand. On the western front battles were at a stalemate, and to the east the front kept expanding, mortar shells becoming more numerous, their aim growing more deadly. Russian tactics improved with practice and they seemed to have a never-ending supply of troops.

In April, a year after arriving and the month during which Johann expected to be sent home, his replacement failed to arrive. So he stayed on, eventually spending his second summer at Kapsukas.

During the long, hot days of August the air around the hospital became permeated with the thick black smoke from artillery fire in nearby woods and fields. The fighting seemed to be deadlocked along this stretch because no sooner did the Germans advance, when they were pushed back. When the distant sound of combat was particularly persistent, extra beds were made ready for the wounded expected to arrive once the guns silenced at nightfall.

It was on one such day of incessant rumbling clashes creating vibrations that shook the infirmary to its foundation that Johann went to town for supplies. The chief provisions officer at headquarters, Captain Fellner, was a difficult man to deal with on a good day, and on this—an exceptionally bad day—it was Johann's poor luck to find the obnoxious man on duty.

Captain Fellner scanned the list Johann gave him. "I wish I could help you," he shrugged before handing it back. "None of these items are available."

"What?" This office had been a constant source of frustration for the hospital; Johann hadn't come here expecting a smooth ride or he would have sent an orderly.

"Thursday's shipment from Tannenberg hasn't arrived yet," Captain Fellner explained, leaning back in his chair and spreading his hands in a helpless gesture.

"Today is Saturday. Where are the trucks?"

"Still in transit."

"You mean the Russians have again ambushed our supplies."

"No. I'm saying they are late."

"And probably in the hands of the enemy."

"Herr Doctor, I didn't say that!"

"All right," Johann shrugged wearily. "I'll just sign for some morphine."

"*Ach!* The last of it was dispatched to the medics in the trenches."

Johann clenched his teeth but otherwise kept his temper in check, and of course he didn't begrudge the men in the trenches access to morphine. "You're telling me that you have no painkillers at all? *None?*"

"That's right."

Johann stared at Fellner in disbelief; this was a new low. "Well, as soon as the shipment arrives, please fill this requisition." He put the list down on the desk and turned to go. "I'll send an orderly to pick it up."

Captain Fellner suddenly remembered something. "Herr Doctor, wait a minute! You can't leave a list. You have to sign an itemized order form. We have new instructions from Berlin." Selecting some sheets from a pile on his desk, he held them out. "If you wish, you can do the paperwork now. It'll save time later."

That last comment spoke to Johann. He took the forms and sat down to attend to this bizarre new order. "Men are dying," he fumed, "and I'm doing paperwork!" His hand flew across the sheets as he filled in the hospital's requirements, copying from his original list and signing each page.

Captain Fellner wondered why a few forms should cause a fuss. "Let me assure you," he said to ease the tension in the room, "your hospital is not being singled out."

"I see. Just stymied with ridiculous regulations." Johann got up and handed over the finished forms.

"Ridiculous? Quite the contrary. These new forms are vital for fair and efficient distribution. We must account for everything. Supplies are becoming scarce and we're deluged with orders from the trenches." Captain Fellner pointed toward an impressive accumulation on his desk. "We are under immense pressure to get provisions to our men in the hinterlands where it's a matter of life and death."

"Supplying the hospital is also a matter of life and death," Johann said, knowing any sentiment was wasted on this man. He had been here often enough to know that this agent didn't consider the hospital a top priority. The wounded could no longer help determine the outcome of the war; therefore it was counterproductive to give them any consideration. It was more important to get supplies to the soldiers who could still make a difference.

Chapter 79

As Johann left the building, he made a snap decision and walked next door to the officers' canteen. If he had to wait for morphine until tomorrow, or until God knows when, he could at least try to get his hands on some brandy to ease his patients' suffering; otherwise this trip to town would have been a complete waste. Of course along with everything else, liquor was rationed, and as he tried to think of some subterfuge to get his hands on a couple of bottles, he realized it might help to display his uniform. Before entering the club, he removed his white surgeon's coat, leaving it outside the door on a woodpile bleached gray from sitting around all summer. Buttoning his military jacket neatly, he also decided to fake an injury; sympathy usually worked in one's favor.

It was early in the afternoon and the lounge was empty except for a burly corporal planted behind the counter, guarding the goods. Evenings this canteen came to life with a bevy of local girls, some serving as barmaids, others picking up extra change from lonely officers who didn't mind a tryst out back among beer crates and other debris. As Johann strolled toward the watchdog at the bar, he did so with an extravagant limp and a formulated pretext, not quite sure how he'd pull it off. But it was key to appear casual.

"I've come to pick up two bottles of brandy," he said, stepping up to the counter clad in green oilcloth battened down with a thousand thumbtacks. He hadn't seen this fellow before and he appeared to be easy game; a pronounced slackness around his mouth indicated borderline idiot. The army had a preponderance of the witless and they were generally kept away from the trenches where they'd be a danger to themselves and to everyone else.

"Brandy, Herr Major?" The corporal clicked his heels together. He'd been trained to recognize rank.

Johann nodded. "At ease!"

"Thank you, sir." The flesh bulging around the man's tight collar undulated as he relaxed his spine. "Did you say *two* bottles, sir?"

"Yes."

"I see. Uh, may I have your voucher, please?"

"Of course." Johann's mind raced to come up with some plausible reason for not having a voucher. This corporal might not be as cracked as he appeared. "Hmm . . ." He searched his pockets with feigned urgency. "Dammit! I know I have one."

"Actually, sir, I can check the ledger." The corporal was happy to oblige a high-ranking officer, and turned to reach for a thick book lying on a shelf, a book Johann was familiar with, one that would expose him. He could buy single drinks to be consumed on the premises, but couldn't get his hands on a whole bottle without a voucher or a notandum in the ledger. Liquor was becoming more precious to the army than ammunition, this corporal staked his pension on its safekeeping, and while Johann didn't begrudge officers their libation, he felt the numbing benefits of a good schnapps was better spent on wounded soldiers; a point he had argued with that brick wall Fellner many times and lost. Not even Herr Director Bergen could peel a voucher off Captain Fellner. A five-star general couldn't twist his arm.

General?

"Come to think of it, corporal, forget the ledger. I just remembered something. The bottles in question are not part of your regular inventory."

"Oh?" The man closed the ledger and turned around.

"It's from General Kinzl's private reserve," Johann lied without the slightest pang of conscience. "It's stored in the basement. We patched up his nephew last week. Saved the lad's life. The general was grateful and wanted to show his appreciation. He sent word this morning that a gift of brandy for the hospital had been set aside in the basement at headquarters."

The corporal looked confused and scratched the back of his considerable neck. The sergeant he'd relieved half an hour ago had not told him about this. But he *had* told him not to abandon his station, which would be viewed as dereliction of duty. He shifted his weight from one foot to the other, neither one was anxious to disobey an order.

"I'd get it myself, corporal, but I've suffered a recent knee injury," Johann persevered, counting on his initial appraisal that this fellow was a born fool. "Steps are out of the question." He removed his hat and limped over to a small round table where a chess game had been abandoned. He pulled out a chair, sat down, and massaged his knee with great ceremony while studying the black king's position. "To the basement, corporal. We haven't got all day." When the man still hesitated, Johann slapped the table, sending the chess pieces flying. "That's an order!"

"Yes sir!" The corporal snapped to attention. A major outranked a sergeant; still, the sergeant's order had been issued first. Which took priority? The corporal was confused. Everyone in the army gave orders, but no one explained anything. He finally decided that the sergeant was elsewhere and would never know if he left for a few minutes. "Uh, sir . . ." he said. "Before leaving my station, I'll have to lock the front door. Not to lock you in, of course, but to guard the entrance against, well, you know, against any unauthorized individual from the outside."

"You're a good man. Dedicated to your duty. See to it. Secure the premises."

"Thank you, sir."

No sooner had the corporal locked up, disappeared along a narrow hallway and started down the ladder to the basement, when Johann got out of his chair, went behind the bar counter and helped himself to two bottles of brandy and some rum for sterilizing instruments. Stuffing the flasks carefully into the inside pockets of his jacket, he rearranged the remaining stock so the theft would not be spotted immediately. Settling back into the chair, he again bent over the chessboard, righting the fallen pieces.

"Sir!" The corporal returned, puffing heavily from his climb up the steep ladder. "I didn't find the brandy. There's nothing down there but spiders." He brushed at the cobwebs clinging to his uniform.

"That's odd." Johann frowned. "The general's message specifically said that his private stock was stored in the basement at headquarters, away from the heat of the day." Although now anxious to leave, Johann forced himself to get up slowly, grimacing convincingly as he put weight on his 'bad' knee.

"A proper place for spirits," the corporal agreed, pursing his fleshy lips. Suddenly lightning struck his small brain. "Say . . . you know what, sir? I'll bet the general meant the basement next door. This officers' canteen is part of headquarters, but not really. If you know what I mean?"

"Hmm, you make a good a point, corporal. I'll check it out." Johann crossed the floor, holding his hat in front of his chest to help hide the bulges under his jacket. "Sorry to have bothered you," he said, waiting at the door for the corporal to unlock it.

As Johann limped away, snatching his surgeon's coat from the woodpile, he almost collided with a couple of lieutenants on their way to the canteen. They saluted him smartly and glanced at his 'war injury' with a flicker of sympathy.

Once he was out of view, Johann walked briskly and somewhat ashamed, next door to where he had parked the hospital's motor lorry. Imagine, being reduced to lying and thievery. Of course, one did odd things in times of war; surely this ranked among lesser sins. Besides, the contraband was not for personal use but as a substitute for basic supplies. Basic? Actually, in all fairness to crab grass Fellner, Ben Tarnoff had recently written that both morphine and ether were in short supply in Berlin as well.

"Damn!" Johann swore out loud. "Damn this useless war!" He gripped the steering wheel in a chokehold, his white knuckles straining against the skin. Revving the motor angrily, he pulled out into the road. As soon as he was free of town traffic, he shifted into neutral and cut the engine. The rest of the way was downhill. He could coast. Everyone was under strict orders to conserve petrol.

Chapter 80

It *was autumn and* by October, casualties along the eastern battle lines were pushing toward catastrophic levels. As the number of fighting men dwindled, bulletins reached all field hospitals, mandating that convalescing soldiers able to walk and carry a rifle, be reassigned to full duty. With that new order, the staff at Kapsukas found little to cheer about when a man recovered. It was earnestly hoped that the fighting would stop before any of their patients became repeats.

The last day of October dawned to a blue sky without a single cloud. As the sun rose, the crumbling brick facade of the hospital gleamed pink in its splendid blush. At daybreak the air was crisp but by midmorning it had turned soothingly warm with the last embrace of a season, *sui generis*, and reluctant to depart. However, before the sun was to set on this benign autumn day, Johann was to be vanquished and feel pain as if he'd been bludgeoned. If he believed that he had experienced the worst at this wretched outpost, he was sadly mistaken.

Due to an inordinate number of casualties deposited on the hospital's doorstep the evening before, he had been in the wards until three in the morning, and no staff member was sufficiently heartless to rouse him at five o'clock for his regular rounds. At seven, he awoke to a beam of sunlight penetrating the slanted attic window and focusing itself on his pillow with prickly heat. From habit he swatted the air before realizing that the tickle was not from the flies that regularly kept everyone company, but rather from the unfamiliar light of the sun, unfamiliar because he always rose well ahead of it.

Turning over, Johann checked his watch and jumped out of bed in a rush of guilt. He made his way down to the one bath shared by all, entertaining little hope there'd be enough hot water for an adequate shower. There wasn't. In his frustration, after suffering a cold trickle, he dropped the only towel available; it fell onto the floor where it promptly absorbed a puddle. Shivering, Johann sought relief in a string of hot curses, struggled into his uniform, and left the lavatory in a distinctly foul mood. He grabbed a white surgeons coat from a closet in the hall outside Ward B and threw the old one into the bin even though it was supposed to have lasted another two days. Thrusting his arms into the sleeves, he put the stethoscope around his neck and entered the infirmary, ready for another twenty-hour day. The nuns were in the process of removing the breakfast trays, some of which were barely touched.

"What's this?" Johann frowned at the plates of black bread with a dollop of bacon grease, accompanied by one hard-boiled egg and something resembling applesauce. "Is the breakfast not to our patients' liking today?"

"Oh, it's not that, Herr Doctor," one of the nuns whispered. "Some of the amputees became hysterical when they woke and discovered the events of yesterday weren't just a bad dream. They lost their appetite."

"Well, that'll never do. Without nourishment, how do they expect to recover?"

"I believe most would rather die here than go home so horribly crippled."

"Something we can't allow," Johann said, ordering the women to take the food back into the ward. "Force feed the men if necessary and account for each and every utensil." He eyed the senior nun, reminding her to be on the lookout for suicides. Ever since the night when a distraught soldier had rammed a fork down his throat, strangling in his own blood, all flatware was carefully collected and counted after each meal.

Nurse Hofmeyer appeared at Johann's side with a cup of coffee. She knew his routine: coffee first, breakfast after his rounds.

"Good morning," she smiled, surreptitiously touching her lips to the rim of the cup as she handed it to him.

Accepting the veiled kiss with a wink, Johann wondered if anyone suspected their affair, or were aware of her regular visits to his room. But, taking a sip of the coffee, he dismissed any and all pleasant musings and began his examinations, starting with a new patient in the bed nearest the door, a soldier who had apparently just been admitted. His face, streaked with tears, was turned toward the cot next to him where a young man lay dead with a gaping hole in his pelvic. He had not lived long enough to have his chart filled in. Two orderlies, unfolding a waterproof sheet, were preparing to remove him. Space was at a premium. The dead were not allowed to linger.

"I'm sorry we couldn't do anything for your friend," Johann said as he bent over the sobbing boy; a gash in his shoulder was ugly but not life threatening.

"He . . . he's . . . n . . . not my friend."

"Oh?"

"He's m . . . my . . . kid brother."

Johann felt a painful twinge in his chest. "In that case, I am doubly sorry," he said. "Now we'd better get you on your feet quickly so you can go home and be a comfort to your parents." As he examined the shoulder wound, he decided that he would discharge this particular patient with an incapacitating internal injury to make sure that he was sent home, not back to the trenches.

Chapter 81

As Johann made his way to yet another cot, a strange crawling sensation on the back of his neck caused an icy shiver to run up his spine. He took another swig of coffee, hoping it would chase the chill. But even as he drank the wonderful black liquid, the only commodity that for some reason hadn't become scarce yet, he was overcome with an odd foreboding and the feeling he was hearing voices. Of course, after a year and a half of this grueling duty, no sleep, little food, his mind could easily be playing tricks on him. He gave himself a mental shake, put his cup down on a surgical tray, and bent over yet another new patient, one he instantly diagnosed with the dreaded and extremely infectious cholera.

"Why in God's name was this man brought in here?" he said aghast, turning a fierce expression on a nurse changing the dressing on a wound of the soldier in the adjacent bed. "This patient must be quarantined!"

"The isolation rooms are full, Herr Doctor," she said.

"Make space somewhere else then! Clear the storage room!"

"Uncle Johann?"

"Huh?" There was that voice again. As Johann turned toward it, his heart slammed against his rib cage with such violence his lungs emptied of air.

"It's me...over h...here..."

Hans? Johann's lips moved, but no sound came as he walked drunkenly toward the voice, thrown off balance by the thought that Hans had landed in this ward. Making his way around pallets and basins, all the while praying his mind was failing him rather than to discover the voice was real, he stopped by a cot and stared at the young man occupying it. Of course this could still be a mistake, a cruel optical trick brought on by a myriad of deprivations. But as he looked at the patient, wishing him to be a stranger, Johann couldn't disclaim what he saw. It was Hans Konauer. For agonizing moments he studied the gaunt, dirty face with the achingly familiar features distorted by trauma. Hans' blue eyes, black and hollow, were searching the surroundings with a frantic urgency as if it was growing too dark to see.

"Uncle Johann . . . is . . . is it really you?" Again the question formed on the thin pellucid lips stretched across teeth protruding unnaturally, presaging death.

Reaching for a limp hand and fighting to keep his voice steady, Johann bent down. "Yes, Hans. It's me. I'm right here."

The young man smiled weakly, his body relaxed, he closed his eyes, his ashen face becoming a mask of contentment as if he suddenly felt safe and free of pain. In the next instant he lost consciousness.

Johann checked for a pulse but the loud drumming within his own chest interfered with a proper reading. "Hofmeyer!" he barked, dispensing with all professional courtesy. "Over here! At once!" It was clear he wanted no one else.

Barreling her way through the maze of cots, picking up instruments, gauze, and a bucket of clean water as she went, Nurse Hofmeyer arrived at the new patient's bed, every pocket in her uniform rattling with instruments, her apron bulging with bandages hastily tucked into the strings. Had the situation not been so tragic, Johann would have smiled at the sight of her.

"Help me cut away his clothes!" he said, his mind still reeling with the seriousness of Hans' injuries. The wound in his hip had been poorly dressed in the field, using a dirty shirt, probably ripped from a dead soldier.

"This patient was brought in early this morning," Olivia Hofmeyer explained as she took a pair of scissors and set about the all too familiar task of cutting through a bloodied uniform. Knowing the young man had lost consciousness and couldn't hear her, she added, "Dr. Bergen gave him a bit of morphine and told us not to bother with him because he wouldn't last an hour. Another patient with similarly wounds has already died."

Johann nodded; he had seen the dead youth.

"Do you want him moved to the operating room?" In view of Dr. Bergen's diagnosis, Olivia wondered why Dr. von Renz was fussing over this hopeless case.

"No. He can't be moved." Removing the crude bandage, Johann cleaned the gash in Hans' side. "I'll have to work on him here. Please bring some iodine and more water. And whatever painkillers you can get your hands on." Johann's eyes traveled the length of the bed to the two limbs under the blood-soaked sheet. "Once I've closed his hip wound, I'll take a look at his legs. If they're as bad as I suspect, he'll be a burning mass of pain when the morphine wears off." Johann reached into his pockets to confirm he had enough sutures for the task ahead.

Nurse Hofmeyer left to fetch the needed items. She returned moments later with everything but the morphine. "Dr. Bergen is guarding it with his life," she said, peeling off the sheet and whatever was left of the uniform around the patient's legs. "He promised to bring it personally in a few minutes."

"Very well." Johann shrugged, long since resigned to the scarcity of critical supplies. Anyway, Hans was unconscious and would feel no pain for the time being.

Johann examined the shattered legs. Pieces of fabric were fused to scorched flesh and both limbs had white bone slivers protruding through the burnt tissue. He exhaled in defeat, wiped his bloodied hands negligently on his white coat, his shoulders sinking along with any optimism he might have entertained moments ago. He sat down heavily on a three-legged stool next to the bed and stared disbelievingly at the mangled mess. No medical miracle known to man in 1916 could mend such damage and this sorry hospital didn't even have an X-ray machine.

"Do you want to amputate?" Olivia asked quietly.

"No. It'll cause him needless suffering and won't save his life. The pelvic wound alone is fatal. He has lost too much blood. It's a wonder he's still alive."

Dr. Bergen came by with the morphine. "Do you know this lad?" he asked, seeing his colleague's stricken face.

"Yes." Johann's voice broke. He cleared his throat awkwardly and dismissed Nurse Hofmeyer with a quick nod. "He is like a son to me."

Dr. Bergen handed him the narcotic. "Use as much as you want," he said and walked away, knowing he could afford to be generous. That young man wouldn't last long enough to make a dent in the morphine.

Chapter 82

Although it was futile, Johann continued to work on Hans, clamping blood vessels, setting leg bones, and fishing out bomb fragments and small stones. He couldn't give up. He couldn't just sit idly by and watch him die. He contemplated double amputation; this in spite of the fact that Hans wouldn't survive the trip to the operating room.

Hans gained momentary consciousness.

Johann reached for the damp rag hanging at the foot of each bed and wiped his hands before fingering the precious vial of morphine in his pocket. But Hans made no sounds signaling pain. He merely looked around the room in confusion before focusing on the person sitting next to his bed. Suddenly he smiled.

"Uncle Johann? I . . . I can't see clearly. Is it really you?"

"Yes." Johann reached for a cold lifeless hand, squeezing it gently to reassure him. "I'm here and I'll stay with you. I've patched you up a bit. You need to rest. Once you've gained some strength I'll go to work on you in earnest." Hating himself for the cheap promises, he hoped Hans was unaware of the condition of his legs and motioned a nun to replace the blood-soaked sheet with a clean one. Thankfully, she was quick about it.

"I'm a mess, huh?" Hans mumbled, sensing the nun's activity.

"Oh, I don't know. I've seen worse." Fighting a storm of emotions, Johann tried to keep his voice light. He touched the back of his hand tenderly to the young face and ran his fingers through the matted blond hair.

"I can't believe my luck."

"Luck?" Johann straightened in the chair.

"Yes. Finding you here. I heard you talking. I recognized your voice but thought I was dreaming because it seemed too good to be true. An old fellow in a white coat slipped me some bitter stuff. Opium, I guess. It made me feel strange. I figured I was hallucinating."

"You weren't."

"I know." Hans smiled before suddenly grabbing at Johann's arm in panic. "Since the opium, I haven't been able to feel my legs. They're still there . . . aren't they?" He tugged at the sheet covering him. "I . . . I still have my legs. Don't I?"

"Yes." Johann helped Hans raise his head and pointed to the outlines under the sheet.

Exhausted from his outburst, Hans sank back down on the pillow. A moment later, as if there existed an urgency to talk, he pulled some air into his lungs and continued to speak despite a gurgling in his chest. "Russians . . ." he said, struggling for every word, "came out of the dark woods like riled boars. They'd shelled our positions for some twelve hours yesterday. We didn't expect to hear from them again before daylight. But there they were. We didn't even have time to shoot off a Verey light. Still, we held them off. They eventually retreated and left some dead friends in front of our trenches. One of them, not as dead as his comrades, blew himself up when we approached to sweep the area for wounded."

"Blew himself up?"

"He had a shell and probably believed we were coming to finish him off. I thought the explosion got my legs."

Johann swallowed past a tight obstruction in his throat. He was remembering a boy, a happy lad with straw-colored hair and sturdy legs, riding a pony around the field by the unfinished terrace, hollering, "Watch me! Watch me!" Laughing into the wind, Hans had urged the animal on without using the crop.

"Uncle Johann?"

"Yes?"

"You were right."

"Right about what?"

"The university . . ." Hans' voice rattled; blood was collecting in his throat; Johann recognized the sound, there wasn't much time left. "Did you know there were days during these past months when I wished I'd followed your advice and signed up for the university instead of the army?"

"You'd be in the war now regardless, Hans. Everybody is being mobilized. The universities have emptied. From *Realschule* and on up. As you can see, I'm here, too; proof they're tapping even the old."

"You're not so old," Hans grinned and closed his eyes. Conversation taxed him. Johann heard his raspy struggle for air. "I'm c . . . cold . . ." he murmured a moment later; pink bubbles and trickles of blood were seeping between his lips.

260

Johann reached for a folded blanket at the foot of the bed and spread it over him, knowing it wouldn't help. "Do you have any pain?" he asked, gently swabbing the corners of Hans' mouth with some gauze.

"No. I'm just c . . . cold . . . and it's so dark. What time is it? Is it . . . is it late?" Hans' eyes were wide open, groping the surroundings like a blind man. "Is it late?" he persisted, as if the time of day was suddenly very important to him.

Johann couldn't find it in his heart to tell him that it was midmorning and a pleasant October sun was bathing the entire ward in a cheerful yellow glow. Obviously, Hans could neither see nor feel it. "It is quite late," he sufficed and took the cold hands in his.

"Uncle Johann?"

"Yes?"

"Don't tell mother what happened to me. Tell her I took a bullet . . . clean . . . quick. I can't bear for her to know the mess I'm in. Please don't tell her."

"All right." Johann pressed the waxy hands and realized Hans knew he was dying.

"Tell grandfather . . . I . . . I was in line for another promotion."

"I will tell him. I'll tell everyone. They'll be so proud of you." Johann tightened his grip on the young hands, hands that had shrunk and felt dry as parchment as if only a thin layer of skin covered the bones.

"I was due for another furlough . . . soon . . . only a few more weeks. I wish I was going home . . ."

Johann stroked the troubled brow. "You will, Hans. You'll go home. I promise you."

Hans smiled queerly. "It'll be so peaceful at home . . . so quiet. It'll be winter soon. I wonder if my sisters will remember to . . . to . . ."

"Feed the birds," Johann finished for him, remembering Hans' elaborate feeding stations.

Hans struggled for more words that wouldn't come. His opaque eyes settled on Johann. A gush of blood poured from his mouth and ran like a sticky red ribbon down into the small of his neck. His head sank heavily into the pillow.

Johann reached out and touched his face. He ran his hand lovingly over the blond hair, brushing it back from the traumatized forehead. Then he brought his fingers down and gently closed Hans' eyes.

Chapter 83

For endless moments Johann sat in quiet, paralyzing disbelief before he finally and with unaccustomed difficulty rose. He was bone tired, couldn't straighten his shoulders, and his legs shook as he fled the ward, wanting nothing more than to pound his fists into the plaster walls. Once in the privacy of the lavatory he washed the blood from his hands, scrubbing them until they were raw and smarted, punishing them for their uselessness. He returned to the infirmary and went directly to the cot where he had left Hans. Another man occupied it.

"Where is Lieutenant Konauer?" he barked at the two orderlies who had just brought in the new patient.

"He's dead, sir."

"I know that! Where is he?"

The orderlies eyed him weirdly. "We . . . uh, we took him outside for burial as per regulations, Herr Doctor. We needed the bed."

"Damn you!" Johann said hoarsely, pushing past the men. "I just promised him that he could go home!"

The orderlies' eyebrows shot up. *Go home?* This doctor had finally flipped. After watching him run from the premises, they immediately went in search of Herr Director to warn him of trouble.

Johann caught up with the funeral possession—a nun and two local male volunteers—a short distance from the hospital. He ordered everyone back to the building. Hans was going home. Deathbed promises were sacred. Johann could not go back on his word. Besides, he had to consider Gerlinde. The thought of her receiving the tragic news was not a pretty picture, but if she could at least have the small comfort of seeing her son laid to rest in Bernau, it might help ease her grief.

Hans' body was being placed on the floor inside the hall just as Dr. Bergen rushed from a rear operating room, armed with a syringe, ready to restrain his colleague.

"What's the procedure for having a body returned to Germany?" Johann asked, cocking an eyebrow at the weapon in Herr Director's hand. "You can put that thing away. I haven't gone berserk. Only God-knows-why."

Relieved to find that the orderlies had exaggerated any bizarre behavior, Dr. Bergen capped the syringe, saying, "There's no policy or procedure. It can't be done."

"Surely some bodies are returned."

"None that I've heard of. We haven't got the manpower or the vehicles."

"Vehicles? I'm talking about *one* body."

"One or a dozen. It makes no difference. I don't have to tell you that corpses deteriorate rapidly. Long distance transport poses a health hazard."

"Well, Lieutenant Konauer is going home and I'm going to headquarters to make the arrangements. Make sure no one buries the body before I return."

"All right," Dr. Bergen shrugged. "But I don't know what you expect from headquarters. They're only going to repeat what I said. As you know, they're not especially receptive to our regular demands. I can only imagine how they'll react to an unreasonable one."

"We'll see." Johann turned on his heel and went outside, leaving the older doctor in the hall, shaking his head.

Chapter 84

Fortunately, no one was using the hospital's motor lorry. Johann got in behind the wheel, gunned the engine, and drove to town in a plume of dust. Speed was imperative. Guilt for abandoning the wounded propelled him, and record setting minutes later he screeched to a halt in front of headquarters. In his hurry he'd forgotten to remove his blood stained surgeon's coat, the stethoscope was still dangling around his neck, and the wind in the open car had given his hair a life of its own. However, he was so fixed on his mission that he was unaware of the appalling sight he presented as he barged through the doors.

"Where can I find the person in charge of transportation?" he wheezed to the sergeant on duty at the front desk.

The man eyed the doctor's bloodied attire and decided that calm discretion was called for. Rumors abounded that things were not terrific at the hospital. This individual confirmed it. "Do you have an appointment, Herr Doctor?" he asked with a patronizing smile.

"That's ridiculous! Of course not!"

"Then, please take a seat." The sergeant pointed to a hard-backed chair in the corner. "I'll see if *Hauptfeldwebel* Mannheim is free at the moment."

"Free?" Glaring at the man, Johann tossed out a few choice words, pushed past him and walked down the corridor, reading signs as he went. He'd been here before. Captain Fellner, held court here. Christ Almighty! An appointment?

"Herr Doctor!" The sergeant was panting at his heels. "You cannot pass along this hall unannounced!"

"Then I suggest you return to your station and announce me. I'm Dr. von Renz."

The man slowed his steps, unsure about how to deal with this. He couldn't very well create a scene by blowing his whistle, nor could he pull out his revolver; after all, this was a fellow citizen and no crime had been committed. Not yet anyway. Turning, he ran back to his desk to ring Mannheim and alert him.

Johann found *Hauptfeldwebel* Mannheim's door and walked in without knocking. The man, telephone to his ear, was seated at a cluttered desk; the wall behind him was hung with military maps freckled with colored pins. Radio equipment standing on a table by the window gave further proof of his importance.

"Ah, Dr. von Renz?" Mannheim replaced the receiver in its cradle, pushed back his chair, stood up and extended his hand, hoping that idiot sergeant out front had gotten this man's name right. Mannheim had no contact with the hospital, didn't know any of the doctors, and was content to keep it that way. "What can I do for you?" Too late he realized his visitor was also an officer; the white surgeon's coat obscured his uniform, something that had obviously escaped that incompetent sergeant out front. Belatedly executing a salute, Mannheim walked from behind his desk to pull out a chair for his caller.

Johann ignored the offer to sit and remained standing. "I have come to arrange transportation for a young lieutenant," he said. "He died this morning in my care and I wish to have his body returned to Germany."

"I see." Having reclaimed his seat behind the desk, Mannheim leaned forward on his elbows and crimped his forehead in an attempt to appear sympathetic. "I'm terribly sorry," he said, "but as you know, that's impossible." Placing his hands together, fingertips to fingertips, he formed a steeple against his chin and squinted in a further display of compassion. "For obvious reasons, our fallen heroes are buried where they die. Of course, we make every effort to send personal belongings home. If you have any special wishes regarding the possessions of the deceased, I'll be happy to handle the matter expeditiously."

Suddenly incredibly tired, Johann sat down. "I did not leave my patients to discuss a watch or a wallet," he said tersely. "I am here to ask you to make an exception in this one case. Naturally, I am prepared to reimburse the army for the expense incurred."

"Herr Doctor, I regret that we cannot make an exception. We don't transport bodies and the military does not accept payment from private individuals. Nor does it cater to personal whims and concerns. We are bound by regulations. If we allowed one body to go home, every family in Germany would demand the same privilege. Our trains would become moving morgues. Imagine the chaos . . ."

Johann rose menacingly; this had been a torturous morning and now this pompous ass was being overbearing. "Don't lecture me!" he said, placing his palms on the desk. "Especially not about chaos. It's something I'm quite familiar with. It's alive and well at the hospital. About the only thing that is. And spare me your precious regulations. Captain Fellner has covered that territory *ad infinitum*. If our hospital had one canister of ether for every twenty useless regulations we've complied with, our entire infirmary would be airborne. This post is rife with inefficiency and hollow promises and has yet to supply the hospital with adequate rations, food, medicine or otherwise. The only thing we get plenty of is paperwork."

Mannheim stood up to gain some ground on this tall intruder. "May I remind you, Herr Doctor, that we here at headquarters suffer shortages as well but manage with what we have. Our orders are to secure the front. With our bare hands if necessary. Though rationed, we are doing an excellent job."

"I invite you to inspect the hospital," Johann said. "You might arrive at a different conclusion."

The transportation officer ignored the galling remark and sat back down, idly shuffling some papers. "There's nothing more to be said. You'll have to excuse me. I really must get back to work. Urgent projects need my attention."

"In that case, I insist on speaking with someone of higher consequence."

Hauptfeldwebel Mannheim winced. "In this department, I'm that person," he said between clenched teeth. "My word is final. While your appeal for the deceased lieutenant is commendable, I must repeat that it is completely out of the question. I am in charge of transporting troops. Live troops. I'm bound by my duty." He threw his shoulders back so the stubborn doctor could have a clear view of the citations decorating his chest. "It would require an imperial decree from Berlin to waive my orders."

Imperial decree? Mouthing the words, Johann was struck by a thought so timely it made him weak in the knees. He sat back down. He just might have Hans' ticket home. Now was the time to cash-in a chit. Why hadn't he thought of that before degrading himself arguing with this individual preening behind a chest full of medals? Years ago, following the throat surgery, Kaiser Wilhelm declared he was in Johann's debt and always greeted him with a wink and exceptional warmth at palace functions. Only Dorrit received a warmer reception because Wilhelm was known to have an eye for beautiful women. But he was also known to have a keen memory and it was safe to assume that as the consummate sovereign he would act upon a favor owed.

"Sergeant Major."

Mannheim looked up.

"I'd like to send a cable."

"A cable? Certainly. Right away." Mannheim picked up the telephone and shouted into the mouthpiece. Somebody at the other end must have jumped, because he had barely replaced the receiver when a wire operator presented himself and walked over to the radio equipment at the window. Sitting down, he clicked in the origination code and waited for the message, his finger poised on the button.

Johann cleared his throat, got up and braced his hands on the back of his chair. "Your Imperial Majesty . . ." he began, formulating his words carefully, keeping them to the minimum required for a telegram, "Kaiser Wilhelm."

The room became a tomb. The wire operator jerked his finger away from the apparatus as if he'd been burned. Mannheim's chair creaked, disturbing the eerie silence, as he tilted forward to stare, flabbergasted, at the brazen doctor.

"Is this some sort of a joke?" he demanded, rising from his seat with an exaggerated effort. "I have no time for games, Herr Doctor." He was turning puce with anger at being taken for a fool. "I am a very busy man. You will please not abuse my patience."

"I must ask you not to abuse mine," Johann countered. "Any interruption will only serve to keep us both from getting back to work."

The fight went out of *Hauptfeldwebel* Mannheim. He slumped back into his chair. "Do you actually know His Majesty?" he asked with a sneer that said he wouldn't believe anything other than a plain and honest no.

"Well enough."

"I see." Mannheim was not surprised with the evasive answer. He motioned for the operator to proceed. What else could he do? His visitor outranked him.

Johann picked up where he had left off. "Respectfully request permission to transport body of Lieutenant Hans Konauer from Kapsukas to Bernau. Speed is crucial. Will await reply at this communications station. Signed Major Johann von Renz, M.D."

As the machine clicked, Johann wondered if Wilhelm would respond to something he might consider a trifling matter. The Kaiser had a raging war on his hands. There was a good chance this telegram would never come to his attention; it risked being buried under the weight of more important messages.

Chapter 85

Hauptfeldwebel Mannheim remained at his desk, drumming his fingers on the blotter, long after his visitor and the wire operator were gone. How had he allowed this von Renz character get the better of him and corner him into sending a bogus wire? To the Kaiser yet! There would be dire repercussions and he would be held responsible because the cable originated from his office. Berlin would not ignore such a prank. Heads would roll. This might be as bad as going AWOL.

That afternoon, when the radio apparatus began clicking, *Hauptfeldwebel* Mannheim summoned the wire operator and stood by perspiring profusely, praying it was a routine war memorandum, not an order to present himself before a military tribunal.

It was not the latter; neither was it by any means routine, far from it. The communiqué was from the Imperial Palace on Unter den Linden and was addressed to Baron Johann Maximilian von Renz. *Baron?* Mannheim tore the strip of paper from the machine. The message was short and explicit:

"Wire received. Permission granted. At the direct pleasure of Wilhelm II space on convoy for the remains of Lieutenant Konauer will be made available. Headquarters at Kapsukas are ordered to comply. Signed Rudolf Breckt, personal secretary to His Imperial Majesty."

Mannheim didn't realize he was holding his breath until he exhaled in a subdued whistle. "Well. I'll be damned!" he mumbled to the wire operator. "No wonder that doctor was so sure of himself. He knows the Kaiser!"

Mannheim took the telegram to the sergeant at the front desk. "Deliver this to the hospital at once," he said. "And have *Oberst* Fuchs send the standard notification of death to the family of Lieutenant Hans Konauer. Tell him to add that the body will be returned home for burial."

"It will? I don't understand."

"You don't have to. It's an imperial order." Mannheim pivoted on his heel and went outside to personally ensure that a vehicle could be on its way to Tannenberg in time to catch the night train to Germany.

And so Hans went home.

Johann would be eternally grateful to Nurse Hofmeyer who, in her resourceful ways, managed to procure a uniform—previously worn—but one that had belonged to a soldier who had died from a single gunshot wound. After carefully cleaning the spot, Olivia patched the hole where the bullet had entered, added Hans' lieutenant stripes to the epaulets, then dressed him, washed his face, and combed his tangled hair. As Hans was placed into the pine coffin delivered from headquarters, Johann commented on the pains she'd taken.

"You are a marvel," he said to her as they stood in front of the hospital, now watching the lorry lumber away, balancing its grim cargo.

"He would want to look good for his parents," Olivia said quietly.

Suddenly and without caring if the entire hospital bore witness, Johann took her into his arms. Standing by the water pump in the yard in broad daylight, he held her in a lovers' embrace. "I adore you," he whispered.

That evening, he wrote a long and difficult letter to Gerlinde and Karl-Heinz. He also wrote Dorrit, suggesting that she leave the boys in Berlin for a few days. "Go out to Bernau . . ." he urged her. "Spend some time with Gerlinde."

Chapter 86

Johann spent another Christmas, such as it were, at Kapsukas. However, since his confrontation with *Hauptfeldwebel* Mannheim, the hospital's food rations improved somewhat and medical supplies became almost adequate.

When two cases of wine were delivered to the wards for the holiday feast, Herr Director Bergen began to seriously ponder the change. With a few carefully placed queries around headquarters, he soon learned that a surgeon at the hospital enjoyed direct access to Kaiser Wilhelm. Inasmuch as Dr. Bergen was a widower from Hamburg with little to enjoy except four grandchildren, and since Dr. Stocker was a garden-variety intern from Bonn with positively no ties to royalty, it didn't take much mental juggling to figure out who did.

January was particularly brutal this year, and February—a short month—dragged its feet, prolonging the icy misery till it seemed the longest month of all. The sky was uniformly pewter and the ground frozen solid, providing a bleak winter landscape where naked, brittle trees groaned in the wind; a befitting sound in this mournful, war-ravaged environment.

Gravediggers had worked diligently during autumn to assure that an adequate number of pits were dug before the ground became rock solid. Even so it wasn't enough. Toward the end of the winter, soldiers went to their eternal rest, en masse, in old bomb craters, their bodies covered by handfuls of pine needles and chunks of dirt pried loose from the lip of the hollows. Still, it was with more dignity than that given those who fell on the battlefields, where the enemy's equipment rolled over the immobile wounded and the dead alike; burying them democratically under tire tracks of ice and snow.

In March of 1917, German battalions advanced to within two hundred miles of Moscow. The Russian plum was within reach, yet there was guarded optimism in Berlin. Reinforcements were needed to keep the lines behind the advancing troops secure, but the men fighting on the western front could not be spared. Furthermore, there was heated talk in military quarters that the United States was about to enter the war, joining up with England and France, which would prove catastrophic for the Kaiser's tired forces.

Chapter 87

A *frigid day in March*, a day as gray as granite and as unyielding, found Johann walking out from the woods behind the hospital, where yet another casualty had gone to his eternal reward in a crater atop the frozen bodies of those who had preceded him. Since that day last October, since Hans' death, Johann had made a habit of accompanying the body of any man who died in his care to its final resting place. A nun—a hurried prayer on her lips—and two orderlies bored with their repetitive task, seemed too callous a ceremony, too small a cortege, for someone who had laid down his life for his country. Determined to lend some dignity to each sad event, Johann followed these funeral processions in full uniform, frequently remaining behind at the gravesite in silent meditation after the others had fled back to the warmth of the hospital building.

However, on this particular day in March, he couldn't linger. Icy gusts of wind whistled through the trees, whipping at his coat and herding splintered tree branches over the rimy crust covering the forest floor. The temperature was such that a deep breath could prove fatal. Blinking against the biting cold to keep his eyelids from freezing shut, Johann bent his head, turned away from the grave, and followed behind the others as they headed back in the direction of shelter. He was just rounding the far corner of the hospital, when he heard the robust roar of a motor lorry coming along the road from town.

"Crazy fool!" he muttered irritably; petrol was scarcer than ever. "Cut the engine and coast, *dammit!*" He was preparing to give the driver a piece of his mind.

The lorry came to a halt in the yard by the old water pump glistening in a new layer of ice, which made it look shiny, giving the false impression that it was brand new. Approaching, Johann recognized the driver, a chap from headquarters, as he jumped out to assist the passenger with his luggage.

Passenger?

Johann stopped dead in his tracks. There was something familiar about the passenger and—in spite of the danger of losing both feet to frostbite—he didn't move. He remained in place, studying the black hair, the solid shoulders, the confident stance and expensive cut of his coat. That man was from Berlin.

Suddenly Johann broke into a sprint. "Kurt!" he shouted, painfully aware of the gulps of frozen air he inhaled. "What in God's name are you doing out here? Don't tell me you volunteered?"

"Afraid so," Kurt laughed as the two friends embraced, slapping each other soundly on their respective backs.

Johann pulled away and gawked at Kurt Eckart; the sight of someone from home took the sting out of the wind; he felt almost warm.

"I weakened under pressure," Kurt explained, taking his bags from the driver and preparing to follow Johann inside. "It was becoming increasingly difficult to go out in public without being mentally flogged for nonparticipation in the war effort. Besides, I was told they needed some competent talent out here."

Johann laughed. It felt incredibly good. It had been so long since he'd laughed that he had all but forgotten the wonderful rippling sensation that went with it.

"Sorry it took me so long." Kurt eyed his friend; Johann had aged, he looked gaunt and, though in full uniform, peculiarly unkempt. "Actually, you can thank Lillian. She insisted I relieve you. It seems she could no longer enjoy Dorrit's company. All she ever wanted to do was read your letters aloud. Lillian was sick of it. No offense, my friend, you have a good pen but my wife prefers cheerful prose. I got this assignment only days ago. There wasn't time to alert you. Personally, I'd rather have gone west, of course. Temperate weather. Closer to home. Regular furloughs. But like I said, Lillian forced this particular placement on me."

"I always knew her to be a peach," Johann said, and meant it.

"No hard feelings at being abandoned out here for so long?"

"That depends on what you're referring to."

It was Kurt's turn to laugh. He laughed till he choked. "Say, how long has it been?"

"Two years."

Looking at the depressing surroundings, Kurt sobered. He had yet to set foot inside the hospital.

Chapter 88

Johann left Kapsukas on the next convoy bound for Tannenberg and the train to Berlin. It had not been difficult to say his good-byes, except to Olivia Hofmeyer.

Bent over his gear, he turned and looked up from his packing, surprised, the morning of his departure when she slipped into his room for a private moment. Closing the door behind her, she leaned against it, holding on to the knob. She figured she had three minutes before they'd miss her downstairs.

Johann took her into his arms. "Olivia, I'll never forget you. I will write . . ."

"No!" she said, pulling away.

"But I need to know that you're safe. God knows how much longer the war will last."

"Letters are not a good idea, Johann. I don't want your wife to learn about us. No harm's been done. Let's keep it that way. Besides, I'll be too busy."

"Too busy to write a few words?"

Nodding, she grinned sheepishly. "I'll be busy convincing Dr. Bergen to marry me."

"What?"

"I am planning to marry Herr Director."

"You are?"

"Yes. It has occurred to me that I'd like some security . . . some happiness once the war is over. I'm tired of fending for myself. I want a husband and the proverbial mountain cottage with a view. And I want some children. Not my own, of course. It's a bit late for that. But Dr. Bergen has four grandchildren and they'll do me fine. I'm sure they'll like to visit us in the Alps. If not, we'll spend time in his apartment in Hamburg where he's rattling around in seven rooms. It's a pity to be alone in such a big place, don't you agree?"

"I suppose so."

"You and I had no future, Johann. I've never kidded myself about that. It's different with Dr. Bergen. He's a widower. He's alone. He and I can build a life together. I respect him, which is a good start. In time I will grow to love him. I've worked with him long enough to know that underneath his gruff demeanor, he's a gentleman. I'm forty-four. Past the age where men fall for me."

"Olivia, darling, that's not true. I . . ."

"Hush!" She put her fingertips against his lips. "Don't make this difficult."

Johann took her face in his hands. "All right. Let me just say that Dr. Bergen is a very lucky man."

"I only hope he'll be unable to resist me."

"That goes without saying." Johann smiled. "You are definitely irresistible. You're a treasure. I wonder if I could have survived out here if not for you."

Again, she touched her fingertips to his mouth. "Good-bye, Johann. I'll not be outside when your lorry leaves." She lifted herself up on her toes and kissed him furtively. "Take care," she whispered hoarsely. "Have a safe journey home. I will always remember you."

He reached out for her but she had already opened the door, slipped through it, and was gone.

Chapter 89

Dorrit met Johann at Potsdam Platz Bahnhof. She arrived with an hour to spare and spent the time nervously pacing the marble floor of the large concourse, occasionally stopping to peruse magazine covers at a kiosk. The butterflies swarming in her stomach didn't allow her to sit down at a station cafe. She was as jittery as a new bride and realized she'd been wise not to take Max and Fritz out of school to meet the train. They'd be chasing each other around in the crowded hall, which would only make her even more nervous. Far better the boys enjoy their father's homecoming at the house.

When the loudspeaker announced the train from Tannenburg, she turned away from the kiosk, dashed across the expanse of the terminal and ran headlong through the designated gate. She rushed out onto the blustery open platform, bumping into travelers and their suitcases.

The locomotive was pulling in, belching smoke as its brakes screeched. Dorrit elbowed her way through the waiting throngs of people. She spotted Johann standing in an open door of the still moving train. Afraid that he might not see her in the crowd, she raised her hand and waved a handkerchief to catch his attention.

She needn't have bothered. He had seen her long before the train came to a stop. She was wearing a sea-green cashmere coat with a black Persian lamb collar. A matching hat was perched at a jaunty angle on her auburn hair. She was even more beautiful than he remembered; he would have had to come home blind to have missed her, no matter the hordes surrounding her.

He jumped down and plowed a path through the people. A moment later she was in his arms. Wordlessly he held her tightly, burying his face in her hair, his heart beating against hers.

Snow was falling in large wet flakes; the kind that fall in late March, the kind that quickly melt.

Soldiers and civilian travelers were stepping off the train, while others rushed to board. The platform soon emptied. A loud whistle sounded and the locomotive jerked forward once or twice before gaining momentum and pulling away toward its next destination.

But Johann was home. Thin, unshaven, gray around the temples, he was home!

CPSIA information can be obtained at www.ICGtesting.com
Printed in the USA
BVOW05*1838070514

352865BV00002B/16/P